ALL RIVERS TO THE SEA
A Novel

All Rivers to the Sea

A Novel

Bodie & Brock Thoene

THOMAS NELSON PUBLISHERS®
Nashville

Published in association with the literary agency of Alive Communications, 1465 Kelly Johnson Blvd., Suite #320, Colorado Springs, CO 80920.

Scripture quotations are from the HOLY BIBLE: NEW INTERNATIONAL VER-SION®. Copyright © 1973, 1978, 1984 by International Bible Society. Used by permission of Zondervan Publishing House. All rights reserved.

Published in Nashville, Tennessee, by Thomas Nelson, Inc.

ISBN 0-7852-8076-6 (hc)
ISBN 0-7852-6814-6 (fl)

99-076010
CIP

Printed in the United States of America

2 3 4 5 6 QPV 05 04 03 02 01 00

For Mama—
Bettie Rachel Turner
With love on your
80th Birthday

Other books by Bodie and Brock Thoene

Only the River Runs Free

Of Men and of Angels

Ashes of Remembrance

Shiloh Autumn

Twilight of Courage

Winds of Promise

To Gather the Wind

Winds of the Cumberland

The Zion Covenant Series

The Zion Chronicles Series

The Shiloh Legacy Series

The Saga of the Sierras

∽ Prologue ∽

"Come all you young rebels and list while I sing,
For love of one's land is a terrible thing
It banishes fear with the speed of a flame,
And makes us all part of the patriot game."

—Traditional

GALWAY CITY, IRELAND, 1652

The hammer blows of the three siege guns began again at dawn. In methodical succession, the battery of English cannons belched fire and vomited sixteen-pound shot. Over Henry Burke's head the wall of the fort reverberated with the impacts, and stone splinters flew through the dust-choked air. His throat was parched, and his hair and clothing were white from the rock powder. There was no water to drink, much less to wash the grime away; there had not been for two days.

"How much longer can we last?" Burke asked Geoffrey Baron, the leader of the Irish troops within the tower.

"I had thought it might be a near-run thing," Baron replied. "Between the thirst and the artillery. But since they have concentrated their fire, the answer is plain enough: the wall will be breached by tomorrow night."

Oliver Cromwell's subjugation of Ireland was nearly complete. From the Puritan warlord's landing in Ulster in 1649 to this, the final assault on Galway City in the west in 1652, the road followed by the English soldiers of the New Model army was paved with massacre and saturated in blood. Drogheda, where three thousand men, women, and children were butchered, was followed by Wexford and another savage slaughter, which was succeeded by Cashel and two thousand more dead.

The discipline of the troops, who had cut off the head of a king, was scarcely challenged by chasing tribal outlaws around the countryside, to quote Broghill, Cromwell's army commander.

All that remained was the reduction of a few obstinate strongholds and the hanging of a few key leaders to cow the rest of the papists, and the Puritan Ironsides could settle down in their homesteads of conquered Irish lands. Besides the rent collected from their properties, the vanquishers could take their ease and calculate the value of their assets, including Irish slaves to be sold to sugarcane plantations in the West Indies.

The round tower that commanded the course of the river Corrib and the road leading northward from the sea was still in rebel hands, but that situation was about to change. English cannons had been battering at the walls for days, and the defenders would soon be overwhelmed.

"How much powder and shot have we?" Hugh Fahey inquired.

"No more than three volleys for the fifty of us," Baron replied.

There were no cannons within the walls of the fort, no way to make a reply to the terrible interrogation posed by Cromwell's artillery, placed out of range of musket shot. Outnumbered ten to one and cut off from supplies, victory for Baron's men had never been achievable. What the final defense of Galway City had accomplished was to buy time for other Connaught rebels to escape to mountain fastnesses and regroup.

"And is it your plan, then, for us to wait for the battlements to be tumbled about our ears?" Burke asked.

"It is not."

"You do not mean to go quietly to hangin' or slavery?" Burke demanded. "My grandfather, then the Burke of Connaught, God rest his soul, disappeared these three years past, and most likely died fightin' roundheaded Puritans. I will never surrender!"

"Nor I!" asserted Fahey, the giant Celt whose antic cheerfulness in battle made even his comrades think him mad.

"And who has said anythin' about surrender? We are too many brave sons of Galway to be lost to a soulless plague of cannons. Now hear me: at dusk tonight a handful of us will attack the guns, screamin' like banshees. At the same time, the others will cut from the sally port and make for the river. With the blessin', some will win free to Connemara."

"I will stay with you," Burke stated in a tone that allowed no argument.

"And I," Fahey added, shaking the double-bladed ax he favored for hand-to-hand fighting.

"It is enough," Baron declared. "All the others go north. The wounded must be carried; leave no one to the mercy of the English!"

Dusk tumbled down the slopes above the Corrib and spilled into the lingering sheen on Galway Bay.

Their work done for the day, the cannons fell silent. Before retiring to his comfortable lodgings in the town, General Broghill exhorted the artillerymen and sentries to keep a close watch on the slumping stone fortress until the night guard detail arrived.

No one seriously expected the deafened, battered, and starving survivors of the Irish resistance to launch an attack against a thousand of the same troops who had cut the hands and feet off the bishop of Ross before hanging him. The tower's defenders had never come out to fight in the open; they surely would not do so now.

Geoffrey Baron gathered his force in the courtyard of the tower. There were protests against his suicidal plan and stoutly expressed desires to die alongside him. "God keep you," he said, "but it cannot be. Burke, Fahey, and I will carry three loaded muskets each. With the rest may you live to slaughter Sassenach invaders on another day."

The plan was simple: the three attackers would stealthily approach and then swoop upon the English guns with as much commotion as possible. When the Puritan troops rushed to the protection of their beloved cannons, the others would make a dash for freedom.

A low wall sheltered the placement of the battery but also gave cover to the approaching Irishmen. From behind it Henry Burke could hear the gunners bragging about the day's accomplishments. "*Joy of the Lord* did good service this day," one of them boasted. "You, brother, should stay abed tomorrow, you will not be needed."

"Just listen to the swaggerer, will you Brother Fortitude?" rejoined another. "As if he did not know that it was *Hurrying to the Spoil* that knocked the capstone off the archway!"

"Nay, brothers both," said a third artilleryman. "Pride goeth before a fall, and besides *Hear, O Israel . . .*"

The intended boast about the third cannon was never completed, for at a nod from Geoffrey Baron, the Irish launched their assault. A brace of muskets were clapped across the top of the wall and just as instantly fired, shattering the peace of the twilight, killing two of the gunners and seriously wounding the last. As the rest of the gun crews stampeded into each other and a pair of English sentries shot each other in the confusion, Baron bellowed, "Ireland and Saint Columba! Donelly, Gehan, McDermot: take your companies and cut off the retreat!"

Howling a war cry at the top of his lungs, and like Baron, shouting orders at imaginary troops, Henry Burke leapt the wall and raced for the nearest cannon. Hugh Fahey did the same, whirling his ax around him as he angled up the hill toward the furthest gun.

A soldier in breastplate and clamshell helmet lunged at Burke with a pike. Burke batted the steel spike aside with the barrel of his musket, then crashed the butt of the weapon into the defender's cheek, felling him.

But before he could again raise the musket, a pair of Ironsides flanked him. One slashed at him with a sword, and the other thrust a pike. From behind him Burke heard Baron yell, "Down, Henry!" and as Burke dropped flat to the hard-packed earth, Baron's wheel lock roared. The opposing swordsman was flung backwards, a fist-sized hole in his leather jerkin over his heart.

Out of the corner of his eye, Burke saw the dagger-tipped pike staff plunging toward him. He rolled aside just as it flashed past, burying its point into the ground where his spine had been. Before the wielder of the lance could draw back for another lunge, Burke rose to one knee and fired his musket.

The stunning recoil and his awkward position combined to tear the weapon from his grasp, but not before it blew the legs from under his opponent.

Up the hill, Hugh Fahey was laughing like a lunatic and laying about him with his ax, spinning it like a sawblade. The Puritan guards, believing that a circle of savage barbarians was closing about them, fled before his onslaught.

Knocking the bung from a keg of gunpowder, Fahey rolled out a trail of explosive dust from the wall to the final cannon. Sprinting back toward shelter, he bellowed for Baron and Burke to take cover. Then, lying on the ground, he snapped a musket next to the furrow of powder, showering it with sparks and igniting a scorching snake that slithered toward the gun emplacement. Fahey barely had time to clear the wall before the racing flame reached the canister. The eruption blew out the wheels of the gun carriage and flung the barrel end for end, scything down a dozen approaching English soldiers.

"Now you may call it *Waters of Babylon*," he mocked loudly, "where you sat down and wept!"

"Reload!" Baron shouted. "Back here and reload!"

The initial charge had produced the necessary confusion. Now, Baron hoped, the trio of Irishmen, protected by the stone wall and firing in turn, could delay the English response to the raid still further.

But it was not to be.

A troop of cavalry swept up the road, led by General Broghill himself. The three wheel locks crashed together, tangling the front rank as a pair of the horses and one of the riders were felled.

Then no time remained as the column of mounted men split apart and encircled Burke, Baron, and Fahey before they could charge their weapons again. All three men were clubbed to the ground, and only a harshly shouted command from Broghill prevented their being spitted on pikes right there.

General Broghill contemplated the three Irish prisoners with satisfaction. "It must feel especially wretched for you to know that your attempt was in vain: not one of you filthy rebels escaped our cavalry patrols. Had this been two years ago," he continued, "I would have happily hanged the fifty of you and fed your remains to the dogs. A year ago I would have hanged you three at least. But now . . ." He made a deferential gesture to the prosperous-looking man in the black silk suit. "Captain John Vernon has convinced me that valuable commerce must not be lightly discarded."

"Quite right, General," Vernon said. "Men aged twelve to forty-five fetch a hundred pound each in Barbados . . . demand much greater than supply. I must furnish three hundred by mid-September or lose my contract."

"So the conquest of Canaan is proven to be complete," Broghill observed dryly. "The merchants are in charge. But just as Parliament commended our treatment of Drogheda as a 'merciful warning against futile rebellion,' I will not allow your insurgency to pass with no merciful example at all. One of you shall go to the scaffold this very afternoon." Broghill pointed toward a clay jug and a row of marbles resting in the bright sunshine on his window ledge. Two were white and the third black. "The hand of Providence will direct the course," he said. "Who draws the black marble dies."

"No need," Baron protested. "I was captain. It is my place."

"Noble sounding," Broghill said with a sneer, "but perhaps a quick end is the lighter sentence? You will draw."

The three balls were placed within the flask, and Broghill presented the lottery of death to each man in turn, beginning with Baron. When the men opened their fists to reveal their fates, Geoffrey Baron had indeed drawn execution. "I have a request to ask of you, General," Baron said. "Allow me to bathe and put on a fresh suit of clothing before I meet the hangman and my God."

Snorting, Broghill agreed, then left the three men alone to make their good-byes.

"If, as I think," Henry Burke said, "you meet my grandfather on the other side, greet him for me and ask him to pray for me. And despite what Butcher Broghill says, there is hope while life remains, so I thank you for my life."

"That I will," Baron concluded. "And I hope you will forgive me if Barbados is hell on earth."

"Forgive you for what?" Fahey inquired.

"The sun warmed the black marble more than the other two," Baron said, smiling. "If the butcher permits, will you help me dress for my coronation day?"

PART 1

"Many waters cannot quench love;
neither can the floods drown it."

—Song of Solomon 8:7

1

There was reason to rejoice in the west of Ireland that October evening of 1844. The harvest was in. No one in living memory had ever seen such a wealth of potatoes from the fields that sloped up from the gentle waters of the river Cornamona. The rocky soil surrounding Ballynockanor and the townlands of the Burke estate had yielded up nearly one-third more than the year before. It was as though the stones themselves had turned to bread. After all, the knobby, russet tubers were the bread of life for the poor folk of Ireland. There was plenty to eat until next July and enough to spare to seed the fields come St. Patrick's day in spring.

From the pulpit of St. John the Evangelist, old Father O'Bannon blessed the people and the fields and the heaps of potatoes. He proclaimed the bounty was something like the loaves and fishes that fed the multitudes from the hand of the Savior. Had not the lady of the manor, Kate Donovan Burke, opened her hand in charity to the folk who had been evicted from the lands of Colonel Mahon?

Now Mahon was dead, his estates passed on to another, while the House of Burke and her tenants flourished. The Lord of Heaven was just and sure to reward the deeds of the righteous. Potatoes were tangible evidence of that reward.

Potatoes were the blessing.

Manna from heaven.

Food for the children of Erin.

Life in Ballynockanor for another year.

And there would soon be other lives in Ballynockanor. Any day Kate Donovan Burke would deliver the child of Squire Joseph Connor Burke. The continuity of future generations in Galway would then be assured. Though Squire Joseph was far from home, his tenants believed he would surely return to share in the joy and abundance of his people. It was as certain as the river flowing to the sea. The sea would bring Squire Joseph back again. It was only a matter of time.

The service at St. John's ended as the evening shadows crept down the gullies of the mountains like long, dark fingers gripping the land. A flock of crows rose from the graveyard and swirled above the congregation as they filed out past Father O'Bannon, then gathered in contented knots. Laughter and conversation blended into one pleasant babble, like the water of the river against the rocks.

One among them raised her eyes to the course of the crows and the shade on the surrounding hills. Mad Molly Fahey had been unusually silent during the weeks of harvest. Her faded blue eyes looked heavenward more often now than ever, and some speculated that the old woman was preparing to die soon.

Molly bent low and whispered to young Mary Elizabeth Donovan, "Where's Kate? Where's your sister Kate?"

Mary Elizabeth replied, "She's home, Molly. The baby's due any time. She's too big to come to mass. Father O'Bannon'll have to take it to her."

"Aye!" Mad Molly nodded. "The babe. 'Tis the babe. And all the tears of Mary . . ."

"Molly'll not pass over till she holds the baby of Squire Joseph," the maid Fern said to the Widow Clooney as they observed Mad Molly brush her gnarled hands upon the heads of Martin and Mary Elizabeth Donovan.

Widow Clooney crossed herself. "Aye. If God gives the simple-minded such a choice, then Molly'll wait till she can hold Squire Joseph's babe in her arms as she held himself."

Molly turned suddenly, fixing her wild gaze upon the two women as though she had picked their voices out from all the murmur and knew they were speaking of her. The crone screwed her face up in a toothless grin and pointed skyward toward the retreating birds. "They've gone to report, y'see?" Molly crooned to eight-year-old Mary Elizabeth.

Mary Elizabeth shook her black curls and nodded. It was well known that the child often understood the meaning of Molly's ravings when the rest of the community was at a loss. "Sure, Molly. The crows, is it?"

Molly tapped the side of her nose. "Aye. The crows. There on the mountain the monster has heard us. He's shakin' his **great** hoary head. He'll take no pleasure in our joy. From the days of St. Patrick he's hated us, sure. Take back the land and banish us forever. That's what he's been waitin' for. Repeal is dead. O'Connell in disgrace. And Joseph . . . come home, lad, to fight for us! Can ye not hear the rumble of his voice? Devour us all, it will, or drive us to the sea!"

At the crackle of her voice clumps of conversation fell silent. Grown men crossed themselves, and children inched closer to cling to their mothers' skirts. Mary Elizabeth grasped her elder brother's hand. A collective shudder passed through the crowd.

Mad Molly was speaking once again. Instead of raving as she had so many times before, her voice was quiet, resigned, and sad. "See there: Angels of light step back as he marches toward us. Rough hair bristles on his head, and he looks upon Eire with fury. Pray for us now and at the hour of our death! The mist of his breath . . . great travail . . . Travail himself shall be given power o'er us. Aye! And all eyes shall grow **dark**. A blight! All eyes grow dark!"

Everyone in Castletown and Ballynockanor had gone to the harvest thanksgiving mass at St. John's. Kate Donovan Burke was grateful for the solitude, pleased that the certainty of imminent child-birth prevented her from making the trip. It was the quiet she had loved, in the old days—leaning her cheek against the warm hide of a moilie as milk thrummed into the bucket. Too often these days, her own thoughts had drowned out the peace of silence.

In the soft light of dusk, Kate stood barefoot among the broken clods on the edge of the harvested field. Last year these same acres had been carpeted in a wide, sweeping lawn that had stretched from the manor house toward the river.

A terrible waste of fine farmland, Kate had declared to the steward, Adam Kane, after Joseph's arrest. What with the Great House burned to the ground and no one but ghosts to stare out through the vacant windows of the rubble, what was the point of twenty acres of grass anyway?

It was a point well made by this daughter of a dairyman. She knew from experience how precious every inch of soil was to families living off as little as a quarter of an acre. Kate declared she had come from the dust and would, one day, return to it like every living creature; but in the meantime she would get all she could from it. The farmers of the townlands and their ragged children could not eat grass. She had witnessed the misery of Colonel Mahon's evicted tenants. She was aware that there were not enough potatoes in Galway to feed the hungry who might come begging at the gates of Burke Hall. And so the lovely lawn was cut away, hauled off in carts, and potatoes planted instead. The field proved to be most fertile, and soon the stable was filled with fine seed potatoes to be distributed throughout the community.

Small wonder the harvest had produced such abundance, Kate mused. After all, generations of landlords had fertilized the ground with the manure of thoroughbreds as the tenants went hungry. Well, she had put an end to the waste. Though lady of the estate, she was still plain Kate, the daughter of Tom Donovan, was she not? Practical

Kate. The Kate who had waded through fire and lost everything but her life. Stretching out the stub of her right hand she considered the two missing fingers and taut, marred skin. For the first time since the fire, her deformity did not matter. She rubbed her bulging belly and said aloud, "Ten fingers and toes. Sure, and all the tears I've shed will not touch you, darlin'."

There was a significant miracle in that, Kate believed. There was so much she had learned, so much she longed to say to Joseph. Glancing skyward she spied the high, wide V of the wild geese flying south. Where was Joseph, she wondered.

She closed her eyes and imagined him near. "Do you remember, Joseph? When we were children? I had a ewe that lost her front leg to Patrick Flanagan's dog. Terrible shame it was. Da was for puttin' her out of her misery, but she was due to lamb. Remember? The poor creature hopped about on three legs. Stumbled on the rocks. Aye. But after a month she had the most perfect lamb. Within a day the wee thing was tearin' round the pasture, then back to its mama's teat. No matter that the dog had been at the old girl . . . the udder full of milk. Her lamb was perfect. So I'll give you a perfect baby. Only come home, darlin' Joseph. Wherever you are, hear me now. Come home to hold him. And myself as well."

There was a chill in the air. Kate had dallied too long in the field. The peat fire on the hearth wanted tending, and soon everyone would be home from mass. Tucking her shawl around her, she stepped onto the shovel-pocked soil of the field. It was warm on her feet, embracing, approving the good use that had been made of it.

As Kate crossed the uneven surface awkwardly, she spied a single, unharvested spud. Stooping to retrieve it, she groaned audibly, caught midway in the bending by her own bulk. Fingers stretched to grasp the thing . . . it was an entire meal for someone, after all, and could not be left to rot.

Scooping it up, she straightened and felt the warmth of fluid course down her leg to seep into the soil around her bare toes. Her water had broken. The advance guard of her travail attacked hard and long from the small of her back and circled like a vise around her middle.

Startled by the fierceness of it, Kate blinked back moisture from her eyes. Irritated, she stared at the spud as though it were somehow to blame.

The chilly gusts of an autumnal afternoon scuttled crablike across Spithead and the Isle of Wight at the extreme south of England. The fitful breezes flung handfuls of sand from the dunes into the water below East Cowes, then capriciously changed direction to churn the waves of the Solent to a froth. Out in the channel a three-masted ship showing American colors struggled to clear Portsmouth harbor.

Tangled in the strands of swirling mist was an evil smell, but it was not the salty decay of castaway seaweed, for this aroma of death came from the heart of the land and not from the shore. A tall, carefully dressed, slender man in his late thirties strode purposefully through a field of drooping potato stalks. To his left and right, across the full expanse of the plot, what should have been vibrant green leaves were withered and scaly—or dead.

In the exact middle of the acreage Charles Edward Trevelyan, assistant secretary of the British treasury, stopped. With deliberate economy of motion he kicked a polished boot toe into the earth at the base of a potato plant, exposing a rotting mass of gelatinous ooze. The reek that spiraled upward made Trevelyan's companion hastily put a perfumed handkerchief to his nose.

Major Denis Mahon remarked, "Putrid stench. Like a ward of gangrenous wounds."

Trevelyan raised an imperious finger in contradiction. "On the contrary, my dear Mahon. That may be the smell of reform . . . the olfactory end of the Irish question."

Mahon glanced toward the receding sails of the ship. "This rot is a bequest from our American friends," he replied bitterly. "It's devoured entire crops in the American south, then France last year, and now it begins here."

"A gift from heaven in disguise." Trevelyan raised his eyes toward Osborne House, the holiday residence of Queen Victoria and her husband, Prince Albert. No doubt the stink of rotting potatoes would also disturb their royal noses.

"The agent of hell itself if it encroaches further into Great Britain than this island, sir. It may mean little on the Isle of Wight, but it would mean everything in Ireland."

"Concerned for your new tenants are you, Denis?"

Mahon denied any misplaced sympathy, then added, "If this should spread . . ."

"If an Irish peasant can feed his brood on a few weeks' labor in his 'prattie patch,' and warm them by cutting free turf in the bogs, what incentive has he to better himself? The potato people *must* change their ways."

Shorter by a head, but no less properly attired than his host, Mahon indicated his agreement. His gesture went unremarked. Trevelyan, his delicate fingers clasped behind his back, was already striding rapidly across the field like a stalking shore bird intent on his prey. Mahon jogged a few paces to catch up as Trevelyan continued, "Mark this: it is the proper duty of men to improve their lots, and improvement means labor. I have no more use for the idle rich with their frivolous pursuits than I do the idle poor. Your cousin Colonel Mahon in Galway was a grasping schemer. It is a pity about his unfortunate death at the hands of that demented Catholic squireen, O'Shea, but nevertheless I am certain you are much more likely to see to the long-term needs of your tenants than he ever could. You will, of course, annex his lands to your own in Roscommon?"

This last was stated as a question, but Mahon had no choice other than to concur. "My steward, a man by the name of Richman, is already on the scene to take charge." Since his words drew a look of sharp criticism, Mahon hastily added, "And I shall be going there myself at once."

The cloaked and hooded figure standing on the deck of the American trading vessel *Nantucket* studied the vanishing wharves of Portsmouth harbor in brooding silence. Over his right shoulder the Isle of Wight likewise diminished. Behind him stood the captain of the vessel.

Captain Nathaniel Coffin, a spare New Englander with sparse words and a bony frame, relinquished his helm to the sailing master and joined the enigmatic form at the starboard rail. "Plaguey winds," he observed. "But tide's set right. London tomorrow. What then?"

The terse question was for the passenger. Joseph Connor Burke, lord of the Burke lands of Connaught, looked anything but ennobled. The borrowed grey cloak covered the ragged and ill-fitting blouse and dungarees from a dead sailor's slop chest and topped a too-large pair of shoes.

What indeed?

Joseph had remained hidden below while the American vessel called at Portsmouth. Its final port of call before recrossing the Atlantic was London. Heading east for the English Channel, *Nantucket* was going in the opposite direction from Ireland, from Connaught, from home, from Kate.

"I can hide among the Irish dockworkers in London," Joseph said. "Learn what I can. No one will think to look for me there while I earn enough for passage back to Galway."

"Are ye dead set on putting yer neck in the noose after escaping transporting *and* being castaway?" Coffin inquired. "Why not come to Boston . . . lots of Irish in Boston. Send for yer missus from there."

Shaking his head, Joseph declined to renew the discussion that had occupied weeks and thousands of sea miles of sailing. If England was as close to his love as *Nantucket* would carry him, then so be it.

He peered out at the passing coast with its lonely stretches of sandy beaches and isolated rocky coves, but it was Kate's face he saw. Not Kate as he had last seen her at his mockery of a trial, her features contorted with anguish at hearing his exile pronounced. Instead Joseph gazed on the memory of a ministering angel, her fragrant auburn hair spilling across his face as he pulled her down to him.

His hands clenched the rail, his body stiffening with the pain of longing. "I will not go to America without her," Joseph vowed forcefully. "I must see her . . . know that she is well. It is worth risking the drop just to be near her again."

Daniel Grogan's farm was on the poorest three acres in the townland of Gilcuddy. His cottage perched on the steep, rocky slope of the knock overlooking more fertile farms and bottomlands bordering the southern banks of the Cornamona.

Only a half mile separated his land from the boundary stones of the estate of Joseph Burke. Misfortune placed him within the perimeter of the south Galway holdings of the Mahon estate. Grogan often looked away to the lights shimmering in Castletown and cursed the luck that he had not been born a wee bit north.

True, Colonel Mahon had recently died a terrible death. In four counties his tenants had celebrated the news. But the word had come from the London heir, Denis Mahon, that all back rents due must be paid upon demand or tenants were to be evicted. The elder Mahon was dead, but he had left the image of his own greedy soul behind to work his will through Denis Mahon.

This was why on a cold, cold autumn night, Daniel Grogan, his pregnant wife, Annie, and three small daughters found themselves homeless and on the road to Galway City.

Dan was only thirty-one, but he looked a gaunt forty years or more. His brown, curly hair and beard were already showing grey. His once bright-blue eyes were sunken and red-rimmed. Annie, now twenty-nine, had been the sixteen-year-old raven-haired beauty of the parish when she married Dan. But thirteen hard years, seven pregnancies, and the death of three infants had taken a toll on her as well.

And the daughters?

Corrie, at twelve, had the disposition of her serious and hardworking father, though she had never been to school. When Corrie thought of heaven, her mother knew, it was always called America. They were going there, her father promised. First to Galway City, it was true, but when he earned enough for the passage money they were going to that promised land where a man could own his own farm and never pay a penny of tax to a corrupt government agent ever again.

The second daughter, nine-year-old Ceili, was aptly named in the old tongue for the gathering of folk for the telling of tales. Brown-haired and bright, Ceili loved a good chat by the fire: a night of stories and the old, old songs. Annie Grogan believed Ceili would remember everything and someday pass on the stories to those who came after them.

Then there was three-year-old Megan, sleeping as she rode on her father's shoulder. Annie hoped little Megan would recall none of the suffering of this land, of what was surely to come. Perhaps one day Megan would go to sleep and wake up in America—wear shoes and own a coat and never go hungry. For now she was too young even to dream of such wonders.

Tonight the air lay bone cold across the bog and hills. The temperature dropped fifteen degrees more when the sun vanished below the horizon.

Annie knew her time was fast approaching. "Dan," she managed to say, "the children. It's so very cold, ain't it? And they're hungry, sure."

At first he did not reply, but the crunching of his footfall slowed. "Jack Reilly keeps a lean-to for his sheep nearby. Will it suit?"

"Smells like rain."

"It does." He stopped in the road, his family clustered around him.

Ceili tugged his trousers. "Mike Trelee lives over there, Da."

Grogan touched her plaited hair. "There's a decree, see, daughter. We're turned out."

Corrie explained to her younger sibling, "Any folk who gives us shelter or aid will suffer a like fate as us. We can't ask."

Annie rubbed her hands across her swollen belly. Her hips ached fiercely. "The lean-to, Dan. Aye. Ye can cut turf yonder, and we'll build a fire. Someplace to rest the night."

In the sable sack of night all boulders, fences, and boundary stones looked alike. Who could tell one thing from another, let alone find a lean-to build into the side of a hill?

Dan Grogan prayed for one shaft of moonlight to show him where he was. Moments passed. In the distance came the howling of a fast-approaching wind. Then there was a flash of lightning, followed by the bellow of thunder.

But it was over too quickly! Grogan cried, "Again, merciful Christ! Show us the place!"

Corrie shouted above the wind, "It's there, Da!"

Grogan turned his face away as the first rain lashed him. Another streak of light illuminated the landscape in one frozen, colorless image. There was the shelter, their refuge! It was no more than a sod roof built over two granite boulders, but it would do.

"Come on, then!" Ceili cried, dashing for the place.

The rain drummed down. The gale pushed against them as they staggered toward the shelter.

2

The wind was up in the west. Martin Donovan raised his eyes toward the thunderheads rolling above the mountains beyond Ballynockanor. The ancient stone cross of St. Brigit was framed against the tumultuous sky. There was an uneasiness among the villagers as they crowded through the narrow gate of St. John's and onto the road that led back through Castletown and onto the grounds of Burke manor, where the harvest celebration would be held.

A firm hand clasped Martin's shoulder.

"I've been watchin' it come. The sky was red as blood this mornin'. It'll be blowin' a gale before we get home, boy," commented Lieutenant Charlie Nesbitt to Martin as the people left the churchyard. Being a Protestant, Nesbitt had stood in the back of the chapel during mass and eyed the approaching storm. "I've sent the Claddagh brothers home to bring in your sister's moilies from the fields."

"Aye, and thanks," Martin said, nodding. Charlie had brought the four Claddagh brothers, Rusty, Moor, Sonny-boy, and Simeon, to the estate after Joseph's arrest. Tonight, Martin knew, there would be lightning strikes in the open fields, and cattle made perfect targets. The Claddagh boys, like bog oak and granite, looked as though they would be impervious to lightning. Mad Molly called the brothers "The Four Horses." Martin had heard them rebuke squalls in the Celtic tongue; even the rebellious skies of Galway seemed to respect them. Likewise, their whispered commands to a cow, a dog, or a stallion were meekly obeyed. To Martin, the Claddagh brothers were wrought from a magical race of giants. There was comfort in their enigmatic presence and in Nesbitt's authority over them. Like Mad Molly they raised their faces to the wind and sensed impending danger. Unlike Molly, however, they did not fear what was to come.

There was murmuring in the crowd as each man, woman, and child studied the gloomy western horizon and gratefully remembered hard-won fields of potatoes gathered and safely stored. There was a question, however, as to whether the celebration should continue or be postponed on account of the impending gale. The combination of imminent tempest and Mad Molly's dire, if obscure, prophecy made them uneasy.

Joe Watty, whose kegs of tavern beer had that very morning been transported to the largest barn on the Burke estate, clapped his hands and called for attention. "Here now! The rain's held off till we could harvest and pray, thanks be to God. What would a harvest festival be without Joe Watty's beer and O'Rourke's fiddle? There's shelter and fine dancin' waitin' for us in the barn of Kate and Squire Joseph! I say . . . What do you say, Father O'Bannon? Shall we cower in our houses, or shall we proceed, then?" The tavern owner turned to the diminutive parish priest.

Father O'Bannon's eyes brightened. "Shall we now? Shall we not! Aye! Play on O'Rourke! I've never known a good Christian Irishman who could not survive a westerly gale with fiddle music, shelter, and a lake of ale to drink! A wind may shake the mighty oak, but we'll never notice tonight if we do a proper job of celebratin'. The Lady Kate is waitin' for us, sure!" With that, the aged cleric hiked his cassock above his bony knees and danced a jig as Mike O'Rourke played "Trip to Sligo." The wind began to push against the backs of the people of Ballynockanor as they sang and sailed up the road to Castletown.

Mary Elizabeth, who loved the howling of the westerlies, skipped through the crowd to Martin's side. O'Rourke's fiddle energized her, much to Martin's irritation. His sister was shrill and excitable on the calmest day, but this afternoon her voice bit through the babble like the edge of a saw. Black curls, finally grown out after her bout with the smallpox, blew forward, nearly covering her face. "It's a grand evenin' then, ain't it, Martin?"

He grunted his reply.

She tugged harder on his jacket. "I was scared they'd call it off. But everyone'll sleep in the straw till it blows over." She leaned her head closer and said in a loud, yet conspiratorial tone, "I was almost ready to tell them about the butter so they'd come ahead."

At this Martin jabbed her ribs. "Shut your face, then, Mary Elizabeth! Will you be tellin' the whole world?"

She dodged his quick hand, stuck out her tongue, and darted away to join the Clooney sisters halfway back in the parade.

"Butter, indeed!" Martin murmured. Most likely Mary Elizabeth had already told every child in the village that they had been churning, salting, and storing up enough butter that every citizen in Ballynockanor and Castletown might take away a lump for the harvest. Quite a gift it was in a world where butter was cash. But then, that was Kate, wasn't it? She was always a welcome neighbor even when they were as poor as everyone else. And there was nothing in the whole countryside as appreciated as a lump of butter, nice and sweet.

It had been going on for weeks. Sister Kate had set the whole household to churning. Fern, the cook, Margaret, and even Mad Molly had been at it. Many was the day Mary Elizabeth had churned until her arms ached and tears ran down her cheeks. Then she begged Martin to take her churn as well as his. Sometimes he had consented just to shut her up. Still, he figured that wee Mary Elizabeth would claim to have churned every lump of the yellow gold on her own and without any help. The butter may have been Kate's gift, but Mary Elizabeth would claim it was made by her muscle. Martin was sure of his younger sister's need to take the glory. It disgusted him completely. There and then he vowed that if she did as he knew she would, he would quietly flatten her when no one was looking. That thought made him smile.

Kate knew something was not right. The contractions seized her hard from back to front. This was not the way it was supposed to be; no, not the way the women in the village said it came upon them. It was too fierce at the beginning. Kate knew it should have been easier at first. The early pains should have been separated by ten minutes or more, not three.

She stumbled into the house, a stable Joseph had converted to a home after the burning of the manor house. Hay hooks and pulleys still dangled from the oak rafters above her. It was a suitable setting for her to give birth, she thought. She had first fallen in love with Joseph in a barn, attending the difficult calving of a heifer. This place had seen its share of mares foaling and most often things turned out well. And yet . . .

Once again the convulsion grasped her spine, emanating outward, then around her middle with excruciating power that took her breath away. She groped for support. Finding a chair, she sank down with a nearly inaudible groan. Where was everyone? Why had she let everyone go while she stayed behind? Foolish! She had approached this hour with the arrogant thought she would handle it without concern.

"Joseph!" His name burst from her unbidden. Thoughts flooded her mind in a babble as the contraction strengthened. Where was Joseph now? Why had he run away just as Adam Kane had sailed after him with the full pardon in his pocket? For the first time since Joseph had been taken from her she felt angry at him. Unreasonable, she knew, but there it was. He should be with her. He did not even know he was about to be a father. He surely would have been there at her side if he had not been such a fool!

Next she called upon Jesus. Then Mary, Mother of God! Had it been like this for the Virgin? No doubt Mary would have told God no when He offered her the choice if she had known about this part of the process. Kate would have more respect for the mother of Christ after this, she decided. Lastly, Kate wished for her own mother. She whispered, "Mama" . . . and then the grip subsided and relaxed.

Kate sighed her relief and sat back, aware her skirt was soaked and a trail of fluid followed her path across the stone floor of the house. The sight of it shamed her. She inhaled with a shudder and stood on shaky legs to find water and a rag to scrub.

One minute.

The kettle hissed on the crane over the peat fire in the kitchen. Kate poured water into a clay bowl and found a rag.

Two minutes.

On her knees she dipped the cloth into the pleasantly warm liquid and scrubbed the slate as she wondered why she imagined the pain was really so terrible.

Three minutes.

While washing the seat and spindles of the chair it came to her that she would finish cleaning up before Fern and Molly and the rest got home. She would put on her long nightshirt, make a nice cuppa tay, climb into bed, and read a bit between . . .

"Jesus! Mary . . . and Joseph!" It came again. "All the Holy Family! Christ have mercy! I'm a coward. That I am!"

For a full sixty seconds she crouched on all fours, discovering that the agony was not as intense in that position. She rocked a bit, letting the weight of her belly ease the tightness of the muscles.

She would not be reading. No. Nor would she be fixing herself a cuppa. Perhaps even the softness of the feather bed was out of the question. Maybe she would stay here, on the floor, remembering the moaning milkcows she had attended in the calving pen.

"Joseph! Mary, Jesus, and . . . Joseph! Why aren't you here?"

Thunder boomed as Kate crept into bed. There was barely time enough between the pains to shed her clothes and don the nightshirt she had been saving for this moment over her head.

As blue dusk closed upon the land beyond the window, the vise gripped her again. Panting, she stared out at the lonely oak where Aidan Clooney, his son David, and young Alan O'Rourke lay buried. Bare, gnarled branches trembled in the wind as they reached heavenward, a mirror image of the roots that plowed down through soil to embrace the bones of men and boys. Life and death were so entwined, she thought, as the contraction locked and tightened. So were agony and jubilation conjoined at birth. Her sister Brigit had died bringing little Tomeen into the world.

Grief and joy.

Joseph had brought Brigit home to the grave and Tomeen home to Kate's arms. She loved the child like her own. For an instant Kate wondered who would care for Tomeen and her baby if the same should happen to her?

But no! In the calving pens Kate had seen a hundred times what she now felt. Confusion, fear, and an understanding of dying had all been reflected in her heifers' wide eyes. When their time came, they each looked to Kate for comfort. She stroked velvet noses and whispered soothing words. There was scarce else to be done. Life's renewal ran its tortured course as a river *must* flow to the sea.

What was it Kate had said to get each heifer through its labor until the creature could finally rest and turn to lick its newborn calf, which lay weak and astonished in the straw?

Kate spoke the words to herself, "There now . . . Kate. Remember, Kate. It'll be all right now. Joy cometh in the mornin'."

And yet she knew the child was turned wrong within her. She would need help. She could not do this alone.

The people of the Burke townlands swept onto the estate and into the barn like leaves piling up in a corner. They laughed and honked like a gaggle of geese going from here to somewhere on the autumn wind. Fiddle and flute called them into the glow and the warmth and the embracing aroma of fresh straw and cattle. Jubilation!

Only Mad Molly had a gloomy expression on her puckered face.

Staring silently out at the storm, she remained framed in the doorway. There was lightning followed by thunder: distant artillery flashes
and a drumroll preceded what she knew was the end of the world.

She began to name names of those who had gone west from
Galway. To America. And then she named names of departed friends
who remained behind forever, whose spirits had joined their fathers
on the team of hurlers in the graveyard of Ballynockanor. There
would be no rousting them, Molly knew.

Dan Grogan cut ragged squares of turf from the bog and dug
a shallow firepit in the dirt floor of the lean-to. The pungent aroma
of peat smoke enveloped the enclosed space. Light, warmth, and
the familiar scent of home and hearth were a comfort to the three
girls. They slept as Annie boiled the last of the potatoes.

Grogan stretched out his hands, gathering heat from the flames.
"There's work to be had in Galway City."

Annie did not look up. "Ceili's lookin' pale, Dan. She's awful
quiet, ain't she?"

"They're wantin' strong backs for loadin' cargo. Sure, and me
back's strong as any man's."

"Little Megan cried for milk b'fore she slept. Where'll we find
milk for her? We haven't a penny to buy so much as a cupful."

"The pay ain't much on the quay. But if a man could work
awhile . . . America we could . . . mebbe, y'know. Three pounds,
six shillin's for passage. Sure, and they won't charge full fare for
the half pints."

"Three pounds . . . half year's earnin's on the farm, Dan. And
that was our best year. If we had such as that, we'd not be here. We
haven't even a penny for buyin' milk. Where'll you find three pounds,
six shillin's, then?"

The hopeless truth struck Daniel Grogan like a blow. He withdrew his hands from the warmth. The light of dreaming left his face.
Crossing his arms over his chest, he tucked his chin. "Three babes
to feed."

"Four soon."

"Half-dozen pratties boilin' there to last us. A bit of salt. Kids hungry. If it was just meself, I could sign on with a whaler."

"But it ain't just you. And you mustn't talk foolishness. Two years at sea, Dan. What about us?"

Grogan winced as the thought of the workhouse crossed his mind. "There's always—"

"Don't speak of it. You know they'd separate me from the kids. You know what it's like in there . . . English poor laws . . . Church of Ireland charity for a bowl of gruel and a stale crust each day. Not a word can you speak or be punished for it. Breakin' rocks and sleepin' in a hall with lunatics and dyin' folk. And they'd keep the babies from me."

"What am I to do?" he pleaded.

The two crouched in silence for a time. Annie brushed Megan's hair back from her forehead. "A wee bit of milk is all Megan wants in the world."

Grogan stood, his head bumping the sod ceiling. "It's lambin' time. Someone'll be tendin' the ewes down the road in the barn where the village used to be."

"Whoever it is, he'll not risk transgressin' the edict. Put his own kin at risk of the same fate as us. Sure, Dan, we'll have no help from any man on Mahon land."

"Any man . . . a man like meself . . . unless his heart's a stone, he wouldn't turn his back on hungry children. A cuppa ewe's milk. It ain't much to ask."

Annie sighed. "A wee bit of milk. I could make soup from the potato broth. Sure, and there's nourishment in the water. If I've got a wee cuppa milk."

A dozen toddlers between the age of fifteen months and two years were herded together into a stall lined with clean straw. Tomeen, his red curls gleaming, was the largest, the strongest, and the most enthusiastic of the captive tribe. He repeatedly clambered onto the bottom slat of the enclosure, whooped and shrieked, then dropped onto the heads of whomever was beneath him. *This is one way to teach a budding Irishman to fight*, thought Martin.

Mary Elizabeth, perched on the top rail of the playpen, observed to Alice Clooney that it was a pity Tomeen had to change from a dear infant into a boy like Martin. And so soon.

Martin, who stood between Nesbitt and Adam Kane, the steward, heard the insult but chose to ignore it. He was fully fourteen, not a boy any longer, and wee Tomeen had a ways to go to catch up with him.

Outside the rain was bucketing, but in the shelter of the barn only the beer was flowing freely. The party had been underway a full twenty minutes. A haze of tobacco smoke from a hundred pipes blued the air. The Claddagh brothers had returned from the pastures, rolled up their sleeves, and washed in the trough. The Four Horses they were indeed, taking to the floor and stomping out their ecstasy in time to the fiddle. The barn shook with the pounding of dancing feet. Martin could feel the bodhran drumming in his chest. Even his lame leg longed to dance. But where was Kate?

As if reading his thoughts, Charlie Nesbitt scratched his grey-streaked black beard and commanded Martin, "Go see to your sister. To Lady Kate, I mean. She should be here with her folk. And don't be sendin' Mary Elizabeth!"

For a moment Martin thought to pass the duty on to Fern or Margaret so he would not miss even a minute of the dancing. But there was the rain to consider. Ladies in the rain. Sighing, he pulled his cloak over his head and made a halting dash one hundred yards through the puddles and burst into the house.

"Kate! Kate! Can you not hear the music? They've all come!" No reply. "Kate? Where've you got to?"

As he stood dripping on the stones of the kitchen, he saw a broken teacup on the hearth. A sense of alarm filled him.

"Kate!" Heedless of his muddy footprints, normally a serious crime in Kate's household, he rushed to her bedchamber. One look at her, ashen and hollow-eyed upon her pillow, told him everything. The hour had come.

He blurted, "They're wonderin' where you are." He suppressed an excited chuckle. He loved it when things got born. Calves, pigs, puppies, and foals: there was something purely mystical about squirming miniatures with squashed faces. Sure, and they all had squashed faces. Wasn't that true, now? Best was the speculation whether the thing would be male or female. Like opening a gift, it was. The Widow Clooney had predicted that the child of Kate and Joseph was a boy. Margaret said a girl. Bets on the matter had been placed down at Watty's Tavern. Kate declared it was impossible to please every fool in the townlands and that any man who wagered on such a thing deserved to lose. But the men of Ballynockanor and Castletown being who they were, the wagers were made, and there was an end to it. Father O'Bannon himself hazarded a shilling in favor of a boy. Mad Molly, who was always right, proclaimed the child would be a baby.

They would know soon enough from the look of it.

"And here you are, Kate. In bed."

Kate raised her hand but said nothing. There was irritation and misery in her glance. Why was he standing there, staring stupidly at her?

"Never mind that," he replied lightly to her unspoken rebuke. "You're in luck, Kate. Every midwife in Galway is kickin' up her heels in your barn tonight." He was also in luck. There would be no midnight ride to fetch the Widow Clooney.

The Widow Clooney, Mrs. O'Rourke, Fern, and Margaret rushed off to attend Kate. The rest of the females gathered on the north side of the barn to discuss in elaborate detail the various multitudes of experiences each had while populating western Ireland. Mary Elizabeth and the girls of the townlands were taken into that fold, where they stared big-eyed and trembling at the prospect of what they must one day suffer on account of Eve's transgression.

Martin leaned upon a keg of beer while the gathering of men and boys lifted glasses to salute Squire Joseph, wherever in the world he might be. Beer for the men and golden cider for the boys. It was a fine night indeed.

"A true bull is our squire! A bull any farmer would envy!" intoned O'Rourke, lifting his glass. A respectful draught was drunk in Joseph's honor.

"Aye!" declared Watty. "One night with the Lady Kate and here we are, drinkin' a toast to his health! To the squire's health then. And to his lady and children. A toast!" This was drunk by all.

Adam Kane concurred soberly, though he was not sober. "And may every ram in his flocks and bull in his herds and stallion too . . . Aye! May every creature follow Squire Joseph's example in the pro-creatin' after its own kind." Here the husky steward lost his place. Overcome with emotion, his lip trembled. "Except, of course, may they not be such fools as the squire and run away when there's full pardon and the warmth of his home and hearth waitin'."

Martin blinked up at Adam Kane. What were they to drink to? Herds and flocks? Procreation? The fact Joseph was a fool?

Father O'Bannon harrumphed and saved the glorious moment. "To his safe return then, God willin'."

There were murmurs of assent as cups were drained dry. Joe Watty set to refilling them. Comments were made about the tragic fact that poor Tom Donovan was not alive to see Kate's baby. And then there was Kevin Donovan, in exile in America and doing very well working on the canals in spite of anti-Irish riots in Philadelphia and New York.

Nesbitt and the Claddagh Brothers remained still. Mad Molly also did not speak a word, but sat upon an upturned bucket and questioned the candles burning in the window of Kate's room.

Shades moved from the bedchamber to the kitchen and back again.

Nearly two hours passed before the toasts deteriorated into talk of politics and hope that O'Connell would revive the movement to repeal Irish union with England. But O'Connell was almost seventy. He could not live forever. Perhaps his movement would die with him? It was mentioned that O'Connell's son, Maurice, was strong and fiery at forty. Maurice was even now in London forming an Irish league to carry the woes of Ireland to parliament. Perhaps Maurice would carry on when the Great Emancipator was gone at last.

O'Rourke picked up his fiddle and played a wordless, melancholy tune that spoke to every heart.

The women's tales of birthing horrors were only beginning. It was an exciting and enjoyable way to pass the time. Thunder rumbled, rain sluiced off the roof. Someone among them asked about Kate's progress. There had been none.

Children, the ones to blame for their mothers' anguish, fell asleep with smiles on their cherubic faces as they lay in the hay.

Six hours passed, and word came back that it was likely to be a long ordeal. The news began another round of discussion about who had the longest labor in the entire county. Two days did not count until the pains were hard. Was it not true that Fanny Michaels had harvested her potatoes whilst her eighth boy, Marion, was on the way? She swore she felt no pain except tightness for two days until the last when the harvest was done. God be praised, and the blessed Virgin too. Fanny had been hoping for a girl to break the monotony; she would have named it Mary. But number eight was another male, so Marion would have to suffice. Perhaps the next time.

Everyone agreed twenty-four hours in hard labor qualified as difficult. There were a few among the group who knew firsthand what that meant: breech, posterior, or perhaps an untried woman whose hips were too narrow. Next came talk of those mothers, sisters, and friends who had died on the childbed. It was inevitable that the dialogue would come to that. The graveyards were populated with Irish women who had lost their lives in childbirth. Such was a common fate and a real concern.

From there a sullen resentment settled upon the females as they glared across the cavernous shelter at their beer-saturated men and snoring sons.

"It's a wonder we don't become nuns, now, isn't it?" said Mrs. O'Rourke.

"Look at 'em! Congratulatin' themselves on their children!" spat Mrs. Watty as she scowled at her husband's customers. "It's their fault sweet Kate's in there sufferin'! And the rest of us as well! No female is safe! Aye! Men! The whole lot of 'em! Night after night they think of one thing! One thing after they've had their pint and their politics! And here we are. And herself in there sweatin' and agonizin' when it comes upon her. Sufferin' race of females we are! At their mercy! Poor, poor Kate."

3

With tiny Megan in his arms, Daniel Grogan walked through the dank slough of the gap toward the lambing barn of the Mahon estate. Fear, not of his own dying, but of watching his children go hungry, had overcome any shred of pride that remained in him. If he had to beg the shepherds for milk, it was best to show them the true desperation of his case. Best show them Megan, small, fragile, eyes too wide and belly swollen from hunger. They could perhaps turn Grogan away, but how could they refuse sweet Megan?

The sun at his back melted into a golden puddle behind the knock. Soon the winds would come again. Grogan prayed for mercy as he stood twenty-five yards off from the barn and envied the sheep within.

"Men of Ireland!" he called, "Hullo to ye!"

It seemed a long time before a narrow, stoop-shouldered adolescent poked his head out from behind the barn door.

"We're armed in here," called the youth. "Come no closer."

Grogan spread his free hand, displaying that he had no weapon.

"I mean ye no harm. Sure, as ye can see, I've a small child in me arms. It's milk I'm askin', not treasure."

Behind the lad, a man emerged. "Ye'll be havin' nuthin' which belongs to the new squire, y'know. Neither milk nor anythin' else of his honor's."

"Just a wee cuppa milk, brother."

"Nay! I know what ye are! Ye're that trash from the high country. Turned out ye was, y'know . . . with an edict upon ye."

"Christ have mercy!" Grogan cried, stepping forward one step.

The protruding barrel of an ancient fowling piece stopped him. "Christ may have mercy, but I cannot! There's an edict against the likes of yeself. Come not a step more!"

"I've a wife with child, brother! Three daughters to feed! No food a'tall. 'Tis only a bit of ewe's milk I'm askin'."

"Ye're squatters, that's what ye are, and me and me son'll not be losin' our jobs and our farm for the likes of yeself."

"For the sake of me children." Grogan staggered forward and dropped on his knees to the ground. "I'm no beggar, but a man as yeself! But I'm beggin'! Upon me knees! For me children . . . brother."

"I'm no man's brother in such a time! If ye were from the same womb as meself . . . I'd not . . . I couldn't."

The youth flinched at the sight of Daniel Grogan in the mud. "Da, y'know, Da . . . Muther would . . . she'd not have us . . ."

The father shoved his son back into the barn. "Enough foolishness! I've pledged an oath to the new squire and his overseer, y'know! Sure, and I've made me mark that I'll not transgress even one small law. I'll lose all if I help, ye know. Some advice now. There are destructives employed by the squire. They'd be pleased to kill ye without so much as a by-your-leave. Move on."

The barn door banged shut. There would be no milk for Megan. Not so much as a drop.

Sundown found *Nantucket* anchored in the Pool of London, under the guns of the Tower. She swung easily at one hook along the south bank of the Thames, while watermen unloaded Moroccan silks and Canary Island pepper.

After full dark she also disgorged her single passenger.

Captain Coffin tried one last time to persuade Joseph to abandon his dangerous scheme, then shook the Irishman's hand and wished him Godspeed. Joseph was set ashore on the low-tide exposed shingle in the frowning gloom of brick warehouses, silent chandleries, and deserted dockyards.

His feet slipping on the filth-covered stones, for the Thames was Victorian London's sewer, Joseph made a dash for a set of steps. He had marked his exit from the river in daylight by noting a sway-backed building whose faded sign announced *Cutter's Wharf.*

At the foot of the stairs he reviewed his meager possessions. Besides his clothing, Captain Coffin had furnished him with a handful of coins and a pouch of tobacco. This, along with a locket around his neck, was his entire stock.

The warehouse smelled of poorly tanned leather, coal dust, rotten fruit, and other less-pleasant things. Between *Cutter's* and a shipyard, a crooked alleyway that tapered from cart-size to shoulder-width pointed inland like a skeletal finger. There was no light except what moon glow penetrated the viscous layer of sulfurous smoke and damp fog that hung upon the city like a shroud. The conditions were good for concealment, but scarcely adequate for one unfamiliar with the surroundings to navigate safely.

Joseph stumbled over a turned-up cobble, stepped knee-deep into a pool of muck, and rammed his knee into an iron brace holding aloft a block-and-tackle. When he turned into the passage that separated *Cutter's* from the next warehouse behind, the overhang of the buildings reduced the light still further.

Rats squeaked and scurried in the gloom, chittering shrilly at this invasion of their freedom. Joseph kicked one accidentally and saw a brief flash of angry red eyes as it sunk its teeth into his shoe before retreating. Joseph resolved that the correct response was to kick harder the next time.

The opportunity was not long in coming. As he reached the end of the lane, his foot again brushed against something soft and yielding.

He unleashed a ferocious blow with the point of his toe, only to have the shapeless mass erupt with drunken curses and spring upright.

"Whyn't ye watch out?" the unknown spouted.

"Sorry," Joseph replied. "I did not see you lyin' there, the way bein' dark and all."

"Irish!" slurred the drunk. "Bleedin' Irish ape. Oy, Freddy, 'ere's another mick makin' free with our territory."

Wasting no time in further apology, Joseph retreated toward the head of the alley, only to find the way blocked by another looming human shape. This one brandished a club over his head and hummed in time to the whistle of the cudgel.

"An' 'e's got coin on 'im, Bill," the alley-dweller addressed as Freddy added, "I 'eard 'em jingle."

Backing toward the wall so the attackers could not circle behind him, Joseph bumped into a shattered barrel. Stooping, he wrenched a barrel-stave free of the hoop and prepared to defend himself.

Freddy rushed in first, swinging his bludgeon in an arc toward Joseph, who ducked aside at the last instant. The blow smacked the bricks beside his head.

Lashing out with the barrel-stave, Joseph caught Freddy a blow on the ear that made the assailant roar and stagger aside. Then, hearing a noise behind him, he swung blindly and managed to hit Bill over the head before being tackled around the middle.

Flailing, Joseph rained a flurry of blows on Bill's back and arms. "Oy, Freddy! Give us a 'and, then!" the assailant demanded as he released his hold and withdrew out of range.

"I think 'e cut me bleedin' ear off," Freddy complained from the darkness.

"Then come 'ere and return the favor with 'is throat!"

"That I will," Freddy replied. This announcement was followed by the recognizable snap of a clasp knife being opened.

Freddy came in more warily this time, knife-hand extended and the blade posed to slash upward into Joseph's belly. The first thrust was batted aside with the barrel-stave, as was the second, but the third lunge jabbed the point of the weapon into the wooden stake, and Joseph's defense was flipped out of his grasp.

Eluding one more thrust of the knife by leaping aside, Joseph found himself seized around the middle from behind. "I got 'im!" Bill gloated. "Just don't cut me when ye stick this papist bog-trotter."

"Bog-trotter, is it?" bellowed a deep, unmistakably Irish voice from in back of Bill. "And who gave you ill-mannered guttersnipes leave to be callin' your betters by rude names?" Another club shrilled through the air, its whine followed by a heavy thud. The grip around Joseph's waist slackened abruptly and fell away.

Freddy had time for one more wild slash with his knife before the newcomer stepped inside the swing and drove the end of his cudgel into the Englishman's midsection. Freddy's breath exploded from him, and as he bent over, the expertly wielded stick was jammed upward into his throat.

Strangling sounds mixed with the running footsteps of Freddy's stumbling flight, but those noises were soon drowned out by the discordant note of police whistles from a short distance away. "That'll be the Thames River patrol," Joseph's deliverer announced serenely. At their feet Bill groaned and thus received his second kick of the night. "I'll be leavin' this trash here as an offerin'," observed the unknown rescuer. "But unless you like the company of magistrates, you'd best be comin' along with me." Grasping Joseph's wrist, he knocked aside a crate revealing a hole in the brick wall that led inside the warehouse. Moments later the two men were three streets beyond the scene of the struggle and Bill's unconscious form.

Twenty-seven hard hours. Ten fingers. Ten toes. Mad Molly had spoken rightly; Kate had delivered a child.

She lay exhausted on her bed. A day had come and gone, and the room was lit by candles again. The figures of the women who had attended her were mute forms in the corner. Martin and Mary Elizabeth waited patiently outside the door. Kate could hear the giggles of Tomeen as he tore up and down the corridor, away from Martin's growling.

There was the baby, partly herself and partly Joseph. Sleep dragged

Kate's senses toward rest, but she resisted, knowing that if she slept they would take him.

Father O'Bannon stood over the child who was wrapped in clean linen. The priest prayed quietly, finishing with the sign of the cross. The Widow Clooney, her round, ruddy face haggard with the ordeal, stepped forward with her arms outstretched.

"Please," Kate whispered, "may I hold him?"

The eyes of the priest and the midwife locked. Father O'Bannon picked up the baby, kissed it on the forehead, and brought the bundle to Kate. She found the strength to take the child, nestling him into the crook of her arm.

"How perfect he is." She examined the tiny hand. The perfect, exquisitely formed nails on the fingers. Brushing her lips across the downy hair she did not take her eyes from his face, a face so much like that of Joseph. The cleft in his chin. Pale lashes. Nose, lips, and cheeks, a miniature of Joseph.

"Aye," Father O'Bannon agreed. "That he is, daughter. Too perfect for this world."

Sleep, her brain commanded. But she fought to stay awake, even as she had fought to bring this child into the light.

"See how much he looks like his father."

A heavy sigh from the priest. "That he does. A fine baby, Kate."

She toyed with the hand. "Big hands like a Donovan, though."

"That's true, daughter. Now you should sleep."

She shook her head in resistance. A single tear brimmed at last and dropped onto the grey cheek of her baby. "You'll take him away and bury him . . ." She clung to the still and lifeless form. "And I'll never again see him if I sleep!" She longed to die as well, to sleep the long sleep with him, to awaken in heaven and watch him run into the arms of Jesus.

"Kate . . ." Father O'Bannon touched her face.

"Not yet!" she pleaded. "Please . . . Martin and Mary Elizabeth must see him, sure. So when Joseph comes home they can say how much his baby boy looked like him!"

The priest gave his assent and Fern, sniffling, opened the door. There were muttered words, a reminder to Martin and Mary Elizabeth that they must be strong, that the infant had not survived. Tomeen, too young to know, burst past the skirts of the women and charged Kate's bed.

"Mama!" he cried, climbing onto the bedrail and attempting to hoist himself up.

Father O'Bannon restrained him with a light touch on his shoulder. "Your mother is restin'."

Widow Clooney came to take Tomeen. "Let him stay." Kate controlled her voice although she wanted to shout. "I need him here, you see." Then she stretched her hand to touch Tomeen's fiery curls. "Here is your wee brother, Tomeen."

Martin, as though he sensed what Kate needed, lifted Tomeen to look into the small face beside her. "Ah, Kate." Martin's voice was thick with grief and pity. "He's beautiful. So like Joseph. See here, Tomeen. Mary Elizabeth, come see the wee babe. His sweet soul is in heaven with Da now. With Mother and the rest. Come here, Mary Elizabeth."

Mary Elizabeth edged toward the bed. As the reality of death struck her, her curious expression cracked and dissolved into tears. "Oh, Kate!" she cried, and ran from the room.

With a strange smile on his lips, Martin handed Tomeen to Father O'Bannon, stooped to kiss Kate and then the baby. "Farewell. Kiss Mother and Da for me." And then to Kate, "Has he a name?"

"I would have called him after yourself if he had lived," she replied.

"Then call him Martin, and I'll live on for him, dear Kate. I'll live a long and happy life for him. I give my word to you."

Nodding in agreement, she let the tears flow freely at last. She wanted to thank Martin. Was he the only one with any sense? She would tell him someday what it meant to her.

He held her hand. "Will you not sleep now, Kate?"

"They'll take him if I sleep."

"I'll take him, Kate. And you must let me."

"I can't be there. He's so very small."

"I'll carry him home to Ballynockanor. Through the home place. Across the fields and then to St. Brigit's cross, which I know you love so well. Then to St. John's. We'll lay him to rest between Da and Mother. He'll not be alone."

Sleep and darkness crowded the edges of her consciousness. She looked gratefully to Martin, knowing he would see to everything. Then she fixed her eyes upon the beautiful, perfect child nestled in the crook of her arm. "Joseph would have been so proud," she said. And then she slept.

The refuge to which Joseph's deliverer took him was on the second floor of a factory that was, by day, a dyeworks. Ground level was rows of vats. The floors and walls were stained with a rainbow of tints that had long since puddled into muddy brown. Overhead all was soot and smoke stains.

The stench of chemicals used to make the cloth accept the dye permeated the air and made Joseph's eyes water. He was grateful to creep up a flight of stairs, even if an unexplained growling rumble grew louder with each step. At the top his conductor nudged open a door that drooped from one hinge like a broken limb and revealed the drying room where during working hours the dyed cloth hung from ropes. But the nighttime view revealed by a few flickering candles made Joseph draw back in alarm. The chest-high cables were festooned with dangling bodies like a macabre display of the recently executed.

Joseph's host chuckled at his reaction. "A penny hang," he reported. "The enterprisin' landlord sees no reason why this expensive cable should go to waste just because it's too dark to work. For a single copper them as has no lodgin's can get out of the London damp." The growling was also thereby explained: the snoring of threescore men suspended under the armpits by clothesline. None of the occupants awakened at the intrusion, and the man observed wryly, "What good can be said of a nation whose greatest contribution to modern life is gin?"

Drawing up a pair of three-legged stools to a candle, Joseph's guide sat down and suggested Joseph do likewise. Beside him, but near at hand, he laid his weapon of choice: a knobby length of blackthorn stick.

The brittle, glimmering light revealed a stocky man of just below

Joseph's height. Green, darting eyes studied him from above a twice-broken nose. "The landlord allows me to stay, gratis, seein' as I keeps order . . . and himself prefers not to come in at nighttime." This was uttered with a smirk. "We can speak freely. Seamus Quincannon," he said, announcing his name. "You've no need to tell me yours. It means no disrespect here."

"Joseph Connor," Joseph replied, omitting the Burke part of his identity.

Quincannon shrugged. "Likely enough. Now tell me this: are you a wanted man?" The hesitation that preceded Joseph's reply prompted Quincannon to add, "I mean here. The peelers cannot be bothered with followin' rapparees runnin' from cattle maimin' in Galway nor Mayo . . . oh aye, I have a knack for recognizin' a man's origins . . . Connaught in your case."

"No," Joseph said. "No one is lookin' for me here."

"Right," Quincannon concluded, slapping both knees with calloused hands. "Here's the drill: you'll be wantin' work. I am the shokelhorn, the matchmaker, if you please. I vouch for you, and you get employment, otherwise never a shillin' will you see. You give me a third of your wages, and I look after your welfare." Raising his hand to still Joseph's protest, Quincannon added, "You need lookin' after, or you'd not be bumblin' into Spice Lane alone, it bein' the border between us and the others."

Despite his position as overseer of the penny hang, Quincannon did not sleep there, nor did he expect Joseph to do so. For the price of one shilling, paid in advance, Joseph was directed to lodgings in Pocock Street that accepted Irish tenants. He was told to report for work at five in the morning.

Foggy lanes and gnawing hunger notwithstanding, long before sunup Joseph labored beside other Irishmen at unloading ships and trundling barrows of goods into warehouses. Looping endlessly from wharfside to the gloomy alleys of Southwark, he counted more than a hundred trips with casks of Madeira wine before he got a break. Then he hastily gulped bread, cheese, and a mug of black beer. He did not bother resuming the count when he was told that all the morning's labor had only emptied the first of five holds of the ship.

It was impossible to carry on conversation while the line was in motion, but after the brief respite, Quincannon picked him out from the others and set him to hauling away at a line that whipped casks up into the storage loft. As the barrels reached the top of their ride, there was a pause for them to be unloaded. The short pauses gave Joseph a chance to question his partner at the hoist.

Brendan Delaney stood a scant inch over five feet, but in spite of this fact (if not because of it), he was the first man to find a reason for brawling, no matter the cause. No one was allowed to take liberties with his stature, yet he was never called by his proper name. A chronic eye inflammation and the resulting perpetually puckered brow caused him to be known as "Squint," and only to this he answered.

"Have you any news from back home?" Joseph inquired politely. "What's the word on Repeal?"

"Repeal, is it?" said Squint, scowling. "I'll give you that for Repeal." He punctuated his scorn with a snap of his fingers. "If I had a drink for every time I heard someone prating of Repeal, I'd be awash in beer over me eyeballs." That these orbs were already yellow and watery crossed Joseph's mind, but he refrained from mentioning it.

"But surely the whole country must be roused after O'Connell's arrest and imprisonment."

"'Tis true it was a scurvy thing, pinchin' the Liberator," Delaney acknowledged, "but they say his cell was the governor's mansion, and Daniel held court every day till his release."

"Release? Released when?"

Delaney, as expected, squinted at Joseph as he muscled the next keg into position on the cargo net. "Where have you been, then?" he inquired. "Bloomin' China? O'Connell and the others was pardoned months ago."

Despite his reluctance at showing too much personal interest, Joseph could not help asking, "And were they all pardoned then?"

Bellowing, "Haulin' away now!" Squint peered closely at Joseph and puffed as the two men tugged on the cable. "As to that, I wouldn't be knowin'." Then he added, "Besides the excitement here is over the trial of the Irish pirates." There was an interruption till the barrel reached the peak of the lift and then, "May God have mercy on their souls, for the English will not."

When Joseph continued to look blank, Squint gave a high-pitched giggle and advised, "Don't try to act like you ain't been away. Sure an' every Irishman in London is talkin' about hangin' of the trans-portees what captured the *Hive*."

Joseph could barely contain the urge to tell Squint everything: how he had been present at the *Hive* mutiny. If Jailer Gann had his way, Joseph's neck would be in a noose as well. Instead Joseph swallowed his amazement and said nothing.

Just as he had promised Kate, Martin saw to the matter. The baby was too small for even the littlest coffin in the shed behind Daugherty's Dry Goods. So Martin took the walnut and maple music box that had belonged to Joseph's mother and removed the bright brass works that played melodies of Bach and Mozart. Mother of pearl violins and flowers were inlaid on the lid, and the name and crest of the House of Burke were set among vines upon the side. The miniature coffin was a thing of beauty and the perfect size to hold the wee, precious treasure of baby Martin Burke.

Laying aside the gears and wheels of music as unworthy for so magnificent a case, Martin determined that he would install the tunes in some other box at a later date. Fern lined the casket with satin. Mary Elizabeth placed a silken pillow in it. And lastly came the tiny occupant, dressed in a white satin christening gown.

Martin carried the coffin himself along the road through Castletown and back home to Ballynockanor.

Through the charred remains of the Donovan dairy barn, where the baby's mother had spent her most holy hours communing with God and the cows . . . across the fields and pastures where generations of Donovan children had played . . . up the slope to St. Brigit's cross to view the beloved valley of Ballynockanor spread out below. Martin showed his namesake in one hour what it took a lifetime to fully love and understand. Or perhaps he was showing baby Martin to the land that must embrace him until the day when Christ would call forth the bones that rested there. Martin and Martin made this pilgrimage alone, but when they came to St. John's, there were hundreds waiting to say farewell.

And so it was done as Kate was locked in merciful sleep.

Father O'Bannon conducted the service. Mary Elizabeth wept and would not be comforted. There was a strange silence as the jewel in the music box was lowered by ropes into the grave. People peeled off in family groups to make their way home. There would be no wake.

Fern took Mary Elizabeth home. Martin stayed with the Claddagh brothers to shovel dirt onto the casket. Mad Molly also remained behind, perching upon a headstone beside Nesbitt as each of the Four Horses took a turn at the shovel. Sonny-boy put his hand upon her bony shoulder and whispered something in the old crone's ear.

Mad Molly replied, saying to Martin, "The babe and all the tears of Mary."

Martin now understood what she had meant. "I see it clearly, Molly," he answered, wiping sweat from his brow and passing the shovel to Moor.

"Nay, Martin. Ye do not see it a'tall." She lowered herself to the ground and scooped up a handful of earth, letting it run through her fingers until it covered the last gleam of the violin. "Three days and her milk will come."

Simeon, an apelike man, glanced sharply at her. He nodded.

Molly continued, "What's a heifer without her calf?" She shook her head slowly from side to side. "The monster on the mountain thinks he'll have his way, but he'll not! Three days until her milk'll come. Her teats'll be full of milk, but no babe to suckle. Hard as stone her breasts'll be. Are there no wee calves in all Ireland, Martin? Not one? Not two? I ask ye? Bein' a dairyman yerself, can ye not see old Molly's meanin'?"

Martin stared at her blankly, then spoke past her babble to Nesbitt. "What's she goin' on about, then, Nesbitt?"

Nesbitt shrugged beneath his greatcoat. "What'd your sister do when a cow lost her calf?"

"Found another." Martin was slowly comprehending. "Another calf . . . lest the heifer grieve and her milk dry up. Or worse yet . . ."

"Die, herself?"

"Another calf?"

"Aye."

Mad Molly held up her fingers. "Three days before the milk comes heavy and painful in Kate's breasts. Aye. She'll long for death, and it may come and carry her away, too, if the Thing has his way."

Martin looked up at the line of faces before him. "Where?"

Nesbitt shoved his hands into his pockets. "There are seven hundred inmates at the workhouse in Galway City. Life and death come hand in hand each day in such a place."

Understanding hit Martin like a thunderclap. "I should go, then. Who will show me the way?"

Moor, dark-eyed and brooding, stepped forward. Placing his massive hands on Martin's shoulders, he pointed toward the road. "God," the giant uttered, sending Martin off on his own.

Three days before the coming of her milk and only the assurance that God would help him find the road. It was a daunting task: find the workhouse and, descending into that hell, find life and the resurrection of hope in a baby.

Martin was no fool. He would not go with God alone to such a place. He would not go on foot. There was no time to walk.

"Saddle me the mare," he told Old Flynn, the stablemaster.

Flynn grumbled as he rose from his rope bed in the tack room. "And who are you to be tellin' me?"

Carrying death and innocence in his arms had given Martin an edge, a courage he had not known was inside him until now. "I'm the head of this house until Squire Joseph returns and my sister, the Lady Burke, is on her feet again. You'll do well to remember it. Think on what work I've been about today and know I'm not a boy after this mornin.'"

The stablemaster blinked back dumbly at him in surprise. "So it would seem."

"Aye. The dappled mare, if you please." The mare was called Savina, after her color, which was neither grey nor dun, but a soft mix of the two. She was fourteen years old, born the same year as Martin, and had wide brown eyes that held a gentleness for children and idiots. When Mad Molly walked past her stall, she nickered kindly. As a result, Molly declared that when she got to heaven she would ride Savina through the clouds.

Martin had ridden the mare every day to check the far pastures. She sensed the weakness of his shrunken leg and acted mindful of his balance. Where another animal might have known his debility and purposely crow-hopped to the left, sending him flying out of the saddle, Savina was thoughtful in her moves. Old Flynn explained away the mare's affinity to Martin by saying she had been trained as a lady's horse—taught the leg cues for a sidesaddle mount. Flynn meant this as an insult, but Martin refused to accept the offense. There was something more about this horse. Molly declared that Savina saw angels on the wind and obeyed them. Martin did not doubt such a thing could be. Had not Christ ridden upon an unbroken colt? Even dumb animals knew things, Martin suspected. Most importantly, her legs were strong as iron. She could go all day at a gentle lope and not lather. Three days there and back again was only possible by this means.

Mindful his own appearance might be important, Martin washed and dressed himself in riding clothes that he'd found last summer in an old box stored beneath a harness in the tack room. The garb had once belonged to an adolescent William Marlowe, the son of the previous squire. The breeches, waistcoat, and jacket were too big, but the boots were almost right and a wool greatcoat hid the flaws. He crowned himself with a top hat, which added six inches to his height and perhaps three years to his age.

He would need money. Mindful that Kate must not know of his impending adventure, he sneaked into the house through the kitchen and moved quietly from room to room to avoid the household staff and Mary Elizabeth. Beneath his mattress he kept twenty new shillings in a leather bag. His treasure. These had been a gift from Joseph the day of the wedding. Martin had saved it, counting each coin once a week, as he dreamed of buying passage to America when Joseph came back to be with Kate.

"What'll I tell Adam Kane?" Old Flynn complained as Martin returned to take Savina's reins and lead her out into the cold afternoon.

"Tell him . . . I've gone to fetch a calf." Martin was in no mood to answer questions. He climbed onto the mounting block and clambered onto the back of the patient mare.

"When will ye be home?" Flynn scratched his beard and peered doubtfully at Savina.

Martin wheeled her toward the gate and the highway. "In time for the milkin'," Martin replied, nudging her to a lope. He called back, "Nesbitt'll know."

∽ 4 ∾

From Pocock Street to the grim bulk of Marshalsea debtor's prison, Joseph was so lost in thought that he failed to notice the increasing press of the crowd. To be released from a morning's labor and have his position held had cost him another precious shilling paid to Quincannon.

Joseph shivered inside the grey cloak. The tremor was not entirely due to the thick fog, though it embraced him like the immersing arms of a sea witch. He had parted from the prison ship *Hive* in mid-Atlantic—had been left adrift when he refused to participate in killing officers and guards. How had it been retaken, and what would be the fate of the rebels?

Piracy was a hanging offense. Many of the *Hive's* transportees had been innocent of the plot to take the ship, but would they be shown any mercy because of that fact? He had to know more.

It was near the approach to the south end of London Bridge that Joseph became aware of the throng around him. The route into the city was always crowded, but this was different. All were moving in the same direction. The mood was festive, as if the travelers were on holiday. Barefoot children darted in and out among their elders, and a pushcart vendor with a smoking charcoal brazier hawked "Ches . . . nuts! Penny a bag. Fresh roasted Ches . . . nuts!"

Joseph had traveled in England in his student days, had even lived in London for a time. He could recall no mass assembly like what he was experiencing. Was it some universal holiday, or a government ceremony of national significance?

When he could no longer stand the curiosity, Joseph plucked a ragged nine- or ten-year-old by the elbow and asked, "Where is everyone goin', lad?"

The boy answered sharply, "Wappin', of course," and, shaking off Joseph's grasp, darted ahead.

"What's in Wapping?" Joseph called after.

The scornful reply floated back over the noisy mob, buoyed and propelled by raucous laughter at such rustic ignorance: "To see the men in chains."

More perplexed than ever, Joseph was at that moment beside a carriage. The forward progress of the conveyance was blocked by pedestrians who would not give way. The impatient occupant alighted to proceed on foot.

The tall man, impeccably dressed in frock coat and cravat, brushed back a lock of wavy, greying hair from his imposingly high forehead and, settling his top hat firmly on his head, fell in step beside Joseph. "It is quite a spectacle, this," he remarked to no one in particular.

Joseph took the words as if meant for him and seized the opportunity to inquire once again about the cause of the holiday air.

"Have you not heard of the celebrated case of piracy involving a prison ship called the *Hive*?"

Answering cautiously, Joseph admitted to possessing some knowledge about the boat in question.

"This is only the final act in the drama," Joseph's sharp-eyed companion noted. "No doubt you've heard how the convicts attempted to sail into Morocco, expecting to exchange their stolen prize for a life of ease and freedom from arrest? The outcome could not have been better contrived if it had been written in a novel! The port into which chance winds propelled them was Mogador, the very place being bombarded by the French admiral de Joinville. Naturally, the Sultan hoped to curry favor with a potential ally . . . us . . . and so speedily threw all the pirates into dungeons and delivered them to our navy with dispatch." This account was uttered much louder than necessary, as if the speaker were on stage and addressing a packed audience, which in fact he was. "The verdict was never in doubt, even if most of the miserable wretches have only had their sentences doubled and are already again on their way to New South Wales. Ah, but the ringleaders . . ."

Wapping was an area of East London, just beyond the liberty of the Tower and squeezed between the Jewish tenements of Whitechapel and the tide-washed muddy shore of the Thames. It could be reached in twenty-five minutes of brisk walking from the north end of the bridge. The pace of travel reduced the amount of breath available for conversation, and even Joseph's garrulous companion fell silent.

The nature of the businesses lining Wapping High Road was characterized by cheap grog shops and slumping brick taverns dating from the days of Walter Raleigh. Contrary to Joseph's expectations, all of these were shuttered and locked, and blue-uniformed constables—peelers—stood guard alongside.

The focus of the migration was reached at last when the banks of the Thames reappeared between tumbledown walls and the charred ribs of derelict ships. Climbing an abandoned cargo crane, Joseph reached a spot where he could look down over the heads of the others on an open space immediately before a flight of steps leading to the water's edge.

The throng continued to grow for a time, and then, from the rear of the multitude, a growl of expectation swelled; hoarse cheering blended with wicked laughter.

The mob parted to admit the passage of a black, windowless coach. A guard sat beside the driver on the box, and a pair of sentries stood on the running board at the rear by the only door. It wheeled in a slow circle, then stopped at the top of the stairs.

From the interior of the Black Maria, Patrick Frayne and Ben Brophy were led blinking into the hazy daylight and the jeers of the assembly. The two chiefs behind the seizure of the *Hive* were well known to Joseph. So was the figure who next emerged from the carriage—in fact, so well and unpleasantly known that Joseph wished he could plunge from his perch and hide, but could not for the clusters of others clinging beneath him.

Jailor Gann, the top of his bald head and the puckered skin of the scar that divided his face both gleaming red, faced the spectators and pivoted in place as if giving the empty, sunken flap of his right eyelid a thorough view of the crowd. In his gruff voice he shouted for attention, and when something like quiet in the first thousand onlookers had been achieved, he turned the proceedings over to an officer on horseback.

The official announced, "Patrick Frayne and Ben Brophy of . . . Ireland." Here his words were overpowered by jeers and catcalls. Brophy babbled and wept. Frayne appeared stoical. "You stand convicted of piracy. Your punishment having been fixed and no appeal possible, today the sentence will be carried out." Dropping his hand dramatically, the officer indicated the mud below. "You will be enchained here until three tides have washed over you. And may God have mercy on your souls."

At that moment Gann's good eye, roving over the spectators, chanced to find and lock on Joseph. Joseph saw the jailor hurriedly approach the chief constable and speak urgently and pointedly.

Waiting no longer, Joseph knocked loose three others as he descended from his vantage point before dropping the last six feet to the ground. As the chatter of police rattles burred behind him, he pushed and kicked his way to the edge of the mob, then wondered which way to run.

A carriage stood there; the same gentleman's carriage Joseph had encountered on London Bridge, together with the same gentleman also emerging from the scene. "Leaving already?" the man inquired. "Most of the others will stay until dark, commenting on the struggles of the living and the changes in the corpses of the dead. But my interest was the mob itself, and I have seen enough. May I give you a lift back as far as the bridge?"

The two men rode in silence as far as Lower Thames Street, where Joseph got out. He thanked his host for the unexpected kindness and asked his name.

"Dickens," was the reply, "Charles Dickens." And the carriage swirled away.

Winds strengthened from the west, blowing clouds away to reveal a moon so full it illuminated Martin's path. The world glowed cold around him in varying shades of colorless grey.

Tugging the hat down over his ears, he tucked his face deeper into the collar of the greatcoat and settled into Savina's confident stride. The course of the moon arched from east to west as numbing hours passed. Twice Martin felt his senses sliding toward slumber. Both times Savina came to a standstill.

At the slowing of the measured gait Martin's head jerked up. He sat a moment, listening to the wind scrape its underbelly across the tops of the boulders. Patting the horse, he mumbled, "Are you weary, then, girl?"

Martin reckoned it must be sometime after midnight. The musky scent of turf smoke was on the air.

Peering out from beneath the hat brim he spotted a faint light gleaming from a dugout built into the side of the hill. Too poor to be called a house or even a cabin, the structure might have been used as a shelter for swine, but tonight it sheltered humankind. Martin was drawn by the promise of warmth, and yet thoughts of Ribbonmen and their rival gangs of Protestant Steel Boys plagued him.

If they made for him, he would ride away. Whoever was inside, they had no horses to pursue him.

Savina picked her way carefully through the stone-littered field.

The gruff voice of a man called out, "Stop where ye are!" The tone contained a warning. "Who do ye be?"

Martin drew up the reins, "I'm on my way to Galway City."

The thin, ragged form was silhouetted in the half-collapsed frame of the doorway. "Then travel on, Englishman."

"I was hopin' to rest and warm myself awhile. I'm Irish, as yourself, and a patriot. God bless all here . . ."

"God may bless who He likes, but God ain't here in this shanty. And there's no good in anyone travelin' a'horseback at such an hour. There's no Irishman these days who rides a horse, except them as is a thief on the prowl or employed by the Crown to torment and evict decent families from their own homes! Ye may be the very devil himself or, if a angel, ye're the angel of death come to take what I have left. Push on . . . or approach at ye own peril. I'll kill any as seek to harm me wife and kids. There's no room here for any but me own family."

Behind the voice was that of a woman, murmuring something indistinct but desperate. Then Martin heard three different cries of young children, groggy yet insistent. This was no gang of rapparees. He breathed a sigh of relief.

Then the nomad spoke again, more gently, at the urging of his woman. "There's a barn three miles farther on. There's two men there tendin' the squire's ewes. It's the lambin' time. Aye. If ye can pay, no doubt they'll take ye in. But without coin neither the Blessed Virgin nor St. Joseph himself could find room at their inn. And such as we? I begged milk for me kids and was turned away. We'd be content with the fodder for their sheep, but there's more care for sheep in Ireland these days than for humanity."

Martin knew his mount and clothing made him the enemy of this family. He knew they were hungry—a man, a woman, and children starving beside the road. Putting his hand to the bag of shillings suspended around his neck, he resisted the urge to share with them. Then his heart cried, "Mercy!" He knew what Kate would do—and Joseph as well. What was one shilling when there were nineteen more? With a single shilling they could buy potatoes enough to survive a month. Milk would still be out of reach, however.

Removing one coin from the pouch he called, "I'm not the devil. Here's a shillin' to prove it. Feed your flock." He tossed it at the feet of the vagabond. It bounced once and rolled into the shelter. With a shout and a mad scramble to retrieve it, the figure vanished into the hovel.

Martin turned away, their exultation ringing behind him.

"'Tis an angel, Dan!" cried the woman. "An angel has visited us this night."

The lambing barn stood beneath the ridgetop, out of the wind in the lee of a hill where a village had existed not long before.

Martin saw what it had been at once—a row of connected stone cabins that had housed perhaps a half-dozen related families side by side. Devoid of tenants, the inner walls were broken through in low doorways, which allowed continuous passage from one space to the other. The rooms that had been home to generations of farmers, children, and children's children, now were a palace for the landlord's sheep. The rubble of other structures told Martin that this place had been spared the wreckers only because it was deemed useful for livestock. The thatch of the roof was thick, the exterior washed in white lime. Martin knew in time the love shown by its former occupants would fade, thatch would rot and fall away, paint and mortar would dissolve. Those who tended the lambs would not repair the leaks or care if the walls took on the look of the stony fields and mossy boulders.

Instinctively Savina knew they had reached the end of a day's journey. She stopped with her head a foot from the doorless entryway at the center of the building. An open fire burned in a pit on the dirt floor. The interior was thick with the haze of turf smoke.

"Halloo the house!" Martin shouted in.

"Who's there?" came the reply as a boy not much younger than himself came to peer out. At the sight of Martin on the horse, the boy doffed his cap. "Good evenin' to ye, sar."

There was an advantage in remaining on Savina's tall back. "You're about the lambin', are you?" Martin asked.

"Aye, sar. Me an' me da. That's all is here." The boy shuffled uneasily. "Us an' the squire's ewes. A dozen. An' a half-dozen lambs so far."

"Where's your da then?"

At Martin's query the boy ducked his head, retreated into the barn, and gave a shout for his father. "There's a young gentleman on his horse here, Da."

The father, a ruddy-faced, tousled man who was an older version of his son, came scurrying. He and the boy gawked nervously up at Martin. "Well, sar," said the father. "Ye're out late. Lost the road, have ye? Goin' on to the new squire's place?"

"What squire would that be?" Martin adjusted his hat and remained regally perched.

"The new squire, Denis Mahon. Though he ain't here an' we ain't yet seen him."

Martin looked off to where the moonlight blazed like a forest fire on the ridge. "So this is part of the estate of the late Colonel Mahon?" Martin thought he had come farther along the way than this grim place. The identity of the former landlord explained the destitute family living in the swine shelter.

"That it is. God rest his honor's soul," remarked the father.

Martin mumbled, "If his honor had a soul to rest."

Father and son exchanged fearful looks. "Ye're out late, sar."

Martin patted Savina on her powerful neck. "On my way to Galway City. My soul could use a rest. Sure, and so could my horse."

The boy, who was barefoot, glanced at the fine boots. The father bobbed his head. "We're shepherds, sar. We've naught but straw and a peat fire to offer ye."

Martin was grateful now for his costume. These two were no different from the poor of Ballynockanor. The sight of tailored clothing and well-heeled boots frightened them. Martin knew they would not pry into the purpose of his travels. "I'll accept your straw and your fire. I'm no stranger to barns and lambin'. Though cattle are more my specialty."

The man chuckled and took Savina's reins as Martin slipped down from the saddle. "I told meself, Big Pete, says I, that's a man for cattle. Squire Colonel Mahon, God rest him, he was all for havin' naught but sheep on these pastures. Sure, an' he kept cattle on his northern estates, near Strokestown I heard. Not grass enough for cattle in Ballyglenkilly, says he. Sheep. There's the ticket."

"And before the sheep?" Martin stretched his crippled leg and limped into the barn. Big Pete followed after, leading Savina. Little Pete led the horse into an empty stall and took off the saddle. Martin knew it would be inappropriate to intervene. He must play the role of a well-off gent or risk being turned away.

"Sure, an' there was a village here. Ballyglenkilly, it were. Gone now. The land is better fit for four-legged creatures than for our own kind. Wherever they go, I says to 'em, they'll surely be better off than they were here in Ballyglenkilly."

Stretching his hands to the fire Martin inquired. "I came across a poor family back up the road."

"Aye." Big Pete stuck out his lower lip. "I know the ones ye mean. Tossed, they were, Lord have mercy. But a man's gotta look to his own. Take 'em in an' . . . the steward'd not like it. Pity though. An' herself big as a ewe ready t'lamb."

Behind them, a ewe stirred in the warmth of the straw. The three settled in around the fire.

Big Pete offered Martin a mug of weak tea and a boiled potato. He accepted gratefully. Little Pete blew on his hands and yawned.

"Sure, an' I'd love t'sleep till spring," said the boy absently.

His father gave him a sharp look, as if to say such talk of sleep might make Martin think ill of him. "When I was the age of yeself, twasn't sleep I was think'in of."

Martin, exhausted from grief and duty and the long ride, finished the tea, tugged his coat around himself, and exhaled with contentment. "Sleep till spring," he repeated as if the thought were a great temptation to him. "We'd miss the ghost stories."

Little Pete laughed. "Ghost stories, sure! Best part of winter. See Da, he's one of us, then."

"You've nothin' a'tall to fear from me," Martin said. "I'll be no trouble . . . sleep till mornin'."

Then father and son relaxed. The elder smoked his pipe, passing it to his son. Martin was vaguely aware when the pair got up to check the ewes in the pens and make sure the newborn lambs had suckled and were warm. Then he drifted off into dreamless slumber.

5

My *dearest Kate,* Joseph wrote. The nib of the quill pen was blunt, mushy, and untrimmable, the ink contained globs of indissoluble pigment, and the sheet on which he was writing was the reverse of a discarded indenture salvaged from a solicitor's rubbish bin. Kate's name disappeared into an initial letter followed by a lump and a smear. It would have to serve.

> *I am well, and you are not to worry. But I have come as near to you and home as I dare. It does no harm for me to tell you that I am in London, as my presence here is already known, though not my exact location. No doubt home will be watched and you followed, so we cannot risk meeting. And so, darling Kate, I am off to America.*

Joseph paused, and three splotches of oily blue added their exclamation points, like teardrops, to the letter. Joseph would not tell

Kate how long he would struggle before leaving for America. It would only fret her and, if the letter were intercepted, might set the hounds on his track.

> *I will do my best to locate Kevin, and together we will arrange your passage as soon as may be.*
>
> *I am told that Daniel is free. If you write to him at Derrynane or perhaps at Merrion Square, he will certainly help you close down affairs on the estate and prepare to emigrate.*
>
> *There is so much more I would say if the means were not so wretched . . .*

Joseph's thoughts on the night following the chaining of Brophy and Frayne were as dismal as the Pocock Street boardinghouse and as black as the Thames. It was almost as if the river water that had taken the lives of the two pirates had likewise closed over his own soul.

Jailor Gann in London and Joseph already recognized! There was no doubt it was so. In recrossing London Bridge he had tried to walk in a casual and unconcerned manner, telling himself he had imagined the identifying look that crossed the warder's face. Yet even as he proceeded with his internal lecture, Joseph found his feet hurrying and his head swiveling to look over his shoulder for pursuers.

The bedroom floor of the boardinghouse was uneven, and his bedfollow, Squint Delaney, rolled over in his sleep and tumbled against a wall. He awoke with a grunt, smacked his neighbor in the back of the head for disturbing him, then went back to sleep. The drunken slumberer never awakened at all.

What had Joseph done? Despite wanting desperately to return to Kate, he had jeopardized his only chance to do so. He had refused free passage to America in order to earn enough money to go straight to Ireland. Now the *Nantucket* was gone, and remaining in London might be too risky to chance. What was worse, Gann knew Joseph's whereabouts and would certainly send word to Galway. Kate and the Burke estates would be watched.

Forcing himself to think rationally, Joseph reviewed what little positive news he had: Daniel O'Connell was a free man. If a letter could be sent to O'Connell, then the Liberator might have a plan. At the very least he would stand good for Joseph's passage money to America. For the first time Joseph admitted the possibility that going to the New World without Kate might be the only practical choice.

But where could Joseph hide to await a reply? How long would it be before Gann and the peelers rousted out the Irish community or found a paid informer to betray Joseph's location? If he were taken, he would be shipped off to Australia like the others from the *Hive*. Or worse still, Gann might lie about his involvement with the pirates and whom would the authorities believe—a prison official or an escaped convict?

It was a long and sleepless night of no answers and the anguished feeling that Kate, so near in his dreams, was now further away than ever.

It was wee Tom who saved Kate that night.

She awoke in darkness, without remembering the sun. When she tried to sit up, the movement made her gasp for breath. Widow Clooney, knitting in a corner of the room, raised her eyes and said, "It'll be awhile. You're torn bow to stern. Sure, and you'll be wantin' to take it slow."

"What day is it, then?" Kate asked, wanting to see the body of her child one more time, uncertain if any time had passed.

"'Twas last night you delivered."

Where had the day gone? Kate put a hand to her brow. Her head ached. Everything ached. How had it gone so wrong? "Is the baby . . . has Martin . . . is it over then?"

Widow Clooney put aside her knitting and rose slowly. "All over, darlin'. Your brother Martin laid the wee babe between your mother and your da. God rest them." She crossed herself. "You'll not be rememberin' we got you up a bit ago to use the chamber pot and change the linens? Hmmm. Sure, you were groggy at that. It's food you'll be needin'."

"Not hungry." Kate turned her face to the wall, wanting to cry out in anguish and rage. How could the commonplace things of life continue as though nothing had happened? How could she eat when the child she had cherished inside her womb would never turn his face to her breast and draw his life from her own? And what meaning did her life have now? She had failed, somehow. Even in this. Her love had not been strong enough to keep the baby alive. "I'll not be eatin'."

Ignoring her protest, Widow Clooney continued cheerfully, "Aye. Food and rest. Time. There's the remedy for grief. Fern killed that wicked rooster, the one leapt out at Mary Elizabeth . . . feathered devil he was. Mary Elizabeth was pleased t'pluck him after the way he went for her. Sure, and he's boilin' in the kettle. Make a lovely soup, he will. I'll fetch some broth." She left the room.

The candle on the window ledge was near to guttering. There was a high wail on the wind. Kate knew the elder ones would say it was the cry of the banshee shrieking from the mountaintop. She sighed, wishing only for one voice to comfort her. "Joseph," she whispered, thinking he must also be dead and wanting to die too.

Behind her, in the doorway, the terrified voice of wee Tomeen called to her. "Mama!" he blubbered, "gark! Scary."

Wincing, she rolled over to see Tomeen in the doorway. His night-shirt quivered with his trembling. He clutched a square of precious sheep fleece, a thing he had named "Ni-Nite," that accompanied him everywhere.

"Ah, Tomeen." Kate's self-pity diminished at the sight of his terror.

"Gark!"

"Aye, it's dark. But you've nothin' to fear, darlin'."

"Sleep wi' Mama." He stretched out his arms as Widow Clooney stepped around him.

"Nay, Tom! Your mother needs her rest. Get back to bed!" Widow Clooney did not look at him but swept over to Kate with a cup of steaming soup in hand.

"Mama! Scary!" insisted Tomeen more loudly. "Mama's bed wi' Mama!"

Pity brimmed in Kate. She pushed back the spoon. "Let him come."

"It'll do him no good a'tall if you baby him."

Kate snapped, "Sure, and he hears the wind. It's enough to scare anyone, that sound. Let him come."

"You're not healed enough to have a child share your bed."

Kate raised herself on her elbow to peer around the ample figure of Widow Clooney. "And that's just what I'd be doin' if the baby'd not flown away. I want Tomeen, I say! He's not seen me in two days. Let him come to his mama!"

Widow Clooney shrugged and, in a patronizing tone, called Tom. "It'll do no good to baby you, boy, but sure, if Mama says so, then bring that scrap of wool."

"His Ni-Nite," Kate corrected holding out her arms. "Come on, lovey."

Relief flooded Tomeen's face. Thumb to mouth, he toddled forward.

Widow Clooney put a hand on his gleaming curls. "Your mama'll drink this broth." She handed the cup to Kate. Then to Tomeen the midwife instructed, "Sure, and you're a big boy. Pee in the pot before you get into bed."

Fear vanished, Tom beamed as he peed in the chamber pot. "Like Matty," he said proudly referring to Martin. "Pee standin' up like Matty."

"Aye," Kate crooned, finishing the soup. "You're a big boy now, Tomeen. Almost two years old."

Widow Clooney agreed. "That he is. Now into bed with Mama, Tomeen. Careful, darlin'. Mama needs her boy to lay very still beside her." She helped him onto the mattress and lifted him close to Kate.

"Sing it, Mama." His request was dreamy. "Sing me Tomeen Cuffs."

His head tucked beneath her chin, Kate snuggled him close. Stroking his soft, clean hair, she began to sing his favorite song:

One night when I was courting,
I went unto a spree.

With polished boots and fancy socks,
I was dressed up to a tee . . .

As she sang, she touched his toes where the fancy boots would have been. He began to giggle.

With tommy cuffs and buttons
and collar white and tall,
I went to meet my Nora
That night at Maxwell's ball . . .

Here he began to sing along in his off-key rendition of the tune. "Tomeen cuffs. Meet my mama . . . mama and a ball!"

When it was done, his lids were burdened with sleep. "Sing again, Mama." He reached up to touch her cheek. "Sing Tomeen Cuffs again."

Kate had forgotten Widow Clooney was in the room. The midwife caught her gaze and held it for an instant. Kate remembered that Widow Clooney had buried her husband and eldest son.

"Did you wake him, then?" Kate asked, knowing.

The woman said quietly, "They never tire of their mother's singin'. Them as goes on livin' need us, y'see, Kate. That's why we go on livin', darlin'. They need us t'hold 'em when the wind howls. Need us to sing Tommy Cuffs again and again."

6

Annie Grogan's labor began just before dawn. She showed little sign of discomfort and gave no signal that there was difficulty.

Near noon, when the moment of birth drew near, Grogan ordered his three daughters from the shelter and delivered the child himself. Annie gave a faint cry at the crowning, pushed one final time, and then lay back, content. And as the baby drew a first breath, Annie Grogan breathed her last.

There was no explanation for her dying, no real reason for it as far as Grogan could tell. Annie had simply given up, quit trying, left him alone with the burden of caring for their children.

"Don't do this to me, Annie, girl. Don't leave me to it alone!" For the second time, his begging went unheeded.

He thought of the lambing barn.

The death of all hope that someone might help.

A cup of milk for a starving child or Annie's life. There was no mercy left in the universe.

"What am I to do?"

He sat listening to the excited voices of his daughters outside as the color drained from Annie's cheeks. A look of peace and joy spread across her face. He envied her. She was beautiful again, as beautiful as the day he wed her.

So this was how it ended.

He wrapped the squalling infant in a shred of table linen, then placed it beside the smoldering fire. It grew calm with the warmth. But he knew the fire would die, and then the baby would die too.

What could he do? He washed Annie's face and hands, brushed her hair, and laid her on the woolen shawl. There would be no coffin, only this plaid cloth for a shroud.

"Da?" Ceili called. "Is it over, Da?"

"Can we see Mother," Corrie asked, "and the baby?"

Grogan emerged from the shelter. "She's flown away," he replied. "Like Granda did. Like your wee brothers, Corrie. Remember?"

"Flown away?" Corrie tried on the words. She knew about death. Could he not say it plain?

Megan cried, "I want Mama."

Grogan wiped his eyes with the back of his hand. His voice cracked. "Megan, darlin'. She's flown . . . y'know . . . Mama's flown away . . ." Megan could not understand, so Grogan gave the stern command to Corrie, "Take your sisters yonder to the top of the knock and wait for me there."

From within came a faint bleating sound.

"The baby!" Ceili tried to dodge past her father. He snatched her up and held her aloft as though he might toss her away from him.

"Corrie!" Grogan ordered, "take them away! Listen! D'y hear me? The baby won't live! It ain't got a chance! Now go . . . get . . . away with ye all! Let me do what must be done!"

When viewed from the hilltop just north of the town, Galway City's workhouse resembled a gigantic belt buckle. The high walls that encircled the complex formed the frame, and the central span comprising men's and women's dormitories was the clasp. In the middle of the compound were the halls given to the grinding of bones into fertilizer and the grinding of men's spirits into dust. Martin, riding Savina in a line of other travelers descending the slope, noticed that when the bulk of the facility appeared in view, all the wayfarers had the same reaction: they crossed themselves and looked immediately away.

The workhouses of England and Ireland were places of last resort. No one with any alternatives left available to them would willingly submit to the crushing labor and domineering discipline. Men were separated from their wives, and children from their parents, but the recently evicted homeless and hungry were housed on pallets alongside perishing tubercular wretches and unresponsive creatures in the last stages of syphilis.

Forcing himself to inspect his destination, Martin studied the groups of raggedly dressed men grouped around piles of rocks in the courtyards. They were thin to the point of emaciation. The swirling winds left in the wake of the retreating storm made the paupers' clothing flap on their bony frames like rags caught on winter-stripped tree limbs. Under the watchful eye of a better-clad and manifestly better-fed foreman, the men pounded one stone against another, tossing the fragments into one heap and selecting larger rocks again from the other. Reminding himself of his mission, Martin quelled his tremors and urged Savina up to the gate.

The mention of Squire Joseph's name, together with Martin's dress and demeanor, gained him admittance by a porter, who conducted him to the workhouse overseer. He met that official in the hallway. Again Squire Joseph's name allowed Martin the opportunity to state his case.

"No, no, no," protested Superintendent Fadge upon hearing Martin's proposal. "This is not a baby farm! We do not sell children. What sort of illicit establishment do you take us for? We offer gainful work in exchange for nutritious meals and adequate housing."

On his way to Fadge's office, Martin had seen hollow-eyed crones sitting in circles doing gainful work for nutritious meals. They were surreptitiously stuffing their toothless mouths with shreds of green, stinking meat plucked from the chicken carcasses they were given to pulverize into bonemeal. The drafty hall was unheated; the women wearing even thinner clothing than the men. Among thirty huddled together around the rotting poultry, Martin saw one blanket.

"But surely," Martin said reasonably, barely controlling his anger and rising gorge, "surely what is best for a child would be a lovin' and carin' home. And would it not be a savin' of precious resources as well?"

Fadge stopped beside a doorless room containing a woman and a child of about Tomeen's age. "Well," Fadge said, sniffing through his long, thin nose, "even if such a suggestion could be considered, it is pointless at this time. We have no infants, you see. The one here is old enough to be removed from its mother and taken to the foundling facility in Kinvarra, as indeed it will be tomorrow or the next day. No infants allowed here." The mother snatched up the toddler and clasped it to her, but Fadge made no comment.

"Don't you have any newborns here?" Martin queried.

"Dear me, no," Fadge said. "The last was over a month ago."

"Only a month?" Martin remembered how long Tomeen had needed Susan, the wet nurse. Perhaps a month was not too old a calf? "Where is he?"

"Dead. Little brutes never thrive coming from such rude excuses for parents. They have no maternal instincts, or they would not be in such unsuitable conditions."

Remembering the music box and the anguished love with which it was attended, Martin's insides twisted into a painful knot. He caught himself from stumbling on the stone of a doorway, his body contorted with retching spasms that stopped short of bringing up his bile.

"Oh, my," Fadge said, backing away. "You must tell the squire that you were ill when you arrived. Mustn't let him think you got sick here. No, indeed."

Slowly wiping his mouth on the back of his hand Martin replied, "I'll be better as soon as I'm out of here." Fadge accompanied Martin to the gate and saw him back aboard Savina. "Where did you say the children are taken?" Martin asked.

"Kinvarra. But you won't find infants there either, I'm afraid. It's the harvest, you see. Plenty of potatoes. Even the destitute can work the fields and get paid with enough to eat. I suggest you come back in January say. Plenty of orphans in January. Pneumonia takes off the mothers . . . and the babies too usually . . . but you might find one then."

Martin was already digging his heels into Savina's flanks and stirring the beast into a very willing canter. Fadge called after him, "Mention me to the squire, and I'll be glad to write to the board of governors. Perhaps an exception can be made . . ."

The storm, not content with the lashing it had recently given the flanks of Connaught, returned with a blustery vengeance. Clouds glowered on Martin as he returned northward, reflecting the gloom that surrounded his heart. He had failed, and he knew it. The clearcut direction of Mad Molly's prophecy weighed on him, but there was no longer any time. The three days would expire, and he could not heap on Kate the additional burden of worrying about his safety.

The rain began pelting again. Martin and Savina both bent their chins into the tempest and forged up the slope.

Jailor Gann emerged from the warren of passageways that connected Newgate Prison with the courtrooms of Old Bailey. He blinked and scowled like a nocturnal predator unexpectedly thrust into sunshine.

In the hall outside Lord Justice Blaine's chambers, Gann met with Police Chief Inspector Appleby, the same man who had been in command of the executions of the pirates. At Appleby's tap on the door there came a bellowed, "Enter!" and soon both law officers stood in the presence of the judge. Blaine did not invite them to sit.

"Mi'lord," commenced Appleby, "you have already met Mister Gann as he gave witness against the pirates. He has come forward with additional information and wishes to be of further service."

Blaine grunted. "I have heard both from Mister Gann and *about* him," the magistrate intoned severely. "What now?"

"Mi'lord," Appleby hurried on before Gann could speak, "Mister Gann attended the executions. While there he spotted in the crowd the face of a fugitive from justice, a convicted felon who escaped at the moment of being returned to custody at the Cape."

"This would be?"

Not liking the fact that his story was not being told by him, Gann burst out, "It is that famous traitor, Joseph Burke, yer honor. He was convicted of conspiracy and transported for life. He is here, sir, and I would be pleased to aid in his capture."

"Stop!" Justice Blaine thundered. "Joseph, Lord Burke of Connaught, is not wanted by the Crown. He was pardoned with Daniel O'Connell and the other Irish traversers."

"But sir," Gann whined, "he was in my charge when he struck me, me, an officer of the Crown."

"That is quite enough," Blaine said coldly. "Lord Burke's pardon was effective before the *Hive* ever sailed. He should not have even been on the wretched ship!" With that Blaine ceased speaking to or even looking at Gann. Instead he addressed Inspector Appleby. "Prime Minister Peel is extremely anxious to conciliate the Irish members of Parliament, which include the pardoned O'Connell and his son, Maurice. The younger O'Connell is even now here in London forming an Irish National Society to which both the Earl of Clanrickarde and Lord Castlereagh belong. Recapture Burke! Instead you are to offer him every assistance. In fact, Appleby, you must deliver this news to Maurice O'Connell personally."

"But he struck me!" Gann babbled. "The Irish dog struck me! He can't go unpunished!" He was still babbling when Appleby, apologizing for the intrusion and promising compliance with Blaine's command, dragged Gann from the judge's chambers.

Cold water sluiced down from the featureless skies as if London were about to be swept into the sea. There was no cheerfulness to the deluge, at least, not for Joseph or the other Irish laborers. In the stews of Southwark there were no cheerful hearths around which to gather, only dripping slums and bouts of mind-numbing toil.

Joseph was once again part of a stream of men hauling freight from shipboard to warehouse. The cargo this time was half-cured cowhides, destined to become the footgear of the British empire. At the moment Joseph wished all men went barefoot if it meant an escape from his present employment. The skins were foul of touch and odor, greasy and alive with vermin eager to abandon ship for a new host and a warm meal. Each man was expected to grab a bale of the things and tote them along the alleyway to the tannery.

Though chilling torrents soaked him from collar to shoe top, the constant drenching was what kept Joseph and the others from throwing aside the hides and tearing at their clothing. Once inside the tannery the air was so full of acidic vapors that no creature could long survive, whether possessing two legs or many. Joseph, once having dumped the skins into huge vats, was free to repeat the process over again.

Beneath his recently cropped hair and behind his growth of blond scraggly beard, Joseph's mind tormented him by repeating mathematical calculations over and over: so many weeks of this agony to obtain passage money to America, prolonged by taking out for Quincannon's share and Joseph's lodging and the necessity of eating at least once a day, if only a bowl of watery cabbage broth and hard bread. No matter how many times he worked the sums, the duration never went any shorter. Worse still, respite from this mental torture only came when he instead pondered that Gann might at any second set on him like a wild dog tearing at his throat, and then he would never see America or Kate again.

On the third pass of the day, Joseph was tramping back from the tannery. He was staring at the mud, ignoring how his shoulders ached and his skin crawled.

Because the line of Irish dockworkers were trudging along in silent desperation, Joseph failed to note a more orderly drumming of better-shod feet until he was halfway down an alley, hemmed in behind and before.

It was not until a voice bellowed, "Stand aside, there! Make way!" that Joseph, startled out of his reverie, looked up to see an approaching file of redcoated soldiers.

Spinning round in alarm, he bumped into Squint, stomping heavily

on Delaney's toes and causing a pileup in those who followed. There
was much cursing in a mixture of English and Gaelic until the next
man back also spotted the advancing soldiers and muttered, "Hist,
Squint. Queen's men comin'!"

Grabbing Joseph's arms with surprising intensity, Squint forced
Joseph to pivot again while urging, "Brass it out! If you run, you're
a right dead'un."

There was nothing else to be done. The troops were only a few
yards away, led by a sergeant with ferocious side-whiskers. Joseph,
as the tallest man in the line, could see him clearly.

The row of Irishmen pressed themselves against the brick wall.
Joseph had only an instant to wonder how many of his comrades
were also taut with the fear of capture before the sergeant stopped
directly beside him.

"You there!" he barked at Joseph. When Joseph did not look up,
he repeated, "You, croppie. Do you speak English? We are looking
for the dyeworks next to Cutter's Warehouse, and we're lost in this
warren of alleyways."

Feeling strangled, Joseph mumbled something, and the sergeant
demanded, "Speak up, then, man. You know the dyeworks I mean?"

From behind him Joseph heard Squint swelling up to go on
the offensive. "And why would you be botherin' us with the
askin'?" the little man demanded. "You lug of a redcoated, thick-
skulled . . ."

The alarm at where this conversation might end galvanized Joseph
into replying, "Indeed I know the place you mean," and he hastily
sketched directions. The soldiers marched away in the rain, and the
column of stevedores returned to lugging hides.

Corrie Grogan watched from the mouth of a shallow cave at
the top of the hill as her father plodded toward them.

"What's he done with the baby?" Ceili pleaded. "Where's the
wee bairn?"

Corrie did not reply. Grasping Ceili's hand, she felt fear. Had the little one died too? Was it buried with Mama inside the hut?

Daniel Grogan did not raise his eyes to meet the steadfast gaze of his daughters. He sighed heavily and sat down cradling his head in his hands.

"I want Mama." Megan toddled to him and placed her hand upon his sagging shoulders.

"Corrie," Grogan ordered, "take Megan."

"Take her where?" Corrie asked.

"Away . . . just away from me awhile."

Anger rose in Corrie's throat. Could he not see Megan needed to be held? Could he not understand they all mourned?

Corrie gathered Megan into her arms. "What's become of the baby?" she demanded. "Is it dead too?"

Grogan did not raise his eyes. "The cold. Tonight. Soon."

"You left it there to die," Corrie spat.

Leaping to his feet, Grogan grabbed her hard by the arm. Megan fell to the ground. Corrie winced with the pain of his grip but stared at her father with unrepentant defiance. Ceili began to weep again.

"And what should I do then? Bring it here to you? So you can play with it until it dies? Corrie! It ain't some poppet. It ain't goin' to live the night! It can't, see? I got nuthin' for it to eat. Mama's dead, and it will die too, God rest its soul!"

He let her go. She backed away, rubbing her throbbing arm, then stooped to comfort Megan.

They all sat down, each in a solitary, unspoken grief.

Corrie rocked Megan until she slept again. For an hour Corrie stared at the shelter on the opposite hill. Her da had blocked the doorway with stones lest some wild dog come and feast on the body of mother and child within.

After a long time, Grogan also fell asleep on the grass.

"Where are we goin'?" Ceili asked Corrie.

"I don't know," Corrie answered truthfully.

"Is Da gonna leave us somewheres like he did the baby?"

Corrie shrugged in response. "I don't know."

"Is it dead yet?"

"Tonight, Da said. When the sun is gone. When it turns off cold."

"Remember how Mama fed the baby bird when it fell from the nest in the hedge?"

"Aye." Corrie did not want to think of the kindness of her mother. The ache was too much. "But shut up."

Ceili did not shut up. "If Mama would feed even a baby bird, what would she say about our own bairn? Da ain't doin' right. Ain't even tryin'. You know he ain't."

Corrie glared hatefully at her father. "He said the bird would die too, but it didn't. It lived, and Mama let it go after summer. Sure, and it flew away. Remember?"

"If it ain't dead, Corrie . . . it'll be freezin' tonight."

Corrie inclined her head slightly. "He said we're sleepin' here in the cave tonight. I'm goin' back after dark."

"Me too," Ceili offered eagerly.

Corrie would have liked the company. It was bad enough going back where Mama lay dead. What if the baby had already died? What if Corrie pulled down the stone barricade to find two dead bodies within? Indeed it would have been a comfort to have Ceili along to hold her hand. But there was a practical matter to consider. If her father awakened and found her gone, she would be punished when she returned. Maybe Ceili and Megan would be punished as well for Corrie's disobedience. "You gotta stay with Da and Megan. Megan'll wake up, and Da'll see I've gone back. So you gotta stay and keep her from wakin' him."

7

The house at which Jailor Gann called was a four-story terrace home on Church Row in Hampstead. The rain dripped from where the elaborately scrolled black ironwork over the gate curved upward to hold the bell jar of the lamp. The curlicues of the metalworkers' trade were mimicked in the pattern of the fanlight above the front door. If the neighborhood was no longer as fashionable as it once was, it was still sufficiently aristocratic for an *Anglo-Irish* lord's London dwelling.

Involuntarily Gann's lip curled in an expression of contempt for such gentility, but he was prepared to submerge his disdain to get what he wanted. Descending to the level of the lower ground he tapped at the tradesman's entry and stood, cloth cap in hand, attempting an ingratiating smile.

The maid who answered took a single glance at the scarred, twisted features and recoiled, throwing up her right hand to her mouth in the sign against the evil eye.

"Would the master be at home?" Gann inquired, his voice having all the pleasant resonance of coal being dumped down a chute. The servant girl tried to slam the door, but anticipating such a move, Gann had already thrust his boot across the threshold. "No need to be uncivil," he complained. "I have business with his honor. Please to tell him Mister Gann, him as has sent round a note, has called as he said he would."

"If you'll be withdrawin' your foot, sir," the maid requested, "I'll go see if the master is at home."

Gann shook his bald head, sending spittles of rainwater flying from his ears and eyebrows. "Bit damp to wait on the landin'," he corrected. "I'll bide inside." And he shouldered both girl and door aside and entered the kitchen. The maid, judging that the master might in fact be better equipped to deal with the intruder, fled upstairs.

Major Denis Mahon, followed by the trembling servant, arrived with silver-headed stick and indignation in hand. "Who the devil are you, and what do you want here?" he demanded.

"Ah, did you not receive my note, then?" Gann asked, staring back boldly into Mahon's angry face. "The name is Gann, sometime assistant to your deceased cousin."

At the reference, Mahon whirled around to the girl. "Leave us," he said. There was no protest of this instruction, and the two men were soon alone. "In your scrawled message you referred to 'unfinished business in Ireland.' If you've come for back pay, you can forget about it. I have no intention of taking on any of my cousin's debts."

"Not a'tall," Gann chided. "It is to your advantage to hear me out. Your cousin, God rest his soul . . ." Mahon snorted in derision, but Gann was undeterred. "Your cousin engaged my services to aid him in . . ." The jailor groped for a word. "Removin' an obstacle by the name of Lord Joseph Burke."

Despite his unwillingness to betray any interest in what Gann was saying, Mahon started and then said evenly, "You have my attention."

"Well, sir," Gann continued smoothly, "this same Burke is in London. I believe you have as great an interest in preventin' him from returnin' to Galway as ever did your cousin. The authorities decline to arrest him."

"Of course they do! Burke's been pardoned."

"Then the more reason to engage the likes of me."

"What do you mean?"

"Indeed, sir," said Gann with the satisfied air of an angler who has landed a monster trout, "for a modest sum, here is what I will undertake to do . . ."

Less than three miles from the Georgian terraces of Hampstead and indeed breathing almost the same air as those of London society attending the theater at Covent Garden, was the notorious community known as the Seven Dials. The acclaimed thoroughfare of Regent Street and the ornate crescents of Regent's Park, developed less than a half century earlier, lay only a half mile away, and yet Seven Dials was a cesspool in the reception room of London.

His pockets jingling with coin and a folded bank draft tucked into his jacket, Jailor Gann knew precisely what he was doing when he entered the lair of dips and rampsmen, of pickpockets and crude street thieves. He no longer wore the dark-blue uniform of his lawful trade, but the arrogant swagger with which he approached the lower end of the lane displayed his sense of command in its absence.

A sundial standing atop a granite plinth marked the intersection of Monmouth and Mercer Streets and the terminus of Gann's journey. Leaning casually on the pillar and picking his teeth with a goose quill was Ben Carp, arranger. For an appropriate fee Carp could arrange the transformation of stolen goods into cash and later recover those same goods for the original owner, taking a percentage of both transactions. He would have sold his own mother, had the price offered been sufficient (and if he had seen her after his fifth birthday). He was a well-known informer, but his services were in such demand that he was tolerated by both the law and the profiteers.

Gann approached the dial and removed a half crown from his pocket. He tapped it on edge as if testing its authenticity. The action drew Carp's interest. "Real?" he inquired casually.

"Real as its mate nestin' in me pocket," Gann observed. "Both of 'em for a chat with some men as will take orders and keep mum."

"How many men?" Carp inquired.

"Two. But no drunkards, mind. They must be able to ferret out some'un for me. Some'un what don't want to be found. And one man must pass for a gent."

Carp shrugged. "Then what?"

Winking his remaining eye convulsed Gann's face into a truly horrid mask. When the contortion relaxed, he said, "Not your concern, eh? Just so's they won't shirk from puttin' down a bloke for keeps." The coin rested between the men's palms.

Whipping a handkerchief out of his breast pocket with one hand, Carp made the gold disappear with the other. "Done," he agreed. "The Clock House. One hour."

Skating on the thin ice of respectability over the morass of Seven Dials, the Clock House pub (whose clock had not worked in a century) stood at the edge of the infamous rookery. It was a place noted for passing counterfeit money and a favorite haunt of the Haymarket dollymops for relieving gentlemen companions of their wallets. Much like Ben Carp's, the Clock House's existence was tolerated by the authorities since it could be easily watched. Beyond that argument, its reputation was so well known that it was clearly a place to beware of, and if one did not . . .

Fancying himself to be smarter than any common criminal mind, Gann arrived at the tavern an hour beforehand and seated himself in the gloomiest corner. From there he could see the entry, the stairs, and the door behind the bar that led to the back rooms. What he did not see was the series of hand signals that passed from the publican to a child employed as a courier. Gann's presence and the fact that he appeared to be alone was reported to Carp before the former jailor had even consumed his first pint of beer.

At the stroke of the chimes of the nearby church, St. Giles, three men entered the drinking establishment, one by each of the three doors.

The first, appearing at the front, was Ben Carp, his top hat inclined at a jaunty angle. The second, who descended the stairs much like an avalanche rolls down a mountainside, was exactly what Gann was expecting to employ: beetle-browed and ponderous of face, neck, and shoulder.

It was the third arrival who appeared out of place. Though he came from behind the bar and moved unerringly toward Carp and the others, the final member of the alliance was slight of build and had boyish features and a certain delicacy of gesture. His hair was drawn forward over his temples in tightly curled ringlets known as jug-loops. He was altogether a prissy sight, and Gann protested to Carp. "'Ere then. None of your nancy-boys."

Carp held up an admonishing finger, gesturing for Gann to be quiet and look again. "Kell Campbell," Carp said by way of introduction.

It was the eyes. Despite the sweetness of his other features, Campbell's eyes had a barely controlled wildness in them, wariness on the brink of a savage outbreak, much as Gann had seen in a cornered badger. Campbell's name was not unknown to Gann. It was rumored that he had dispatched thirteen men in Liverpool by slitting their throats with a razor. Now he was in London.

The four men gathered around the table. Campbell offered Gann an engaging smile without softening his eyes in the least. The thickset man, aptly named Oxfoot, called loudly for a pitcher of stout.

"Before we proceed," Carp said smoothly, "there is the matter of my fee."

Gann paid the remaining half-crown of the arranger's toll, announced, "Be off with you," and Carp took his leave.

"What's it to be, then?" Oxfoot asked. "A cosh job?" The thug thumped a fist the size of a mallet on the table to emphasize his meaning.

"First," Gann instructed, "we have to locate him. Joseph Burke. A lord he, but on the run."

Oxfoot snorted, and Campbell commented, "Only three of us to canvas four or five million? Can you narrow it down?"

"He's papist Irish and likely hidin' with his own kind south of the river. Sooner or later he'll try to contact some'un for help . . . one Maurice O'Connell by name. Here's O'Connell's address."

Oxfoot could not read, so Campbell read aloud, "The Hampshire? That's near here. Leicester Square."

"Right," Gann concurred. "We start the lurk tonight."

The flames of the peat fire burned low at the mouth of the cave. Daniel Grogan lay apart from his daughters, curled beside the warm coals as he slept.

It was cold, Corrie thought as she sat up and nudged Ceili. Perhaps the baby was already dead. A day without food. Hours without warmth. A whole lifetime of suffering, it was, to one tiny and helpless.

"I'm goin'," she mouthed, pointing to Megan and then at her father.

Ceili frowned, sitting up and hugging her knees to her. "I'll keep the fire."

"If he wakes, tell him I've gone to use the chamber pot."

Corrie tucked a scrap of paper with its scrawled message into her pocket. Then she stepped over her father and out into the night.

She carried no torch. The sky was blank, overcast and moon-less. It was a quarter mile down the hill and across the swale to the lean-to. Corrie had spent the afternoon memorizing the narrow cow track that led down and then up again to the shelter.

Behind her Ceili stirred the embers and tossed on another brick of turf. The glow swelled up and spilled out onto the hillside, faintly illuminating Corrie's path for the first steep fifty yards. She scurried ahead, coming to the furthest extension of light within moments. On the way she talked to her mother.

"What do I do, Mama? Show me what you want me to do."

There was no audible answer, but inside her head Corrie heard her mama's voice telling her to always do right, and the answer would come when it was needed.

Where was the path? She needed that answer now.

Glancing over her shoulder, Corrie studied the reassuring pin-point of firelight from the cave. Far off in the distance to the south she caught the glimmer of another light. The lambing barn. But what lay ahead was obscured.

"Straight ahead, Corrie," she instructed herself. "The fire at your back. Mama and the baby are straight ahead."

Easy enough to say it, but she could not see the way. She barked her shin upon a stone. Was she off the trail? Dropping to her knees, she touched the ground. Grass! She had wandered into the field. Should she go to the left or the right? Fat drops of rain splashed against Corrie's cheeks. Heaven was keening, Corrie thought. Had the baby died then? Was Da right? Should she turn around, forget about her plan, and return to the warmth of their shelter?

"Which way, Mama?" Lightning flashed behind her, giving her a fragment of vision.

Then: "There it is!" She stumbled forward onto the trail as thunder boomed and reverberated from the far hill.

Three times more the flash of lightning showed her the way until she stood at the stone barricade that blocked entry into the tomb where living and dead lay together.

It was long past nightfall when Martin arrived back at the lambing barn. Big Pete and Little Pete were into the lambing. Smoking and chatting around their smoldering peat fire, they crouched in the open barn door. Their voices carried on the frigid, still air. Martin could see them there, perfectly framed in the portal. Little Pete blew into his hands and raised his head to listen.

"Whist, Da! Someone's comin', sure."

"Shod hooves, it is. That'll be Martin Donovan, y'know."

Little Pete stood and stretched, then called out, "Is it Martin Donovan there?"

Martin cleared his throat and hollered back, "Aye. That it is." He felt cheered by the greeting, as though father and son had been expecting him and were glad he had come back.

Big Pete joined his boy as Savina plodded up the path. "You look a sight. That grand hat of yours . . ."

"The rain," Martin said wearily.

"Aye. Pelted the beaver in that hat right to death." Big Pete was grinning. "Not a cold rain though. Me and Little Pete was just commentin' on it, y'know. Not a terrible rain a'tall."

Martin raised his hat to them. The stovepipe effect of it had begun to list to the right from the pummeling it had taken in the deluge. His coat was also nearly soaked through, and the chill was beginning to sink into Martin's bones.

"I could do with a cuppa." Martin slid off Savina. The horse followed him into the barn and went straight to the stall where she had spent the last night.

"Ah. That's a fine animal," Big Pete waggled his head in admiration. "Will she take off her own saddle as well?"

"I'll see to her," Martin said as Little Pete turned a confused circle, not knowing if he should tend the horse or make tea.

Little Pete made tea as Martin rubbed Savina down and fed her.

"A fine animal, y'know, ain't she?" Big Pete said again as he leaned on the rails of the stall.

"She is," Martin replied, rubbing and rubbing the steaming hide. Then, "So how's the lambin' goin'?"

"It's . . . y'know . . . lambs . . . lost one, we did. The ewe was goin' mad. Twins from another, so we skinned out the dead'un, slipped the hide upon the extra, an' made it suck the ewe who'd lost her lamb. She never knowed the difference. Did she, Little Pete?"

Little Pete came with the tea. "Never knew, y'know? The wee thing is suckin' away back there in another's skin. And herself never knew."

Martin's failure once again came to the front of his thoughts. He did not offer proper congratulations or even comment on the wonder of it. Thoughts of Kate's milk coming in tomorrow and no babe to suckle made him frown and stick his lower lip out.

Big Pete gave him a sideways look and then cast another look at Little Pete. "Your business . . . in Galway City? It went grand, then?"

Martin breathed in deeply, determined not to speak of it. He accepted the tea from Little Pete and made his way to the fire.

The two joined him, offering him a potato and munching silently for a while. Big Pete made his way down the line of penned sheep, then came back and reported that all was well, entirely well.

Outside a westerly roused up from the sea again, stirring the grass and whistling through the rocks.

Martin wondered how Kate would be taking it. Certainly the force of it would have settled in on her. When the wind came on like this, would she think about the baby alone in the churchyard? It made him shudder. And then he thought of Joseph, wherever he might be. Well, and he had never even known about the baby. Would he grieve for something that had happened when he was gone?

Brooding on Fadge and the workhouse, no babies to be taken home and loved, he yanked off his boots and warmed his feet by the fire. Big Pete and Little Pete looked at his scarred and shrunken foot, wanting to ask him. But they were too polite.

And he would not tell them. Such matters were too solemn for men who could talk of nothing but the sheep and the steward and the weather.

"The wind is up again," Big Pete commented.

'The rain'll be fallin' sideways," Little Pete added. "Through the door, through the very door."

The shriek of it grew more fierce until the rain became a lashing torrent. Little Pete got up and shut the barn door, but wind skirled in beneath it and rain drummed on it, like wee hands knocking to be let in.

"Them other folk," Big Pete mumbled. "Down in the glen in the swine barn. They'll be havin' a time of it."

"I think they cleared off, Da. Their fire's gone out anyway."

"Them an' those kids. An' herself as big . . . y'know . . . as, as . . ." Words failed Big Pete.

"The steward would have our necks if we let them in. Sacked," Little Pete said definitively.

"That he would," said Big Pete, blinking at Martin's crippled foot. "Fire. The fire's gone out, y'say?"

"Aye," said Little Pete flatly. "Out entire."

"So they've moved on. Good. Well then . . ." Bit Pete raised his eyes to Martin's shoulder and pressed his lips together to keep himself from blurting something out. It came anyway. "Fire . . . I see you was burned, was you?"

"Aye." Martin did not draw his foot back nor take the conversational bait.

Silence. Waiting for a story. Big Pete tried again. "An' your business in Galway City, was it? Y'know, did it . . ."

"It did," said Martin.

"That's grand." Big Pete's voice trailed off.

Then the wind began to sing. The three looked up sharply and saw they all had heard the melody. Martin tugged his boots on, and they jumped to their feet. The wind had changed.

Little Pete said, "They say this place is built upon an old fairy rath."

Savina nickered as she did when greeting someone familiar. Ewes stirred and lambs bleated, restless in their pens. There was a racket in the back of the barn where the latch on the shutter broke and the thing banged to and fro.

"Somethin' back there, then," said Little Pete fearfully.

"It's nuthin'. Nuthin'," his father answered, taking up a pitchfork. "We'll close the shutter is all."

Martin felt his hands go clammy as the trio moved cautiously toward the end of the barn.

Here a ewe was on her feet, her lamb standing clumsily beside her. There another ewe clambered up and moved away when her lamb tried to suckle. The flock was uneasy. The needles of rain sliced through the cracks in the shuttered windows.

Then came something like the cry of a human child. Frail. Bleating. Was it a lamb?

Little Pete crossed himself against the evil thing and clutched Martin's sleeve. "They say the fairies make human sounds . . . draw folk to fall down wells an' such. Sailors to jump an' drown in the sea! It's there! Somethin' in the feed trough at the end, so it is!"

Curiosity and wonder seized Martin, made his legs stumble forward when Little Pete warned him not to go. Big Pete, frozen at his son's explanation, stood like a stone in the aisle.

It was like pitch, and the shutters were bang, banging, but Martin could see something moving in the straw, hear that feeble human cry. His eyes wide, he stooped over the wee thing and gasped, "Look here!"

Big Pete and Little Pete shuffled to the fore, their mouths working in fear. They peered down in unison.

Big Pete gave a low whistle. "First time I've seen such a thing."

"A changeling child," Little Pete declared. "The fairies brought it here! An evil thing it is!"

But Martin knew better. He closed the shutters and reached down to touch the newborn infant. It was crying and crying. It was wrapped in rags and still wearing the dried film from its mother's womb. There was a note pinned to the tattered shawl that served as its blanket.

"It's a frozen little thing." Martin gathered the baby easily into his arms and pushed past the thunderstruck father and son to the fire. He unpinned the scrap of paper with letters scrawled in charcoal upon it and read aloud:

> *HER MAMMY DED*
> *CANT WACH BABY DIE TO*
> *HAVE MERCY TAKE CARE OF HER*

Little Pete looked, then looked away, then decided it was a human thing after all.

"She must've perished, poor woman," commented Big Pete. "Aye. They've buried her out there somewheres an' left the babe for us to care for. Well, I've got mouths enough to feed. Eight at home."

"You think they've buried the mammy out there? Her bones an' all . . ."

"An' all the bones of everyone who ever died in Ireland is out there! Shut up, Little Pete. We've enough to deal with. This one'll have to go. The poorhouse'll know what to do with it." Big Pete was in no mood for terror. There was the reality of this unwanted infant. "Nuthin' like this has ever . . . y'know."

"She's hungry like." Martin slipped his finger into the baby's mouth. She latched on and fell silent. "There now. That's fine! She's sound and healthy. Like a new calf, she is."

"What'll the missus say?" Big Pete worried. "She'll want to keep it. Cursed luck!"

"Fetch me ewe's milk." Martin knew what had to be done.

"Sure, an' it won't survive on ewe's milk long. Give it the skitters. Better boil it. The milk, that is. God in heaven, what'll we do with it? She'll get attached, sure. An' there it'll be. It'll die, an' I'll have the wife's tears to deal with."

"I know a woman who lost a child," Martin said softly, as though he were talking to the child. "Her breasts will be full tomorrow, and she'll be waitin'. How she'll welcome this tiny one!"

"Glory to God!" cried Big Pete. "You'll take it away before me wife sees it? An' you know a woman, an' she'll nurse the thing then?"

"Aye." Martin could not take his eyes off the miracle in his arms.

Big Pete snatched up a bucket and shoved it into Little Pete's hands. "Fetch ewe's milk, lad, an' hurry. It's a starvin' little thing. An' bring that clean fleece to wrap it in."

8

Joseph, me boyo," said Quincannon expansively, "you look as though a hundredweight of scrap iron is hangin' round your neck and you're tryin' to swim the Shannon. Is life altogether so bad, then?"

Shaking his head, Joseph thought about how he could frame a reply that was polite to this kindly meant pleasantry and yet give away no real information. "I am a long time from home," he said. "And my prospects of returnin' there are distant indeed."

"And don't we all have that same notion, and me with the threat of fourteen years transportation hangin' about me if ever I set foot upon Ha'Penny Bridge again? But here now, I've had a bit of luck with another business venture of mine. Come with me, and I'll stand the shot for a round of drinks. We'll sing 'Dear Colleen Bawn' and cry in each other's beer."

"I'm not much of one for the drinkin'," Joseph replied, "and my singin', I'm told, sets dogs to bayin' at the moon. But if your celebration includes food, then I'm your man."

The duo found Squint Delaney eager to make a third, and the group soon settled into the Pig and Whistle, already crowded with Irishmen who even had a bit of pocket change to spare. Flynns and O'Flahertys sang and laughed with Murphys, Daughertys, and Burkes. A plate of smoked herring was not exactly Joseph's favorite fare, yet at the time it was the most delicious meal he could recall since it was not cabbage soup. In a short time conversation flowed like water. Because of Joseph's years in school in Dublin, he could speak knowledgeably about Quincannon's Dublin neighborhood. They talked of the river Liffy and St. Stephen's Green, but it was Squint who burbled in his pint and mourned the green hills of County Clare.

Even though Seven Dials had a choice position that gave the underworld easy access to the nobs and swells of the West End, it was not London's largest criminal rookery. Pride of place in that respect went to Bermondsey, south of the river, cheek by jowl with the Irish settlement. Called the "Venice of Drains," Bermondsey was even more dangerous and sinister. Unlike St. Giles, where the bobbies traveled in pairs, after sundown they did not venture into Bermondsey at all.

Oxfoot guided Gann through meandering lanes, cuffing aside a pair of drunken brawlers and leading the way to Onion Street at the south edge of Irishtown. "You wait here," he instructed. "I'll bring back one as can sell us some information." Then he vanished.

He reappeared five minutes later with a swarthy, black-haired, earringed man in tow. "This is Gus," Oxfoot reported. "He's a gypsy, so even the Irish let him pass. He's a screever see, writin' fake papers, and he hears things."

"How do we know he won't sell us out?" Gann growled.

The smile on Oxfoot's face could not be seen in the gloom, but the sound of it was in his voice when he said, "'Cuz Gus knows I know where to find him."

"Sure, Oxfoot," the gypsy agreed. "I voker what you say. I never cross you."

"Half a crown," Gann said, "if you can tell me where to find a papist . . . name of Joseph Burke."

"Burke?" Gus repeated. "Burke is common enough with these Irishers. What Burke you mean?"

Gann gave a brief description of Joseph and concluded with, "He likely makes out that he's shanty-born, but he comes from money. His talk will give him away."

"I hear such a one speakin' tonight."

"Where?" Gann demanded, pouncing on the words.

"Not far. Pig and Whistle."

Hiding across the alley from the entrance, Gann watched the Pig and Whistle with the rapt attention of an owl eyeing a burrow in which he has already marked the sounds of an unsuspecting mouse. He dispatched Oxfoot to keep a vigil at the rear, but there was no reason to think Joseph knew he was being hunted. It was turning out so easy! Gann would get his vengeance and get rewarded at the same time! He could pay off the accomplices much earlier than expected and keep even more of Mahon's expense money. It was also even possible he could string the major along and extort more commission for a job already done.

As Gann settled in to wait, the rain that had lately slackened decided to keep him company. It dripped from the leads of the narrow overhang and streaked his face with black. The windows of the pub glowed with warmth, fellowship, and the sounds of good humor. Gann hated them more for it. "Idol-worshipin' swine," he muttered to himself, ducking his head back into the collar of his coat and leaning back against the wall.

Oxfoot likewise propped his bulk against a wall, in the angle between a house and a brick fence that served as both the boundary of the knacker's yard and the men's room of the pub. Oxfoot took no notice of the odors of his outpost, though the mixture of offal and urine was staggering. The sounds coming from the pub mingled with the night air, the increasing patter of raindrops, and the lowing and coughing of ancient sheep and antiquated horses to be slaughtered in the morning. "Dumb brutes what don't know what their lot is," Oxfoot said to himself. "If they was men they'd be lookin' for escape tonight, instead of waitin' for the ax."

A latched door at the rear of the Pig and Whistle popped open. Since it was half a flight above the ground, Oxfoot had only an instant to see that the silhouette emerging was tall and young in the face. Then he heard it.

"Don't be long, Burke, me boyo," called a voice rough with the drink and hoarse from laughter. "And don't be sneakin' off. Whose turn is it to buy the next round, anyway?"

"Ah, you'll be knowin' who," returned the exiting form. "Trust you to never lose track of that."

The tall man descended the stairs and headed for the knacker's wall.

Oxfoot could not believe his luck. He wondered how generous Gann would be and how much he would have to share with Kell Campbell to protect his own throat. Waiting until he heard the rustle of cloth and the fumble of buttons, Oxfoot stepped up behind Burke. The increasing drumming of the rain covered his approach. From the pocket of his coat Oxfoot drew the tool of his trade and smashed the cloth sack filled with lead shot into the man's head and neck. The force of the blow was so great that, instead of felling the victim, the stroke propelled him into the bricks. Oxfoot heard the unmistakable crunch of teeth and bone, and then the prey collapsed in an unmoving heap.

There was plenty of time to help himself to the contents of Burke's pockets: a miserable handful of coins, a religious medallion around the mark's neck, and a folded scrap of letter to be examined later. When Gann asked, Oxfoot could truthfully report that Burke had nothing on him.

The pub entry opened again. "Here, now, Burke. What's become of you? Did you lose your way?"

Oxfoot did not bother slinking. He merely hopped the fence and strode boldly away from the scene. He knew what confusion was about to follow.

"Who's there?" yelled the voice from the stairs, accompanied by the sound of boots thumping downward. Then moments later, "Paddy, Liam! Come here at once! Some'un has done for poor Jimmy Burke! He's dead!"

The mob from the Pig and Whistle gathered around the corpse. Quincannon took charge of the investigation, and no one disputed his right.

Squint Delaney bent over the body. "His skull bashed in from behind," he noted in the light of a lantern brought out from the pub. "No fair fight, this."

"None of our own better have done this," Quincannon announced fiercely, "or when he comes to my hand himself will curse the day he was born. Who knew this man?" he demanded.

"I, sir," responded the one who found the body, one Aaron Murrow, by name. "Me, Paddy, Liam, an' him come from Westport together."

"Did any of you see some'un follow him outside?" Quincannon inquired. The response was negative. "Well, then, was he wavin' money around in the Pig? Could they have been layin' for him outside?"

The three bereaved friends exchanged a look of consternation and shook their heads again. Aaron continued to act as their spokesman. "He was not a flash cove, was Jimmy Burke. Quiet an' harmless an' barren as a Mayo poor box."

Joseph, who had until that moment been hanging back, grasped Aaron by the elbow. "Burke, did you say?" he asked, looking down at the light-brown hair of the corpse, matted with blood. The man might have been his twin in height, if younger in age. "Quincannon, I may know somethin' about why this happened. But it's murder. Should someone not fetch the constable?"

A rippling undercurrent of hostility greeted this suggestion, and as if the mere mention of the title might summon officialdom, the crowd began to disperse. "You do not understand the way of it,"

Quincannon corrected. "We tend our own parish here. The constables are English and think it sport to do us down when they can. If we ring in the peelers, it is we who will suffer and not those who did this to poor Burke. No, we will find who done this and deal with him in our own way."

Drawing himself upward, Joseph said grimly, "Then you must hear what I think, so you will know what you may be facin'. My name is also Burke, Joseph Connor Burke. I escaped from the *Hive* and later from my warden, a monster named Gann. He spotted me the other day at the hangin', and it may be that this Burke was mistaken for me."

Squint Delaney refused to believe it. "The crushers would not flatten your head without warnin' and then run away. If you are such a fiercesome rapparee, would not this Gann come with the army and smoke you out?"

"I do not understand it myself," Joseph admitted, "but the confusion of names and persons is too close to be happenstance. It is better for you to be warned of what may follow."

Joseph and Squint looked expectantly at Quincannon, waiting for him to pronounce judgment. Joseph prepared to be told that his continued presence would cause unwanted attention from the authorities and that he should take his problems elsewhere. Instead Quincannon repeated thoughtfully, "Joseph Burke. It has a familiar ring to it. Why do I know your name, Burke?"

"My troubles came about because I am in with Daniel O'Connell and the Repeal movement."

Snapping his thick fingers, Quincannon barked, "Joseph Burke! Of course! Lord Burke of Connaught, is it not?"

Joseph agreed to the title.

"I have heard you mentioned in the same breath with the Liberator himself. But the traversers, includin' the great O'Connell, have been pardoned, have they not?"

Joseph explained that his trial had been held separately from the others before the judge called "the hangman of Kilkenny" and that he had been tricked into a life sentence. "And I also face the charge of assaultin' an officer of the Crown."

"This Gann?" Quincannon interjected.

"Himself," Joseph confirmed. "Likely enough I am lookin' at hangin' instead of only transportin'."

Both Quincannon and Delaney nodded soberly at this assessment; they knew of others who had suffered similar fates.

"It was an error not to assault this Gann more permanent-like," Squint said in a tone laden with self-evident wisdom.

Quincannon and Joseph ignored him.

"If they are on to you, and willin' to bash your head to prevent the bother of another trial," Quincannon mused, "then the only answer is this: you must leave the country at once."

Joseph agreed, commenting that he had reached the same conclusion, but then revealed he had not the funds with which to purchase passage to America.

"But you're a lordship," Squint objected. "You must have piles of the ready!"

"Shut your gob," Quincannon ordered. "I'm tryin' to think." Then to Joseph he continued, "How 'bout if I front your tariff?"

Looking around at the smoke-stained walls of the Pig and Whistle's innermost room, Joseph replied, "It is kind of you, that thought. But who knows when I could repay the debt?"

"Is there no one who would go surety for you?"

"I could write to Daniel O'Connell. He would stand good for me. But it would take too long and might compromise him to be correspondin' with a criminal."

Once again enlightenment brightened up Quincannon's face. "What about this, then? Maurice O'Connell, Daniel's son, is in London. Could you be applyin' to him for aid?"

"Maurice is here?" It was Joseph's turn to be astonished. "I never thought . . . I grew up in the O'Connell household. Maurice is like an elder brother. Yes, he will certainly help me if he can a'tall."

"Well, there you are then," Quincannon concluded. "You write him a note. Squint here will carry it. And there's the *Syria*, bound for Quebec at the turn of the tide, tomorrow noon. You'll be on it."

"Canada," Joseph repeated in a puzzled tone. "I had thought America."

"And would you stay here to have your throat slit and that fine ship waitin' on the turn even now, when you can walk to America once you've the ocean behind you? Besides, is not the fare to America five shillin's and Canada only three and six?"

Finally Joseph smiled. "I'll pen the note to Maurice, but there will be time enough to send it 'round in the morning."

Taking a clay pipe out of a wall rack, Quincannon thumbed the bowl full of tobacco, lit it, and admired the fragrant cloud of smoke with a satisfied air. "Tip this Maurice as to who you are without writin' the name or what your destination is. That way no one is compromised."

"Compromised," Squint Delaney repeated. "By St. Patrick, you've a gift with the language, Quincannon!"

9

Just before dawn on the third day Kate was awakened by the scent of roses and the gentle murmuring of Mad Molly at the foot of the bed.

"Is it yourself, then, Molly?" Kate asked.

"Aye. That it is."

Kate was aware of the throbbing fullness of her breasts, the dampness of her gown. "And you've brought roses? So late in the year?"

"Before sunrise. Aye. For the babe."

Kate winced. Did the old woman not understand? Had no one explained to her? "Where did you find them?"

The reply was a reverent whisper. "There'll be no potatoes to bring ye soon enough. But roses they sent ye, Kate darlin'. The sisters of the St. Bride's. They showed ol' Molly where they was. A pretty bush full of blooms, it were. Saved from the frost in the shelter of the convent."

Sisters? St. Bride's Convent? Molly had been wandering again.

This time to the remains of the ruined monastery. The nuns had
been gone for centuries, raped and then massacred by Cromwell's
army. The building had been demolished. The garden roses that the
sisters had planted still blossomed in a wild thicket every year, however. Some in Galway believed the flowers were a sort of miracle, a
reminder of hope and resurrection.

"You've wandered far then, Molly."

"Far. Aye. And wide! They bade me . . . that is, the sisters did . . .
to remind ye . . . to give ye these from their garden, they did. Saved
'em for ye from the beginnin' of time." The room began to lighten
as Molly crept closer and placed the bouquet on the comforter.
"Last roses of summer, they be. Mind the thorns. No roses on
His crown. Just thorns. 'Tis dark what lies ahead. Sure, the tomb
is always dark. But there's hope on the third day! His own dear
muther . . . poor darlin', she looked into it expectin' death. But
He's alive in the garden, don't ye see? Here I be! Here I be! Not
dead a'tall!"

Kate did not answer. She could not. Emotion stopped her words.
Molly's muddled attempt to comfort brought tears to her eyes. After
a time she managed to thank the gnarled woman.

"'Tis nuthin'. A bunch of roses . . . roses is all." Molly patted her
arm. "There now. Martin's comin', Kate darlin'. I'll be goin' back
to meet the lamb on the road if ye don't mind."

At the first light of day Savina was saddled. Martin rigged a
sling lined with soft wool to carry the newborn.

Big Pete passed her to Martin. "Mind the wee head. That's it,
that's it. Them heads can't be bobbled around."

Little Pete said soberly, "I was hopin' it would look a bit better
after we cleaned it up some, y'know."

"They're ugly at this stage," reprimanded Big Pete. "Mashed faces
an' such like."

"Aye. Pointed heads." Little Pete's eyes narrowed as he rumi-
nated on the looks of newborn humans.

But Martin's pained expression brought a gushing of assurances from the elder. "Ugly it is, but it'll come 'round, right enough. Sure, an' it'll take on human features. Me da, God rest him, when he laid eyes on Little Pete here, said he must be a monkey out of King George's zoo, y'know. An' look at Little Pete now."

Martin had seen enough of Little Pete that this was no comfort. "I know how it is." Martin carefully placed the infant into the rig, where she would be protected by the warmth of his body. He looked down at her face. Perfect, pink, and peaceful in sleep. He thought these fellows had been too long with the sheep to know what a beautiful baby was.

"An' don't be forgettin' the jug of boiled milk there. An' the sugar tit to feed her."

The sugar tit was a worn leather glove with a hole in the tip of a finger. Filled with milk, the glove had been used to feed orphaned lambs. It had served this human lamb too. She was full to the brim and content to sleep against Martin.

"It'll be out for a few hours at least. Did you hear the belch of it? You'll be nearin' home when it comes 'round. When it wakes, change its nappies. Sure, an' ewe's milk'll give it the skitters, an' then you'll have a raw bottom to deal with if you don't change its nappies. An' daub a bit of whiskey on its stump, like I done with the lambs. The thing'll dry out an' drop off in ten days or so. Just keep the whiskey on it . . . and y'know . . . to keep it clean, or the whole belly will go rotten an' it'll die, sure."

Martin supposed Big Pete was a good father. "You're a good man," Martin said solemnly, shaking hands with the shepherd.

"I've done this a time or two. Six times. Lord of mercy, it's grateful I am you're takin' it so me wife . . . y'know . . . she'd say what's another mouth to feed, but another mouth is one more too many."

"Well, I'm thankin' you both." Martin slapped another shilling into Big Pete's hand. Little Pete ran back to fetch three more potatoes for Martin to eat on the way.

"Home, Savina." Martin fixed his eyes on the brightening sky. Cloudless, it was; breathless and washed after the rain.

Dressed in his best kit, Kell Campbell had loitered across the square from the Hampshire all the preceding evening without being harassed by the bobbies. He had a line of patter that amused the shop girls, deploring the prices of imported fabrics. He made infrequent, inexpensive purchases of handkerchiefs—wipes, in the street jargon—and the like, to keep the shopowners from becoming suspicious.

In between his forays inspecting goods and when the shops closed, Kell strolled around the area looking like a swell. Since that part of London was frequented by streetwalkers and those seeking their acquaintance, he was noted but not bothered by the patrolling peelers.

Kell had actually entered the lobby of the Hampshire, where he let it be known he was waiting for friends who were supposed to accompany him to the opera. His presence was acceptable.

What these diversions had in common was that he never lost sight of the front of the hotel. The awaited Joseph Burke did not appear, and Campbell continued his vigil.

Whenever he grew impatient, Campbell fingered the bone handle of the folded razor in his right coat pocket. He found the feel of the smooth material to be soothing. Eventually it became so late that he knew O'Connell had turned in for the night and retired himself.

Like a dutiful sentry, Campbell was back on watch early the next morning. He caught sight of the scruffy Irishman as soon as Squint Delaney entered the square. Squint seemed out of place and betrayed his own unease by walking up and down in front of the hotel several times before entering. It was with amusement that Campbell noted how the grimacing man was immediately escorted back out by a pair of disapproving porters and a scowling desk clerk.

When shoved by one of the Hampshire employees, Delaney shoved back. His speech grew louder, plenty loud enough for Campbell to overhear: "Let go of me, you right Cockney bugger!" Squint announced to the world, "I have important business with himself, the Maurice O'Connell."

Kell Campbell was instantly all attention. While pretending to examine a poster advertising the latest attraction at the Covent Garden theater, he moved closer to the group.

Clearly the hotel clerk was taken aback at the use of a distinguished guest's name. The present irritation was only dirty, bog-trotting Irish, but Irish nevertheless. What if O'Connell really did have an appointment with this hooligan? Even well-to-do Irish looked as if they dressed from a rag bin or a missionary barrel in the eyes of London society. The Hampshire deskman made his decision and stated firmly, "Allow me to take Mister O'Connell your calling card and see if he will receive you."

"Now you've spliced it," Delaney agreed. "Take him this note. I'll wait for a reply."

This was it. Campbell knew it. His fingertips tingled with the sense of being on the trail of his quarry. He stroked the razor handle with increasing fervor.

In a short time Campbell's clairvoyance was rewarded when a dressing-gown-clad Maurice O'Connell emerged from the hotel at a dead run. He went straight to Squint Delaney and at a volume that suggested no need for secrecy demanded, "Where is Lord Burke? What is the reason for this cryptic note? I recognized the author at once, but why did he not come himself?"

Delaney knuckled his forehead and bowed. "Your honor," he said, "it's on this wise." What followed was accompanied by many furtive looks and pointed glances at the hovering desk clerk, but in such a low voice that Campbell could no longer hear. He edged closer.

Despite Squint's imploring looks, O'Connell's words boomed as loudly as his father's: "But doesn't he know he's been pardoned? He is runnin' from his own salvation! From Cork to Capetown and back, my father and others have been tryin' to locate the Burke to tell him 'Go home!' And . . ." O'Connell slapped his forehead hard enough that Delaney winced at the impact. "By the shade of Brian Boru! He doesn't even know he's goin' to be a father. May be already. Can you get word to him?"

"Yes sir," Delaney hedged. "I'd be glad to give him the message, see? Only it's like this: he's taken ship for Canada. He's goin' aboard right now."

O'Connell, despite his dress, took charge and commanded the hotel manager to whistle him up a hansom cab. "I'll send the police ahead and follow myself at once. There's no time to lose."

With that conclusion Kell Campbell heartily concurred.

The whole long night Corrie Grogan crouched beneath the eaves of the barn. Peering through the cracks of the shutters she had watched their clumsy efforts to feed her baby sister. Listening to the conversation of the men within, she memorized the features of the well-dressed boy who held the infant with such a look of joy and wonder on his face. He had an awful gimp to his walk. His features were sharp and his dark eyes sad, as if he were much older than his years. He was kindly with the baby.

All would be well, she knew.

Now, as the rider carried her baby sister away to the north, she tracked his progress for a full two miles. Jogging along behind, she waited until he stopped to let the dappled horse drink from the river. Only then did she dare to show herself.

"Hullo," she said, ambling from behind a copse of brushy trees into the open.

Startled by her appearance, the horseman patted his mount and eyed her with resentment. His free hand curved protectively around the sling holding the baby.

"Mornin'," he replied.

"What you holdin'?" She clasped her hands behind her back and walked cautiously forward.

"A baby."

"A baby, is it?"

"Sure. That it is."

"Where's its mother?"

"I'm takin' it to its mother."

"Is it far away, then? I mean, its mother?"

"Not far." He looked away from her impatiently.

She saw the Burke crest emblazoned on the flap of his saddle bag. "You're lucky if you live on Burke land," she remarked.

"Who told you such a thing? And what business is it of yours, then?"

"It's on your saddlebag."

He jerked his chin in acknowledgment.

She looked back at the bundle in his arms. "You'll take care of her, won't you?"

The pain of comprehension filled his eyes. "You're . . . you were in the lean-to."

"I was. Mother's died."

"Did you write the note?"

"I'm glad 'twas yourself who found her. They might have let her die, y'see."

"She'll be loved. Tell your da."

She did not say she would tell her father anything. It was her da, after all, who had left the baby to die. "I'm glad 'twas yourself."

"You won't be comin' back for her?" His expression changed to sudden fear.

"There's two others beside myself. All girls, we are. Me the eldest. We was tossed from Mahon's land. We're goin' to America. Da don't want the wee thing. Never worry about that."

Relief showed on Martin's face. "She'll be cared for."

"I know't."

He reached awkwardly into his pocket and drew out yet another shilling. "For your sisters, then. For your trip to America." He tossed it to her. It thumped on the dirt.

Corrie scrambled to retrieve it lest it bounce and roll into the river.

The riders spurred his horse on across the ford.

She watched him go for a while. Content, she pulled her shawl close around her and ran back along the road to find her family.

∽ 10 ∽

For Joseph, everything was happening too fast. From the drudgery of counting bales, kegs, and days to the abruptness of this departure . . . it was overwhelming. Joseph joined a queue of other emigrants waiting at the foot of Mill Stairs to board the *Syria*. An hour earlier the assembly had been told to be ready to board soon. The captain was said to be a stickler for punctuality, yet the advertised departure time had come and gone without the embarkation happening, much less the sailing.

The wharf was crowded with a hundred or so chattering passengers, comparing notes about going to the New World, about forests and farms and Red Indians, about relatives who had already made the crossing and how much better life was there. For Joseph's part, he found he could not look at the ship without shuddering; it reminded him too much of the prison transport *Hive*. Though he did not dispute the wisdom of his present course, he could not help but resent another voyage that was taking him further from Kate. At least he was not in chains this time.

The crowd's murmuring grew until finally the delay was explained: the ship's purser was in a row with someone at dockside. Twelve thousand gallons of drinking water had been contracted for, and only half that amount had been delivered. The purser argued that if they did not sail within two hours they would miss the tide, and the captain would see to it that heads would roll. The carter who delivered the water shrugged and said it was impossible to produce the rest of the water in less than four hours.

It seemed to Joseph that the two men would come to blows soon. When the first bobbie appeared on the scene at the head of Shad Thames Street, he wondered if the policeman had been summoned or had merely heard the disturbance and come on his own initiative.

Then the second peeler who appeared beside the first was joined by three uniformed others and a well-dressed portly gentleman who gathered the officers together and gave them orders, accompanied by much finger-pointing and arm-waving.

It was a search party, and Joseph had no doubt the target of the quest was himself.

Ducking behind a heap of discarded netting, Joseph sought an escape route. The lower dock on which he stood had only two gang-ways leading up to the level of the road and a pair of bobbies already at each end. Their chief and the remaining officer approached the purser, likely armed with a description of their quarry. Joseph men-tally kicked himself for having appeared early at the ship. He should have waited until they were ready to cast off and then made a dash for it. Now he was trapped.

Stooping down as if tying a boot lace, Joseph hastily inspected the area under the pilings to which the floating dock was attached. A single, slim length of timber was spiked from piling to piling and ran backwards into the gloom under the wharf. The area would be searched, but maybe there was another way out.

Then he saw it: at the extreme rear of the structure the seawall supporting the wharf was not solid. A disused flight of steps tumbled into the murky water but also led upwards into shadows. It might come to a trapdoor under a warehouse or to another passage. It was the only chance.

A glance over his shoulder toward the ship revealed there was no time to waste. The police official was engaged in conversation with the purser, who nodded vigorously and scanned the passengers at the same time.

Extending his foot onto the thin plank, Joseph tested it to see if it would bear his weight. When it did, he ducked under the overhanging wharf.

One step, then another, clinging to the upright pilings for support, Joseph advanced into the darkness until the gap between posts was too wide for a handhold. Joseph would have to rely on balance alone; there was nothing in reach on which to steady himself.

The most improbable things came to his mind. He saw himself as a boy walking the high stone fence that separated the apple orchard from the canyon of the Cornamona. Beside him, urging him on and applauding his success was a dark-haired girl: Kate Donovan.

"Ah, Katie," he murmured. "If ever you held a kind thought for my balance, I hope you're havin' it now."

Three more paces to another piling, then two, then one, then a firm grip on another beam. Not far to the stairs now.

A creaking sound behind him. No chance to turn and look, and then no need. A shout: "There he goes! Under the dock."

A clatter of pounding feet was accompanied by a voice shouting, "Joseph Burke! Halt! Come back!"

No need to balance now. Plenty to hang on to as Joseph raced forward. Only one more plank to cross to the steps.

Suddenly, disaster! The board broke under him with a sharp crack, dumping him into the slimy water. It was shallow, but Joseph's feet stuck fast in the mudbank. He struggled forward as the yelling and the noise of pursuit closed in from behind. He could hear his name being called over and over, but he shut his ears to the sounds and labored against the drag of the clay.

The closest of the pursuers abandoned the plank and jumped deliberately into the river, splashing and floundering, but gaining.

Joseph yanked one foot free of the grasp of the ooze. Then the other came loose, minus a boot which the Thames claimed as its tithe.

He was at the bottom of the stairs, scrambling up them on hands and knees. The passage led upwards towards a square of darkness outlined by light—a trapdoor. Escape was still possible.

Flinging himself up the last of the steps, Joseph heaved against the trap. It would not budge! Either it was bolted, or a heavy load pressed on it. There was no other escape. The closest officer was even then wrestling with the mud in only knee-deep water a few yards back. To either side two others had outflanked Joseph to prevent his doubling back.

He hoisted with his shoulders, his neck bowed under the load. The pursuers were saving their breath for the chase, but the nearest was close enough that Joseph could hear his breathing, could hear the sucking sounds made by the mud as it reluctantly released each footstep.

"Open!" Joseph demanded. "Open!"

Then miraculously, it did. As it sprung back with dramatic vigor, Joseph shot halfway through the opening. The answer to the unexpected release was found in the person of a smiling, curly-haired, coatless young man who peered over the panel from behind. "Burke?" he surprisingly inquired.

Without thinking Joseph responded, "Yes."

In that instant the unknown slammed the trapdoor down again, pinning Joseph to the steps. His head, arms, and shoulders were clear, but he could not move. There was no breath left in him to protest as a palm splayed across his face and yanked his head backward.

Something flashed in front of Joseph's eyes, and then there was a moment of fiery burning pain that stopped amid curses from the attacker. Frenzy at the searing in his neck filled Joseph with incredible energy. Gathering his legs under him, Joseph leveraged himself upright, sending his lighter assailant sprawling onto the warehouse floor. Joseph rose to his feet.

There was a bare fragment of time during which Joseph and his enemy regarded each other from a few feet away, then from both the trapdoor and an entrance to the street, the room boiled with shouts and racing footsteps. The curly-haired man dashed away, bolting through a broken window and out of sight, even as Joseph was surrounded by policemen.

Three miles from home, the newborn awoke with an indignant bleating. In the shelter of an abbey's ruins Martin carefully dismounted. Leaving Savina to crop the grass that grew where the choir had been, he cleaned the child as Big Pete had instructed and fed her ewe's milk from the nipple of the glove. The nursing was awkward. More milk spilled that was consumed.

"Three miles more, darlin' girl."

Behind Martin came a chuckle, and then Mad Molly spoke. "Not a calf . . . nay . . . 'tis a lamb ye've brought home."

Martin started and turned too suddenly, dislodging the sugar tit and causing the infant to cry a protest.

"Sure, and you've wandered off, Molly!"

"Nay. Been watchin' for Martin, I have. Standin' yonder on the hill. Saw ye comin' with the babe." The crone shuffled forward to peer into the infant's face. "Ewe's milk, is it?"

"That it is. Hungry, too, but it's a battle to suckle."

"Give him no more of that. He'll colic, and heaven help us." Molly shook her head in disapproval and took the baby from Martin. She held the infant with the expertise of one who had spent a lifetime holding newborns, Martin observed. Molly was mad, but she had not forgotten the art of burping a baby. A dozen pats, a half-dozen circular rubs upon the back, and the child let out a tremendous belch.

Molly chortled gleefully. "Fine! Fine! Fine it is! And wouldn't Tom Donovan be proud of such a belch!"

"That he would." Martin was glad to have her take over for a time.

"Sure, and whiskey was mother's milk to your old da, Martin. Mother's milk! Aye!" She kissed the tiny cheek. Her conversation with the miniature human was remarkably lucid. "Ye'll have the real thing soon enough, darlin'. Kate's full to burstin', she is. Such breasts! Swelled and hard as stone. Milk runnin' out upon her gown! Soakin' the sheets. The misery of it. No babe t'suckle. Poor girl. Never a complaint from her though. Bears all with dignity. A regular Guernsey. Two gallons a day, and all the butter ye can eat in a year." She danced a circle and coaxed another burp from the newborn. "Did ye hear that, Martin?

Choirs of angels sing in a baby's belch. An intelligent child, this."

Martin held his knees and rocked back. "You think Kate'll like her?"

Molly stopped short and peered into the face of the child. "Her, is it? Ah, well. A pretty wee she-thing ye've brought. Should've known that. Sure."

"Do you think Kate'll mind? There wasn't a boy baby a'tall to be got at the workhouse. I found this one in a lambin' barn."

Molly chortled and screwed up her face in thought. "Mind? Mind, did he say? See how pretty she is. It'll have brown, brown eyes like its mother. Golden hair like its da. Old Molly should have known what ye was, darlin'. Sure, and what'll we call ye, little bird?"

The child fell silent at Molly's question. Gazing up through the roofless ruin to the azure sky, the babe seemed to be watching a flock of wild geese flying in a wavering V toward the south.

Molly stooped and put her ear near the mouth of the newborn as if she were hearing a secret. "Aye. Sure. And a fine name, that. So . . . Thought ye were a goner, did ye? Ready to fly away was ye? Hmmmm. True, true, true. Martin's a good lad, he is. But ye'll like your mammy best. Aye. And ye'll never lack for a good meal, neither."

Joseph was bundled in two blankets and a rug and propped in a corner of a carriage across from Maurice O'Connell. Appleby, the portly Police Inspector, approached and peered in at the window. Joseph's neck was swathed in layers of handkerchiefs. A narrow red stain on the cloth traced a line for about four inches from under his left ear toward his Adam's apple, where it stopped.

"Joseph," Maurice O'Connell implored for at least the tenth time, "we must get you to the hospital."

"There is no need," Joseph protested again. "Stop fussin' over me, Maurice. The cut is not deep and has stopped bleedin' already."

"You are a lucky man," observed Inspector Appleby.

"Yes," agreed Joseph, fingering the newly scarred lead pendant around his neck that had intercepted the slice of the blade.

"I have dispatched my men throughout the area with your description of the assailant," Appleby said in an official tone. "If he's gone to ground anywhere near, then we will find him. A sneak thief with a murderous bent, no doubt. We found a flash coat that must have been his. The pockets were stuffed with those wipes serving as your bandages. Too many for any honest gent."

Responding to the doubtful look on Joseph's face, Maurice said, "But you think differently, eh, Joseph? Do you have any reason to believe someone would want to kill you in particular?"

Nodding slowly, Joseph said, "But nothin' I will speak of yet." Then, with greater animation, he requested, "Tell me again how it is I'm a free man."

"You are like the drownin' man who struggled against bein' rescued," Maurice suggested wryly. "Your pardon came soon after my own father's, but the news was too late gettin' to Cork to stop *Hive* from sailin'. Since then I hear your steward . . ."

"Adam Kane."

"Kane has been scoutin' half the globe lookin' for you and . . ." O'Connell slapped his right hand to his heart in a dramatic gesture so like his father's speaking style that Joseph had to smile. "Can you ever forgive me, Joseph? I've clean forgot the other news. Congratulations! You're to be a father."

First it was the disgusted sound of Widow Clooney's voice that roused Kate from her fitful sleep.

"Martin Donovan! You're all over filth! You'll not be goin' into your poor sister like that! Nay! I say, you'll not be takin' that thing into her! Found it, you say! Found it! 'Tis a changeling! The fairies have . . ."

Then there was Mad Molly, home again from her wanderings. "Moira Clooney! Hush! Ye've been a bag of wind since first I know'd ye! Ye're a gale! A Norther full-blown, that's what ye are!"

Widow Clooney replied indignantly, "Upbraidin' by a mad woman is no upbraidin' a'tall! Now hear me!"

Mad Molly answered back with the loud imitation of a howling wind. "And there's to ye, Widow Clooney! Poor Aidan died to escape your naggin', 'tis a fact!"

Then there was Martin, desperate, pleading. "You'll wake . . . hush . . . all day long it's been . . . hush!" His voice cracked. "I'm the man of the house, and I'll see her!"

"Man, is it!" Widow Clooney was outraged. "Give the thing to me! You'll not take it in to her! Her milk will dry up in no time, and she'll . . ."

Kate struggled to rise. There was no part of her that did not ache. Swinging her feet to the floor, she stood shakily and shuffled to open the door.

Mad Molly laughed. "It'll be decided by and by! By and by, ye'll see herself come in and then . . ."

Kate threw back the door and glowered angrily at the group gathered beyond the threshold. There was Charlie Nesbitt and two of the Claddagh brothers hovering in the background behind Martin. Fern had her back to Kate while Molly, Martin, and Widow Clooney stood arguing to the fore.

Widow Clooney looked up sharply at the vision of Kate. "Back to bed with you!" the red-faced midwife commanded.

Molly cackled. "Now we've won it! There's herself to come see!"

Everyone else looked up guiltily.

Kate fixed her stern gaze on Martin. He was splattered with mud that half-concealed his riding clothes. "And where have you been, Martin Donovan?" Kate snapped, leaning against the lintel.

Martin worked his mouth soundlessly, finally blurting, "Galway City."

Kate demanded, "Galway City, is it? Without a word? Without a by-your-leave?"

"Sure, and you were sleepin' when I left, y'know, Kate?"

"Without a note?"

Martin glanced furtively at Nesbitt who gave a weak shrug. Martin hesitated, then said, "I went to fetch somethin' for you, Kate."

"Aye. Charlie Nesbitt told me. A calf . . ."

Molly interrupted. "A lamb! A wee lamb!"

"And I've been sick with worry about you," Kate finished.

Silence. More furtive looks.

Fern turned, a bundle cradled in her arms. "A lovely wee thing it is, Kate."

A baby? Kate felt the room spin around her. What had they done? And why?

Widow Clooney rushed to her side and clasped her elbow. "Now see what ye've done! Can't let the woman grieve and get over her tragedy? For shame! Fools! All of you!" She aided Kate back to the bed. "Poor girl. Poor Kate! What were they thinkin'?"

Mad Molly cried out loudly. "Wake it up! Wake it up! Angels of heaven!"

Kate felt sick. She laid her head upon the pillow. "What has he done?"

"Ah, Kate," Martin proclaimed remorsefully. "I thought . . ."

Then came the feeble bleating of the newborn in Fern's arms. "Hush. Hush, darlin'," Fern urged. "Martin, take it. There's a wet-nurse over in Tuam."

The baby's wail increased in volume. Kate's breasts throbbed, tightened, and then a flood of milk let down, soaking Kate's night-shirt and the bed.

Widow Clooney exclaimed, "Lord have mercy! She'll drown in it! Bring a towel!"

Kate began to weep. She covered her ears, but the infant's hungry demand would not be shut out. What madness had possessed Martin to think she could ever . . .

Martin touched her on the shoulder. "I'm takin' it to Tuam, sister. I'm sorry. I thought it would help. And when I found it, well, she's so hungry. Two days old she is, and never a proper meal."

"All the way to Tuam," Fern muttered. "Be lucky if it makes it that far."

Kate turned on her back. The flow of milk increased. "Look what's happened!"

"A baby's cry," replied Widow Clooney sagely, "still makes these old teats stand to attention." She whirled around. "Get the child out of here!"

The cluster of onlookers moved en masse toward the exit.

Kate sat up. "All the way to Tuam, is it?" she queried. "Bring it here! I say! Give the wee thing to me!"

"Bring it here then," commanded the Widow, taking the baby

from Fern. "Men out, if you please!" She took the squalling infant from Fern. Was that a wink that passed between the two women?

Mad Molly smacked her gums in glee and twirled around. "All men out! Out! Out! Out!"

Widow Clooney slipped the baby into the bed beside Kate. It was little and so very new. Tiny fingers were spread and quivering with outrage.

"Poor thing," Kate crooned, untying the neck of her gown and guiding the infant to its first proper meal. It latched on with a fierceness that made Kate wince.

"Look at that, will you?" whispered Widow Clooney. "It'll take a stick to make it turn loose!"

"Just as natural as anythin'," agreed Fern, leaning over to look.

"A fountain of blessin'!" exclaimed Molly. "Where's Mary Elizabeth? She should see the wee thing! Where is she?" Molly fled the room.

Widow Clooney closed the door behind her. "Ah, Kate! 'Tis a sorry thing your brother's done, bringin' this foundlin' child. Its poor mother perished and itself left in a feed trough in a lambin' barn. Or so he says. It would have died. Might yet if it ain't fed properly. Nuthin' yourself needs. But he meant good. Forgive him. He meant no harm to you. You're doin' well. This'll give the sad wee thing a chance to live until Martin can find a place for it. Do you need any help in the matter?"

Kate frowned and touched the fine velvet hair. The tiny head fit into the palm of her hand. "I learned a thing or two workin' in a dairy my whole life." Without meaning to, she kissed the perfect ear. Then the cheek and the forehead. The baby girl drew a ragged breath of contentment and burrowed deeper into Kate.

The relief was palpable.

The infant girl slept peacefully in the crook of Kate's arm.

"Dear stranger," Kate whispered, stroking her cheek.

Mary Elizabeth called from the corridor, "Can I see it, sister Kate?"

"Come in, Mary Elizabeth."

The child entered the room on tiptoe and came to the edge of the bed. "It's a wee girl, is it? Martin said he found her in a manger in Mahon's lambin' barn."

"Mahon's barn, was it?" Kate asked. She had not heard that grim detail. It could be no surprise that a child would be abandoned in such a place since many families had been turned out on the road to starve in that part of Galway.

"Aye. A miracle, like. Thunder, lightin', and wind. Then there she was." Mary Elizabeth pressed forward for a better look. "She's a pretty wee thing. Rosebud for a mouth. Don't think they'll want her back, do you Kate? And you won't send her away to the nurse in Tuam with Martin? Widow Clooney says she'll most likely die if she ain't warm and fed good."

Kate did not reply. She adjusted the blanket so Mary Elizabeth could have a better look. "Sweet. Aye. She is . . . indeed. That she is."

Mary Elizabeth grinned broadly, then giggled. "What'll we call her?"

"I hadn't thought." Kate knew no one would come to claim the child. She also knew Martin would not be taking her to Tuam. Suddenly protective, Kate held the newborn closer. "I had some names in mind . . . in case we had a girl. I thought maybe . . . Dora."

"Dora." Mary Elizabeth nodded. Then she glanced at Mad Molly's roses nestling in a tin pot on the window ledge. "Dora . . . Rose . . ."

Kate touched the infant's lips. "Dora Rose, then."

"Aye. She's pretty like a rosebud in spring. But it ain't spring and sure, like Molly findin' roses all a'bloom in such a gloomy time . . . well, she's a grand surprise to us, ain't she like? Like a bloomin' miracle, sort of?"

"It's a perfect name, Mary Elizabeth."

The two were pleased with the naming of Dora Rose. Smiling, Mary Elizabeth hung on the mattress to admire her new niece and contemplate years of getting to know Dora Rose better.

11

From the imprisonment and torments of the previous year, Joseph was so thin his cheekbones threatened to poke through his skin. Nevertheless he felt energized, as though years were dropping away with every passing mile.

Though morning had not yet arrived when the packet made landfall off Dalkey at the entrance to Dublin Bay, Joseph was already on deck and peering through the gloom toward the land of his birth. At the docks a trio of ships were being loaded with grain: barley and oats for shipment across the Irish Sea to English mills and bakeries. Few Irish tenant farmers could afford such bread for their own tables, but even so, a crop for export meant employment for thousands of laborers and a few more shillings at home. The port bustled with commerce, and it was clear that the autumn of 1844 held the promise of an even brighter New Year, 1845.

The O'Connell townhome in Merrion Square likewise bustled with visitors and guests. Daniel O'Connell, on being told the news of Joseph's return, startled the elderly Bishop of Meath by bursting out of their meeting to sweep Joseph up in a huge embrace.

"Joseph, my boy," O'Connell boomed. "How glad I am to see you again! We were afraid your martyrdom had come. How much you have suffered for the cause! And what is the meaning of the bandages around your neck? Were you nearly hanged and only spared at the last second?"

Before Joseph could answer even one of this flood of queries, O'Connell was struck with remorse at keeping his protégé standing. The Liberator changed to demanding that Joseph not speak until he had eaten something.

Over a lavish meal Joseph was regaled with O'Connell's account of his trial and imprisonment and the subsequent appeal. A committee in the English House of Lords had agreed that O'Connell had wrongfully faced a jury packed by his political foes and overturned the guilty verdict.

Despite rumors that the Emancipator was in a decline after his incarceration, Joseph could see no evidence of it, apart from a greater whiteness to the almost seventy-year-old's hair and a tendency to ramble. "Next spring," O'Connell boasted at the close of the meal, "we will breath new life into Repeal! Monster meetin's to put even the one at Tara into the shade! We have the support of all the Irish! Even those in Ulster who have hung on the longest to the Union are speakin' of a federal system where Irishmen govern Irish affairs. I tell you, Joseph, a grand day is dawnin'! But did anyone tell you of my speech this afternoon? And the one in two days at Conciliation Hall? And will you be our chief collector for Galway again?"

"Daniel," Joseph protested, "may I not go home first? I hear I may have more family there than when I left."

"Of course, my boy," bubbled O'Connell affectionately. "I'll send you off in my own coach and six this very day . . . fastest team in Kerry. Only . . ." O'Connell paused and looked at Joseph slyly. "But the team can't be got ready till after my speech today. What do you say? You'll stay and hear it, yes?"

What other choice was there?

In the event, the speech delivered from the second-floor balcony of the Merrion Square home was vintage O'Connell. The Liberator told the massed crowd of twenty-five thousand packing the Dublin streets, "Tell everybody you meet . . . say this is my command: Protestants, Catholics, Dissenters . . . Irishmen of all classes. Let us combine for justice and freedom for all of Ireland."

By dusk Joseph was spinning off toward Connaught, the whir of the coach wheels and the clatter of hooves playing a counterpoint to the clamor of his thoughts.

In the front room of the New York City lodgings that he shared with seven other Irish immigrants, Kevin Donovan read over the letter from his sister Kate for yet a third time:

> *. . . so you see, dear brother, how much we need you to remember us in your prayers. Joseph may no longer be a hunted man, but we have no way to tell him so and to get him to come home.*
>
> *Daniel O'Connell vows to take up the cause of Repeal again in the spring, but for now an Irish parliament remains out of reach. I mention this not because I care much for the politics but because it means your exile must continue. How I do long to see your face!*
>
> *Martin and Mary Elizabeth send their love . . . you cannot imagine how tall they are both grown. In answer to your question, I have not heard from Jane Stone and do not know what is become of her.*
>
> *Your loving sister,*
Kate

Henry Kennedy, one of Kevin's roommates, burst into the apartment in a high state of agitation. He was waving a newspaper. "Have you heard the news?" he demanded, thrusting a copy of the Irish paper, *The Defender,* under Kevin's nose.

Knocking the arm aside, Kevin retorted, "I've had my fill of bad news, thank you. Only one letter from my Jane while I am stuck here diggin' sewers. Leave me alone."

"But this is important!" Kennedy insisted, pushing the crudely printed sheet forward. "More riots in Philadelphia. They are burnin' churches."

They, Kevin knew, referred to those in the anti-Catholic, anti-immigrant movement called the "Know-Nothings." Henry Kennedy was an active member of the Ancient Order of Hibernians, the secret Irish society formed in response. *The Defender* was published by the Hibernians.

Despite Kevin's avowed lack of interest, he nevertheless scanned the headlines. "Two Churches Burned," the paper reported. "Many Houses Also. Twenty Dead in Three Days of Fighting." The broadsheet went on to note that the Know-Nothings vowed to drive the Irish Catholics out of America once and for all.

"It's Philadelphia, not New York," Kevin declared. "What do you want me to do about it?"

"You know New York's Mayor Harper is one of them. Bishop Hughes has already had a meetin' with the mayor to warn him against unleashin' his hooligans here, but the bishop still wants us to come to St. Pat's tonight."

Galway Workhouse loomed fortress-like before them. The Grogan family made their way toward it through the paupers' graveyard. Unconsecrated ground, it was nothing more than a rocky field pocked with sunken earth where the bodies beneath had rotted away.

Corrie Grogan knew this was the end of fine dreams about America, the end of all hope that their family would find a new life in a new land. A pipe dream it had been, to believe they would board a ship and sail away to happiness. Of the three sisters only Corrie was aware of what this place meant to them.

Daniel Grogan spoke soothingly. "Now me beauties, yer da'll have to leave ye here at this big house awhile."

The word *forever* echoed in Corrie's brain.

"But I'll come back for you."

Liar.

"Soon as I've earned enough to buy passage for us all to America."

Liar.

"There'll be plenty of food for ye here."

Liar.

"And Corrie, ye'll get schoolin' here, no doubt. Just as ye've always wanted."

The stream of deceptions was more than Corrie could bear. She halted beside a mass grave where the earth sagged, and not one marker could be found to identify those who rested beneath. She had heard of this. Mama had spoken of the smallpox epidemic, which had taken half the workhouse population only a short time before. Old people and children, mostly.

"Mama didn't fancy us comin' here, Da!" Corrie challenged.

"She's nothin' to say about it," Grogan countered threateningly. "Come on, then."

"Mama said they'd separate us if we came here." She stood her ground.

"Shut up!" Grogan ordered as Ceili's expression changed from acceptance to fear. "Ye're scarin' yer sister."

"It ain't a good place!" Corrie pleaded. "People die here. Lots of 'em." She jerked her hand toward the grave. "See, Da."

"That was a long time ago."

"What if the fever comes again?"

"Ye'll not be better off beggin' on the streets. At least I know they'll feed ye here. Ye'll have a roof over yer ungrateful head!"

"You're leavin' us! Like you left the baby!"

Grogan slapped Corrie across the cheek. "Shut yer gob, then!" Ceili began to sob and then Megan. Corrie remained still as stone, hating, hating, hating her father!

Grogan drew back from her. "I've no choice! D'ye hear me? No choice! I can't do what's got to be done with the three of ye hangin' on to me . . . always needin', needin', needin'! I can't manage without Annie." He gave Corrie a shove. "Take yer sisters to the gates!

They're hungry, ain't they?" Turning on his heel, he did not embrace them but strode away. "I'll come back for ye. I swear it."

The turreted cornices of the otherwise boxy form of St. Patrick's Cathedral lifted their spires above New York City's downtown between Mott and Mulberry Streets. The churchyard, first dedicated in 1815, was surrounded by a ten-foot-high brick wall. On that night in 1844 the normally deserted graveyard was filled to overflowing with more than three thousand Irishmen, most of them about Kevin's age.

There was much grumbling and brandishing of shillelaghs in the crowd. The sentiment most often expressed was that the throng should not wait to be attacked but rather carry the fight to the enemy. "Burn the mayor's house and his worthless self too if we can catch him," was the drift of the rhetoric.

"Quiet down, then," commanded Bishop John Hughes from the top of the church steps. "You are gathered here to defend against a riot, not to start one. I'll have no charges of hooliganism laid to our score."

Hughes, an imposing figure with broad shoulders, a high forehead, and dark hair, shook his finger in admonition as he spoke. "I have already met with Mayor Harper," he said. "I have warned him that any attack on Catholic churches will be met with force . . . and the result will turn New York into another Moscow."

There was a widespread murmur of approval at this harsh pronouncement. Only one generation earlier, Moscow was burned to the ground by its residents rather than let it fall to the invading army of Napoleon Bonaparte. Bishop Hughes, derisively called "Dagger John" by his enemies for the hand-drawn cross affixed to his signature, was a straight-talking clergyman who had his origins as a laboring emigrant from County Tyrone.

"Now Mayor Harper promised there will be no trouble, and accordin' to himself this meetin' was unnecessary." Widespread groans greeted this bit of crack, and Bishop Hughes was grinning as he added, "But I told his honor that as much as we thanked him for his assurances, we would hold our little gatherin' just the same. Now I want you to go and set up sentry parties for each parish church. Ten men on watch and the others within call will be ample. Three nights runnin' should see us safely through this crisis. Now before you go . . ."

Knowing what would follow, the mob of hardworking, lean-faced, angry men knelt for the benediction. "May God keep us all in peace and freedom," Hughes intoned.

After uneventfully patrolling the streets around the cathedral until three in the morning, Kevin and Henry Kennedy were allowed to go home to bed.

They were jumped a block away from their dwelling by a gang of Know-Nothings.

Half a brick whistled out of the darkness, thumping painfully into Kevin's side. Back to back, shillelaghs in hand, he and Kennedy faced four thugs armed with broken bottles and barrel staves. One of the attackers was two paces nearer than the others. Kevin abruptly ran at the man, swinging his stick over his head and slashing it downward. The assailant jumped aside, but not before the club struck him on the point of the shoulder. Yelping, he dropped the glass shard he was holding and hopped away.

Leaping back toward his friend, Kevin parried a blow from a paling, then jabbed his weapon into the midsection of the second opponent. As the figure doubled up, Kevin slipped his grip down to the end of the club and whirled it into the man's chin.

Two down.

At a cry for help, Kevin turned to see that Kennedy had been driven to his knees. A Know-Nothing raised a brick in two hands and plunged it toward the Irishman's head. It smacked into Henry's skull with a sickening thud, and Kennedy collapsed on the pavement. The aggressors turned toward Kevin.

Even though facing two opponents, Kevin did not retreat. His shillelagh spinning around him, he advanced, shouting in Gaelic at the top of his lungs. A wild fury on his face, he might have killed the two men had they not fled from him, dragging their wounded comrades away.

Kevin knelt beside Kennedy. Henry's scalp was bleeding profusely, and his eyes would not focus, but he was alive and conscious. Kevin helped him to stand. "It's a good thing you are a hardheaded mick," he said. "Come on, let's get you some help."

On the way to the parish infirmary Kevin said, "I've made up my mind. I'm goin' home."

"What?" Kennedy said, taking his hand away from his wound long enough to look anxiously at Kevin. "Was it I who was knocked in the head—or you? Did you not tell me it was worth your life to ever return?"

Through gritted teeth Kevin explained, "I did not go back when they killed my father. I did not go back when they burned out my brother and sisters. But if I have to fight for bein' Irish even in America, then by St. Patrick I may as well fight at home, where it matters."

∽ 12 ∽

The workhouse was a charity of the state church of Ireland, which was to say, the English church. As such, it was distantly administered by a board of governors, Anglo-Irish landholders, most of whom lived in London, some of whom had never been to Ireland. Structured along the same brutal lines as the English workhouses and orphanages, the day-to-day business of maintenance and care was left in the hands of local officials.

Mr. Fadge, superintendent of the establishment, delegated the care of children to Reverend Banbreak.

Banbreak, a young English clergyman, had barely graduated from divinity school and after some scandal could not find a suitable post. The impoverished nephew of a London-dwelling absentee Irish landlord, his mother had entreated the board of governors for a meager post for her son.

The position found for Reverend Banbreak was children's administrator for the Galway workhouse. There was only one slight problem: Banbreak detested children.

Banbreak's stipend of seven pence half penny per head per week was ample to keep the young residents fed and clothed. But Banbreak considered that sum too extravagant for an Irish child, which meant two-thirds of the amount could be siphoned off into his own pockets. In addition to this embezzlement, the older children were rented out as laborers. Some broke rocks into gravel for the roads. Others, less strong, were taught to sew and given the opportunity to stitch the uniforms for Queen Victoria's sailors. Banbreak also pocketed the cash received for the labor done. What remained from the bounty was converted into thin soup, gritty porridge, and rags to wear.

In exchange for the privilege of working in a useful manner, being shoddily clothed, and fed barely enough to survive, the youthful inmates of the Galway workhouse had to meet one requirement concerning spiritual matters. It was this directive that Banbreak explained to Corrie, Ceili, and Megan.

"It is my duty as chaplain to see to your spiritual well-being. Unbaptized pagans are not welcome here."

Corrie, who could not bring herself to look into the face of the fierce cleric, said, "My sisters and myself were baptized in the parish of St. Matthew, Connaught, sir."

"Catholics."

"Aye, sir. A good Christian family fallen on hard times. Our mother is dead, y'see."

"Catholics!" Reverend Banbreak peered down his long nose at the trio of sisters. "It'll never do. Papists are not fed at this workhouse. The charity of the church does not extend to the unwashed idol worshipers."

Ceili said in the Irish, "What's he saying, Corrie? What's the man mean?"

This lapse into the Celtic tongue brought an outpouring of rage from the reverend. His round face reddened. Pale eyes bulged with fury. "It . . . IS . . . FORBIDDEN . . . to speak the devil's language within these walls!"

Ceili asked more softly again in Irish, "What's wrong with him, then?"

The cleric raised his walking stick as if to strike Ceili. She flinched as it whistled past her ear and smacked against the stone floor. "You! If you expect to break the bread of our charity . . . IF you expect our generosity . . . UNDERSTAND THIS . . . you will not speak the language of demons here ever again!"

Corrie, horrified, stepped between Banbreak and Ceili. Megan, pitifully skinny and frail, whimpered and buried her face in Corrie's skirts. "Sir," Corrie pleaded, "my father has gone off to find work."

"Deserted you!" roared Banbreak. "Typical drunken Irish. Leave their brats to the kindness of others, is it?"

Corrie was too hungry to argue. Megan would die without food and warmth. "Sir, tell us what it is we must do to stay. What to feed my sisters and myself?"

"Convert to the one true church."

"And what church is that?" Corrie asked.

"Impertinent waif!"

"Sir . . . we hunger."

"Then cleanse your souls by denouncing the Catholic church and its follies."

Ceili, puzzlement on her face, said, "Sure, and Mama said we must be good Christians, sir."

Imperiously, Banbreak lifted his chin. "I am certain I can feed your deceived soul as to what a good Christian is." His eyes narrowed. "Would you like bread, Megan?" he queried the littlest Grogan.

She nodded fearfully. He chucked her under the chin. "You'll follow the rules then, eh?"

The three sisters nodded, though none of them could know what rules Reverend Banbreak had invented for children who entered this sinister place.

No matter how fast the carriage raced across the Irish countryside, Joseph's thoughts leapt ahead of it.

Kate . . . after all these months . . . Kate. And a life that was neither of them alone but the two of them together, as they had always meant to be one and inseparable. Their oneness had taken so long to achieve! His years of wandering, the struggle to redeem his birthright, the terror of the smallpox, the necessity of overcoming Kate's doubts: all had finally been resolved before the altar. And then: prison and exile!

Through the months of enforced separation, Joseph had kept his sanity by holding fast to the dream of returning to her embrace, and by never giving in to despair and desperation. But now that he was actually on the road, he was consumed with frustration—almost panic—at the least delay. Stopping to rest and water the team was intolerable; Joseph paced ahead of the coach and was picked up en route, as if that would somehow bring the fulfillment sooner.

Wave upon wave of images of her assaulted him: Kate seen from afar working at her father's dairy. Kate in her shift as they struggled together to bring an awkwardly turned calf into the world. Kate on their wedding day. Kate as she had come to him in prison.

He shivered.

Joseph's eyes snapped open at the inner vision, as if even his thoughts were too private to take place anywhere away from her side. Joseph pounded on the wall of the carriage and bellowed, "How much longer?" though he knew the answer as well as the coachman.

"No more'n an hour, sir," the driver yelled back.

The hour passed with agonizing slowness, though the boisterous team seemed to have caught the eagerness of their passenger. The alarmed citizens of Castletown leapt out of the way of the speeding rig, never dreaming they witnessed the homecoming of their hereditary lord.

Then it was the drive beside the home fields and the tree-lined rock wall that marked Burke Park. *At last!* Joseph wanted to shout as the rear wheels skidded around the turn beside the gatekeeper's cottage and into the drive.

There were the tumbled remains of the burnt-out manor house and beyond it the former stable, the renovated Great Hall of the Burkes.

Joseph saw all of this but took in none of it. It was like asking a man who looked at himself in the mirror every day if he saw the color of his eyes.

What if it were only a dream from which he would awaken to find himself back on the *Hive* and carried away from Kate forever?

There was only one sight that would satisfy Joseph's longing and quell the fearful pain swelling up in his chest.

And then, suddenly there she was: Kate, beside the front door, with a baby in her arms!

Joseph was out of the carriage before it had even slowed, much less stopped . . . running toward her, sweeping her to him, holding her tightly and carefully at the same time.

Then both spoke at once.

"Ah, Kate."

"How can you . . . I had no word . . ."

"Cannot believe how glad . . ."

"I missed you so."

"And the baby! How I wish . . ."

And then there were no words at all, just an embrace that went on and on and on, an embrace joined by Tomeen around Joseph's knees, Martin and Mary Elizabeth on either hand.

Joseph sat in the rocking chair beside the window as he held Dora Rose gingerly in his arms. The afternoon light was gold behind him.

Kate remained on the edge of the bed. She had to tell him, she knew. He could not be left to believe that this was the child she had given birth to exactly nine months since they had made love in the Galway prison. But his eyes were so bright, so filled with awe and joy at the miracle! How could she destroy his delight so soon after his homecoming?

Yet if she did not speak up, would he think she meant to deceive him?

"'Tis a long, long, time since I held one so tiny," he said, grinning. "Not since Tomeen was a wee babe. I was afraid I'd break him too. Now he's such a big boy."

"He's been a blessin' to you, Joseph? Has he? I mean even though he's not your own?"

"But he is."

"I mean . . ."

"Aye, Kate. I know what worries you, and it needn't. Dora Rose will not take Tom's place in my heart."

Kate shook her head curtly. "That's not what . . . I'm . . . What I mean to say is . . ."

Joseph shifted the infant to his shoulder and patted her back. "Well? Say it then."

"What I mean is . . . she's . . . Dora Rose is . . ."

"Is?"

"Joseph, I gave birth . . ."

"That's plain enough."

"Joseph!" Her voice sharpened. "Look at me, will you?"

Startled, he raised his gaze. His smile faded at the sight of her brimming eyes. "What is it then, Kate? Sure, I've been gone awhile, but there's nothin' you can't tell me, girl."

She clasped her hands together and stared at the floor. "The baby . . . he was a boy."

"Was?"

She replied with a stiff nod. "Widow Clooney said he would have been fine and healthy, but the cord, you see . . . around his neck three times like a rope. And he was turned wrong. He lived a few moments only." The words tumbled out at once as Joseph's features froze.

Tears came unbidden, flowing down her cheeks and falling on her fingers. "And y'see, Martin found her and brought her home to me . . . I couldn't send her away. And the truth of it is, Joseph, I didn't want to. I . . . need . . . her."

The room was silent. Beyond the closed door Kate heard the clanking of the kettle on the hearth as Margaret cooked supper.

Joseph closed his eyes and lay his cheek against the velvety head of Dora Rose. In a soft voice he spoke to the infant. "The angels brought you to us then, Rosie girl. Aye."

Kate blurted, "Sure, and I couldn't let you go on thinkin'."

Joseph locked her with his stare, and she saw his grief. "If only I could've been here for you, Kate. If only . . ."

"I held him only a bit, Joseph. He looked so much like . . ."

"It's all right."

"Like you."

"We'll have other children. Sons, Kate. Don't cry."

"So much like you. I didn't want them to take him, but when I awoke, y'see . . ."

"We have Tomeen to raise then. And God has sent us a fine little rose." Joseph came to sit beside Kate, putting his arm carefully around her as if she might break. "I'm home now, darlin'."

Kate leaned heavily against him. All the pain and weariness of the last months began to drift away. "Ah Joseph, Joseph! I was afraid I'd never see you again!"

"Here I am, love. For you. For Tomeen. For our wee Rosie girl. I'll never leave you again."

It was the Widow Clooney who took Joseph to the kitchen for a cuppa and told him the way of it.

"'Twas a hard, hard time she had of it. She might of bled to death from it. Some have, and some have died who've not had half so hard a time. So y'see, Squire, it may be that she should never have another child. And 'twould be pure folly if she was to get in the family way now, y'know? Do you hear me?" Widow Clooney looked at the smoldering peat fire and frowned as she chose her words. "You're lucky she's alive a'tall. 'Twould kill her sure if she was . . . and it took no time a'tall for you . . . one night together and she was . . ." She grasped his arm. "You'll need to take the vow for a time like Father O'Bannon, y'know . . . Do you take my meanin'?"

Joseph jerked his chin downward once. "I thank you, Widow Clooney. You're a woman . . ."

"I hope I am that."

"Tell me, what'll she need from me? What can I do?"

"If my Aidan was alive, God rest him, he'd tell you."

"Sure, and I know he would. A good man, Aidan."

"Since he ain't here, then I'll tell you what I'd tell him to be tellin' yourself, Squire. Aidan, I'd say, tell the squire to keep his hands in his pockets and his mind on the farm, if you know what I mean."

"And I'd thank him for the advice."

"See you do more than thank him, Squire. Aidan had twelve children by me, minus David now, God rest his soul, and knowed when enough was enough."

"Yes'm."

"And furthermore, Squire, no need bringin' up the subject . . . that the child died. 'Tis guilt she'll be feelin' about such a failure. Dead baby . . . Like a failed harvest to a man. There's a burden for a woman to carry. Keep your mouth shut on the matter."

"That I will." Her warning went through Joseph like a knife. There was so much he wanted to say to Kate.

"God has seen fit, seen fit, he has, to give you a baby girl. Never mind . . . a foundlin'. Martin brought her home. There she is, sucklin' at Kate's breast, and might have been your own child as far as you knew. Forget entirely the child you've lost. Be glad for the child you've found."

Again Joseph nodded, though he felt his throat tighten with sorrow. Pity for the little one who did not live. Must the life of tiny Martin Burke never be remembered? Forget the son he and Kate had borne together? Pretend their baby had never come into this world even for an hour? Could Joseph close his heart to what might have been? A son! Part of himself and part of Kate! Did he have Kate's eyes? Joseph's chin? Did he have the hands of a Burke? The nose of a Donovan? Never to ask meant never to know. To forget meant never to have said farewell properly.

"For Kate . . ." he stammered. "My silence . . . It's what Kate needs, is it?"

"Aye. She's got herself a baby girl at the breast and never more needs remindin' it ain't the child she brought into the world." She put a finger to her lips as if her voice would carry back and smite Kate's heart like a cudgel. "Martin saw to the buryin'. A fine lad, Martin. Now then, if you've got a tear to shed . . . Well, Squire, sure, you're supposed to be more sensible than ordinary menfolk. Ain't you?"

He did not reply but looked out the window toward the barn.

Martin, standing beside the door, waved tentatively, no doubt guessing at what the Widow Clooney was saying to Joseph.

Don't speak of it!

In his nightshirt Joseph emerged from the wardrobe adjoining the bedroom. Having washed in a wooden tub, he was drying his hair so his voice was muffled under the cloth. "I will never take bathin' for granted ever again," he said. "Why, for months after you came to the prison . . . that is, there were times when I would gladly have changed my skin if another had been . . ." His face reddened from scrubbing, appeared from under a hood of toweling. Kate was lying on the bed facing him, propped on her elbow. She was nursing baby Dora Rose. "K-Kate," he stammered, turning abruptly around as if inspecting the wall.

"She's just dropped off to sleep, dear thing," Kate said, smiling down at Dora Rose. "She is puttin' on the weight now, but you should have seen her that first day. She looked and sounded feeble, but no longer. Molly says my milk must have the goodness of the earth for her to grow so. She's been well behaved for you, Joseph, but she can bellow loud as Tobin's bull if she's a mind to. Is anythin' wrong?" Detaching the sleeping child from her breast, Kate relaced and tied her gown.

"No," Joseph said awkwardly. "I . . . it still feels strange to be home, like I might waken and find myself back on the *Hive* or somewhere. So often I dreamed about bein' here with you and . . ." Dangerous territory, his dreams. His words subsided, and he stood clumsily beside the bed.

"Do y'see what a perfect rosebud mouth she has?" Kate asked. Dora Rose heaved a sigh of infant contentment as she nestled in the crook of Kate's arm. "Would you like to hold her?"

Staring down into the face of the sleeping child, Joseph recovered his composure. "She is a rare beauty indeed," he agreed.

"Joseph," Kate inquired slowly, "there was no way to ask your permission before doin' this . . . taken' her in, I mean. I know you'd never send her away, so I won't ask. But is it . . . can you love her?"

"Of course," he said, allowing a warmth of tender reassurance to flow from him. "She and Tomeen." The red hair of the toddler was a tumbled mass of curls where he lay sleeping in his crib at the foot of the bed.

Pointing to a fleece-lined basket nestled between the bedframe and the wall, Kate indicated that Joseph should tuck Dora Rose in there. Then Kate folded aside the coverlet and scooted over to make room for her husband. "Are you ready to come to bed?" she asked.

Widow Clooney's warning thundering in his head, Joseph was suddenly aware of a crushing load of guilt. What kind of beast was he to be gripped by desire so soon after Kate's ordeal? And what sort of danger would Kate's life be in when . . . if . . . she became pregnant again?

"No, I . . ." He faltered. "I don't want to jostle you." Over Kate's protests he made a heap of clothing and blankets into a nest of sorts on the floor. "I'll be fine here. Better by far than anything I've slept on in months."

"Joseph," Kate said softly, "won't you hold me?"

Cautiously, reluctantly, Joseph blew out the lamp and crawled in beside her. Brushing his lips quickly across hers as one would test the hot rim of a cup, he held her at arm's length and said abruptly, "Good night, then, Kate. What a day this has been. I'm just done up."

When Dora Rose awoke sometime in the small hours of the morning, Kate found Joseph wrapped in a quilt, fast asleep on the hard planks of the floor. He did not awaken as she nursed the infant.

She was disappointed he had not wanted to spend his first night home in bed beside her. Had the privations of the last months robbed him of his desire for her, she wondered? Was it the loss of their son that made Joseph look away from her, as though he could not bear the thought of holding her?

All she had wanted through the ordeal was the comfort of his arms around her. Tonight she consoled herself by remembering what the old ones used to say when a child was lost from a family:

Men grieve differently than women. The dead turn
their backs on us forever and walk away from us toward
the light. A woman walks with them for a while, call-
ing, calling in sorrow, and finally turning back to life
again. A man stays behind, busies himself with mun-
dane details, wishes living were not so hard, and waits
awkwardly for his woman to come home to life again.

Kate knew something about loss. How many years had she sor-
rowed for the deaths of her first husband, mother, and infant brother
in the fire? How many times had she made pilgrimage to St. Brigit's
cross to embrace the past?

It was Joseph who had called her back to loving again. Perhaps,
Kate reasoned, he needed time to grieve. Time to chase after the
image of what might have been. His heart would come home to her
when he was finished. She would have to be patient, set aside her
own need and longing, let him wander that long road alone.

Dora Rose had her fill. Milk trickled from the corner of her mouth
as she dozed contentedly. Kate was in no hurry to slip her back into
her bed. The infant lay warm against her, content, living proof that
love was stronger than death.

Alone in the churchyard of St. John the Evangelist, Joseph
stood beside the grave of Martin, the infant son whom he would
never meet in this life. It had bucketed rain all morning, and Joseph
had remained at Kate's side. But when around noon the torrent
finally abated, he could wait no longer. Across the hills and valleys
he trudged, his head uncovered and bowed.

Raindrops hung suspended from the tips of the bare willow
branches like unshed teardrops.

He stood for a long time beside the heap of earth and stones. The
rain had already beaten in and flattened the mound until it was
scarcely different from the rest of the rocky ground. The space of
disturbed soil was small, hardly as much as a man might turn to plant
a single rose bush.

"Martin," he offered softly, "Martineen. It's your da. I'm glad your uncle has brought you here, to be with your grand-da." Then to the headstone beside the place he said, "Tom . . . take care of him, will you? He's so tiny." The hollow place beneath Joseph's breastbone gave way to a wrenching sob, and he dropped to one knee in the sticky clay. "I'm sorry I wasn't there for you," he said. "My son . . . my boy."

Digging into the sod, Joseph squeezed both fists tightly around handfuls of earth, even as his eyes squeezed out another offering of tears.

Peering around him, he carefully selected the largest flat stone from the mire. Brushing it free of the clinging clay, he set it upon the grave. "This is for not being able to hold you close and put you over my shoulder and pat your wee back," he said. "Each time I pass by I will tell you of somethin' else . . . bouncin' you on my knee . . . or ticklin' you . . . or just watchin' you in the arms of your mother."

Joseph clamped his jaw against the pain caused by the last image and, for a time, could not speak.

Then: "Your mother thinks she failed you, that she harmed you. Speak to the Lord about her, will you, Martineen? She loves you so and is hurting so much. Will you do that for your da? And Martin . . . it won't be so very long now, will it? Till we can all be together?"

The clouds atop the Maumturk mountains parted slightly, making a faint halo around the peak. Raindrops, sprouting from the willow twigs, captured sparks of the light, each a rainbow in miniature, waiting to blossom.

PART II

"O! Dublin sure there is no doubtin'
Beats every city upon the sea,
'Tis there you'll see O'Connell spoutin',
And Lady Morgan making tea.
For 'tis the capitol of the greatest nation,
With finest peasantry on a fruitful sod,
Fighting like devils for conciliation,
And hating each other for the love of God."

—Traditional

13

It was icy, but the sun was shining on that Sunday morning when the handsome new squire of the Mahon estate passed through Ballynockanor and by the chapel of St. John the Evangelist.

Early mass and the christening of Rosie Burke had just ended.

The citizens of the parish crowded round the proud parents to congratulate them on the beauty of their wee daughter. Outside in the brilliant day the Claddagh Brothers hefted Tomeen and his playmate, Fern's adopted son, Robert, into the air, tossing them from one to another.

Martin, feeling quite satisfied with himself, sat observing the celebration from the top of the churchyard fence. From there he had a fine view of the living parishioners and the quiet resting places of the dead. He could plainly see that the pile of round pebbles on top of baby Martin's headstone had grown considerably. Joseph had been having more conversations with the little one of late about worries no one understood but Joseph himself.

Ah well. But there was no time for sorrow on such a day as this. Rosie's dear smile had charmed everyone, especially Tomeen and Mary Elizabeth, who played with her like she was a doll. Nowadays Kate was always humming. Joseph dandled the baby girl on his knee at all hours and did his bookwork with her propped up in the crook of his arm.

All of this, Martin knew, was because he had found her and brought her home to the grieving Kate. It pleased Martin immensely. He was congratulating himself when the rumble of wagon wheels along the road turned his head.

There, in an open carriage drawn by a team of four and bearing the family crest of Mahon, was the new squire, Major Denis Mahon, the heir to the Mahon lands. Behind his vehicle were three farm wagons heaped high with potatoes and drawn by stout shire horses.

Martin had heard the fellow was coming. Somehow he did not expect to see him today.

The caravan came to a halt at the gate of St. John's. Martin swung his legs around to turn his back on the squire.

"You, there," called the coachman. "Boy."

Martin pretended not to hear.

"I say, you, young fellow . . ."

Martin saw Joseph look up. The proud grin faded at the sight of Mahon's coach. He drew himself erect, bowed slightly to Father O'Bannon, passed Rosie to Kate, and marched to the newcomer. The whole community then glanced up and, in one unified harrumph, followed Joseph out to see who and what was traveling on the road on Sunday.

"Hullo, there." Dennis Mahon smiled broadly as he stood and extended his hand to Joseph in a most cordial manner.

Joseph reciprocated, introducing himself.

"I'm on my way home, you see," explained Mahon. "I've brought seed potatoes to my tenants. I understand there is much oil to be spread upon these troubled waters in the West."

The meeting was short. An introduction. An exchange of pleasantries. No more than that. Then Major Denis Mahon was on his way again, spuds dripping from his wagon and spilling along the edge of the road.

Pure English was the general impression. Handsomer than his predecessor, the women agreed.

Leave it to Mad Molly to get to the heart of it all, however. Kicking off her shoes, she galloped after the procession, gathering potatoes in her apron. Martin was sent to fetch her. He hung back awhile as she charged into the road in front of the carriage, crossed herself against the evil eye, and began to pitch potatoes at the squire and his steward, Mr. Richman.

"Take that! Ye devil, ye! Come not this way agin! Come not with darkness, fire, or blood! Come not upon the road through Ballynockanor! The eyes are dark! I see it all! They've told me all, ye see! Molly knows what ye're about!"

Martin gave a whistle, interrupting the tirade. "Come along, then, Molly!"

"Ah, Martin." She threw one last spud at the coachman, hitting him squarely and knocking off his hat. "Is it time for cake, then?"

The weeks since Joseph's return turned into months. Still he did not come to Kate's bed at night. He remained aloof, apart from her in every way. He had to stay up and work, he told her, as the hours of an evening wore on. He promised he would be along later, but he did not come to bed. Often in the morning she found him fast asleep with a book over his face on the couch in the study.

Several times she had tried to tell him of her longing for him, of the passionate dreams that awakened her to the sound of her own sighs. Of how when she reached out and found the bed empty beside her she buried her face in the pillow and wept. But when she opened her mouth to speak of it, he somehow read what was coming and turned the subject deftly to O'Connell, the politics of Repeal, the price of butter, or the constant rain.

When the death of their son hung heavy on her soul, she grieved alone, knowing Joseph did not want to think of what might have been. Little Rosie and Tomeen became her comfort. And Joseph was a loving father, even though he had become a stranger to Kate. She wanted to give him a brace of children to love, but his interest in her seemed to have perished with the baby.

It was at Margaret's suggestion that Kate moved Tomeen and Rosie out of her bedchamber and into the adjoining room.

Margaret approached the subject head-on. "Too many kids in the bed, y'know. Tends t'dampen a man's interest in makin' more. They're all alike at heart. Selfish as a mewin' infant. Don't want t'share the milk with anyone else, if y'take my meanin'."

Kate did not say that Joseph appeared to have lost interest in that particular delicacy. Why speak of it? Was it not clear to everyone in the house that her husband shrank back at her touch and looked everywhere but at her when she entered the room?

The week before in the market square she had seen Mrs. Watty gossiping with the Widow Clooney. Their heads leaned toward one another, mouths and eyebrows worked excitedly as they chewed some titillating information. As Kate approached, they each looked up guiltily and fell silent. Their ruddy faces froze in false smiles as they greeted her. It was plain who and what they were discussing.

What man would want to make love to a woman as disfigured as Kate? The squire had one look at her in the altogether, and that was enough for him. Killed his desire. And what's the use of it? She shouldn't bear any more children as it is. You know what they say about a woman who can't deliver a live child . . .

Kate saw, rather than heard, this discussion. As clearly as ink upon a printed page, the whispers in the market square followed the text of her own thoughts and fears.

Joseph no longer loved her.

Dublin! Beyond the quays the city spread out in a fan of Georgian terrace houses, low brick tenements, and church steeples that scratched the belly of the glowering sky. The river Liffy divided Dublin in two.

The spires and domes of Trinity College to the south were plainly visible that afternoon.

Kevin Donovan shouldered his dufflebag as he strode through the shoppers of Henry Street toward Nelson's Pillar at the intersection of Earl Street. He clutched the one clandestine letter he had received from Jane Stone nearly six months before. It had taken nearly half a year to reach him in America. Ten pages of cramped writing on the thinnest onionskin paper, the epistle was filled with vows of her undying love as well as sweet details of her life in Dublin without him. It was the stuff that eased the long ache of homesickness and brought the sights and scents of his homeland back to him each time he read the words. The paper was worn out from his reading. He knew each line by heart and had come to imagine himself back in Dublin, tracing the steps of her daily shopping routine.

Kevin had it all planned. A lovely plan it was too. It was Thursday. This afternoon she and her mother would have ladies from church to the house for tea. At three o'clock Jane would make her way to Downe's Cakeshop where she would purchase cakes for tea. Kevin would come in behind her and wait patiently at her back. When the shop assistant asked what he required he would say that he wanted a wedding cake, that he had come home from America to wed the only girl he had ever loved. Then Jane would hear his voice, spin round, and fall into his arms. Away he would carry her to the church where they would be secretly wed! Then home again to Galway!

Kevin shouldered his way into the crowd at Downe's. Being a head-and-a-half taller than anyone in the shop, he scanned the place for sight of Jane. She was not there.

"Can I help y'sar?" queried the shop girl.

Kevin considered asking about Jane Stone. Had she been in? Did she still come to the shop on Thursday? But he did not. The scent of baking breads and cakes made his mouth water. He remembered he had not eaten since he shared his last meal of hard tack on the schooner *Estelle* the evening before.

Tipping his hat, he dug in his pocket for a coin. "A dozen penny cakes, if you please."

The shop girl wrapped his purchase in brown paper and made

eyes at him. He was a handsome man in spite of the brown stubble of beard on his chin. "Eat them all yourself, will you? Or plannin' to have tea?"

Several young women in the room giggled.

"I've been away . . . in America, y'know," he said exchanging money for package. "Too long since I had a bit of Irish cake."

"America!" was breathed throughout the shoppers. All eyes turned to look at him. It was seldom these days that anyone came home from America.

"All the way across the seas to buy penny cakes at Downe's, is it?" teased the woman.

He blurted, "No. I've come back to be married."

He regretted giving this information out so readily. It ruined his script for later when Jane came into the shop. Now everyone knew he was home to be married, and the line about buying wedding cake would not do.

The shop assistant sighed. "Married is it? Have you met the lucky girl?"

Kevin blushed as the ladies laughed out loud. "That I have," he declared. "And I've had it in my mind to buy the weddin' cake right here."

He left the shop feeling satisfied. At least the crack about wedding cake in Downe's cakeshop had not been wasted entirely.

Munching on the small feast, he took up his position in a nearby doorway where he would have clear view when Jane came to the establishment.

∽

Cradling baby Rose, Kate walked a few paces behind Joseph and Tomeen. They were a vision, father and son.

Carrying Tomeen high on his shoulders, Joseph's long legs reclaimed the rocky ground that sloped down to the bend of the river. The child's chin pressed tightly against the top of his father's tousled blond hair; tiny hands clasped together on Joseph's forehead.

Kate raised her face toward the sun. Clouds scudded across the sky like sailing ships. Joseph laughed aloud at nothing at all and at everything. It was as though the breeze of Galway against his face somehow carried the memory of their separation out to sea.

"Faster, Da!" Tomeen cried.

Joseph turned and winked at Kate, then jogged a few steps and galloped a circle around a stone. Tomeen whooped with delight.

How long had it been since she had smiled like this, since she had not been afraid that even a moment of joy would end in sorrow? Fear of what *might* come had stolen even the most beautiful *now* from her.

But there were her men: Joseph, swooping and soaring across the ground like an eagle, and Tomeen, spreading his arms like a fledgling riding upon the wings of his da! It was no dream, this! The springtime she had longed for had come at last on this chilly March afternoon.

Kate let the triumphant song come into her soul. It warmed her like the first warm breeze thaws dormant branches, stirs sleeping squirrels from dreaming, pipes life to dance again upon the frozen earth. The darkness of her thoughts shifted into the light; all sorrow lifted into a song of praise.

"Sure, and when I was a wee boy like yourself, Tomeen," Joseph remembered, sweeping his arm across the acre of land where they walked, "there were apple trees planted here on this slip of land beside the river. And I would climb them and pick the apples too. Remember Kate? Do ye?"

There was music in Joseph's memory. Fiddles and pipes and tin whistles played in her head. Kate kissed Rosie and whispered, "I remember the apples. Sweet and crisp they were. Cider at the harvest dance."

Joseph's face was bright with recollection. "We'll plant an orchard here again. Why not? Right here where the river curves! Just where it used to stand! Aye! We'll plant it again! Bushel baskets of apples. The ground is right for it. By the time Rosie is old enough to be climbin' trees . . ."

"I wanna climb too, Da!" Tomeen exclaimed, as though rows of sturdy apple trees were already standing on the slip.

"And so you shall!" Joseph declared, swinging the child over his head and lowering him to the ground.

Kate sat on a boulder as man and boy examined the plot. Like a honeybee mapping a flower, Joseph paced the empty acre and imagined the nectar that would flow from it. A farmer measuring his acre of ground—an ordinary thing, it was. The stuff men discussed over a pint at Watty's Tavern.

But for Kate it was resurrection day! An orchard by the river! Apple trees growing again on the slip where the river curved! It was today and tomorrow and a hundred years from now, great-grandchildren climbing trees in the summer and tasting the harvest Joseph imagined on that day.

Beginning and ending wove a tapestry of hope across the barren field. Joseph's voice was as miraculous to Kate as that of one long dead coming into the kitchen to ask for a cup of tea.

∽ 14 ∾

It was nearly half-past three. Kevin Donovan had devoured his entire packet of penny cakes, and yet Jane Stone had not made her usual Thursday appearance at Downe's Cakeshop.

His belly ached. It had been months since he had enjoyed anything as rich as Dublin teacakes. Kevin hoped she would come soon. The combination of too-delicious dainties and the excitement of anticipation made his head spin.

Leaning against the rough stone facade of the greengrocer's shop, he wrapped his woolen greatcoat tighter around himself and glared up at the sky. The afternoon light was already growing dim. By four o'clock it would be nearly dark, he knew.

Where was she?

Had he missed her? Could it be that in an instant when he had glanced down to choose between a cream cake or a current cake Jane Stone had slipped into Downe's, made her purchase, and slipped out and away?

Wadding up the brown paper, he tossed it into the road and strode back beneath the shadow of Nelson's Pillar and toward the shop. His jaw was set. If he had somehow missed her, he would ask the shop assistant right out where Miss Jane Stone resided. He would march boldly to the ladies' tea and pound upon the door. He would carry Jane away despite the shrieks and hysteria of her mother! Kevin had been waiting for this day, this very hour, for too long to be denied. It was after three o'clock, and Jane was late!

He ferreted his way into the crowd, looking to the right and to the left. Suddenly, the dull sunshine picked out a gleam of gold beneath a dark-blue bonnet!

Jane! Her eyes were downcast. Beside her, and a bit behind, walked a dour-looking Church of Ireland minister with a broad hat and a white forked clerical collar. Jane acted preoccupied. Did the minister accompany her? Kevin dismissed his concern. The tea Jane had mentioned in the letter was always a Thursday church affair. Perhaps the prelate was part of the gathering, come to offer words of anti-Irish comfort to the uncomfortable Anglos forced to dwell in the Sodom of Catholic Dublin.

Jane did not see Kevin. She entered the shop with the cleric at her heels. Kevin waited a few moments and then, dodging a carriage, crossed the road and peered into the window.

The same shop girl was there. Ladies crowded the counter like cattle at the trough.

The bell above the door jingled as Kevin entered the shop. He was drenched with sweat in spite of waiting outside in the freezing weather. Snapping off his hat, he ran his fingers nervously through his thick brown hair, and took his place at the end of the queue.

Jane was still in front of the parson. The fellow leaned down and said something to her. She nodded, standing on tiptoe to look at the goods on the shelves.

The shop girl spotted Kevin as she made change for a thickset servant in uniform.

"Sure, and you've come back so soon," she teased him.

His mouth was dry, his hands shaking. "Aye" was the only word he could force out of his throat. Jane did not turn around to look at him.

"Ate all your penny cakes, have you?" the shop girl queried playfully.

"Aye . . . I mean . . ."

"Not married yet, are you?"

Kevin swallowed hard and burst out, "Nay! But I've come back to fetch the weddin' cake we were discussin', as well as to fetch the very bride I've come home from America to wed."

Jane Stone's eyes widened. Her jaw dropped as she turned with every other customer to see who it was that was shouting about marriage.

She gave a little shriek. Not a sound of joy, but horror. Her gloved hands flew to her mouth. "Kevin!"

"Jane!" He shouldered his way through the ladies. The pastor drew his breath in sharply and narrowed his eyes in a threatening, unfriendly way.

"You!" shouted Jane's companion. How did he know about Kevin? "You! Get out of here! Stay back, I say, or I shall call a . . ."

Kevin paid him no mind. "Jane," he called as he struggled to break through the throng. "I've come home to marry you, Jane, darlin'!" He fumbled for the letter and held it high. "It's Thursday!"

The cleric planted himself in Kevin's path. "Call the constable! This fellow is a . . ."

Jane was ashen. "Kevin," she whispered. Her eyes rolled back in her head, and she fainted.

The press of the customers held her upright as the cleric fanned her and called her name. "Jane! Jane! Darling! My dearest wife!"

Kevin halted. "Wife." He repeated the word like an epithet, a vile thing in his mouth. "Wife?"

The parson shrieked, "My wife! That she is, you rapparee!"

Jane slithered to the ground, disappearing from view at the feet of the onlookers.

Outside came the shrill of a constable's whistle.

Women with sympathetic faces jostled to open a space for Kevin's escape.

The assistant shopkeeper sprang around the counter and grabbed Kevin by the arm. "Aye. Out the back. She's Missus Stapleton, wife of Reverend Stapleton. No weddin' for you then. Get out now. Out the back if you please!" She shoved a loaf of warm bread into his hands. "No weddin' cake neither."

The frigid air was like a slap in Kevin's face. The door of the shop slammed behind him. One police whistle was joined by others in the front of the shop by Nelson's Pillar. Kevin shook his head and sprinted down the alley in the opposite direction.

Following his encounter with Jane Stone, or Mrs. Stapleton, Kevin wandered about Dublin in a haze. Somewhere he got a brown bottle from which he drank freely until the mixture of liquor, bile, teacakes, and despair made him vomit in an alley. He shattered the remaining whiskey on the cobbles, but the fog in his thinking accompanied him still.

What was it he had relied on to keep him alive while in America? Had it not been the dream of marrying Jane, of making a fresh start with her in a land of freedom and justice?

It was an illusion. He knew that now. If you were an Irish emigrant, guaranteed freedom and reliable justice no more existed in American than it did in Ireland. And as for Jane? How long had she even thought about Kevin before entertaining, *welcoming* advances of the scrawny, pencil-necked, prating, pious Protestant? Safe in the arms of her own kind! Bad cess to her, then, and her kind.

But what was there left for Kevin?

His nocturnal rambling carried Kevin onto Ha'Penny Bridge. At the center of the span he faced east, then looked downward at the placidly swirling water of the Liffy. Ripples on the surface reflected the three-quarter moon that hung overhead. Each eddy appeared only for an instant before being reabsorbed into the stream. A footstep in a brook left no trace; rivers kept no memories of intrusion. And a few miles away, the impatiently rushing water, having left its origins on mountain or in fen, embraced the sea, and its identity lost forever.

Kevin stretched one leg over the iron railing. His pant leg caught on a spike and tore as he yanked it free. He felt foolish.

Hearing the sounds of someone approaching from the south, he hurriedly exited the north end of the bridge and turned toward the white facade of the Custom House. Like any other Dublin visitor he peered up at the sculpted heads that formed the keystones of the arches and gates. Shadows cast by the moonlight made the faces, each one representing an Irish river, sneer or simper or smile at him.

All except one.

The features of one allegorical stream appeared kindly, welcoming without mocking. Against his will, Kevin studied the benevolent countenance, seeking a clue to its identity. Unreasonably, Kevin decided it was the Cornamona. It said to him that home was still in Ballynockanor.

He told himself that this was another illusion. Yet, he could not shake the thought that Galway held something for him, some answer to his needs. Despite the danger, he would return to Connaught.

The choice was a simple one for Corrie Grogan and her sisters: they could stay in the workhouse and starve to death slowly, or leave and starve quickly on the streets.

Corrie chose to stay.

Every day Reverend Banbreak uttered his before-meal prayers of "God Save the Queen and protect the right noble members of the order of the Bath . . ."

Corrie prayed for one thing only: that Da would come and carry them away from this place of hunger and torment! That Da would bring the tickets for passage to America! That he would throw open the gates of the Galway workhouse and call their names and gather them into his strong arms again!

It was Father O'Bannon's counsel that Kate sought when Joseph grew more distant to her.

Tears came in spite of her vow not to cry.

"There, daughter," consoled the old priest. "Just tell me what it is."

"We've not . . . he's not . . . I can't . . ."

"Aye." Father O'Bannon nodded. "Sure, and it's easy to understand when you've been through so much."

A fleeting doubt passed through Kate's mind. Did the priest understand what she was trying to tell him?

"He seems so . . . different . . . since he came home."

"Sure. Sure. That he would. An ordeal it was. Bein' away from his world so long."

"I can't . . ."

"Of course you can't, daughter. Such an ordeal you've been through yourself. He'll have to understand now, won't he? A man *is* a man after all. Oh, I hear their confessions, and it's not a pretty thing."

"What I mean is . . ." Her mouth could not form the words, the very private information that Joseph had not slept with her since his return. Nor did he seem to want to.

"Sure, and I know what you mean, exactly, daughter. Be patient with him. He's a good man. Deprived a long while. It's no wonder he's feelin' the way he's feelin' toward you."

Did that mean it was natural Joseph would not want her, or that he would, Kate wondered?

Father O'Bannon worked his toothless gums together. "Marriage is a holy estate. No room for wantonness."

Kate blushed at this. She was wanton. She was wantin' Joseph. She ached with yearning for him. Why did he not want her in return?

"Aye, Father. I'll try to be patient."

"Well, you know how a man is. You were married and a widow, Kate. Sure, I've no need to tell you a man is altogether a different color horse than a woman. Aye. Scripture says marry if you lust."

"That I did, Father. And so I did."

"It's understandable. The loss and all."

"I have . . . needs, y'know."

"Sure, and you would, after everythin'."

"Will you have a word with him then, Father?"

The old man patted her on the arm. "As if he was my own dear son. Sure, I'll explain it to him."

Over supper Kate wondered aloud about the two-day absence of Nesbitt and two of the Claddagh boys, Simeon and Moor. "And did you know they'd be away, or is this a wild scheme of their own concoctin'?" she inquired, twirling a silver spoon in the dish of finely sieved oat porridge she was feeding baby Dora Rose.

Joseph cleared his throat and avoided looking directly across the table at Martin. "They're away to Galway City," he said calmly. "I expected them back today but tomorrow should see them here right enough."

"To Galway City," Kate repeated, narrowing her eyes. "What's in Galway City then?"

"Just a few supplies . . . for an experiment I have in mind, don't y'see. An agricultural experiment, you might say." He rattled his coffee cup and pushed his chair back from the table as though anxious for the meal to conclude.

"Well?"

"Well, what?"

"Joseph Connor Burke!" Kate's voice had an air of amused exasperation. "Why this mystery? Is it a secret lodge you're formin'? With secret handshakes and passwords?"

Martin choked on his last bite of boxty bread. Kate reached over and thumped him on the back, rather more enthusiastically than was strictly necessary.

"No, no," Joseph protested. "Nothin' like it. I want to get the trial underway before I explain further, that's all."

Kate hummed into her teacup and tapped her foot. Calling to Fern to clear the table, she said to her sister who was feeding Tomeen, "Come along then, Mary Elizabeth. Let's leave these conspirators to their plottin' before keepin' mum strangles them to death."

Her nose in the air, Mary Elizabeth could not resist getting the last word. At the door of the dining hall she sniffed, "Men!" and departed with a flourish.

It was after midnight that Nesbitt's voice called hoarsely from outside the window, "Squire! Squire! Are you awake, then?"

Joseph's feet slapped the plank floor before the second cry and shortly after slid into his waiting boots. If Kate had been less groggy, she might have wondered at her husband's apparent wakefulness. But as it was she murmured, "Joseph?"

"Hush, darlin'," he urged. "Don't wake the babe. It's just a minor matter to see to. I'll be back soon." And he slipped out of the room.

She roused enough to peek out the window. By the glow of a single lantern bobbing at the end of a slender pole, she could make out the shadowy forms of men and a pair of wagons heaped with lumpy, canvas-covered loads.

Kate, so attuned to Dora Rose that even a tiny change in the rhythm of the child's breathing brought her to instant attention, nevertheless took Joseph's assurance at face value and returned to dreaming.

At grey dawn she awoke. Joseph was still missing, and his side of the bed was cold; he had not returned from his nocturnal errand.

Nor were any other menfolk to be found about the place. From Martin to Old Flynn and every age in between, none of the trouser-wearing class presented themselves for questioning.

The babies were fed and bathed, and the morning's chores eased into the noon hour before Joseph, dirty and disheveled, reappeared alone.

Meeting him at the door, Kate said, "If you were any other man, I'd be smellin' the poteen and refusin' to waste sympathy on your achin' head. But since it's you, I'll wait to see what you have to say."

His face flushed with excitement, Joseph grabbed her in his arms. "I'll do better than tell you," he replied. "Get your shawl, and I'll show you," and he loaded her into the now-empty wagon.

On the road leading to the Cornamona Joseph was cheerful but as mysterious as ever. He deflected Kate's questions and took her teasing abuse with evident delight. Then as the rig drawn by Savina approached the ridge where the lane plunged downward toward the water, he suddenly demanded that she close her eyes and keep them so.

Kate leaned back and braced herself against the descent as the dappled horse carefully picked its way downward. A few minutes later Joseph urged the animal off the track and onto a level patch beside it. "Now," he said.

There, just below her and standing like clumps of muddy, grinning scarecrows, were the missing males of Burke Park.

There, too, lining the inch beside the stream, in both directions up and down, stood row upon row of apple saplings, their spindly trunks braving the breeze along the Cornamona. From the top of each sprouted a bare handful of green leaves, the earnest money on the future life waiting to burst from within.

Kate exclaimed with pleasure and clutched Joseph's hand. "But how? When?"

"Our orchard," he said. "We stayed up the long night to see them well and truly planted. One hundred trees for our children's children's children to climb, harvest, and remember us by."

It was not from the hill crowned with the cross of St. Brigit that Kevin studied the outlines of Ballynockanor and Burke Park. Instead he stood on a knoll on the other side of the river, above the ditch planted thick with apple saplings.

There were two reasons Kevin avoided the stone monument.

The first was because he knew it to be a place of pilgrimage, particularly for Kate. As dearly as Kevin longed to rejoin his family, he also felt clearly that he could not. Since being seen and recognized in Dublin, his illegal return to Ireland could already be known to the authorities. If they wanted to take him up, they would certainly be watching Ballynockanor.

Kevin realized he was not important enough to require much attention on his own behalf, but he also knew from Kate's letters that the British government had been eager to attack Joseph, had succeeded, and would no doubt welcome an excuse to turn Kevin's sisters and brother out of their home, as well.

The second reason Kevin stayed away from St. Brigit's cross was more personal. On the morning of his first return to Galway he had been atop the hillock at daybreak. There, spread out below him was the destruction of the Donovan homestead: the burned-out remains of cottage and dairy. The crumbled walls, already sprouting grass, sagged inward like an untended grave. In fact, the whole effect was like looking at the imagined corpse of his father, tragically murdered and left unburied. The sight made Kevin seethe with rage; it made him fear for himself and the others that he would do something foolish.

And so emotion and good sense combined to prod him into seeking a more cheerful view.

Though Burke Park also showed devastation in the vacant swathe where the Great House had stood, the ancient hall, once a stable and now again a home, bustled with life.

Several sturdy men came and went, as did a sprouting youth that Kevin could scarcely believe was Martin.

Two other sights amazed him even more.

When he saw Kate with a baby in her arms, he assumed it was Tomeen, whom Kevin has last known as an infant. But when a red-haired toddler played peep-boo with Mary Elizabeth from behind Kate's legs, he knew the baby she held must be hers . . . hers and Joseph's.

Which led to the last surprise.

Joseph was home and plainly fearless of arrest. His tall, blond form could be seen striding about the yard, giving orders and riding over the fields. How he had come to be saved from exile Kevin could only guess at.

It added up to fierce pain and awful confusion. He wanted to go to them, to be with them, but could not. He would allow himself one more day of looking at the homely, cheerful, obviously prosperous scene . . . views to savor wherever his path would lead.

Joseph paced the length of Father O'Bannon's cramped kitchen, then back again as the priest studied him. The elder man's near toothless mouth was puckered with concern.

"I'm goin' mad, Father. Stark-ravin' mad for wantin' her!"

"Sleepin' in the same room, are you?"

"Sure. She won't have it any other way. Opens the covers, invitin' me. I've been sleepin' on the floor." Joseph held up his right hand as if he'd swear an oath to the truth of it. "But the sweet scent of her. I'm goin' mad!"

"You can't expect her to want to do her wifely duties, lad. She's been through an ordeal."

"That she has."

"Well, then. You'll need to practice patience with herself. Charity, you might say. Kate's in no state to be gettin' in the family way again so soon."

Joseph mopped his brow. "I should leave."

"Can you not sleep elsewhere, then?"

"It's a contest, see. I stay awake although I'm bleary-eyed. She tries to outlast me. Thank God above for Rosie. Kate can't keep her eyes open when the child starts to nurse."

"Aye. That's a blessin'." Father O'Bannon rubbed his chin. "Well then, here it is. I charge you . . . Lust is a terrible thing, Joseph Connor Burke."

"Aye, I'm in the grip of it."

"God has given you this trial to test your patience and your love. Do you love her?"

"With every ounce of myself, Father!" Joseph's features contorted in agony.

"You'll need to exclude . . . hear me now . . . a few ounces of yourself from love for a time . . . if you take my meanin'."

"I should sleep in the barn."

"You never would have made a priest," Father O'Bannon said with a sigh.

"And so I married."

"And you'll be bound to live like a priest until your woman is strong enough again. Control! You'll not be layin' a hand on her, if you please. She came to me in a pitiable state. I told her the straight of it. Said I'd speak to yourself on the matter. So. Think of her as you would a sister."

"When she's nursin' Rosie . . ." Joseph did not say what happened to him when he watched her put the baby to her breast. How he longed to be cradled in her arms.

"Leave the room then! Avert your naughty eyes, if you please." Father O'Bannon raised his finger in warning. "And I'll be hearin' your confession, remember."

"I'll have to bathe in ice. Wear a blindfold."

"Whatever it takes. Be patient with her. It may take a year . . . or more." He dropped his voice. "You'll not be wantin' to put the poor girl in danger, Joseph."

∽❍ 15 ❍∽

There had seldom been rains like those that came in spring
1845. Kate's milk cows should have been grazing on the hillsides
by St. Patrick's day. Likewise, the seed potatoes should have been
in the ground by then. But all things had gone wrong. The warm,
bright days of spring and early summer never came. After the plant-
ing, summer broke though only briefly. In the West warmth yielded
to lashing wet winds across the bleak fields, refusing to let the crops
or pastures sprout properly. The world was bone cold on the bog
and over the hills. Turf that lay spread to dry remained wet and
ungathered. Hayricks were damp and sodden, ruined in the fields.
Some of Kate's cows wandered off and died, trapped in deceptive
mires that promised lush feed and offered death instead.

July the twenty-third was typical of the uncertain weather in
Connaught. From a morning that dawned cheerfully sunny and
pleasantly warm the day progressed rapidly back to wintry gloom.
The clouds above the Maumturks, swollen with rain, bristling with

thunder and lightning, waited only long enough for the clock in Castletown's market square to finish tolling twelve before rolling across the valley like a juggernaut.

Kate, Mary Elizabeth, and Fern organized a relay to bundle damp bedding off the clothesline. They had scarcely finished before rain was bucketing, sluicing off the slate and finding new points of entry to drip into the hall with little splashes on the flagstones.

Martin, driving in the cattle from Blood Field, felt the temperature drop. His sweater, unneeded and tied on Savina's back, was soaked before he could don it, and still the temperature plunged. Before an hour passed the rain stopped, but by then he was stomping his feet to get feeling back into them and tucking his hands into his armpits to aid his blue fingers. By the time he and Savina reached the barn, the plumes of their frosty breath hung about them and crystals of frost hung from Savina's muzzle, the tips of her ears, and Martin's hair where it stuck out from the brim of his hat.

Joseph, writing in the room he used as a study, looked up toward the west as the storm progressed from threatening to furious assault, and then, like a phantom army claiming its conquered territory, rolled downward to fill the valley of the Cornamona with dense mist.

When he walked outside into the strange afternoon twilight, the fog absorbed all sound. His own footsteps echoed hollow and distant, as if he were listening to someone else a great distance away. The moisture-laden air was so thick it was difficult to breathe. Nor were humans the only creatures oppressed by the gloom. On the stone fence that separated the house from the potato patch sat a row of hooded crows and a single merlin falcon. These hereditary enemies, instead of flying exultantly high among the peaks, shared a brooding truce; they were silently grounded and somber.

No cattle lowed, no chickens or geese announced their presence, no wild things chittered or chirped.

Joseph, though not a superstitious man, turned on his heel and reentered the house. Once there he lit candles and lamps and heaped peat bricks on the fire till it blazed up, banishing the unnatural shadows from the hall.

$\backsim\!\infty\!\backsim$

As the dense fog settled over the valley, Mad Molly would not be consoled. The world was silent, except her. There was no motion or movement that was not somehow muted, except for that of Molly in the kitchen with Kate, Margaret, Fern, baby Robert, Tomeen, and little Rosie. Martin and Mary Elizabeth entered as the commotion swelled.

"I told ye so . . ."

Kate snapped at Fern, "Take the babies out. She's scarin' them."

Fern gathered up the infants. "Aye, she's scarin' me, she is."

Molly babbled at the rafters, "See here now. Do ye intend t'kill us all? All of us now, is it?"

Mary Elizabeth ran to Kate and clung to her. "Widow Clooney said she's been goin' on like this for two days. Father O'Bannon tried to catch her in the churchyard where she was speakin' to the departed."

Molly was more disheveled than usual. Her hair was soaked, and her tattered clothes covered with mud. She was weeping hysterically between bouts of gibberish. The old woman had been missing for three days, always a cause for concern.

"Molly, darlin'." Kate put a hand on her shoulder.

Molly shrugged it off. "The eyes are all gone dark, y'see now, Kate? Y'see what it is ol' Molly's been tryin' to tell ye? Who would know we'd run short. Ah the babes! The babes! What're we t'feed the wee ones?"

"Sure, sure." Then Kate urged Martin, "Run—fetch her daughter and Father O'Bannon. Tell them to hurry."

Molly tugged at her hair and rocked back and forth on the hearth as Martin and Mary Elizabeth tore from the room.

"Ah, Kate! We'll none of us survive! The river flows, don't ye know? It carried off man and beast, grass and flower, to the sea. Always to the sea! It's over for us. They warned me what was comin'! Angels saw what they did."

Kate tried to reason with her. "What who did?"

"The Rich Man and Travail. The new squire himself. It's in the potatoes they brung! His gift to the tenants, said he. Poor Molly saw it! The eyes gone dark! They put the dead among the livin'! In the earth! In the field! We couldn't stop 'em, Kate! And it's too late for us all. They knew! Them as had the power knew! They knew what it meant to the common folk when the eyes went dark! How they rejoiced! How they danced upon our poor dead prattie patch! Death to Ireland, sang he!"

It was a full two hours before Martin and Mary Elizabeth returned with help. By then Molly sat quietly drinking a cuppa with Kate at the kitchen table.

Much later Kate confided to Joseph, "We'll have to do somethin' about the way she wanders off. She's likely to get hurt one day."

Joseph passed an unpleasant night, plagued by sullen dreams and nameless fears. He awakened several times, sweating, with his heart in an uproar of palpitation. Each time he assured himself that nothing tangible was wrong, that his feeling of dread was merely compounded from the sense of choking to death on the leaden air and Mad Molly's foreboding pronouncements. As never before he understood the presence in the mass of the plea: "Lord, free us from all anxiety." He offered the same prayer himself and finally managed a dreamless slumber in the last hours before dawn.

He awoke to the cadence of many booted feet drumming upstairs. Then there came a frenzied hammering at his bedroom door and the voice of Charlie Nesbitt crying, "Squire, come quick!"

"What is it? What's happened?" Throwing back the bedclothes, Joseph stuffed his nightshirt into his trousers and headed for the door. To Kate's apprehensive query about the disturbance Joseph replied that she should shoot the bolt and keep the children inside while he investigated. Then he bellowed again, "What is it?"

Clustered on the landing as he threw back the oak panel were Nesbitt and all four Claddagh boys. "It's the potatoes, sir," Nesbitt answered nervously.

Joseph thought he had been made the butt of some unexplained and completely ill-advised prank. Anger mounted to his face, but before he spoke again, Nesbitt urged, "Come see for yourself, Squire. It's terrible."

The turf smoke from the now guttered fire still hung heavy in the hall, so Joseph noticed nothing amiss until he reached the entry. One pace outside, however, and his sense of smell was so assaulted that he gagged and threw up his hand as if to ward off a physical blow. The stench was overpowering. Even Joseph's time locked belowdecks with two hundred unwashed prisoners . . . even his time with the reeking hides at the London tannery . . . nothing had ever prepared him for this reek.

Grimly Nesbitt led the way toward the lushly flourishing potato patch. Nothing was immediately visibly wrong, except that the thick growth of dark green leaves appeared coated with white powder, like a light frost, though the morning was nowhere near cold enough.

Vaulting the stone wall, Joseph laid hold of the first stalk to which he came. Near the base of the plant was a previously unseen brown spot, no bigger than a shilling. Despite the loose, muddy soil, when Joseph tugged at the stem the plant stretched, then tore apart at the tan blemish.

Dropping to his knees, Joseph dug into the earth.

When he reached the level where the tubers should have been fist-sized and growing toward harvest weight, the upwelling of stinking, sulfurous odor almost blinded him.

Reaching toward another dirt clod, he closed his fist instead around a slimy lump of rotting potato. A black, viscous ooze squirted between his fingers. The next root dug up was the same, and the next, and the next, till nearing the bottom of the hole Joseph came across a few marble-like whole tubers, barely enough to fill the palm of his hand.

"Get everyone up at once," he ordered. "We've got to save what we can."

"Everyone, sir?" Nesbitt repeated.

"Everyone. Margaret . . . Martin and Mary Elizabeth. Leave only Kate to care for the babies. All the rest must dig as though their lives depended on it."

At midday the rainstorm that had been hovering over the Cornamona Valley like a carrion bird scenting the odor of death, swooped in for a closer look. Mocking raindrops plopped noisily on Martin's head when he lifted it from yet another potato mound. They scurried busily into Mary Elizabeth's collar as she labored to fill a wicker basket with tubers, some of which were no larger than the drips themselves.

Joseph, standing hip-deep in a hole, was grateful for the cleansing feel of the moisture from the sky until he licked his lips and tasted destruction and decay. He spat, trying to clear his mouth of the bitter loathsomeness, but found nothing on which to wipe away the rot; nothing that was not itself coated with the foul slime.

The labor was backbreaking as well as heartbreaking. The potato patch, so lovingly tended and so bountiful in expectation was almost entirely lost. Joseph estimated that the harvest would be about a tenth of what had been expected. Instead of bushels heaped with spuds . . . baskets that represented food for a year . . . there were mere handfuls of the roots, the largest no bigger than eggs. Instead of making a satisfying meal out of two or three, a man would have to devour a dozen of these dwarfs just to take the edge off his appetite.

Worst of all, and yet unspoken by any of the dozen laborers in the patch that day, was the clear vision that the disaster would be worse elsewhere. The Burke income, though sadly depleted, still provided for meat and grain and cheese and butter. Joseph knew it was not so for others, even among his own tenants. A quarter of the Irish lived on potatoes alone. Three meals a day, day in and day out, they fed themselves, their children, and their livestock on pratties.

Perhaps the blight was not widespread. In 1821 and again in 1832 the potato crop had also been afflicted. The plague those years had been devastating in Connaught . . . the West always seemed to be the hardest hit . . . but it had been less severe elsewhere. Perhaps it would prove so again.

One of the Claddagh boys—it might have been Simeon, but the figure was smeared from head to toe with mud and ooze making it impossible to tell—staggered forward with a heaping basket of rescued roots and set it on the stone wall, then returned with an empty pail to continue the toil.

The rain came harder, filling in the moundholes with bog. Joseph heard Mary Elizabeth shout, and then she began to cry. She was stuck in the ditch, exhausted, and unable to pull her feet free from the clinging clay. Joseph and Nesbitt hoisted her loose, then sent her into the house to clean up and eat something.

When the girl returned, she carried a covered hamper and distributed a parcel to each laborer: leftover potatoes boiled the night before. Dull-eyed, Joseph and the others devoured the sustenance in silence while standing in the rain, then returned to their efforts.

Adam Kane rode up just as Joseph added a fistful of gravel-sized tubers to his basket. "I'm sorry I was not here," Kane apologized, jumping into knee-deep mud next to Joseph. "I started back as soon as ever I could."

"Never mind that," Joseph said. "How bad is it elsewhere?"

Kane looked stricken. "It's bad, Squire . . . worst I've ever seen. This whole end of the country is cursed with it. People wailin' that the end of the world is come. And then there is the young Mahon's land."

Joseph snorted. Doubtless Mahon would be the only one spared the ravages of the blight. He said as much to Kane.

"Oh, no, Squire," Adam Kane explained. "The plague must have hit Mahon land first. There's no crop left there a'tall. His tenants will be eatin' the thatch from their roofs before the month is out."

Daniel Grogan came to the gates of the Galway City workhouse as he had each month since he had left his three daughters.

"If y'please, yer honor," he said, holding his battered hat in his hand as he implored the Reverend Banbreak, "may I not see me girls this time?"

Banbreak regally addressed the man. "You know the rules."

"But they'll forget me. And sure, they've grown enough under yer honor's kindness that I'll not recognize them, neither."

"Are you ready to remove them from our protection?" Banbreak queried.

Grogan lowered his eyes. "Yer honor knows I can't feed 'em. Got no way to support 'em yet."

With a shrug Banbreak sniffed and said coolly, "Well, then. You know the rule. Indigent children may not converse with parents or relatives. To see you would simply upset them."

"Then tell me how they fare."

"Well. They are learning the reward of diligent work. They flourish upon English charity. Therefore English rule shall be the law of their existence."

"May I not see 'em on the sly, like? Through a crack in the door? Where they'll not see me, but I'll know they're in health, yer honor?"

With a dismissive snort, Banbreak waved Daniel Grogan away as though he were a fly in front of his nose. "If you wish to see them, you shall have to take them away with you. That is the rule."

This was a rule Grogan could not get around. "Will ye tell 'em their da has come by? That I love 'em dearly. Pray for 'em daily. That soon we'll be off to America."

"False hopes, is it? Has something changed? Passage to America, is it? Then you must surely be capable of feeding them as well."

There was a threat in this observation. "Just a bit of hope, yer honor. No harm."

"Indeed there is harm. We provide your daughters what you cannot: the hope of daily bread. Your pipe dreams will make them discontented. That is the reason we do not allow communication between your sort and the inmates. For the last time, I say do not come back until you are ready to retrieve your children. You are a nuisance, Mister Grogan, and your entreaties fall upon unsympathetic ears."

And so, as he had done many times before, Daniel Grogan left without seeing his beauties even for a moment.

ᗞ 16 ᗞ

Daniel O'Connell's Dublin home was full of men shouting and waving their arms, each striving to outdo the other with the urgency of his message.

In his prime O'Connell's histrionic talents would have enabled him to sweep the room with a glance that demanded silence and obtain it; to punctuate a biting phrase with a singular tilt of his chin and fill countless headlines, to offer his personal opinion and sway millions.

Joseph saw in the Great Liberator a man who could no longer perform any of these miracles, who was but a likeness of his former greatness.

The emergency meeting to which Joseph had been summoned had two purposes: the first was to assess the extent of the potato blight throughout the country; the second, to evaluate the impact of the plague on the effort toward Repeal.

Rather than a commanding figure to whom everyone deferred,

O'Connell appeared sunken in on himself, like an empty sack flung carelessly over the arm of a chair. In part, the change was due to Daniel's age; he was seventy, after all. Another portion of the evident depression owed its onset to the potato crisis and what it meant.

But the largest single contributing cause to the Emancipator's despondency was the unraveling of the Repeal movement in front of his eyes. His friend Osborne Davis was dead, had only been dead two days. The fiery cofounder of the voice of Repeal, *The Nation,* and a staunch Protestant supporter of Irish nationalism, was dead at little more than thirty years of age.

While the contrary voices argued and cajoled, Joseph drew his chair closer to O'Connell and spoke quietly about Davis, of whose demise he had only just heard. "How did he die, Daniel?"

O'Connell shrugged his stooped shoulders. "They say pneumonia, but that is an old man's way out. You know he never fully recovered from the poisonin'."

Joseph had been present when Davis was nearly killed by an assassin's dose; Joseph had, in fact, been the intended victim. "I'm sorry to hear that," he said. "I know he would want the work of Repeal to go forward."

Again O'Connell made a dismissive gesture. "Repeal? Repeal is done for. Between the plague and the prime minister, the lid of Repeal's coffin has been nailed shut."

Despite the harshness of the imagery, this turn of phrase was so unlike the O'Connell of old that Joseph encouraged him to explain. "The other Young Irelanders—Smith-O'Brien and his group—have allowed the British government to do somethin' Davis and I never permitted: they let the movement be divided on religious grounds. Where once we were for Ireland, pure and simple, now we must say Irish Catholic, Irish Protestant, Irish Dissenter. And this late catastrophe. We would have rebuilt the movement, but facin' this . . . I tell you, Joseph, if I were a young man, I would leave it behind and go to America. The game is not worth the candle."

Dismayed at the depth of hopelessness in O'Connell's startling words, Joseph could think of no reply, so it was the Liberator who returned to the announced subject of the meeting. In louder and

firmer tones, an effort that clearly cost him physically and emo-
tionally, he called for attention and indicated that each man present
should report on the degree of the blight in his home county.

The summary was frightening: the rot had attacked the crop in
eleven counties, with the harvest only beginning in the rest and the
full magnitude not yet known. The severity did vary from place to
place, light in Donegal to more than half the crop lost in Monaghan,
and worst of all in the West.

"Then what's to be done?" O'Connell asked. "There will be
terrible sufferin' come winter if we do not get busy."

"The Corn Law must be repealed so cheap grain can be shipped
into Ireland without high duties," one contributor said.

"There should be public works projects payin' enough for a man
to feed his family."

"We need a country-wide moratorium on rents so the people can
buy food to replace what they cannot grow," offered another.

"We must stop the export of wheat, oats, and barley to England
and keep the foodstuffs here," said a fourth. "And they must be
priced so the poorest tenants can buy."

O'Connell held up a wrinkled, blue-veined hand in a request for
silence; this time, at least, it was respected. "Do you know what is
wrong with what you have proposed?" he asked rhetorically. "Every
single idea, as proper as it is, requires the consent of the British government and the support of the landlord. Now stop talkin' and start
thinkin'. While we must and will hammer on Westminster to come
to our assistance, it is clear Ireland must do for Ireland—or else
Ireland will assuredly starve. Begin again: what steps can we carry
out ourselves?"

In the brilliant light of morning, Kate saw Joseph in the churchyard. His back was to her. His head was bowed as he knelt beside
the grave of baby Martin.

So he had come here from his meeting with Daniel O'Connell.
While Kate had stayed awake the long night through and paced and

prayed, he had come home to the grave of their son rather than to the comfort of her arms.

For the first time Kate realized she envied wee Martin for the place he had taken in Joseph's heart. What Joseph would not dare say to her, he shared with their dead child. At mass on Sunday Kate had counted three dozen pebbles at the foot of the headstone.

She was grateful she had left Tomeen and Rosie at home with Margaret. Raising her chin she pushed back the groaning gate and entered Joseph's sanctuary. He turned and looked up at her, his face drawn and haggard.

"Kate." There was no surprise or happiness in his voice as he spoke her name. He did not rise. It was plain to her that she had interrupted him, and he wished she had not.

"I did not sleep last night, hopin' you'd come home."

"The meetin' went longer than I expected." He blinked into the sunlight behind her and looked down at the heap of stones. Why did he not tell her what had happened?

"Have you told Martin about it, then?"

Joseph's lips curved in a sad smile. "It's a strange comfort to me to come here, somehow."

His reply angered her, but she controlled her emotions. "Aye. Easier to talk to the dead than with the livin'."

A frown creased his brow. Had he caught the disapproval in her tone? Perhaps not. "That it is. I'm glad he'll not have to suffer what we must."

Stupid! Granite-headed man! Could he not see her standin' there? Needin' him?

"Some things we suffer by our own doin'. Or lack of doin'."

"And some by the will of God."

"Ever the priest, aren't you, Joseph?"

"I hope I can . . . accept all things patiently."

"What things?"

"We're in for hard times. People will die before it's finished. All things, Kate."

She could contain herself no longer. "Accept all things, is it? A coward's excuse."

His dreamy reverie was smashed. He stood, dusting off his trousers as though the interview were at an end. "Excuse me? Coward, is it?"

"You heard me, priest. Here you crouch, envyin' the peace of the dead . . . at least they have no need of passion."

"Or pain." He turned away from her. "It's the absence of pain I envy!"

"Then, pray for a new heaven and a new earth if you like. Most likely it'll not deliver us tomorrow. That'll come in time, and we'll see it too, by Christ's mercy. Meanwhile the potatoes are rotten, politics have gone sour, our tenants . . . old friends . . . will go hungry if we accept this sufferin' as God's will. Accept the devil's doin' as God's will? Accept hunger? Christ fed five thousand. Accept sickness? He healed the sick and raised the dead. Accept! That's the devil's lie! Pray instead for a clear eye and a firm plan to bring your people relief. Work hard to make this hard life better for as many as you can. Heaven'll not be on earth till Christ brings it to us. Meanwhile it's in your hand to show Christ's mercy. Accept the work God has given us to do. Then do it!"

Her words shamed him. He hung his head. "You're right, Kate. I was only speakin' platitudes."

"Blarney!"

"Always. I was feelin' sorry . . . for myself mostly."

She cocked a steely eye at him, "Is that so?"

He nodded. "And what about . . . you?"

"What about me?"

"Are you . . . have you been . . . well?"

Her anger was unabated. What right did he have to shift the subject from himself to her? "I've no self-pity, if that's what you mean."

"That's not . . . I didn't mean to . . ." His gaze shifted to the mound of earth.

"Rosie is my own as sure as I carried her nine months in my womb. She nurses at my breast. It's my own milk that nourishes her and makes her grow. I'll not live in the past—or in a present that never existed. That's the way Kate Donovan accepts the will of God. I live today . . . now."

He backed a step from her. "You're a strong one, you are. The very thing I love about you."

Love! He spoke that sacred word as flatly as if he said, "There's a bird on the fence."

Her mind spun out a dozen retorts, but she repeated none of them. "Well, then. I'm glad you're safely back. There'll be plenty to do." She turned away. "I'll leave you to your devotions."

She left him there beside baby Martin's grave. He did not call her back. When she emerged from the chapel, his horse was gone.

The Galway City docks were crowded with gangs of men hoisting seven-stone sacks of spring crop oats into cargo vessels bound for Liverpool. The rain, which had progressed from pelting to lashing, continued unabated. The storm was as furious as the foreman overseeing the loading, as if the two were inextricably linked.

"Keep that tarp cinched down tight!" Denis Mahon's steward, Ross Richman, bellowed. "Hurry up and get these bags loaded before the wet spoils them! Put your backs into it! There are plenty of hungry men looking for work. If you can't do any better than this, don't bother coming back tomorrow!"

On one end of a hundred pounds of grain, Kevin Donovan, bearded and hooded against rain and recognition, grunted, "One . . . two . . . three . . . heave!" as he and Daniel Grogan hefted the load onto a cargo net.

"Blast Squire Mahon and his grain and his driver!" Grogan said with venom. "No roof nor food for me family but the workhouse, but more money to line his pockets from sellin' grain in England."

Kevin kept his mouth shut. He did not want to attract attention to himself.

Grogan continued, "Richman looks right through me like he don't even know me name when 'twas him gave the order to turn us on the road. And now me Annie's dead. How I'd like to catch him alone on a moonless night!"

"Shut your gob before somebody does it with a rope 'round your neck," warned the third member of their work gang, Blue O'Hara. O'Hara was a massive man, barrel-chested and strong as three others. What his Christian name was, no one had the courage to ask. He got his moniker from the egg-shaped cobalt stain over his left cheekbone. It was said the mark resulted from the discharge of a pistol that nearly blew off O'Hara's head and the powder got under the skin. It was also said that O'Hara's attacker had his head removed from his body by a single twist of Blue's arms. No one felt compelled to ask about the accuracy of this assertion either.

"It's me family I care about," Grogan complained in a lower voice. "They won't let me see me girls. How will I ever put me family back together again?"

Kevin, remembering how his sister Brigit had died after being in a workhouse in Dublin, was sympathetic to the man's plight, but kept his peace.

The remaining member of the work crew was a good-sized but soft-looking man named Mickey Morton. Kevin already knew Morton was a slacker, stumbling over imagined obstacles so as to miss a turn in the loading queue and failing to put all his force into hauling away at the block and tackle. Because Morton continued to work on the docks, Kevin suspected him of being a paid informer.

"Things will be better after Repeal," Morton offered. "They say Daniel O'Connell is gettin' ready a new round of monster meetin's. They say the one at Cork will be the biggest yet."

"Repeal!" Grogan snorted.

Morton's comment sounded transparently worthy of an amateur agent provocateur, so Kevin could not resist disagreeing. "Repeal is done for," he said. "When Prime Minister Peel said he would support secular schools of higher learnin' for Ireland, he knew exactly what he was doin'. Now the Protestant Young Irelanders say maybe Peel isn't so bad after all, while the Catholics continue to hate him. If Peel can split the movement over religious issues, then he's already won."

"Who cares about schools?" Grogan demanded. "All I care about is feedin' me family and then gettin' away from this accursed land to America."

"I've been to America," Kevin retorted without thinking. "It's no better there than here if you stay in the cities. If you go, plan on headin' West without stoppin'."

Morton and O'Hara studied Kevin with interest, and Kevin abruptly stopped speaking.

The net heaped to capacity, the four men hauled away at the tackle.

As the load swayed to its peak before being swung over the side of the ship, the block at the end of the beam creaked ominously. The ring by which the pulley was attached pried apart and the mass of grain sacks plunged downward.

"Look out!" Kevin yelled, leaping back. He never knew what made Mickey Morton stumble forward, as if he had been pushed from behind.

With Kevin, Grogan, and O'Hara clear, Morton absorbed the total weight of the mound. He was crushed beneath it, several of the sacks bursting open like overripe fruit and burying the man entirely except for one outflung arm.

"Get this cleaned up at once!" ordered Steward Richman. "Any grain lost or spoiled will be stopped from your pay. You three better hope the dead man's share covers it!"

As Richman turned away, Grogan stepped after him, his fists clenched. Kevin intercepted him from one side and O'Hara from the other. "Leave it be," O'Hara said. "I think the both of you are men I can use. What say I stand you to a meal after quittin' time tonight, and you hear what I have to say?"

Since Joseph, Adam Kane, Nesbitt, and the others were occupied with helping the people of the Burke townlands recover from the blow they had suffered to their food supply, an important duty fell on Martin's slim shoulders. Because the potato crop was merely a fraction of its usual bounty, it was more important than ever that it be preserved intact.

The usual method of storing spuds for the year was to dig a pit, line it with straw, cover it with earth, and raid it from time to time as needed. In this year of biblical catastrophe, nothing was as usual and much bigger precautions had to be taken.

Martin was given the task of poring over the reports of the scientific commission sent from London and the instructions transmitted in the *Gardeners' Chronicle* for the conservation of potatoes. He understood that whatever the manor house did would be copied by the tenant farmers. They were eager for instruction, grasping at any way to respond to the disaster.

"Dry the potatoes in the sun," Martin read. It was all well and good to advise that step, but the sun was unreliable in Galway of late. He spread the marble-sized pratties on the floor of the hall, then spent a day and a night turning them until they were thoroughly dry.

"Mark out a space on the ground six feet wide and as long as needed," the article continued.

The *Chronicle* went on to advise about trenching, leveling, lining the floor with a mixture of straw and lime dust, building a pyramid of potatoes mingled with lime and straw, and covering the whole with blocks of turf. Once completed, the mound, which looked remarkably like the burial chamber of a vanished Celtic chieftain, was said to be impervious to damp inside and out and guaranteed to safeguard the nutritious qualities of the remaining crop.

The editorial concluded by saying that if the instructions were too complex to be understood, the peasant should ask his clergyman or landlord to explain them. Martin decided he would not read that passage to his friends and neighbors.

It was a significant audience from Ballynockanor and the Castletown environs that gathered around to watch Martin perform. Joe Watty was there, the Widow Clooney, even Patrick Boyle, the celebrated tenor from Cong. After all, everyone had a prattie patch, everyone had been hit by the plague, everyone was anxious about the coming winter.

They studied, listened, nodded, and approved what they saw. Then Boyle, who was from a city and could be excused for asking such a thing, said, "And where, in faith, do we come by such a quantity of lime dust?"

There was much clearing of throats, but no one offered to relieve Martin from the painful duty of answering. "Ah . . . ," he replied, shuffling his feet, "you can get what you need from the white-wash . . . of the walls of tossed cottages."

Between Nun's Island Street and the road leading west from Galway City towards Salthill, on the Claddagh side of the Corrib, was a backwater alley named Fish Lane. It was there that O'Hara led Kevin and Daniel Grogan to a public house called *Monk's*. Its undistinguished exterior of worn stone and shabby thatch was echoed by an equally faded interior that consisted mostly of low beams and scarred wooden benches. But to Kevin the aroma of hot stew and fresh-baked bread more than made up for any lack of grace in its furnishings.

O'Hara was evidently known there, as he nodded to the innkeeper and led the way behind the bar to a snug barely big enough to hold them around a single table next to a smoldering peat fire. Waiting only until three mugs of porter and three bowls of stew had been delivered, O'Hara asked if Grogan was curious about the meeting.

"Only if it means money in my pocket," was the reply. "Ten pounds is the passage money to get me and me girls to America—as much more to see us started on our new life there. Say twenty pounds in all. Even before Richman docked me for today's accident, it would still have taken me three years to save enough. By then who knows where me daughters would be . . . or if they'd be alive. I'm for anythin' that makes it possible sooner."

O'Hara indicated that Grogan should eat and drink while he posed the same question to Kevin.

The young Donovan's reply was more cautious. "It depends on what you've in mind," he said. "I thought I wanted America, but I was wrong. I thought I wanted a woman in Dublin, but she didn't want me. Right now I'll listen to anythin', but I'll not be sayin' yes or no without thought."

"Fair enough," O'Hara declared. "Did you ever hear of an English rapparee name of Robert O'Lockesley? Some called him 'Robin Hood.'"

"And who has not heard of 'Rob from the rich and give to the poor?'" Kevin replied.

"Just so," O'Hara agreed. "In this land is it not the landlords who are the rich? And do they not oppress them as work the land but cannot own it?"

"Like Mahon?" Grogan growled into his mug.

"And who might these poor be whom you'd be aidin'?" Kevin inquired.

O'Hara clapped a beefy hand on each man's shoulder. "Does not Holy Scripture teach that charity begins at home? Why should we not take out for our expenses before extendin' our benevolence elsewhere?"

Kevin announced, "Are you some kind of Ribbonman or Whiteboy? I will rob English landlords, but I want no truck with them who say they are fightin' for a cause by maimin' cattle and burnin' hayricks."

"No politics!" O'Hara vowed. "Where's the profit in that? What I propose is business, pure and simple. Friend Grogan here has a goal in mind; perhaps you do too. We partner together, share and share alike, and go our ways when the time comes."

"And what of the law?" Grogan asked belatedly.

"I judge you are men from these parts as I am myself. Can we three not lead English law a merry chase?"

"And how do you know one will not sell out the others?" Kevin asked softly.

O'Hara did not reply at first. He merely picked up an iron fire poker and casually bent it into a horseshoe shape. "Do not think that what happened to Morton today was an accident," he said. "Is everything clear to you?"

Kevin and Daniel Grogan nodded.

"Good," O'Hara said. "We'll meet back here tomorrow night and make plans."

"I have not said in or out," Kevin said, stirring his bowl of stew with a wooden spoon.

"I think you have," O'Hara concluded, draining the jar of stout and grounding the cup with a thump. "I think you have."

After partnering with Blue O'Hara, Kevin understood why the rapparee continued to work at the Galway City docks. The port was a natural source of information about the movement of wealth around the west of Ireland. Though O'Hara explained that to commit a robbery within the precincts of Galway Bay was unthinkable, "foulin' their own nest" as he put it, the news of commerce gleaned there was invaluable.

It was on the docks that they first got word of a squire by the name of Farrell, who was selling off a brace of prize bulls from his herd. Farrell, who hailed from Adare in county Limerick, was delivering the livestock to their new owner at the port of Foynes on the lower Shannon.

"It is of no consequence what happens to the bulls thereafter," O'Hara declared, waving his hand in dismissal. "May their hay be sweet and the heifers cooperative. But what we care about is Farrell and the route he will take back to Adare."

So it was that O'Hara, Grogan, and Kevin were watching nearby when Squire Farrell received his payment in gold on the quay in Foynes; and, having scampered over the hills, they were already hidden in a thicket beside the road outside the village of Adare.

It was a perfect time for wickedness. The weather, which had been briefly warm and sunny, had turned cold and wet yet again. Across the swale the night wind howled through the cloisters of the thirteenth-century Trinitarian Priory and wailed in the turrets of Desmond Castle on the banks of the river Maigue.

"Why don't he come?" Grogan hissed nervously.

As if in reply, the shrieking breeze dropped just long enough for them to hear a rapid clopping of hooves.

"What if he's armed or has picked up a guard?" Grogan worried.

"All you need to do is watch the road," O'Hara instructed. "I'll do the talkin', and Kevin will catch hold of the bridle. Draw up your mask."

When the arriving carriage was only a few paces away, O'Hara drew a dragoon pistol from a leather pouch and cocked the hammer back. Jumping into the center of the roadway, he thrust out the weapon and demanded, "Stand and deliver, or your next breath is your last!"

Squire Farrell checked his horse for a second before deciding to whip up and charge past what appeared to be a lone assailant. In that moment of indecision, Kevin ran up on the opposite side. Grabbing the leads, he pulled the animal's head to the side so that even when the lash descended, the roan could only buck and plunge.

"Don't be a fool," O'Hara said, advancing and pressing his pistol against the third button of Squire Farrell's waistcoat. "Get out of the coach."

Blindfolded and gagged, Farrell was led off the road and tied to a tree, after which the carriage was unhitched and dumped out of sight into the river below the bridge.

They took turns riding the pony while the other two trotted alongside until they were some distance away, then it was abandoned to find its own way home.

By morning the three rapparees were back in Galway City, and the following night they divided up twelve pounds in gold.

17

The deputation led by Joe Watty included the Widow Clooney and the fiddler, O'Rourke. When Fern answered the hesitant knock at the front door of the hall, Watty asked in a diffident voice if they could speak with the squire. She invited them to step inside, but they refused, and Fern, disturbed by the solemnity, bustled away to seek Joseph.

He came downstairs at the same time Kate emerged from the kitchen wing, and both saw the throng gathered in a semicircle outside the door. "Come in, then, Watty, Missus Clooney," Joseph called from the steps. Kate hurried to her husband's side, gesturing for their neighbors to enter.

"A handsome offer," Watty returned, "but no. Things must be done in the proper form . . ." then he repeated, "in the proper form," as if he had lost his place in a rehearsed speech.

As Kate and Joseph reached the doorstep, the entire gathering knelt on one knee. Most already had their hats in hand, but those

who did not swept them off. Those who had no headgear knuckled
their foreheads in the age-old gesture of fealty to a hereditary lord.

"Get up!" Joseph said in shock. "Widow Clooney, O'Flaherty.
My friends! Get up."

Kate, flushed with embarrassment at the scene, urged the same,
and when they would not, she knelt beside Missus Clooney.

O'Rourke poked Watty in the back. "Get on w'it," he goaded.

"You see, your lordship," Watty continued, "we are here on behalf
of the townlands. We, that is, the tenants of the Burke estate, have
come to beg a boon of you."

"Go on," Joseph said kindly, knowing how hard this was.

"Well, sir, we wonder if you would consider . . . that is, we respect-
fully request that you . . . since the potatoes is bad, would you be
willin' to hang the rents due this Gale Day? There's none of us can
pay all we owe, and some cannot pay a'tall."

His face lightening at the words, Joseph said, "Is that what this
is about? Get up, all of you. I'm sorry to put you through this, but
I thought you already knew. I have no intention of enforcin' the
rent collection until this plague is past."

With much shuffling feet, the deputation rose, showing relief.

"What is more. . . ," Joseph began, then said quickly, "but come
in, come in. You should not be standin' outside in the cold."

Kate helped Widow Clooney and the older members of the group
to places by the fire.

"It is good you came," Joseph noted. "I have somethin' I want
to do, and you are the ones to help with it. In my possession . . .
they were actually my grandfather's and father's and have not been
lately used . . . but I want to share them with you. What do you
think?"

"Er? What is it you'd be sharin', Squire?" Watty asked.

"Sorry . . . the fowlin' pieces, of course. There are four of them
together with powder and shot. What with the rabbits and the ducks
on the estate and in the bogs, we can feed many families."

Now it was O'Rourke and others who looked shocked. "D'ya
mean to say you'd put weapons in our hands, Squire? Is that not
against the law?"

Joseph said simply, "The necessity is too great not to use every resource."

"And d'ya mean to say you'd allow us to poach . . . shoot . . . animals on Burke land?"

"With only one proviso. We must not waste, and we must see that the game is distributed fairly. You look like a responsible committee to carry out such a task. I'll leave it to you."

Joe Watty was not too stunned by this proposal to allow his chairmanship to slip away entirely. Interrupting O'Rourke's agreement to Joseph's condition he vowed, "Leave it to us, Squire. The committee will meet in my tavern, and all will be done as is fittin' and proper."

Monk's Public House was crowded with sailors of the Ballyvaughn fleet. The fisherfolk, driven into Galway harbor by an unrelenting spate of storms that turned the fishing grounds into a seething cauldron, were ashore, drowning their woes in beer instead of seawater.

O'Hara, Grogan, and Kevin occupied the snug. Grogan had drunk more than was wise for him and was blubbering about his babies in the workhouse. Kevin and Blue O'Hara ignored the man, instead concentrating on gleaning what they could from the gossip.

Most of the news was gloomy. For men who earned their living netting herring and mullet, to be trapped ashore meant no income. Worse still, the schools of fish had abandoned their usual haunts for deeper water, making the pursuit even more dangerous. And if that woe were not enough, the market was drying up; no one had money to buy fresh fish.

A blond-bearded, hawk-nosed captain, whose visage and manner suggested his Viking ancestry, slammed his mug of porter down and groused, "And what d'ya think? When I went to the gombeen man to take a wee loan, he would only allow me six shillin's, and that only if I would leave a net in charge. A net, mind you! With what does he think I earn my keep?"

"So?" inquired another. "What did you do?"

The truculent Viking descendant deflated with a shrug. "What could I do? A man's gotta eat, does he not? I give my second-best net in pledge till the next good catch."

O'Hara nudged Kevin and indicated with a pointed look that the conversation had taken an interesting turn. Kevin nodded. Grogan continued to stare into his ale and mumble.

"Curse that gombeen man for a usurer anyway," said a lean, hard-faced captain in the sleeveless tweed jacket of an Aran islander. "Did he not take me da's watch in pledge and give me three shillin's for it, and it worth a crown easy?"

A growl of general agreement went round the room. Times were hard and money scarce, but at least one citizen was prospering. The Ballyvaughn gombeen man, a pawnbroker by the name of Seamus Goree, was roundly reviled as a flagrant profiteer.

"Sure, an' he is practically coinin' money," said a sailor, sniffing through his bulbous, bright-red nose. "You never saw the like of it. Goree must be the wealthiest man in Ballyvaughn."

Laying a sausage-like finger across the end of his nose, Blue O'Hara winked at Kevin. "The wealthiest man in Ballyvaughn," he repeated in a low, meaningful tone. "What d'ya think of that?"

It was outside Lem O'Shaunessy's dry goods shop in Castletown that Joseph was assaulted by Major Denis Mahon. Joseph, who had just finished consulting with the textile store owner about acquiring a large quantity of cheesecloth, was on his way next to see Joe Watty when Mahon approached.

"You there, Burke!" Mahon shouted. No pretense of polite neighborliness here. "A word with you!"

"What is it, Major?" Joseph asked wearily, not welcoming the hostile-sounding interruption. His mind was on a scheme proposed by the *Gardeners' Chronicle*. The composition claimed that the pulp of diseased pratties could be milked for the starch it contained. This starch water, squeezed through filtering cloth like cheese was drained of whey, and could then be dried and mixed as a "lengthener" with bean-meal or flour and baked into bread.

"Is it true?" Mahon demanded.

"Is what true?"

"Have you armed your tenants? Great Scott, man, have you taken leave of your senses? What will you do when they turn on you?"

It was in Joseph's mind to retort that such a worry might be justified in regard to Mahon's tenants, but he refrained from the comment and said merely, "Ducks and rabbits feed families who would otherwise go hungry."

"But it's against the law! Irish peasants are not to own weapons of any kind!"

Grudging the wasted breath and time when every daylight hour was precious, Joseph nevertheless disagreed. "They do not own them. I have allowed my tenants to use them as tools, like turf spades or hay rakes."

"But you have armed the peasants in defiance of the law! You can be arrested for treason!"

Shaking his head, Joseph retorted, "The lords of Burke have always held the position of magistrate over our own property. As long as the fowling pieces are only used to hunt Burke wildlife on Burke land, there is no violation of any statute. Now if you'll excuse me, Major."

Mahon caught Joseph by the arm. "By thunder, you'll regret this. Don't you know our class must stick together?"

"Forgive me, Major," Joseph replied coldly, plucking Mahon's fingers loose as one might remove a loathsome insect, "but I prefer to never consider myself part of any class that includes yourself."

Leaving Mahon sputtering with rage, Joseph put several paces between himself and the major, but not far enough to not clearly hear the snarled conclusion: "Next time I'll bring my driver's assistant. He's an old friend of yours by the name of Gann!"

Ballyvaughn lay on the southern curve of Galway Bay. It was close enough to the Galway City docks that Kevin questioned the wisdom of carrying out a robbery so close to home. Blue O'Hara reminded him that since Ballyvaughn lay at the end of a dirt track dead-ending at the sea and was part of the barren rocky expanse known as the *burren*, it was really only accessible from the ocean. "And you heard what them fisherfolk had to say," O'Hara continued. "Would you be thinkin' any of them will lose a wink of sleep over the robbin' of the greedy gombeen man? Or that any of them will run cryin' to the constabulary for the poor pawnbroker's sake?"

Grogan, having already counted his share of the loot taken from the "richest man in Ballyvaughn," was clearly in favor of the scheme. "Are y'losin' yer nerve then, Kev? If y'are, just say so, and I'll take yer share for me and my girls."

"Who's losin' whose nerve?" Kevin demanded, bristling.

"That's the fightin' spirit," O'Hara cheered, nearly knocking his partners down by clapping them on the backs. "Only save it, save it, for the comin' struggle."

The home of Seamus Goree, the gombeen man of Ballyvaughn, lay just at the edge of the town where the limestone plateau called the burren dropped abruptly into the waves. Even that despoiler of all things Irish, Oliver Cromwell, found the burren to be not worth the trouble of conquering. The Lord Protector examined the region and said he found "neither tree to hang a man nor soil enough to bury him," such being the main concerns of the Lord Protector.

From their cave hiding place behind Goree's cottage, Kevin looked out at the single stunted and twisted hawthorne that adorned the landscape and commented, "The richest man in Ballyvaughn lives in one of the ugliest spots in Ireland."

"Shut your gob, then," O'Hara challenged. "Here he comes."

It remained broad daylight when Seamus Goree drove his two-wheeled cart up to the door of his one-room cabin. His pony stopped without being ordered to do so, and Goree alighted and in a twinkling loosed the pony to fend for itself among the rocks. Extracting a large iron key from his pocket, he unlocked the door and let himself in, closing the portal behind him with a clank that was audible up on the hill.

"D'ya hear that," Grogan demanded. "Who but a rich man would be lockin' his door like that?"

"So what do we do now?" Kevin asked O'Hara.

"We wait," was the reply. "We could not know he'd be alone when he came home, and the country so open that we could not follow without him seein'. Even if we can't break in upon him, we can catch him unawares in the mornin'."

When morning came the three rapparees were stiff, hungry, and foul-tempered. Looking at the wisp of smoke rising from Goree's cottage did not improve their humor since they had spent a fireless night. The smell of black sausage frying in a skillet did not lighten the mood either. "He better open up quick," Grogan growled, "or I'll break in his door to steal his breakfast!"

At last the door did open, and the three robbers, scarves over their faces, thrust Goree back inside and made him sit on the floor, which the victim did without argument. The room was festooned with nets, lanterns, a compass, two brass telescopes, and fishing tackle of every description. There was so much gear that the single square of slate where the gombeen man crouched was the only unoccupied space. "Where's your money?" O'Hara snarled. "Be quick, or we'll twist off your head and dump your body in a cave!"

"Don't hurt me," Goree pleaded, raising his hands but hunching even lower. "I don't have any money. Who has money this year?"

"Don't lie to me," O'Hara yelled, backhanding the man.

"If we kill him, he can't tell us where the money is," Kevin warned. "Let's search the place instead."

Nets and fishing tackle, compass and lanterns were soon flying, but no money could they find. "It has to be here somewhere," Grogan lamented.

Kevin turned slowly around in place. "Have you noticed," he asked, "how still the gombeen man sits? Like he's rooted in that spot."

"Right it is!" O'Hara roared, catching Kevin's point at once. In the next instant the gombeen man was himself sailing through the air while Grogan and O'Hara lifted the slate flag before the hearth. Under the stone was a metal box.

"Please don't take my money," Goree begged.

O'Hara ripped open the container with his bare hands and out fell six shillings and nine pence. "Where's the rest?" he bellowed.

"That's all there is, I swear. Look around you. When I have cash, I lend it out. But this year nobody pays me back, nobody! Can I sell nets to the same men who pawned their lanterns? No!"

Comprehension dawned first on Kevin, then O'Hara. Grogan was complaining that there must be more money hidden somewhere when Kevin explained how things really stood.

Emboldened by how deflated his attackers appeared, Goree said, "Let me join up with you! Just over the way, at Doolin, there's a gombeen man who must be coinin' money, and I can get you past his locks. Or what about the Kilfenora butcher? He's got a rich wife. Take me with you, will you? I hate it here!"

O'Hara had to threaten to kill the gombeen man three more times before he would leave off following them.

The time had come.

All of last year's potato crop was eaten, stretched, and extended with oats and Indian corn and eggs, to be sure, but gone, just the same. It was time to break into the barrow and begin using the pratties that had been saved from the rot.

Bushel basket in hand, Martin approached the south face of the long mound. His plan was to make an opening as small as possible in the wall that got the most sun and was most sheltered from the rain.

Mary Elizabeth was by his side. She was proud of her brother's know-how and praised the symmetry of his engineering to all who would listen. Now she was counting the turf bricks as he carefully lifted them aside, almost as if it were a jigsaw puzzle that had to be reassembled in only one way.

"One, two, three," she intoned. "Four, five, six . . . and the bigger one there is number seven, Martin. Put it on top of the others."

When the entry was wide enough to admit Martin's head and shoulders, he began removing handfuls of lime-laced straw. "See how dry it is," he said to his sister, with a touch of self-satisfaction in his accomplishment. "Not a single drip can have got past that."

"Ten straw, eleven straw, twelve straw . . . Martin!" Mary Elizabeth interrupted herself. "What's that smell?"

It could not be . . . must not be.

Throwing aside his caution together with an armload of packing stuff, Martin plunged into the mound. Worming his way further inside he encountered an inky, sticky mass of goo where the potatoes should have been.

As he reemerged from the pit, covered in ooze, reeking like a sewer and crushed with gloom, Mary Elizabeth reacted to her brother's appearance in the only way possible: she shrieked at the top of her lungs. It was a wail of loss heard inside the Great House.

It was a howl of hopelessness that echoed throughout the district as mound after mound was opened to reveal not wholesome winter food but masses of stinking rot. From Ballynockanor to Cong, across Galway, Mayo, and Sligo, through Cork and Wexford to bounce off the walls of Dublin, there was such a cry of despair as rivaled what must have crossed Egypt at the death of the firstborn . . . and why not? It was the death cry of a generation.

That evening smoke from the peat fires lingered above the hearths and filled the houses of Ballynockanor and Castletown with the earthy musk-like scent of smoldering turf, concealing the stench of rotting potatoes.

"The air's too thick outside." Joseph prodded the coals in the kitchen with a poker. "The smoke'll not go up the chimney, Kate."

"If the weather doesn't clear, I'll not be doin' the washin' tomorrow."

Margaret, Fern, baby Robert, and Adam Kane were off in Tuam to visit Fern's parents, leaving the Burke family alone in the house. It was a welcome relief for Kate to occupy herself with ordinary household tasks.

She cooked a supper of stew as Joseph helped Martin with geometry at the table and Mary Elizabeth sat on the floor and played at building blocks with Tomeen and Rosie. All had wandered into the kitchen one by one and stayed. Kate preferred it that way. Like the old days it was. In spite of the gloom it was comforting somehow. Kate could almost imagine Da and her mother looking on in approval.

Mary Elizabeth said absently, "Fern and Adam'll come back engaged."

Martin glanced up sourly. "You know everythin'."

"Aye," Mary Elizabeth said, "she's takin' him home for approval."

"Poor man," Martin muttered.

"I heard Margaret tellin' Flynn as much. Adam's goin' to ask for her hand. They're to wed and go to America. Maybe go where Kevin is."

Kate swung the crane from the fire and tasted the gravy. "Not a surprise."

"Aye. America. Not gloomy like here. No potato blight, neither. The sun shines everyday there," Mary Elizabeth babbled.

In disgust Martin broke the lead of his pencil. "More light to kill the Irish by if the newspapers and Kevin's letters are half true."

Joseph closed the book and stood, stretching by the window. He said nothing for a long while. The conversation and speculation between the children about the marriage of Fern and Adam continued.

Kate could see Joseph was worried. "What is it?" she asked in a quiet voice.

He half smiled as if speaking his mind would embarrass him. "Today in the field I thought about the plagues of Egypt. Wondered if the Hebrews had frogs in their kitchens and swarms of . . . y'know . . . along with the Egyptians. Then I thought, well, it was God's people who had to leave Egypt, wasn't it? The people who built the land left. The landlords stayed behind, didn't they? Masters of all they surveyed." He shrugged and looked away out the window into the greyness. "What'll they eat? What'll they feed the livestock?" He pressed his fingers on his brow. "I miss the light."

"This'll pass."

"No. I mean I miss the heady days when we had a hope of freedom. It's over, Kate. At least for now. O'Connell is done. Losin' all the crop like this is puttin' a bullet in the brain of our hopes for Repeal. Said if he was young again he'd board a ship and go to

America to seek his fortune. He as much as told me so. The English have beat us. And now . . . it's as if the land itself has taken sides with wickedness against us."

"You're feelin' the weather. The potatoes."

"Maybe."

"Everyone's on edge."

The unfriendly banter between siblings confirmed Kate's remarks. She took Joseph's hand. It was moist but unresponsive to her touch. A vague fear filled her. She had never seen Joseph so soul-weary. She led him from the kitchen to his study and closed the door behind them.

"You have to talk to me, Joseph," she demanded.

"I didn't want this . . . this responsibility. So many people, you see."

"Me and the kids."

"I'm not meanin' you."

"You wanted to be a priest."

"Aye." He turned away from her.

"You've been livin' like one since you came home."

He grimaced as though this topic pained him. "It's just that . . ."

"We're livin' like brother and sister, Joseph! Not man and wife."

He stared at the spines of the books. "Kate . . ."

"Look at me, you lout!" she said, suddenly angry.

"I can't."

She grabbed his arm, hard, digging her fingers into his flesh. "If you don't love me anymore . . ."

"No! It's not that!" He spun around, grasping her shoulders. His eyes were full. "Kate! Kate!"

"Don't *Kate* me! Talk to me! You've not been the same since you came home! Am I . . . is it my scars? Did I . . . the fact that your son died when I should have given him life? Has it made you stop lovin' me? I can't . . . don't understand why you won't . . ."

"I'm afraid . . ."

"Afraid of what?"

"Losin' you." His expression was like that of a toddler being left by his mother at the neighbor's house against his will.

"Losin' me?"

"They said . . ."

"Who said?"

"Widow Clooney. When I came home, you were so ill. She said you could die . . ."

Kate scoffed. "I'm healthy as a . . . I have been healthy these many months. And willin'. Eager, you might say."

"That if you had another child . . ."

"I want another child! I want ten or twenty children, but I can't manage it by prayer alone, sir!"

"That you might die from it. Kate. I couldn't bear it if I hurt you." He fell into her arms.

She stroked his head and whispered sweetly to him like he was Tomeen waking up from a bad dream.

ᗡ

I want the light," Joseph whispered as Kate cupped her hand around the flame. "I want to see your face."

She nodded and came to where he sat on the bed. Two candles burned on the table, illuminating them in a golden light. She could see his hands tremble as he drew her to him and kissed her mouth. Smiling, she untied the ribbon at the neck of her gown.

"That day you were takin' in the wash," he said.

"Nuthin' between the two of us, Joseph Connor . . ." She finished the thought. "Not even the sheet."

"I've been dreamin' of it, Kate darlin'." He crushed her against him and kissed her fiercely.

"This is no dream," she returned breathlessly.

Joseph made love to her, tender and slow, his gaze never leaving hers. Like the strong current of the river he caught her, pulling her into swirling eddies, drifting through fragrant pools.

Hours passed.

The candles burned low.

At last he slept in the cradle of her arms, his head beneath her chin. She could not sleep. Tears burned her eyes. She stroked his back, her fingers brushing across the furrows of scars left by the whip. Strong wrists bore fleshy welts where the manacles had worn away his skin. A line four inches long marked the path of the razor that had nearly taken his life on the docks of London. As Kate bore the wounds of her tragedy on her body, so Joseph would carry the reminders of injustice and suffering to his grave.

Her love for him was fierce, and so was her fury at his enemies.

And with the loss of the baby? There were recent wounds in Kate, unseen. Wounds too deep, perhaps, to ever heal. The why of it pounded her soul.

She tried to remember what Father O'Bannon said when she survived her own inferno and others she loved did not . . . when she was ashamed to show her scars . . . when she could not look anyone straight in the eye, nor kneel before the living God without reproaching Him for her suffering.

What was it that had made her lay the bitterness aside then? She had confessed her rage at heaven, and as penance the old priest had commanded her to write a letter to herself about the crucifixion and the Blessed Virgin. It had seemed silly at the time, but how those words had changed everything.

What could ease the pain of these too-fresh wounds that filled her alternately with fury and grief?

She rose from the bed and carried the guttering candle to the desk. Opening the drawer she rifled through a sheaf of papers until she came to the single yellowed sheet she had written upon years ago. The words on the page were awkward at first. Ink from the nib had dripped a trail like tiny footprints from one word to another.

> *Scars. Visible. Invisible . . . A badge of honor in heaven.*
> *The wounds of the risen Christ . . . hands, head, side*
> *and feet. Touch them and believe.*
> *Hide in them and live.*
> *Cherish your scars, Kate. They make you more like Him.*
> *Proof you've fought the battle here below.*
> *Christ crucified, the only begotten Son of God sacrificed*
> *for you. And at the foot of the cross, most human*
> *of all agony. His mother watched Him die.*

Think on it! To stand helpless while the child she loved suffered and died! And her suffering did not end when He cried, It Is Finished! She took Him from the cross and buried Him. Her child. Aye! It all speaks of heaven and of earth. Of what you must suffer while you're here. He died and rose, but sure, you must tremble at His loneliness and the darkness of that final hour.

And His mother.

Can you remember her as well?

Grieve like Mary at the grave for all you cannot understand.

Give up to God the hopes your love has begotten.

Mourn at the tomb of what you've lost.

Then give up to God what you cannot change.

Remember there will be Easter morning.

Resurrection.

Hope in that alone.

Bear your scars with joy.

∽ 18 ∽

Kate found Joseph in his study. Spread out before him on his left hand was a detailed map of the Burke estate. A portion at the top of the map, the area just under the crest of Ben Beg, was circled in red. On Joseph's other side was a thick, leather-bound statute book. Looking over Joseph's shoulder, she saw the passage to which it was open: *Corn Law Regulations.* Scribbled numbers in red ink covered the margins of both book and map.

Joseph was muttering. The words were audible, but scarcely made sense. "Two hundred acres at . . . no, that's no good. A penny a pound for a hundred tons is . . . but if I give up the headwater of the Camanach, it'll be worth more . . ."

"And what devilish incantation are you utterin', then?" Kate teased.

Jumping as if shot, Joseph spun round in his chair with a guilty expression on his face. "I didn't hear you come in," he said.

"Obviously," was the dry rejoinder. "And is this secret formula somethin' you'll need to confess to priest or wife?"

"Wife," Joseph admitted slowly, his features puckered as if he had bitten into something sour. "I intended to discuss the matter with you, but I wanted to be clear on it myself first. It's to do with the potatoes, or rather the hunger that will come from their lack."

Her lightness shelved by the serious tone, Kate drew up a chair and sat down. "Is it so bad, then?"

"It will be. Over the whole country, full half the crop, at the very least, is gone. What the people will eat this winter . . . If only I'd had time to work on the wheat plantin' and the other grains! If only we had planted more barley this year."

"But we did not," returned Kate practically. "What must we do so no one starves?"

Joseph clasped his wife's scarred hand. "You have been through so much already that it should be easier for a time."

"And where is that promise written?" Kate scolded. "But you are not a man to despair if any way can be found. What have you discovered?"

Clearing his throat, Joseph explained, "You know that England does not want cheap foreign grain competin' with what English and Irish landlords produce. The tax on imports is what keeps the price high."

"And keeps poor Irish tenants from bein' able to buy even grain grown here," Kate added with bitterness. "Oats get shipped to England to fill landlord pockets, not Irish bellies. Oh!" she said suddenly realizing she had indicted Joseph and herself.

Joseph grinned. "Not us, sweet. Anyway, what I want is a source of cheap grain to feed those with no potatoes left to eat."

"And have you found one?"

"I think so," Joseph said, closing one eye and holding up the statute book. "By a strange oversight, Indian corn—*maize* it's called some places—is exempt from the tax. That is to say, it's not mentioned at all."

Excitement growing in her voice, Kate asked, "And is it cheap?"

"About the same as potatoes."

"And can we afford to buy enough to make a difference?"

This time Joseph's affirmative reply was longer in coming and accompanied by a grimace. Involuntarily his glance fell on the map, and Kate suddenly understood.

"Barrevagh. You're thinkin' of sellin' Barrevagh to the O'Sheas."

"You know the state of our finances as well as I," Joseph said. "There is no way to come at that much cash without partin' with somethin'. Barrevagh is the Burke holdin' furthest away and the most cut off from the rest. And the Widow O'Shea has a good heart. She'll not be for tossin' the village. What do you think?"

Kate threw her arms around Joseph's neck. "I think *you* are the best-hearted person." She slid into his embrace on his lap. "And the handsomest in the whole West of Ireland."

"Only the West?" Joseph teased, kissing her.

It was not commonplace for any prime minister of England to go to the office of a subordinate, but in the case of all things Irish, the commonplace was often turned on its head. In this instance Prime Minister Peel was meeting with the permanent assistant secretary of the treasury, Charles Trevelyan.

Trevelyan, as the highest-ranking civil servant in the British government, was more or less immune to political change, and inasmuch as the Treasury was the single most important department, he was a force to be reckoned with.

For these reasons, and because the matter involved the expenditure of government funds, Peel approached Trevelyan in his office at the Exchequer.

Peel was in a shaky position politically, and both knew it. The prime minister's support within his own Tory party was eroding because Peel favored easing trade restrictions so that grain for Ireland could be made less expensive. This was a distinctly un-Tory stance.

The strained relationship between the two was compounded by the fact that neither liked the other: Trevelyan had such an inflexible belief in his own correctness that he endowed his every opinion with insufferable self-righteousness.

"I want to discuss the situation in Ireland," Peel said. "I have a relief scheme I want to put forward."

Trevelyan accepted as his due that the prime minister was consulting privately with him. Though Trevelyan was not on the Relief Committee, he held the purse strings, and he intended to hold them tightly indeed. "Quite," he said curtly. "The movements of Providence are indeed wondrous. I believe that this present crisis will do more to modernize and improve the moral and political economy of Ireland than a hundred years of the status quo . . . as long as the fuzzy-headed and soft-hearted in authority do not circumvent the process by which the Irish will be civilized."

Peel stared. Trevelyan spoke of the starving Irish—and the work-houses were already filling, though the hungry times had scarcely begun—as one would a savage from the jungle or a wild animal facing domestication. "Surely you do not mean we should let people starve?"

Trevelyan dismissed the assertion as unimportant. "People have always starved in Ireland, and they will continue to do so as long as the lazy peasant subsists on unreliable potatoes grown by a few weeks' work a year. This present situation strikes at the heart of the problem. Eliminate Irish dependence on the potato, and you have moved the superstitious, papist, tribal Irish closer to joining the modern world. But come, my views on this are well known. What is it you wished to ask me?"

Peel gritted his teeth in the face of such bigotry. Peel was himself adamantly opposed to Irish self-rule, but he did not hate the Irish people. Moreover, if the unrepealed union of England and Ireland meant that the Irish were citizens of Great Britain, then surely a famine required Great Britain's assistance. He forged ahead. "Relaxing the trade barriers to allow less expensive grain to reach the hungry is proving to be difficult to accomplish; it may never happen. But the laws apply only to a specific list of grains, wheat, barley, oats, and not to Indian corn as grown in America. I intend to purchase cheap Indian corn to distribute to the needy . . . not to give away, but to sell as near cost as possible."

"Certainly not! That would be a politician's trick for circumventing a wise law *and* the will of Providence!"

"You forget yourself, sir!" Peel exploded.

"And you forget that one day after you propose such a scheme you would no longer be prime minister! Do you think I will support such an ill-advised plan? Do you think I will allow a secret distribution of funds? I would denounce you through the halls of government."

Not surprised by Trevelyan's response, Peel had already put in motion his own secret expenditure of funds to purchase corn. But soon he would need Trevelyan's approval to expand relief efforts. "There is another facet to this," he said, trying a different tack. "In the west of Ireland, certain landlords, Joseph Burke and others, have gone so far as to sell property to obtain corn for their tenants. How will we keep the Irish gentry in favor of the Union if the government lets them bear the full burden of relief?"

Trevelyan was not impressed with the argument. "As I said: a clear example of fuzzy-minded thinking. This Burke you speak of is a rabble-rouser who is already in the camp of the Repealers. Nor will he be swayed by a flagrant misuse of government funds. No, Prime Minister, I will not support you in this matter."

It's come," announced Tomeen loudly, skipping into Joseph's office. "Mama says 'Tell Da it's here!'"

"What is?" Joseph asked tersely. Interrupted in the casting up of the estate's accounts, he sounded much harsher than he intended and over his shoulder he saw the red-haired child's lip quiver as the joy of being a chosen messenger drained away.

"Come here, Tomeen," Joseph said, laying aside his quill pen and turning around. "Come sit here in my lap, and tell Da what's come."

Tomeen, ever ready to sit in Joseph's lap and too irrepressible to be downcast for long, soon recovered his feeling of importance. "Mama says it's the corn."

"Blessed day," said Joseph, breaking into a smile and sighing as he pushed back the ledgers. "And just when I couldn't find another penny to spare."

"I've got tuppence if you need it, Da," Tomeen said brightly. "Want it?"

"Lord bless you, no, not today, but thank you, Tomeen. Now let's go see somethin' come all the way from America!" He swept the child upward toward the ceiling with a rush that brought a squeal of delight. "The only flyin' boy in the world," he said, laughing, invoking a familiar game. "Let's fly like a hawk down the steps!"

Four wagons, their beds sagging under the weight of heaped sacks, were drawn up in the yard by the Claddagh boys. Moor, in the lead rig, had a stranger beside him on the seat. "Squire," he called. "This is Mister Butterman, of the United States of America."

Butterman, whose compact, thrifty frame did not fit well with his name, nevertheless had a buttery smile and manner. "Squire Burke," he said, extending his hand and pumping Joseph's like he was ringing a school bell. Tomeen bounced up and down on Joseph's shoulder. "Butterman. O. G. Butterman. Obadiah Gideon, but folks call me Ogee. Pleased to make your acquaintance, sir, mighty pleased. And your son's. Fine-looking boy, fine."

Grinning through his confusion, Joseph said, "A pleasure, sir. And how do you happen to be ridin' with my grain?"

"As to that, no mystery a'tall. I'm the new European agent for the Consolidated Cereal Company of Baltimore, Maryland. I made the crossing with the goods, so to speak. Wanted to meet all the customers in our new territory."

"Welcome, indeed, Mister Butterman. Will you stay to supper?"

"A pleasure," Butterman said, beaming. Then, turning to Kate, who had just emerged from the house with Martin and Mary Elizabeth, he said, "And am I correct that this lovely person is Lady Burke? Charmed, charmed."

"Mister Butterman," Kate said, seeing the gleaming excitement in Joseph's eye, "we have been eagerly waitin' for this day. If it's not too rude, may we look at the corn?"

"Certainly, ma'am," Butterman agreed. A clasp knife appeared in his hand from a trouser pocket and slit a six-inch gash in the topmost sack. From it spilled a flow of brilliant yellow, hard as pebbles, dried corn.

"Pretty rocks, Mama!" Tomeen shouted.

Joseph set the boy down, hefted a handful of the grain, and frowned.

"Is anything the matter, sir?" Butterman inquired. "I assure you it is top-quality flint corn. First-rate. Fattens hogs like nothing else. Good for chickens too."

"Mister Butterman," Joseph said, "do I understand that it is all like this . . . kernels? Is none of it already ground into meal?"

Already shaking his head before Joseph finished asking the question, Butterman explained, "Can't ship meal without a lot of spoilage. Moisture is death on ground corn. But this is prime. No spoilage here."

"What was it you called it?" Kate asked. "Flint?"

"Yes, ma'am, that's right. Flint corn, Indian corn. Same thing. Takes special blades to grind it. Regular millstones . . . well, you'd have to grind it twice over before humans can . . . say, you wasn't going to feed this to people?"

"Yes, Mister Butterman, that is our intent," Joseph admitted.

"Whew! Big job. Guess you'll be glad to only have the one shipload."

"I beg your pardon?"

"Oh, we saw the *Dorset* in midcrossing. She was the ship carrying your second request. But I have to tell you, sir, the demand has shot up so much, I'm afraid Consolidated can't fill your order at the original price . . . maybe not at any price. Most all this year's stock is already gone. French government is clamoring for more, too, but I can't even supply them for another ten months at least."

Martin was put in charge of making the Indian corn into something usable as food for people. When he first encountered the flinty kernels, his response was, "The Red Indians must have different teeth altogether than Irishmen . . . or else no teeth a'tall after the age of five."

There was no mill closer than Westport for the grinding of the grain in large quantities, and when queried about it, its superintendent was skeptical about the ability of his millstones to handle such impenetrable nuggets.

Nor was it possible simply to do the job in smaller amounts at smaller mills. After recording the wettest year in living memory all the way through July, the subsequent months of 1845 were bone dry. The rivers and streams fell below their usual flow, and the small mill on the Cornamona stopped grinding altogether.

According to the *Gardeners' Chronicle,* Indian corn was perfectly nutritious, but it took considerably more preparation than boiling potatoes. The first method suggested was crushing between two flat stones, then mixing with grease and boiling into a slurry.

Martin, working all day and into the night in the barn where the corn was stored, succeeded in cracking three bushels into small enough granules to be edible. It was, he said to Mary Elizabeth, "Miserable hard." The local limestone rocks were flat enough to be handy for pounding, but they chipped almost as much as the kernels and left the cracked corn full of grit.

The second method suggested was of soaking the grain overnight, then boiling it for an hour and a half and eating it with milk. Treated that way it was edible . . . barely.

"Joseph," Martin said. "I know you put me in charge of the corn, but I need your help."

The answer, when it occurred to Joseph, seemed obvious: He would sell more land to the O'Sheas. At the exorbitant price of fifteen shillings apiece, Joseph purchased hand mills for the grinding of flint corn into meal, which could then be mixed with potato flour or bean flour and baked into bread. Buying enough mills to supply the people of the Burke townlands took most of the proceeds of the land sale, but as Joseph said, "It is this year we have to be concerned about. Next year will have to take care of itself."

∽ 19 ∽

The inmates of the Galway City workhouse secretly called the porridge, made from bright yellow Indian corn, Peel's Brimstone. Poorly ground, it had the consistency of gravel mixed with water. Hulls and sharp fragments of the kernels did not digest well, leaving those who consumed the mixture with bleeding dysentery.

Nevertheless, at a cost of one penny per pound for the cornmeal, Reverend Banbreak found that the children in his care could be fed for one tenth of the amount provided for them. He was growing prosperous even as they grew more thin by the week.

The waning of 1845 increased the number of inmates at the workhouse. The potato crop failure led to nonpayment of rent, which was followed by eviction, starvation, and ultimately this last resort.

Corrie, Ceili, and Megan Grogan found themselves surrounded by children who, like themselves, had been abandoned. Those who entered the domain of the Galway workhouse with their parents had been separated from them by the official policy that isolated male from female, parents from children. Corrie often remarked that God was good to let them be born girls. They slept together at least.

The sleeping platform became so crowded with newcomers that they could only lie on their sides. In the night the hacking coughs of the ill were ignored. Every morning the fever, which marched shoulder-to-shoulder beside starvation, claimed a half-dozen little ones. Always there were more to take their places.

Light had been out for hours. The fire was dead. Moisture from steamy breath rose, condensing on the ceiling and dripping on the inmates like rain. The Grogan sisters were packed together on the dirty straw of the sleeping platform with one hundred and twenty other girls.

Megan was coughing again. It had come upon her three nights before. She was feverish, hot as fire, and yet she shivered against Corrie.

"It's cold," Megan whimpered.

Corrie pulled her sister closer and stroked her head.

"I want . . . Da . . . ," Megan whispered hoarsely.

It was against the rules to speak after dark. Corrie shushed her, but she was rambling.

"Want . . . Mama . . ."

"Hush, now. Don't say it," Corrie soothed.

Racked by a fit of coughing, Megan began to weep.

From somewhere down the row someone shouted for her to shut up.

"Want . . . to see . . . why doesn't Da . . . Corrie! Corrie! Sister . . . why doesn't Da . . . America, he said. He promised!"

The sound of the latch and the circle of lamplight made Corrie clamp her hand over Megan's mouth. The coughing continued behind her fingers.

Banbreak's sharp voice awakened them all. "What's this? Who's talking? You again?" He came directly to the Grogan sisters. "You!"

"She's ill, sir!" Corrie pleaded.

"Ill, is it? We have rules! There are rules!"

Megan cried, "I want Mother!"

Banbreak reached down, grasping her by the hair. He jerked her upright to her feet as she shrieked, "Mother! Da! Corrie! Where's Da?" Her eyes gleamed with the fever.

Corrie tried to struggle upright. Banbreak pinned her down with the silver tip of his walking stick.

"You'll stay here!" he threatened. "'Tis attention she's needing, is it? Very well. Attention she shall have. An example to brats who think it permissible to awaken the house. Selfishness! Self indulgent!" He raved as Corrie pleaded for Megan to remain.

Carrying Megan beneath his arm, he bustled from the room, bolting the door behind him.

Fever had taken twenty-three in the workhouse along with Megan Grogan. There was no proper funeral. For so many there could not be. Most of the indigent dead were elderly or children like Megan. Most were without relatives.

A long pit was prepared for their grave. A handful of relations stood shivering beside Corrie and Ceili as the bodies were placed by a crew of the strongest inmates in the bottom of the pit. They were wrapped in rags, any usable clothing having been stripped from them for use by other inmates.

A lock of hair protruded from a sparse shroud covering the form of a child.

"There," Ceili said, pointing miserably. "She's there."

Corrie, unable to utter a word, nodded in response. Megan was wedged between two larger bodies. *An uncomfortable lot*, Corrie thought irrationally, as though the dead needed comfort. She wanted to shout at the inmates laying out the dead, "Can't you give her a bit of room?"

But Corrie said nothing, did not weep as Ceili wept.

Megan had found her bit of room, her peace with a God who said suffer the little children to come unto me. Megan had suffered. Aye. That she had. And now she was gone to Jesus.

Reverend Banbreak marched pertly to the rim of the burial pit. Directly opposite Corrie and Ceili, he did not notice them. The wide gulf of the grave separated them. He did not look in as the work of unloading and positioning bodies continued. Adjusting his hat and his spectacles, he opened his book and began to read in a low, uninterested monotone. The voices of the workers and the sound of spades obscured the words.

"What's he sayin'?" Ceili said, sniffing.

"Readin' the rules," Corrie replied.

Banbreak's book snapped shut. He tossed a handful of earth onto the centermost bundle. "Dust to dust," he intoned. Bags of lye were opened and sprinkled over the bodies.

So this was all there was to it. Raising his eyes for the first time, Banbreak spotted Corrie and Ceili. "You can rejoice. Your baby sister is with God . . . His will entirely that you came to us and converted to the truth. Though her body decays, her soul is redeemed, saved from the papist tommyrot of Catholicism."

Corrie hated him so. Rejoice, he said. He, who whipped Megan for asking for another bowl of porridge. He, who, in the name of God, pulled her hair and made her work when the fever was upon her. He, who did not let Corrie come to her when she called from her deathbed.

Banbreak saw it in her eyes. "Why do you stare so?"

Corrie looked down at the dead, who lay between him and herself. She knew something for certain as her eyes fixed on Megan and then raised defiantly to the vicar. She replied in the Gaelic, "You know not the same Christ we know. He who holds Megan now is not your Lord."

He did not understand her, of course. "Impertinent! You know it is forbidden to speak your pagan gibberish! The rules! The rules! I'll have you . . . get back to work." Her steely gaze put him off.

Again, in the Gaelic, she responded, "You will give me no more orders. Tell me no more about the Lord you know not."

"No supper for you!" He raised his finger.

She smiled. Raised her head. The dignity of a royal Celtic ancestor shone through her expression. "I renounce England. I renounce you. And your queen, who makes herself head of an invented church." The insult was complete. Corrie would speak no more the tongue of her oppressors. In the ancient language she added, "We will go back to you never more. Though I perish, I will live and die a true daughter of my church and Christ."

Ceili whispered fearfully, "He'll beat us, sure."

Corrie took her sister's hand. The Irish of her voice was like music. She sang the words to Ceili, remembering how things had been in the old days. "God is not in that place, Ceili. We will go back nevermore. We must find Da."

"What'll we eat?"

Corrie backed away, keeping her eyes on the vicar who was white with outrage. "The bread of Christ," Corrie said. "The bread of truth. The bread of suffering."

As Reverend Banbreak shouted at them, calling down the wrath of his unloving God upon their frail shoulders, Corrie led Ceili away. Away. Away. Away from that terrible place.

So Burke has sold more land, you say, and is using the proceeds to feed his hungry peasants? How extraordinarily stupid of him."

"Exactly so," Steward Richman agreed. "It is the high grazing land on the north of Burke property. He sold it to the widow of Squireen O'Shea."

Mahon's face clouded. Not only would he have liked to own that real estate himself, it was an additional poke in his eye to see it go to the Catholic O'Sheas. After all, Squireen O'Shea had murdered Mahon's cousin before committing suicide. The Mahon estate should be the one to receive compensation, not the heirs of the murderer!

"How long can he keep this up?"

Richman shrugged. "How high is up? They say he got a good price on a shipload of Indian corn, but that won't last forever."

"How can we see that Burke's corn runs out faster than he planned?" Mahon mused aloud.

Richman's thinking took barely a second to complete. "By sending him more hungry mouths than he can handle?"

"Precisely! If we speed up the pace of evictions, we not only clear the grazing land we need, but we can deliver a starving mob on the doorstep of Joseph Burke!"

"Glencrag is already two weeks in arrears. We were going to give them another two weeks. Shall we cancel the extension?"

"At once! Set the whole village on the road tomorrow if possible."

"Excuse me a moment, Major, while I consult our chief destructive." Stepping to the door of the office, Richman called, "Mister Gann, would you come in here please?"

It was with understandable confusion that Joseph received the word from Charlie Nesbitt that Mahon tenants had come to the manor and were asking to speak with him.

The truth was readily explained.

Footsore, weary, dripping pots and kettles, blankets and babies, the dazed Glencrag villagers had the look of being lately emerged from a battlefield. Three dozen people crowded into the Burke barn to escape the cold. They had few provisions and fewer belongings.

"He promised us more time, did the driver Richman," said a woman supporting an infant on each hip with a third child riding her back. Her feet were unshod and bloody. "Then this mornin' at dawn they come . . . that Richman and a whole gang of destructives . . . said our time was up . . . said we had to leave or they would pull the cottage down around our ears. And they sent the devil himself to do the work. Horrible-lookin' thing with his face all . . ." The woman stopped abruptly at the sight of Kate's scars, and Kate instinctively covered her throat with her good hand.

Margaret made clucking noises as she helped the woman ease the small girl off her back. Kate handed over a cuppa and told Fern to see to the babies.

"Thank you," the woman said. "Me husband, that's him there lyin' beside the barrow. Got a clout upon the head when he tried to resist, didn't you, Sean?"

A man with no color in his face but a bloodstained cloth wound around his head nodded wearily. "I asked to speak to the squire, I did. Said it must be a mistake, that we were promised more time. He didn't even answer me, that one. Just swung a short club and knocked me down. Kept at it, too, like he liked doin' it."

"Would have killed him if not for Richman callin' him off like a dog. 'Enough, Gann,' he said, or else me Sean'd be dead in the ditch, I swear to heaven," the woman concluded.

"And did none of you ever get an answer?" Joseph asked the stableful of battered refugees.

An elderly man spoke up. He stood with difficulty, supporting himself with a blackthorn stick in each hand. His forehead and his shock of white hair were creased and soiled from the leather strap that supported his backpack. "They did none of them speak except askin' for hammers or more rope. Went about their work as mum as any fell spirits that ever came out of hell. Tore down beams, tore down walls, warned us to never go back inside an' went after the next."

"And how does it happen that you all came here?" Kate asked.

The patriarch continued to speak for the group. "Took us right to the edge of Mahon land, they did. Then said, 'let Burke feed you an' shelter you, for you'll get nothin' from us but beatin'.' You see, Squire, we didn't know what else to do. We had nowhere else to go."

20

Burke Hall echoed with laughter as Rosie, attempting to feed herself, got as much of the mashed mixture of boiled potato and cabbage in her hair as in her mouth. She was past a year old, and high time she learned. At least that was the theory. Mostly it felt good to have a reason to smile.

Tomeen, as a mature boy of almost three, looked disapprovingly at Rosie from where he and Robert played at trading smooth stones beside the hearth. "She's gone and mucked up her frock," he said scornfully.

"She's still just a baby . . . and you watch how you speak," Kate scolded.

"Yes, Mama," he replied

Leaving Fern to mind the children so a squabble did not result in bruised heads, Joseph gathered the others around himself. It was understood that the easy banter of the dinner had to give way to practicality. The council included Kate, Martin, the Claddagh boys, Nesbitt, Kane, and Father O'Bannon.

"There is no easy way to say this," Joseph began, "so straight out is best. What with the failure of the stored potatoes . . ." Martin hung his head in shame. "Which no one could have foreseen or prevented," Joseph continued, "the amount of Indian corn I have already purchased may just be enough to see us through . . . may be, but with no certainty. We need to buy other provisions, and we cannot wait. I am going to sell off the townland of Ballydoo and use the money to buy food."

Stunned silence greeted his words. More than one of the guests looked at the pratties spattered on Rosie with a different eye.

It was Father O'Bannon who inquired, "And who will the purchaser be? Not, I'm prayin', Major Mahon, whose land is next to the east?"

"No." Joseph said with satisfaction. "I am happy to say that it will stay out of Mahon clutches awhile longer. The Lady Fiona Shaw . . . some of you know who she is . . . has agreed to take on the lease."

Quietly O'Bannon asked, "And will she guarantee to keep the tenants?"

"There is no way anyone can make such a pledge in times like these," Joseph answered truthfully. "Now here is my query for you all: every sale of Burke land raises the specter of eviction and puts fear in the tenants. If you are asked about this, can you in good conscience say it was the only course that would protect the greatest number? It is not too late to stop the sale, and I need your support."

"How many people live in Ballydoo, Squire?" Nesbitt inquired.

O'Bannon had the number. "About threescore," he said. "Includin' a half-dozen widows. Joseph, are you certain it has come to this?"

Joseph studied Kate's face and received a nod of encouragement in return. "I'm afraid so."

"And if the good people of Ballydoo are tossed, will you take them in? Your father, may he rest in peace, the Burke of Connaught, would never have set any of his people on the road."

Again a look at Kate. "We will take them in," Joseph said. "But I fear another meetin', for all Burke folk, is in order."

A blanket of leaves covered the grave of Martin Burke. Joseph gently placed the stone of his offering upon the mound. Already the ground had begun to subside. The year of mourning was past. The earth sighed and settled beneath the weight of grief.

Most beloved soil, heart of myself, first breath of love between me and Kate . . . you know your father well now. Littlest among the great cloud of witnesses, but not the least, in innocence you look down on the life you never lived.

Joseph spoke aloud then, clasping his hands. "Your sister Rosie is over a year old now. Aye. A pretty thing she is, and bright . . . as you would have been. Talkin'. Callin' me Da and your mother is Mama. She doesn't know times are hard. Smiles all the time, she does. Sunlight she is to us when no sun shines. I hold Rosie and think to myself that she doesn't know what's come upon Ireland. It came to me just now, as if I saw you . . . a strong baby boy a year old, smilin' just the same as herself, and callin' me Da. I wish it could've been so. Can't think of what might have been. Mustn't." Joseph faltered. Words came hard. He missed this child more as the days went by, longed more for him than he had even in the beginning.

Clouds drifted above like ships sailing. "I'm doin' all I can, you know. But it won't be enough, baby boy. Not nearly enough." Joseph bowed his head. "You lived an hour. You sit with those who've lived a thousand years and more. You're wiser than I am, baby. Because you see the end, don't you?"

Joseph inhaled deeply. "There's the land of Ballydoo. Lady Fiona Shaw has agreed with me on the matter." He frowned. "Am I becomin' a hard man? Well I must, mustn't I? I'm left with no choice. To save some I'll have to turn my back on the rest. Can't save the whole world. Can't save Ireland, God help her."

Joseph touched the pyramid of smooth pebbles with his fingertips. "So many children like yourself . . . livin' through what you'll never live through. Smilin'. Givin' joy to their folk. What of them?" Joseph cradled his head in his hands.

Somehow the face of every hungry child in Ireland had taken on the identity of this tiny child who lay beneath the clay. "When they ask for bread, will I leave them a stone? See? Turn my back upon them, y'see. In the end . . . walk away. From where you sit among the saints, do you see it all as if it's over? Christ will come again. Why not now? I long for it, baby. You'll understand, won't you? And forgive me? Forgive? I can't feed the five thousand folk Mahon's tossed. Or the hundred thousand evicted on the roads or the million who marched to Clontarf with Daniel O'Connell. They'll become the dust of Ireland. They'll find their rest in this earth. Raindrop by raindrop their dust will wash away. Join the earth's passage to the sea.

"As for us? Five hundred souls in this wee valley. 'Tis all I can manage. My own tribe. Five hundred souls within these gates. When the little ones I shut out . . . when they go hungry . . . fly away to watch it unfold from above, will you explain to them that your da had no choice. None a'tall in the matter. Can't feed them all . . . isn't that I don't love . . ." His voice broke.

It began to rain.

The latest round of evictions in western Ireland had swelled the transient population of Galway City to bursting. The streets were crowded with other people, who, like Corrie and Ceili, were searching for something. There were more beggars than those who could offer charity.

The two sisters ferreted their way through the crush to the docks. It was here, Corrie recalled, that Da had told them he might find work.

Stacks of grain sacks, barrels of Irish butter, kegs of whiskey made from Irish grain, and mountains of foodstuffs lined the wharf. It was true what Corrie had heard: there was no true famine in Ireland, only hunger. The only crop lost was the one that had fed the poor folk for generations.

Starving men, women, and children milled just beyond the quay, their hungry eyes fixed upon the food they had grown that was going to feed other people far away while they went without.

To counter the possibility of riot, armed guards patrolled the bounty being exported to England. They were young men, mostly. Hired by the agents of absentee landlords, they were empowered by the magistrates to shoot to kill at the first sign of riot and looting. Corrie noted pens of sheep and cattle likewise awaiting loading for transportation to England.

Ceili licked her lips as the aroma of oats drifted to them. "It's like at the workhouse, ain't it, Corrie?" she asked. "Like when Banbreak was eatin' chicken while we ate Peel's Brimstone."

"Aye," Corrie agreed bitterly. Trying to distract herself from the gnawing emptiness in her stomach, she took Ceili's arm. "Look for Da, Ceili. Stop thinkin' about food. We'll not have anythin' a'tall unless we find him. We've got to find him. Tell him about what was done to Megan."

"He won't make us go back, will he?" Ceili worried.

"We won't go. Not ever. No matter what he says."

With this assurance, the two searched the faces of the stevedores. Daniel Grogan was not among them.

Two hours passed and then three. Cargos were loaded on one dock while on another, emigrants slowly moved up the gangplank of a ship.

"Where are they goin'?" Ceili asked a fresh-faced boy of about thirteen.

"America," he replied wistfully.

Ceili smiled. It was the first smile Corrie had seen on her sister's face since Mother had died. "Well then, I'm goin' there, too, one day," Ceili said. Then, leaning close to Corrie, she remarked, "I never seen anybody really go, y'know. Always heard of it, but there they are, like. Really leavin'. Really goin' onto a ship. You think we'll find Da, Corrie?"

"Aye. We'll find him," Corrie replied, but she was not so certain. Two dozen queries of men at the docks offered no hope. None remembered seeing Daniel Grogan, but then, men came and went with the tides in Galway City. Perhaps, some suggested, he had gone on a ship, sailed with a whaler to the South Seas. Or perhaps he was already in America.

Dispirited, at dusk Corrie turned her eyes to the tower of the Church of St. Nicholas. "What day is it?"

"Sunday."

"Sure, and Da's at mass, then. Remember how he said he'd never miss a Sunday mass. Never miss prayin' for us."

Ceili hung back. "What if it's one of their churches then? They'll make us . . . what do they call it . . . before we could eat . . . they made us . . .?"

"Convert," Corrie finished.

"That's it." Ceili looked pained. "Like Banbreak made us do. And if it's our old church . . . even if Da's there, the Lord Jesus'll be angry with us for turnin' away from the church."

"Everyone's hungry enough nowadays they'll all say they're Protestant just for an ounce of soup. There's only one true church, Ceili, and that's the one where love is. Maybe where Da is . . . Mercy, there's the ticket. Y'know. Da said Quakers have it, and they ain't Catholic like us, nor are they Church of Ireland. Some of the others too. Baptists. Banbreak treated them just as bad."

"I'm scared to go there." Ceili hung back.

"We'll look inside. If Da, Jesus, Mary, and Joseph ain't there, we'll go away."

Ceili agreed to this bargain. Approaching the edifice, Corrie scrambled up the steps and peered in. The place was packed. Jesus, Mary, and Joseph were there in that place.

"It's our own," Corrie explained to Ceili. "We'll wait here until mass is finished. Da'll be comin' out." Peering around the corner, she spotted a second entrance. "Now go wait there for him. I'll stay here."

Mass was ended. Streams of folk came out blinking in the sunlight. Daniel Grogan was not among them. Corrie dashed in, crossed herself, looked around the vast empty hall and then ran to find Ceili.

Ceili sat upon the gravel walk, her face downcast. "He wasn't among them, Corrie."

Corrie plopped down beside Ceili. "Where shall we go?" she muttered, feeling hopeless for the first time.

Perhaps they would die quickly on the streets, as Banbreak had threatened.

Ceili seemed strangely calm.

"I listened, see. The priest said a special prayer for Daniel O'Connell and for Joseph Burke in the West who was holdin' out for his people."

"Burke."

"Aye. Da was always wishin' . . . remember Corrie? Da always said he wished he was born a few miles north, for then he'd have been a Burke man and all would've been well."

Corrie read the plan in Ceili's eyes. "What is it you're thinkin'?"

"Maybe Da's gone there. We could see the lights of Castletown from home. I want to go home, Corrie."

∽ 21 ∽

In the life of Ballynockanor many gatherings had been held at the chapel of St. John the Evangelist: children were welcomed into the community of faith, marriage partnerships were enacted, solace was given for departed loved ones who had gone on before. The little church also had seen its share of other meetings, having played its role in organizing the relief efforts when the potato crop had failed before.

The strain of the present circumstance showed on everyone's face, but most on Father O'Bannon's. "How are you keepin', Father?" Joseph asked.

The elderly priest shook his head. "I never thought it would come to this," he said. "When the English barred the road and hoped we would all die of the smallpox, I said to myself, 'They have no charity in them, God help them.' But I never looked to see a time when the ones lackin' in charity would be us!"

The discussion that had been raging for three hours already was winding down as there were no longer any doubts about the verdict.

"Are we agreed then?" asked Adam Kane. "The Burke lands are to be closed to outsiders and the roads guarded. We can feed and care for our own, but not if everyone evicted from Mahon property . . . and others . . . comes here to be cared for."

"Who then is my neighbor?" O'Bannon quoted with a shudder.

Kate was one of those who had resisted the proposition the longest. She had seen the weary mothers, the ragged children, the haunted-looking men. She knew what despair accompanied having nowhere else to turn.

But in the end, she looked down at Rosie and Tomeen and studied her sister when she thought Mary Elizabeth was not noticing and imagined them starving. She saw them with sunken eyes and starvation-bloated bellies, and she hardened her heart in favor of her own. "There is no choice, Father," she said at last. "We can feed all who come, and in a month we will be upon the road beggin' ourselves. Or we can do this thing and make it through."

At the last, though Father O'Bannon was hoarse with misery and none of the womenfolk were dry-eyed, it was concluded. Ballynockanor and the Burke townlands would shut themselves off from the world. No one from outside could enter, and if one chose to leave he could not return.

It was not long after the meeting at the chapel of St. John that Adam Kane approached Joseph, hat in hand. Joseph was inspecting the apple trees planted beside the river. For the steward to ride out meant he had some message and Joseph, though he hated to see it come, was not at all surprised at the content.

"The trees are doin' well, Squire," Kane observed. "They have taken hold."

Joseph agreed, then waited for Kane to continue.

"I love it here," the steward said. "Not just Connaught, but this very spot. It was in my mind, had things been different, to ask you could I build a cottage here on the knock for Fern and me. Robert too, an' such little ones as God may bless us with. 'Tis a grand view across the river an' up into the mountains beyond." Kane sighed to a stop.

"But it isn't to be?" Joseph asked gently.

Shaking his head, Kane continued, "We're young and strong, Fern an' me, an' we have no family here, beggin' your pardon, Squire, for you've treated us like family, I don't mean that. But now's the time for us, don't y'see . . . before more family does come . . . to go to America. And besides," Kane hurried on, anxious to finish now that the subject was broached. "You've plenty of help with Nesbitt an' the others an' plenty of mouths to feed too. If we go, there'll be two less for the Burke estate to carry."

"Adam," Joseph said, using the steward's Christian name, "you are welcome to stay as long as you wish. The Burke estate has never begrudged you a mouthful and never would, but I understand what you are sayin'. Was my duty not so plainly to be here, Kate and I would be lookin' to emigrate too."

"Then'll you'll let us go without ill feelin's?"

Ruefully Joseph said, "With sorrow at the partin' but blessin's on your head. You are a true man, Adam Kane, none better, and I wish you well."

Kevin was thoroughly disgusted with himself. He had entered a life of crime because he felt angry with the world and ready to take it out on the wealthy. But robberies like the gombeen man had netted fewer shillings than working on the docks, and he scorned O'Hara's offer of another meeting at Monk's in favor of wandering around Galway City alone and thinking.

Perhaps Grogan did have the right idea. Maybe it was best just to acquire enough money for passage back to America. All the Irish who could manage the tariff seemed to be going there anyway. If he approached Joseph and Kate and explained that coming back home had been a mistake, surely they would come up with the fare.

As soon as the notion occurred to him, Kevin knew he could not do it. Joseph was already being spoken of as the one landlord in

Galway who would sacrifice his fortune to save his tenants. How could Kevin, who had already been safe, if not happy, in America, show up with his hand outstretched for money?

He plopped down moodily on a bench on Dock Street, near the intersection with Petticoat Alley. A man whose cast-off trousers were held up with a piece of rope and whose elbows and knees protruded through rents in the paper-thin fabric sat down next to him. The two exchanged no words until another figure rounded the corner, whistling.

With a jaunty air the new arrival inspected the crease in his stovepipe leg breeches, adjusted the waistband, and straightened his black waistcoat. "Just look at him, will you?" Kevin's benchmate spat the words as if the subject filled him with loathing, then put action into his speech by spitting forcefully on the ground.

"What about him?"

"That's the Reverend Mister Banbreak," the observer said, sarcastically enunciating every word. "A greater hypocrite never walked in shoe leather."

"That's a clergyman?" Kevin asked. "Comin' out of Petticoat Alley?"

"Or so he calls himself. Goes up there regular. Takes off his collar like nobody don't know who he is anyway. They say he favors Big Maeve."

"He looks pleased with himself."

"And why should he not? He takes the bread out of the mouths of orphans at the workhouse and spends the take on whores. Hey, what's your hurry then?"

Leaving his informant with his mouth agape at the sudden departure, Kevin was racing after Banbreak and thinking furiously. The cause of this abrupt decision was simple: in the realignment of Banbreak's waistcoat and trousers, Kevin had glimpsed a significantly thick money belt. But how to separate the clergyman from his previously stolen wealth?

In the event it was absurdly simple.

Banbreak's leisurely stroll took him into Eyre Square. Kevin sprinted ahead and ducked into an alcove in the brick wall shaded by willow branches. As the reverend neared the spot, Kevin judged that the area was clear enough and proceeded to hiss urgently. "Psst! Reverend!"

"Who's there?" Banbreak demanded, waving a silver-headed cane in the air like an amateur duelist.

Careful to keep his face shielded by the treelimbs, Kevin said, "Big Maeve sent me. She said you left this on accident, and she sent me to return it."

"It? What it?" Banbreak inquired, stepping a pace forward.

With one lunge, Kevin grabbed Banbreak's outstretched arm and yanked the man into full forehead contact with the brick wall and an unexpected transition into unconsciousness.

Satisfied no alarm had been given, Kevin stripped the money belt off the body and wound it around his own much-slimmer waist.

Only when he was safely behind a locked door did he discover that it contained forty pounds in gold.

The wedding of Adam Kane and Fern was a quiet affair. The celebration and dancing lasted only one night, for the next morning they were to leave the pleasant valley forever.

The folk of the townlands gathered to make their farewells to the couple and to their Robert.

Tomeen, who did not understand the why of it, told Robert he would see him in the morning. Kate did not try to explain.

"We'll see ye on t'other side." Molly raised her hands to the heavens and blessed Fern, who had always had a kind word for Molly, no matter the circumstance.

Fern, weeping, daubed her eyes, and kissed Kate, Rosie, and Tomeen. Then she took one long last look at the hills. "I know this is the last I'll lay eyes upon my home . . . upon all of you," she managed.

"Here's a letter for Kevin in New York." Kate pressed the envelope into Fern's hand. "Write us, will you? When you're settled."

Fern, for the first time in her life unable to speak, nodded.

"That we will." Adam hefted Robert and took Fern's arm. "Pennsylvania's the place for us. Fine farmland there, it's said. I have cousins there. A grand country."

"Aye. So I've heard. The West. God bless you then. We'll write all the news," Kate promised.

Joseph cleared his throat and pumped Adam's hand. "One day these troubles'll pass. Pray for us when you think of it, friend. Godspeed."

"Aye. And you for ourselves." Adam and Fern shouldered their few belongings.

The road beyond was empty. Father O'Bannon blessed them in the name of the Father, Son, and Holy Ghost. He charged them to live their lives as though the whole host of heaven was watching and to raise their children in the old, true ways as they had been taught.

As they passed, Margaret broke into sobs. Molly embraced the cook and led her away.

This was the moment. A tremendous cheer rose from the citizens. O'Rourke raised bow to fiddle and began to play.

> *Many a day to night gave way*
> *And many a morn succeeded,*
> *Yet still his flight by day and night*
> *That restless mariner speeded.*

The folk of Ballynockanor and Castletown began to sing the ballad as the Kane family reluctantly turned their backs on home and walked away to the West.

∽ 22 ∽

It was dawn. When the sun rose shining in the molten east, Kevin knew a storm would follow by the end of the day. He considered leaving for Galway City before the rain came to Ballynockanor and made the memories he took with him sodden. But he stayed.

Planted in the shade of a granite monolith, he gazed down at Joseph's apple trees. Not much bigger than spindly weeds, they represented Joseph's hope, this investment in the next century.

"Wish I had his luck," Kevin said aloud.

A voice croaked behind him. "It ain't so grand as all that, Kevin! And did ye eat up all the frog bread I baked for ye?"

Mad Molly Fahey! Kevin spun around to see the woman crouched and peering down at him from the top of the outcropping. "You're quiet as a cat, you old loon!" Kevin exclaimed.

"It's me shoes, Kevin." She extended her bare foot toward his face.

He caught his breath. She had startled him, frightened him by her unannounced arrival. What if someone came looking for her? Someone was always looking for Mad Molly.

"Are you alone then, Molly?"

She guffawed and winked at the air. "Did ye hear what he's askin' me? Askin' if Molly be alone? Never! Can't ye see 'em hoverin' there, Kevin Donovan?"

The air was empty. "I see no one but yourself."

"Then ye're a blind man livin' in a world of fools."

He nodded. At least he could agree with her on that count. "That I am, Molly."

She leapt to the ground and plopped down beside him. "I'll sit awhile beside ye then."

"You're welcome. But you know I'm not really here, Molly."

She laughed again. "Think I'm a loon, do ye?" She pinched him hard on the arm. "Ye're real enough for the hangman."

"You mustn't tell anyone I've come."

"Where's the fun in that?"

"If I'm caught . . . they'll truss me up."

"Aye. They'll catch ye, Kevin, and truss ye up. Into the gaol they'll toss ye. And there'll be the gallows."

"Stop it now."

"But a little child shall lead them. Choose only one! Aye. Christmastime it shall be. Certain death! Freedom! Choose only one! The reward, it is. Promised. They'll have to pay what's due. A little child shall . . ."

"Hush now, Molly. I'll not be listenin' to your gibberish."

"Sure." She seemed satisfied. "I've said what there is to say. And all I've said is true."

"You're a strange old bird." Kevin looked away toward the gleam of the sun.

"Aye." She reached into the pocket of her apron. "A potato for ye, Kev? They'll soon be no more for any man. But I've saved this one for ye."

He took it gratefully. "Thanks. And did you know I'd come?"

"Aye. Angels sang of it from ages past. They told me. And that ye'd be goin' agin soon."

"That's true," he said around the potato. "You'll not tell anyone I've come?"

"What'd ye take me for, a fool?"

"Swear it."

"Aye." She waved a paw dismissively. "But ye'll be needin' to speak to Martin."

He paused mid-bite. Yes. Martin could be trusted to hold his peace. Martin could give him the news, the facts, without letting anyone know.

"Sure. I've come to see Martin."

"I knew it already. But where will ye meet him?"

Kevin studied the landscape, the familiar places of home. "Kate wrote that Da is buried beside Mother."

"A good man, your da. Hated the English like a true patriot, he did. They killed him for it."

"I fancy goin' there. One last visit. Me and Martin used to play leapfrog over the headstones."

"A fine place to play, it is."

"It'll have to be after dark though. You think Martin'll be afraid if we meet in the graveyard?"

"Nay! Not Martin! Meet among friends? B'fore midnight?"

"That's fine. Ask him to bring food, will you? I've a powerful hunger."

Molly grinned toothlessly and emptied four more potatoes and an apple out of her pockets. "Angels above! Look here! They told me ye'd be needin' a wee bit. No tea though, Kev. Couldn't sneak out the kettle."

He was there on the hill above the orchard," Molly exclaimed to Martin. "'Twas the dear brother. 'Twas Kevin Donovan himself."

Martin's belly went cold and tight at the crone's revelation. Hadn't Da appeared to Mary Elizabeth in the instant of his death? Loonies like Molly and wee children often saw things that weren't there at all. But Martin knew such things might be there—only not seen by folk in their right minds.

Molly was not in her right mind. She saw all sorts of things, pleasant and unpleasant alike.

"'Twasn't Kevin," he protested, fearing Kevin had died in America and then in the blink between heaven and earth had come home for a last look around.

"Aye! Martin Donovan! 'Twas Kevin Donovan himself! Standin' there on the hillside in the full glory of the day lookin' down and wishin' he could come home."

"Molly, are you daft?"

"Aye. But even so, 'twas Kevin I was seein'."

Martin asked the dread question. "Is he dead then?"

"Dead!" howled Molly. "Dead is it? Are ye daft?"

"That I may be for listenin' to yourself."

"Ye'd better listen," she chided, "young pollywog! Half grown are ye! One day ye'll be a frog. Aye! One day!"

"God help me then, for you'll roast me up and grind me to powder to use in frog bread!"

"Well. Well, well, well . . ." She scratched her head and looked behind her. "Now ye've done it, Martin! Now ye've made me lose it."

"What have you lost?"

"Me thought. It's somewheres hereabouts. Somethin' about . . . frog bread . . . America . . . AYE!" She leapt up in the air exultantly. "Kevin's come home! He has indeed."

"His ghost most likely."

"Nay. 'Twas himself. The very same Kevin who lit out of Ireland with an edict chasin' him."

Martin surrendered. There was no talking sense to Molly. When she had something fixed in her mind it became the north star, the light by which her brain navigated. "So Kevin's come back, has he?"

"Ye saw him too?"

"Not a'tall. You saw him, Molly."

She nodded her grizzled head vigorously. "Aye. That's what I said. I saw Kevin Donovan there. Standin' on the hillside, he was. Wishin' he could only come home."

"And why does he not?"

"They'll toss him in the gaol, sure, ye fool!"

"What's he want then? You said he brought a message."

Molly clasped his arm in the fierce grip of urgency. "Aye. Swore me to secrecy he did. Molly, says he, swear ye'll tell no one but me dear brother Martin. I swear it, says I. So what does ye want, Kevin Donovan, says I?"

Martin had heard this part of the tale once through but still had not got the message. "And what are you to tell me, Molly?"

Suddenly crestfallen she answered, "Ye're t'meet him . . . some-place . . . a place . . . he said ye'd know it."

"And where is the place?"

"I've forgotten it. He said ye'd know."

Martin squeezed his eyes shut. "Perhaps I'd know where it was if you'd tell me the place."

"He said ye'd know it."

Martin, half-believing the woman had indeed met Kevin in the flesh, controlled his urge to shake her. "When?" he asked gently. "When is this meetin' to happen? Can you tell me that much anyway?"

"Aye. Aye. I remember when it is. The where of it ye'll have to figure out on your own." She counted slowly to thirteen using fingers and toes. "Before midnight, said he. Tell him meet me in the place . . . leapfrog! Martin'll know it . . . before midnight."

Steward Richman's smile stopped short of gloating. It was well that he held back the final ounce of exultation because Joseph already wanted to smash his fist into the short man's cocky, mus-tached face.

The Mahon driver was in Joseph's stable examining horses to purchase.

Feeding horses while humans went on short rations was nothing Joseph would tolerate. Also on Joseph's mind was his promise to Father O'Bannon about the villagers of Ballydoo. If they should be evicted, God forbid, where would he house them? The stable would have to be cleaned and prepared for human occupants.

The irony of it was not lost on Joseph: the loss of the potato crop had reduced the Irish peasant population to eating fodder intended for pigs and living in barns built for horses.

"What about those two draft horses?" Richman asked, eyeing the brawny shire animals with calculation. "Though they look a bit over-worked, Squire Mahon might be prepared to offer . . ."

"Never mind what he might offer," Joseph said. "They are not for sale."

"Oh," Richman said, sniffing. "But the black hunter is? Getting back to the moiling in the soil, delving in the clay, eh? An Irish lord is never far from an Irish peasant, is he?"

"I'll give you Irish peasant, you Sassenach dog," Old Flynn said, bristling and snatching up a turf spade. Over a friendly pint Old Flynn might have passed a remark identical to Richman's, but he was not about to allow an Englishman to insult his lordship to his face.

There was a growl of warning from outside the barn, and Gann's twisted visage appeared. His stout club was in his hand.

"Get that man off my property," Joseph ordered.

"That man is my assistant," Richman replied.

"Mister Richman," Joseph said with stell in his words, "Gann will leave at once, or there will be no horse-tradin' a'tall. I want him outside my gates in one minute."

Eyeing Joseph to see if there would be any weakening in his resolve, Richman finally said, "That will do, Gann. Go out to the road and wait for me there."

Holding the turf spade at his shoulder like the battle-ax of a Celtic warrior, Old Flynn marched to the door of the barn to ensure that Gann obeyed.

"Now as to that dappled mare," Richman said, reasserting his control over the situation, "I can go as high as twelve pounds."

"The price we discussed was twenty, and she is worth twenty-five."

The gloating was back in Richman's eyes. He knew Joseph needed the money and the only possible buyer for horses was Major Mahon. "That animal has some age on her," he said, "and she looks scruffy."

Studying the brushed, curried, and alert-eyed Savina, Joseph almost retorted that Richman could take his twelve pounds and . . . join Gann on the road. Instead he sighed and said, "Fifteen?"

"Twelve," Richman returned firmly. "And that makes one hundred eighty for the lot."

"Less than half their value," Joseph muttered under his breath.

"What was that?"

Unwilling to let the Mahon steward carry a triumphant report back, Joseph said, "Tell the major to take care of these animals. They are the best in the county."

Richman said, "Shall we exchange the money and bills of sale in Castletown? I'll take the livestock today, of course."

"Mister Richman," Joseph replied dryly, "Castletown is fine . . . and we'll exchange money and stock at the same moment, if you please."

The worried voices of Kate and Joseph drifted out from behind the closed door of their bedchamber.

It was nine o'clock when Martin slipped out of the house. There were English patrols out traveling the road in twos and fours, looking for curfew violators and drifters, mostly. For safety's sake, Martin would take the shortcut, skirting Castletown and winding over the knock four miles to Ballynockanor.

It was black as pitch, but Martin needed no torch to light his way back to St. John's. His legs had long ago memorized the path. Kate often joked he could walk the whole long way in his sleep. It was true. Gathering cattle from the high pastures, he knew how many steps it took to travel from one point to the other.

A westerly wind sprang up. Not a cold, cold, wind, but chill enough to make him gather the collar of his greatcoat round his cheeks and tuck his head in defense. On the breeze he could smell the peat fires of Ballynockanor. That and the aroma of bogs and swales and the crisp mint leaves that grew along the Cornamona guided him sure. Even if blindfolded he could find his way home by the scent alone.

Kevin had written of his longing for the smells of home. Now, unless Molly had gone off completely, Kevin was here, waiting, enjoying a noseful of all that was common and familiar.

The thought of Kevin made Martin quicken his uneven stride. One step. Two. Skip, skip, skip.

He was panting when he reached the crest of the hill. Laying a hand on the rough, weathered stone of St. Brigit's cross, he paused, gulped air for a moment, then let gravity speed his way down the slope.

It was near midnight when he reached the stone enclosure surrounding the graves. He tried the gate. It groaned horribly on its hinges. Martin halted, hesitated at the noise, and then remembered that Father O'Bannon was half-deaf and that the wind would make the whole world groan on such a night.

Slipping into the churchyard, he crossed himself and mumbled the Our Father against any evil that might be lurking about the place. His mind raged at Kevin for choosing such a point of rendezvous. Reminding himself the dead hereabouts were of a friendly, neighborly sort did not help. His hair bristled at the crunch of his own footstep.

Down the nettle-choked path past the Watty family plot and the O'Briens' mossy headstone, he approached the place where most of the Donovans lay in a cozy, cluttered patch.

"Kevin!" he whispered hoarsely.

The breeze rattled twigs in the hedge. Leaves in the lone oak tree made a rasping sound. Martin's mouth grew dry. Molly had made the whole thing up, he decided. Sure she had! The old biddy had been prowling the graveyard for years. No doubt she remembered seeing him and Kevin playing leapfrog over the crooked stones and had called it up when she was talking this afternoon.

One more attempt and then Martin would leave.

"Kevin! Don—"

Martin shrieked as a firm hand grasped his shoulder from behind and a broad, calloused hand clamped down over his mouth, muffling the cry.

"Shut up, y'fool!" It was Kevin. Not dead. Not a figment. Same clod as ever. "I'm gonna let you down. It's me. Myself. Kevin. Stop kickin'! Shut up! Will you be quiet if I let go of your face?"

Martin, stifled, nodded desperately. Kevin released his grip, sending Martin to the ground in a fit of coughing. "Kev!" he managed. "Still yourself I see . . ."

Reaching through the inky night, Kevin grabbed his brother up again, holding him close, dripping tears and kisses on his face. "Martin! Martin! Ah me wee Martin! Joseph and Mary, Martin! You've grown a foot!"

Martin's irritation vanished. "You! Sure! Kevin! What are you doin' here!"

"I've come t'Da's grave. T'pay my respects," he said. "Sure, I dare not come in the daylight. I've been longin' so since Kate's letter . . . the trouble . . . damn English murder ol' Da . . . I've had it in my mind to take a few of 'em before I go!"

The two brothers, unable to distinguish the faces of one another, linked arms and moved instinctively toward the headstone that marked the grave of Tom Donovan. As they sat on it, Kevin traced the letters with his fingers until he was convinced that Da was truly gone. He wept a bit more, wiped his nose on his sleeve, and asked questions for an hour as Martin responded with every scrap of news.

"And you see, Kev, there's nothin' here for anyone anymore."

"Beyond the boundary of Burke land the world is ten thousand times more harsh. I see it everywhere," Kevin reported. "I was in hopes things had not gone sour here as well."

"He . . . Joseph . . . he's doin' what can be done. But it's goin' downhill fast. I've been thinkin', wishin', I could join you in America. But you're back. You've come home to nothin' but hunger and despair. Why?"

Kevin spoke of Jane Stone, of what a fool he'd been. Then he said he'd had good fortune in America. He had turned his hand at a thing or two, and perhaps he could help Joseph out.

Cash is what I'm talkin' about, boyo." Kevin clapped Martin on the back. "Here." He hefted a bag of coins into Martin's hand. "Forty pounds and some odd. Just a bit of what . . . well, take it . . . there's plenty more where that came from."

"But Kevin . . . forty pounds. Nearly a year's wages for ten men. Enough to feed ten families. How'll I explain that to Joseph?"

Kevin sat awhile in brooding silence. "Just stash it somewhere. Somewhere where he'll find it sure. Him or Kate. I don't know. In an old boot or a hatbox or . . . think like Molly would think. They'll believe it's a gift from heaven above, they will." He clapped Martin on the back. "We've been here hours. Look. I'll come back."

"When?"

"A month. You know the mossy round stone beside St. Brigit's cross?"

"Aye." Martin knew it. It looked like a ball that had been frozen into granite. There was some legend about it too. Molly could tell it.

"The round mossy stone. I'll turn it when I'm in the neighborhood, like. A signal. At the dark of the moon. Look to it. I'll have a bit to add to the Burke storehouse, I will. But you mustn't tell 'em I've been here. Swear it."

Martin raised his right hand and spoke an oath upon his father's grave the he would not tell where the money came from.

23

Think like Molly?

Martin tucked the money pouch into his trousers as he made his way along the track to the house. Exhilarated by the thought that Kevin would be back with more within the month, Martin fairly flew up and over the hill.

For the first time since the days before the potato mounds had spoiled he felt happy. There would surely be enough. And enough was as good as a feast!

But where to hide the loot so it would be sure to be discovered?

Beneath a loose board in the stair? But there were no loose boards, he reasoned. Could he not make one loose? Well then, would he not be caught prying the thing up?

A list of possibilities cascaded through his mind. Dismissing each as obscure or impossible or foolish, he reached the confines of Burke Park without a solid plan. It occurred to him that he could march into Joseph's office and present the pouch to him as something

Martin found. But Joseph, being Joseph, would want to return the treasure to its rightful owner.

It was nearly dawn when Martin staggered, weary and footsore, up the lane to the house. The soft light in the east cast a pink glow on the windows of Old Flynn's quarters in the stable. Martin heard the nicker of Savina in her stall.

Flynn would have a kettle on for tea. The old man was always up before the sun.

Martin entered the warmth of the barn. The scent of hay and horses was a comfort to him after his night of wandering.

Flynn was at the far end of the stalls, forking hay into the mangers.

"Up early," Flynn greeted him.

Martin did not mention that he was up late. "I could use a cuppa," Martin asked.

"You and every beggar on the road to Dublin," Flynn replied cheerfully. "Me sister in Kerry says the place is crawlin' with 'em."

Martin did not want to hear the report. "Just a bit of tea."

"That's what they say. Tea before food. Well, the English have made us addicted to the stuff, then set the price."

Martin sat on an upturned barrel. "Aye. Terrible, it is."

"The same as happened here with the storage has happened in the North. All of Ulster'll be goin' hungry."

"Sure. So Squire Joseph says. But a cuppa . . ."

"He's sellin off a few of me beauties. The hunter, sure. The carriage. That sweet dappled mare you're s'fond of."

The news jerked Martin awake. He leapt to his feet. "Sellin' Savina?"

"Aye. Keepin' two of the shires for the haulin' and such. But the rest . . ."

"But why?"

"Have y'no eyes t'see, Martin?" The bent man asked sadly, stopping and leaning on the handle of the pitchfork. "Folk is goin' hungry. And here I am, feedin' ten horses. They're me own children, these nags, but I can part with 'em if the Squire says it must be so. He has a point. Aye. And the tack as well. It'll fetch a price in Dublin."

Martin moved through the gloom of the barn. "Is it as bad as that?"

"Aye." Flynn returned to his chores.

Martin hung on the top rail of Savina's stall. She lowered her head for him to stroke her forehead. "Is there nothin' to be done?"

"It's settled. Mahon's man came by yesterday evenin'. Now there's a monster for ye. Turn out his own people and buy horses . . ."

Martin was out the barn door and into the house. He stumbled up the stair and pounded on the door of Joseph and Kate's bedchamber.

"Wha . . .? What is it?"

Furious, Martin threw back the door. Joseph and Kate struggled to sit up. "You're sellin' Savina to Mahon?"

"Aye." Joseph rubbed sleep from his eyes. "I meant to tell you . . ."

"To Mahon!"

"It can't be helped."

"How much?"

"Twelve pounds."

"Twelve pounds!" Martin exclaimed. "She's worth twenty!"

"Aye. But we'll not get that. She's got years on her. And Mahon needs mounts for his men."

"Like equippin' the enemy, it is! The best horse we own."

Kate said imperiously, "We? Martin, where've your manners gone?"

"Sell her to that . . . the devil himself. He's turnin' folk on the roads by the thousand." Martin tried to steady his voice. "Better she dies than belong to the beast."

Joseph tucked his chin in shame. "We need the money, Martin. It can't be helped."

"Better . . . better you shoot her! I'll shoot her myself!" Tears came. He brushed them back. "Look you! It's a shame! Sell her to Mahon! Send her to heaven!"

"There's nothing in a dead horse. We need the cash." Kate backed up Joseph. "It wasn't your decision. Joseph's lettin' his own horse, the black, go as well."

Beaten, Martin glared at them.

"You should've told me. I could get . . . I know a man . . . down the road he is . . . forty pounds he said he'd give for her."

"Forty," Joseph said, startled.

"Aye." Martin raised his chin defiantly. "Forty. Tack and all. He'll ride her away too. Out of Galway. An honorable . . . honorable . . . Irishman."

"Forty pounds?" Kate gasped.

The string of lies rushed from Martin's mouth. "Forty. He's lost his . . . I saw him . . . on the road. He's campin' by the river. Saw him yesterday. A merchant. Irish from America. Needs a horse." His brain was reeling. He could track Kevin if he left now. Find him. Give him Savina to ride.

"Have you signed the bill of sale?" Kate inquired of Joseph.

"No. And Richman lowered the price after he saw her. Broke all bargains, but I thought there was no choice." Joseph pressed his lips together. He narrowed his eyes. "An American?"

"Aye," Martin lied. "He'll be headin' out this mornin'. May be gone. May be. But maybe I can catch him . . . if I ride out now."

Joseph hesitated, then gave a brief nod. "Mahon'll have one less Burke horse in his barn. Go, then."

Savina caught the excitement of her rider. Snorting, she galloped hard from the gates of the estate. Her breath came in steamy bursts. Martin urged her on, reining her off the road and onto the cattle track. Never breaking stride, she flew up the slope of the knock with St. Brigit's cross the destination.

From that high vantage, Martin hoped he could spot Kevin—a solitary traveler headed . . . where?

Martin leapt from the saddle, leaving the horse to stand panting as he clambered up the stone face of the cross. Shading his eyes, he searched the sunlit east as morning shadows stretched to the west.

Martin prayed, "Dear God. Sweet Jesus. Me brother, Lord." But Kevin Donovan was nowhere to be seen.

Beneath him were the charred remains of the Donovan homestead and the rest of the village of Ballynockanor. St. John's glistened white in the morning light. The road was a thin ribbon through the stony fields. But Kevin was nowhere to be seen; he had vanished. Martin should have expected it.

Crestfallen, Martin climbed down from the edifice and remounted Savina. The journey down the slope to St. John's was slow and sorrowful. Martin slapped the pouch of coin at his waist. What was he to do? He had forty pounds, but he also had the horse. Joseph would sell her off to Mahon sure as anything.

Tying Savina to the iron gate of the churchyard, he entered the unlocked church. Father O'Bannon was not about. Martin crossed himself, genuflected, and knelt to pray. The topic was the selling of his horse to the devil. Perhaps the Good Lord would see fit to have Savina toss Mahon or one of his fellows off a precipice or kick an English visitor's head off?

"Well now, Lord, I've got a horse to sell, and no one to sell her to," he said aloud.

From behind the pillar at the front of the church the rumpled figure of Kevin Donovan popped up.

"Martin! Is it you, then? I fell asleep. Fast asleep. Foolish of me. Came in out of the cold and couldn't help myself. Should've been miles down the road by now."

F orty pounds." Martin upended the money pouch onto the dining table in front of Joseph's breakfast of porridge.

Joseph nodded once, gazing at the money with a pained expression on his face.

For an instant Martin thought he saw a hint of moisture in Joseph's eye.

"I'm grateful to you, Martin. For your quick wit."

Martin replied in a steely voice, "She'd not have done well under the spur of any who belong to Mahon."

Joseph raised his eyes to the boy. "This'll pass one day . . . these hard times."

"And so will judgment day come," Martin replied bitterly. "If only I could live to see it."

"Aye. You've a right to be upset. I should've told you."

"Sure. Forty pounds. Will you be keepin' the other land then? With the other horses, it's enough for the provisions?"

Joseph spread his hands in helplessness. "Martin," he said halt-
ingly, "Martin, you couldn't be thinkin' . . ."

"How much is it, then?"

"Eight hundred pounds. Eight hundred pounds will buy enough
to feed only the five hundred who live here in the townlands for one
season."

Martin blinked at him in disbelief. So the sacrifice of Savina and
all the other horses had changed nothing. The highlands would be
sold, and there was an end to it. Five centuries of Burkes had owned
that land. A handful of herding families lived there. What would
come of them?

"What else . . . who else . . . what will you be sellin' to them? Who
will lose their homes? Who sent to the road? Who go hungry here
in the parish?"

"We'll hold onto all we can. Feed all we can."

"It's myself you're blamin' for the spoilage."

"Never. It was the same everywhere."

"Folk'll go hungry. Or you'll sell their homes for the cash. Evict
them same as Mahon done."

"I'm not Christ Almighty, Martin," Joseph said angrily.

"I'll be rememberin' it from now on." The boy clenched his fists.
"I want to leave this place."

"Leave?"

"Go live with Kevin. I want to see my brother."

"America." Joseph inhaled deeply.

"It's Kevin I want to see. The blood of an Irishman runs through
his veins." The implication was clear that Martin considered Joseph's
attitude less than Irish.

Joseph did not respond to the insult. "I need you here."

"Another mouth to feed."

"I need your help."

"I'll not be tossin' my neighbors from their homes."

"No. But there'll be food to distribute. I need you here, Martin."
Joseph motioned to the jumble of coin. "You did well. This'll see
to the feedin' of ten families. Sellin' Savina . . . You did well, Martin."

Martin hung his head, aware of the deception. He could have

given Joseph the forty pounds, and Savina could have gone to Mahon for another twelve. Three more families might have been fed with the extra cash. "Not as well as I might, if the potatoes hadn't . . ."

"I'll hear no more of you blamin' yourself!" Joseph clasped his hand. "Haven't you heard? All was lost in county Tyrone in the North. Kerry and Wicklow and Cord too. A few seed potatoes is what's left. 'Twasn't yourself, Martin. 'Twasn't God that done us up. Just the way of it. And we'll have to do what we can to save all we can."

Martin thought of Kevin, of next month at the dark of the moon. He would have to be here till then, to bring whatever treasure Kevin brought. Then he would leave forever.

Galway City had lost its bustle and vitality. The port city was strangely silent, and many of the businesses were not only closed but shuttered. Within the Church of St. Nicholas off Shop Street, Daniel O'Connell rubbed his hands over the single brazier of glowing peat bricks that struggled vainly against the cold enclosed by the fourteenth-century stones.

"And do y'mean to say you're goin' to patrol the roads, Joseph?" Daniel asked. "I know what you're sayin', about Mahon and others of his ilk castin' their unwanted tenants on your doorstep, but closin' the borders? A drastic step, that. What if Mahon takes it to law over freedom of commerce? He can force you to open the roads."

Joseph disagreed. "I've reviewed it thoroughly. Castletown and Ballynockanor are Burke land over which I have high and low justice. Traffic must go around by Clonbur or Maam. It isn't only the food, Daniel. There's also the sickness to think on."

O'Connell nodded somberly. "And you say none may go out and come back again? Then you're shuttin' yourself in too? We will . . . I will miss your counsel, which I am more in need of than ever."

Attempting to lighten the mood Joseph teased, "And when did you ever need help makin' up your mind, Daniel?"

"Things are changin', leavin' me behind," the aging Liberator admitted. "The fire-breathin' radicals, the Young Irelanders, are harder and harder to contain. Their calls for reform grow so violent they might be Ribbonmen in name as well as attitude." Then, changing subjects, O'Connell said, "You know Peel almost fell?"

"I heard something of it, yes."

"Went so far as to resign because his own party would not back him on the import tax changes. I never thought I'd have a kind word to say for 'Orange' Peel, but cheap grain is what Ireland needs. Anyway, the Whig, Russell, could not form a government, so the queen called Peel back again. He's on shaky ground though. Beyond the one shipment of corn he'll not challenge Trevelyan again."

"Meanin' Trevelyan is in charge of Irish Famine Relief?"

"Meanin' the devil himself has his claw on Ireland's throat! There will be no more corn and precious little help for Ireland. But every time a Young Irelander shouts about fire and sword, they gain another vote for a coercion bill: 'Keep the Irish down.' God help us, as if we could be any more down than we are."

The two men stood and shook hands. O'Connell looked around the carved stone memorials to long-dead Irish chieftains, their marble faces placid despite hacked-off noses and limbs. "Cromwell's men did that," Daniel said, pointing out the wanton vandalism. "Stabled their horses in the nave too. But the Ironsides are not the famous visitors I prefer to think on here."

"No?" asked Joseph. "Then who?"

"Christopher Columbus," O'Connell replied. "He worshipped in this place before sailin' west to discover the New World. Maybe here is where he got his inspiration to go on one more day's sail instead of givin' up too soon. And thanks be to God for it. The best hope for Ireland lies that way instead of east in England."

Outside in the swirling mist that swept off Galway Bay, it was hard not to think about leaving the troubles behind and going to the New World, one in which there was no English law, no Mahon, no Gann, no famine. The carved skull, a momento mori, over the church-yard gateway grinned mockingly at him.

Turning toward the high street and home, Joseph saw a tall young man pass by the intersection. In the midst of his reverie in which politics, hunger, and America were mixed, it took a moment for the observation to penetrate his thoughts. The passerby looked like Kevin Donovan—leaner, harder-looking to be sure, but the same strong features with which Kevin reflected kinship to both his da and to Kate. But it could not be. Kevin was off in that New World, blessings on him.

When Joseph reached the corner of the road, the look-alike had disappeared. Perhaps the attraction of America had presented a greater resemblance than really existed. Joseph dismissed the matter from his mind and mounted the broad back of the shire horse.

The quickest road home from Galway City led through Oughterard and then on to Maam Cross, but Joseph decided to follow instead the older road that lay along the shore of Lough Corrib. It was, he reflected, a peaceful, beautiful scene, and facing the coming confinement, he had need of storing up beauty for remembering later.

The land through which he rode was Mahon property. He gave that no thought until, rounding a bend, he came across the smoldering ruins of a handful of cottages, not only tumbled but burned.

His jaw tightening, Joseph nudged the shire horse into a lumbering trot off the road and into what remained of the village.

A dog lay clubbed to death outside one of the ruins. A heap of stones from a collapsed wall buried a straw doll. Its head and one arm protruded from the crush in mute appeal.

Joseph knew this place: Turlough, it was called, after the renowned twelfth-century Galway king of the same name. A pitiful place it was, of rocky soil, barely clinging to the slope and in constant danger of being swept into the lake. The Turloughers supplemented their farm produce by fishing. As far as Joseph knew, they asked for nothing, expected nothing, and previous landlords had not felt any need to disturb a lifestyle that had not changed in six hundred years . . . till now.

Feeling his rage climbing, Joseph experienced a new determination to see that Ballynockanor never fell into Mahon hands, no matter what the cost. The sound of a horse neighing with fright just beyond the hill added to Joseph's sense of urgency and spurred him toward the outcry.

As he crested the rise, there was Jailor Gann, mounted on Joseph's favorite black hunter. The man, clearly an incompetent rider, was sawing the bit back and forth and bouncing from side to side in the saddle. The confused animal pranced about, hopelessly confused.

As Joseph watched, Gann swung a short club by a leather thong at the top of the black's skull. With a sudden rear and twist, the horse unseated Gann, dumping him across a heap of stones. The hunter, spirited but trying to please, stood as he had been taught and allowed Gann to catch up the bridle.

With one fist seizing a double-handful of reins, Gann proceeded to beat the defenseless black with his club, across the nose and alongside the ears. No matter how much the horse bucked and struggled, Gann continued to yank down on its head and pummel it with the stick.

The next moment Joseph was thundering down the incline, the placid shire horse absorbing his rider's emotion. From a few feet away, Joseph dove over the wither straight at Gann.

The thug turned at the instant of Joseph's leap, so Joseph's shoulder hit the man in the chest, knocking him to the ground under the black. The hunter, yanking free of Gann's grasp, stomped on his midsection twice before plunging away.

Then Joseph was on top of Gann, pinning the man down. With both fists flailing, Joseph landed blow after unanswered blow on Gann's nose, forehead, and chin. Cringing and begging for Joseph to stop, Gann drew his hands up to cover his face and rolled about in an attempt to dislodge the attacker.

But Squire Burke would not be pried loose. When his strokes bounced harmlessly off Gann's clenched fists, Joseph transferred his aim to chest and belly. All the harbored resentment of mistreatment during his imprisonment and onboard the transport ship surfaced at once at Gann's abuse of the protectionless black hunter.

At last Joseph stopped, not because his anger was exhausted, but because his knuckles were swollen and bruised, and each blow caused pains to shoot along his arms.

Getting up, Joseph walked away from the blubbering Gann without looking back. Speaking quietly to the nervous black, Joseph's familiar voice calmed the animal as he removed the reins and the saddle and dumped them on the ground. Slapping the hunter on the rump, he shouted, "Go on with you! Get away, go!"

Then Joseph retrieved the unperturbed shire horse, which had grazed among the rocks throughout the struggle, remounted, and rode off toward home.

24

Joseph grunted with exertion as he heaved at rocks too big for him to lift.

It was one of the same stones that the English troops had used to imprison the smallpox sufferers of the Burke townlands, the same stones across which Kate's father had been shot to death. Panting with the effort, Joseph stopped and contemplated the boulder. Perhaps it was on this very rock that a soldier who had fired one of the fatal bullets had leaned.

The choice of this exact spot on the road west to construct the barricade made perfect sense, because the embankment met up with the stone walls enclosing the fields on either side. The ramparts were thus complete.

On the other side of Castletown, Joseph knew, a similar scene was being enacted, and he could have been there, supervising that construction, or at the one up the Ballynockanor road that led over the mountains. The Castletown folk and the villagers understood the need. They went willingly to the task of locking the door against starvation and disease and applauded Joseph's courageous decision.

But instead of going where it was easier, Joseph had chosen to assist in the building at this grief- and anger-laden spot. He had a sense of a duty he would not shirk, even though Martin eyed him with suspicion and Mary Elizabeth gave him no more than a glance in passing before looking away. They did not understand, of course. How could they? Joseph himself did not comprehend how he had been reduced to this pass. Two years before he had been a leader in the movement to unite Ireland into a single nation; now he was a tribal chieftain again and nothing more.

One of the Claddagh Brothers—Simeon it was—came up beside him to help roll the stone into place.

Unbidden, Simeon began to speak as if in reply to Joseph's thoughts: "Sure, and there came a time when Noah had to draw in the gangplank, Squire," he said. "It did not mean he was a cruel man, nor a hard-hearted one. But when the rain beat down and the fountains of the deep were loosed, it was those inside who were saved. I'll speak to Martin and Mary Elizabeth about it."

The Burke townlands were bounded at their southern extremity by Lough Corrib, so there was no threat of invasion from that direction. The north likewise posed no terrible worry because of the mountains that lay between Ballynockanor and the O'Shea lands over the border in County Mayo. Sonny-boy undertook to keep a watch on the high pass. He could go for help in the village if needed.

In the direction of the setting sun lay the wilds of Connemara and beyond that, the sea, but the Galway City road also ran that way and required attention. Just west of Burke Park, at the embankment rebuilt by Joseph, Simeon had his station, aided by Rusty and Moor and Martin.

It was from the east that the largest number of travelers could be expected. That way led to the populations of Roscommon and Sligo, and also to the remaining Mahon villages that everyone expected to be the first to be tossed.

Outside of Castletown, where the delta of the Cornamona spread out into impassable marsh, the guards assumed their position.

Charlie Nesbitt, together with Paddy O'Flaherty and the fiddler, O'Rourke, took turns at that location. The road was blocked with stones, and a pair of wagons rolled across it. Watch was kept from the tower in the town center and an alarm bell rang when men approached, just as if there were a fire. Up to the gorge of the Cornamona and down to the marsh, the stone walls of the fields formed a continuous barricade.

Every rampart had a regular rotation of villagers assigned to it. No man or boy over sixteen years in Ballynockanor or Castletown was excused from duty unless aged or infirm.

Joseph distributed fowling pieces to each of the three ramparts, reserving one for himself, but he only allowed the Claddagh men or Nesbitt to handle them. Joseph inspected the Castletown barrier and delivered the muzzle-loading weapon to Nesbitt himself. "You know that this is for show," he cautioned. "I want no shootin'.' "

Nesbitt acknowledged the order. "Understood, Squire," he said. "It makes us look shipshape, like."

Kate and Margaret, aided by Widow Clooney and other womenfolk of the townlands, put up meals for the men on watch: cold boiled potatoes and soda bread.

On its first day of operation, the Castletown barricade turned away three families who were on their way from Ballinrobe to Westport: three men, four women, and eight children. All were adequately dressed and did not seem haggard. "Will you give us the road, then?" the leader of the group asked. "The landlord gave us a choice: take the passage money offered and go to America, or stay behind and starve. Is that really a choice then, I ask you?"

With Joseph watching, Charlie Nesbitt cleared his throat and said, "It is not. But all the same, you'll have to go back and go 'round by Cong, for you cannot come through here. It'll not put you more than a day out of your way."

"Can you give us food then?" was the next question. "We've only what we can carry and precious little it is."

Nesbitt swallowed hard, looked at Joseph, and then said, "No, I'm sorry, but no. We have no food to spare. You may rest awhile by the river, but then you have to move on."

Three hours later Nesbitt was standing next to Moor at the rampart when his stomach growled. As if answering, Moor's insides likewise complained of emptiness. "Did I not see you get your meal from Lady Burke some time ago?" Nesbitt asked, looking slyly at his companion.

"You did," Moor said, returning a knowing look. "And three potatoes and a loaf of bread was not enough for you either, it seems. Or could it be that yours went the same way as mine?"

"Yes," Nesbitt acknowledged. "But I'll not be sendin' more food toward Cong unless they return the favor."

Throughout the morning, Corrie and Ceili crouched in the hedge waiting. At last the brawny, dark fellow in the rough tweed cloak took his leave of the boy sitting on the blockade.

"May we go now? The boy'll give us somethin'," Ceili asked. Her once-clear eyes were sunken and rimmed with red. Lips that had readily smiled and sung the old songs beside the hearth were cracked, crusted, and swollen.

"Wait awhile," Corrie said. "See if the ugly man comes back. He'll run us off the place sure if he catches us." Adults were always more fierce than the young ones, Corrie had learned.

"But the boy . . . will he not? See. He's got a gun. Like the English."

"He's no Englishman. I know this boy," Corrie replied.

"Know him?"

"Aye." Corrie was certain of his identity, though she did not know his name. "The mornin' after Mother passed . . . the baby . . . I followed . . . remember?"

"Followed?" Ceili could not understand what her sister was saying.

Did she not remember the story of the boy who had ridden away with the newborn in his arms? "The limp it is which makes me certain. Kind eyes. Gave me the shillin'. He's got a heart, sure. Such as himself, he'll not be turnin' us . . . sisters of the wee baby girl . . . turnin' us away."

Touching Ceili on the shoulder, she started to rise from their concealment, but the clattering of coach wheels made her draw back.

Martin rested upon the stones of the barricade while Simeon patrolled two miles along the length of the estate wall and then back to the post again. At midmorning the Galway mailcoach arrived, halting outside the heap of boundary stones.

Jack the coachman blasted the bugle, hung a leather pouch of newspapers and correspondence upon the signpost, and retrieved a bag of Joseph's outgoing mail. With a wave to Martin, he backed the team, turned the coach, and drove away.

As the rattle of iron wheels diminished, Martin jumped from the barricade onto the road and retrieved the mailpouch.

Joseph had been waiting a week for news from the outside, for letters from O'Connell and information of the spread of the potato blight and the epidemic of fever that accompanied the malnourishment. Was there any word about possible government relief?

Clambering back onto the barricade, Martin opened the flap and peered inside. There were four newspapers and an assortment of letters. Martin dared not take the bundle to Joseph until Simeon returned to keep watch on the road.

Carefully lifting the top newspaper from the bundle, Martin half-removed it to read the columns.

"Plague Nearly Universal." "Potato Blight Much Worse Than Expected." "Storage Opened to Find Complete Loss." "Many to Starve by Spring."

This was nothing new.

Where was a plan to help? A way to feed the people left with nothing?

Martin thought of the late nights Joseph had remained in his study, pouring out requests for aid for the west counties to London and the authorities in Dublin Castle. What use was all that when the government simply considered the suffering of Ireland an act of God and a boon to commerce?

Ireland without the Irish!

He bitterly crammed the sheet back into the bag.

Mary Elizabeth called from twenty yards away. "Is that the mail then?"

"Aye," he responded.

"Joseph was hopin'." She jogged to the barricade. "I brought you and Simeon a bite to eat. Biscuits and a jug of tea." She passed a basket to him, then climbed up after.

Her face blanched as she glanced beyond him up the road. "Who are they, then?"

"Who?" Martin whirled around, expecting to see a gang of vagrants.

Two thin girls, ragged like scarecrows, stood staring from the heap of warning stones. They neither spoke nor moved, but clutching hands, they simply looked at Martin and Mary Elizabeth with weary eyes.

"What do they want?" Mary Elizabeth said.

"You know what they want," Martin replied, depositing his lunch basket on an outcropping of rocks out of view of the hungry urchins. He picked up the fowling piece and cradled it across his lap. "There's likely a whole tribe of their kin lurkin' in the hedge, waitin' for us to . . ." He frowned and called out to them, "Get on with you. This here's Burke townland. Nobody who ain't from our parish may enter."

They did not budge or speak. Their clothes were rags, tied together. They had no coats. Their feet were naked.

Mary Elizabeth lowered her eyes in shame. "The smaller one there, she's not older than myself."

"And you'll be no older than herself if we open the gates to feed such as her," Martin retorted. But the tug of pity was strong in him, churning his insides, causing him to feel angry at them for being in such a pathetic state.

A silent standoff ensued for the next half-hour. Martin would not eat while they were there watching. Mary Elizabeth would not leave. They would not go away. Nor did they attempt to come closer.

Simeon, his cheeks ruddy from the brisk walk along the border, leaned against the barrier, rested his arms on the top, and studied the two interlopers on the far side. His eyes blazed like fire.

"They haven't tried to come in," Martin said, feeling ashamed that he had not driven them away, that he did not have the stomach for it.

Simeon said in the Gaelic, "They will not try."

"What'll we do then?" Martin asked.

Mary Elizabeth added, "I've brought lunch for you."

Simeon, never taking his eye from the sisters, said, "I will not be eatin' today."

Martin understood him. "Nor I." His brow creased with concern. If they broke the rules for some, would not others come? "What if they have family . . . others . . . waitin' in the hedge there?"

"There is none but these two. I saw them comin'. They came alone upon the road. Came to see you, Martin, though you cannot know why for a time. A rare beauty, that one." He inclined his head toward the tallest of the two girls. "Fair hair. Ivory skin. The image of St. Brigit, is she. Pure of heart was Brigit. And this one. Descended from the kings of Ireland. Nobility. See it there upon her brow? Brought into the dust by those who cannot know who we Irish be. Or how we fought the pagan hordes to carry the name of Christ from our shores to all the world. Look to her, Martin—she, still beautiful in her poverty. Martin, she is your nation and your tribe and your life."

"But . . . what should we do?"

Simeon turned his searching gaze on Martin. "I cannot tell you. We brothers of Claddagh stand guard upon the house of Burke. The promise was given. No plague is permitted to come near this dwelling. We cannot speak for those who come to this haven and must be turned away. What does your heart tell you?"

Mary Elizabeth was already taking off her cloak.

Martin followed her example, stripping down to the knit sweater and moleskin trousers. "I have another coat in the house."

Simeon, who had never smiled once, let his thick lips curve upward as he swung around and walked briskly back along the border.

Martin waited until he disappeared over a low hill.

Cupping his hands, he called out to the sisters. "Come ten paces."

The fair-haired girl tugged her brown-haired sister forward then halted.

Martin climbed down the rugged stone face of the blockade. Mary Elizabeth passed him the food basket and their outer garments. These he gathered and carried toward the girls.

"There's fear of the plague here. I can't let you in. Tell no one," he instructed, then hesitated. "Have I not? I've seen you before."

"Aye." The tall girl nodded.

"Where?"

She did not answer at first, but eyed the greatcoat and then the boot of his lame leg. At last she said in the Irish, "The baby girl. She is well, sir?"

"You!" He started to reach out. "That day by the river . . . Aye! The baby. Rosie's her name . . . She's well."

She drew back from him.

Lowering her chin slightly in acknowledgment, the girl gathered the gifts, passing the heavy cloak to her sister and donning Martin's greatcoat. She asked for nothing more. Not refuge. Not even shelter for the night. Not for a shilling or a penny. Crossing herself, she bowed to Martin. "Rosie, is it?" she repeated, smiling gently. "Meself and me sisters . . . we owe our lives to you from this day onward. May I live if only one day to repay the debt. Long life to you, sir. God's blessin' upon your head, sir. The mercy and peace of Christ upon all in this place."

With that she took up the basket, linked her arm with that of her sister, and turned back along the highway to Galway.

∾ 25 ∾

It was a mercy, Joe Watty said, and no one disagreed with him, that the hardest winter since '28 had come to Galway. Looking out the tavern window at the swirling snowflakes that were already accumulating on the ground, Watty said, "This'll block the road better than any stones or bricks or guards. If the highways can't be traveled, there will be no one to be turned back."

This sentiment was almost universal in Castletown and Ballynockanor. Though no one had shirked their duty, no one liked to look into the faces of women and children and tell them there was no shelter and no food to be had, to move on.

So when the gales blew down from the Seven Bens and clogged the passes with snow, when the mailcoach could not travel and what few letters there were came by horseback, when days passed and the flood of homeless and hungry slowed to a trickle and then stopped altogether, no one complained about the cold or the damp.

It was also a mercy, some said, that the flow of news from the outside had dried up. The last reports were of food riots in Cork and Skibbereen, of bodies found by the roadside with no mark upon them but the skeletal touch of the Reaper, and worst of all, of illnesses, sweeping across the land like the snows.

"Fevers," most of them were called, typhus and blackwater and recurring. A village that went to bed whole could wake up decimated, and in days be deserted of all but the dying. Castletown and Ballynockanor, remembering the smallpox, collectively shuddered.

It was a mercy that the snows closed the highways. "Amen to that," said Joe Watty. "And may they stay closed till spring."

The spectral form that appeared at Castletown out of the howling blizzard was too nearly frozen to cry out.

With the north wind that swept down the ravine of the Cornamona piling the snow eight feet high above the stone walls, most of those on sentry duty had retreated inside Joe Watty's tavern.

Only Charlie Nesbitt, faithful to the letter of Joseph's instruction, still patrolled the rampart, stamping his feet and pounding his hands on his biceps to keep from freezing.

When he first saw the dark patch lying on the road to Ballynockanor, he did not know what it was. It was as though a freakish blast of the storm had tossed a bundle of rags onto the midst of the otherwise blank expanse. Then as Charlie wiped the snowflakes from his lids and shaded his eyes against the gale, he saw the bundle reach out an imploring hand.

Tossing down the fowling piece and leaping over snowdrifts, Nesbitt ran to the now-motionless form. The man seemed to weigh no more than the thin black cloth that barely enclosed him. Scooping him up, Nesbitt slipped and skated back to the lights and into the embracing warmth of Watty's.

The ale was long since gone, but those men gathered around the big center table shouted with dismay when Nesbitt knocked O'Rourke aside, pushed Rusty out of the way, and sent their mugs of tea crashing to the floor.

"What's?" Watty demanded as Nesbitt deposited a load of something in the center of the table, then "Holy Mother of God!"

It was Father O'Bannon.

Rusty and Moor chafed O'Bannon's hands and feet while Watty spooned tea into his bloodless lips.

The good priest's life flickered like a candle. His eyelids twitched, but his heartbeat was so fluttery and ragged as to be impossible to count. It was some time before they knew if they were gaining any ground or merely watching for his last breath.

O'Bannon's first words, when he could speak at all, were not for himself. "Widow Clooney . . . fires out . . . sick. Roofs . . . children . . . others too. Must bring in . . ."

The words were garbled and halting, but the meaning was clear: Ballynockanor was not proof against the worst winter in living memory. The villagers, as many as remained alive, would have to be rescued.

The relief expedition undertaken by the residents of Castletown on behalf of their Ballynockanor brothers and sisters took on the flurry and vigor of a holy war, a fervent crusade. It was as if the pent-up guilt at having turned away so many strangers at the gates needed to be assuaged in one massive outpouring of energetic redemption.

Mounted on one of the shire horses, Joseph led the way through the drifts. On a sledge hitched behind the animal perched Martin and a heap of blankets, turf spades, and sacks of cracked corn. Behind Joseph, guiding another similarly loaded draft animal, was Charlie Nesbitt.

There was a break in the storm, and the passage of the sledges broke enough of a trail through the mounds of snow for others to follow on foot.

It was a hard pull up the hillside out of the river valley and across the slope toward Ballynockanor . . . or where Ballynockanor was supposed to be.

The roof of the chapel had collapsed inward, and Father O'Bannon's cottage could not even be seen for the heaped-up snow.

But it was the disappearance of Widow Clooney's place that gave Joseph the most concern. From the churchyard he should have been able to see her rebuilt cabin just below the crest of the next hill across the way.

It was Martin who voiced the thought. "Clooney's place is altogether gone. Vanished. Can they still be alive under that?"

While other rescuers dispersed around the village to dig out other homes, it took Joseph and Martin two more hours to traverse the intervening valley. The sun was already sinking behind the Maumturks, and the icy fingers of another threatening blizzard raised gooseflesh on their necks. Only the barest stub of a Clooney chimney protruded from the snowbank; no welcoming curl of smoke showed above it.

Fearing the worst, Joseph instructed Martin to wait with the shire horse.

The boy refused, and the two used turf spades to dig into the wet hillock above the remembered doorway. No sounds came from within.

When they reached the door at last, Joseph found that it hung crookedly from one hinge, the gap filled with untrodden snow. Putting his shoulder against it, he forced his way in, expecting to find twelve frozen corpses inside.

Instead the tumbled interior was as devoid of life as the windswept plain outside. "Where?"

"Joseph!" Martin called urgently from the shoveled out-ramp of ice. "Look there!"

The youth pointed toward the further hill, toward the furthest extent of Ballynockanor, toward where the Donovan home had been before cottage and barn had been burned. There, where no one could possibly be living, winked a small, orange glow against the lengthening shadows.

Widow Clooney answered their halloo in a shaky but resonant voice. "We are here, and praise God we are alive!"

Three of her children were ill with the fever and all of them starving, but none had perished. "When our roof fell in, we came straight here," she said. "We found a way into the cellar below the collapsed dairy barn, and we've been burnin' cow chips from the manure pile ever since. Sure, and it don't smell as nice as good turf brick, but with so many of us crammed in, a fire warms the place."

By the time the snow flurries came again, all of Ballynockanor had been removed to the stables at Burke Park. Not one of them had been lost.

"Travail has come upon Ireland, and the eyes have all gone dark . . ." Mad Molly's dirge never changed. A people better fed might have had the energy to be irritated at her gloomy refrain, but the refugees of the Burke townlands were too beaten down to care about a mad woman's litany of nonsense. The more immediate concern was food.

The former residents of Ballynockanor not only lived in Joseph's barn and outbuildings, but they looked to him to feed them as well. It was no longer possible to snare rabbits, and the ducks had long since left for more hospitable climes. The stores of Indian corn were shrinking, as was the meager supply of sound potatoes.

There remained the seed potatoes, purchased with almost the last cash Joseph could scrape together and kept in a locked and guarded cellar. Joseph stood on the entry steps leading down into the cold but dry space. "Thank the Lord these have not taken the blight," he said to Charlie Nesbitt. "It must be because they are not from around here. Golden Wonder, they are, and rightly named, it seems. Connaught folk always plant Kerr's Pinks because they say the Goldens bust up in the boilin'. No one will mind that now, I imagine."

Nesbitt frowned and wove his fingers together behind his back, a habit learned as a midshipman. "But if we eat the seed potatoes, what happens next fall?"

Prancing up and down the steps between the two men, Molly Fahey sang, "The eyes of the Lord are on the righteous, and His ear is attentive to their cry . . . sure, and we've cried a'plenty, and the eyes have all gone dark . . ."

Gently Joseph and Nesbitt grasped her elbows and hoisted her insignificant weight out of the way without even interrupting the discussion.

"I have fought this off as long as I could," Joseph said. "But how can we worry about next autumn if we cannot live past spring?"

"It's the eyes," Molly said with a note of exasperation in her chant.

"Of course it is, Molly," Joseph replied, for the first time letting irritation with her creep into his voice. Joseph waved his hand over the cellar. "The news from outside reports that people are fightin' over scraps . . . for a one cut-up bit of potato no bigger than your thumb. I want the guard doubled outside this door, Charlie. We cannot chance . . ."

A thunderstruck expression illuminated on Joseph's face like a flash of lightning on the heights of Ben Levy. "What is it, Squire? Are you taken ill?"

"No!" Joseph fairly shouted. "It's the eyes! That's the answer. No bigger than your thumb!" And he laughed.

Nesbitt looked from the jubilant Joseph to an enthusiastically nodding Molly. Perhaps madness was contagious. The look on Nesbitt's face told Joseph of an inner debate: Would the squire come along quietly even though he had, poor soul, lost his wits?

Controlling his outburst, Joseph said, "It's all right, Charlie! I'm not suddenly fey, though I should have the label 'simpleton' branded on my forehead."

"Oh?"

"You are a seafarin' man and so excused, but I am supposed to know these things. Look here," he instructed, stooping to grab a fist-sized Golden Wonder. "See . . . five, six, seven . . . seven eyes on this one potato. Planted, every one will send up a shoot."

Nesbitt looked torn between humoring his master and going for help.

"Jefferson's work on farmin'," Joseph said. "He says plantin' the eyes together with a cut-out piece the size of your thumb grows a healthy stalk."

Comprehension dawned. "And the rest of the prattie . . ."

"Can be eaten! That's the answer. Potatoes to feed us and to plant for the next crop both."

And Molly clapped her hands as she sang, "The eyes have all gone dark!"

PART III

"*The Water is wide—I cannot cross o'er*
And neither have I wings to fly
Give me a boat that can carry two,
And both shall cross my love and I . . ."

—Traditional folk melody

26

The summer of 1846 began with hope and ended in despair.
Across the breadth of Ireland, gentle April rains revived the blighted
fields, and the May sun warmed the land so the June crops flourished. Villagers congratulated themselves. There had only been seed
potatoes enough to plant half the usual acreage, but the dark green
vines grew so thick that people spoke of an overwhelmingly plen-
teous crop—a banner year, the fat year after the lean instead of the
other way around.

In the Burke townlands Joseph watched the baby apple trees bud,
sprout leaves, and go into blossom. But mostly he studied the cal-
endar and the fields burgeoning with the creepers that foretold a
bountiful harvest of Golden Wonders under the soil.

The refugees from Ballynockanor moved back to their village and
started the labor of repairing their roofs and cutting turf to dry
against the next winter season. There was even talk of devoting a
week of thanksgiving to restoring the Church of St. John, after the
harvest was in of course.

As the twenty-third of July approached, Joseph and Kate held their breath and prayed clear through the anniversary of the blight.

No freakish storm lit the summer sky, and no sinister fog descended from the heights.

The *Gardeners' Chronicle* did report a few cases of potato blight, but called the number "insignificant." It suggested that accounts of renewed plague were exaggerated with "every blemished potato being turned into a fresh outbreak of the disease."

Things looked so improved that Trevelyan wrote an order directing all supplies of relief provisions, all public works projects, be shut down by August 15.

Of course there were thousands of evicted homeless wandering the land, and fever continued to stalk the places where they congregated, so the Burke lands remained isolated and guarded, though the mood at Watty's Tavern turned against it.

Then came the morning of the first of August.

Joseph and Kate slept with their bedroom windows open to cool the upper chambers after the heat of the day. They awoke to the sound of Tomeen retching in the chamber pot beside his cot. "I be'd sick," he said between gags. "It stinks, Mama!"

And it did. The unmistakable stench of rotting vegetation permeated every bit of the hall.

Joseph clad in his nightshirt, dashed outside, praying for a different explanation than what he feared.

Beside the stone wall he encountered Nesbitt and Old Flynn. Flynn was weeping, as if he had lost a dear friend. Nesbitt said nothing and merely turned from watching Joseph's approach to facing the field again. Where healthy potato vines had curled the night before, there remained nothing but withered, drooping leaves.

"Like a fire passed over this place," Joseph said, his head sagging onto his chest.

The catastrophe was universal. From Clontarf to Castlebar, from Skibbereen to Sligo, the entire potato crop of 1846 was lost. Kerr's Pinks or Golden Wonders made no difference to the outcome.

After the closing of the government soup kitchens in Galway City, Corrie and Ceili followed the human scavengers down to the seashore to look for food. As the icy water of the Atlantic lapped their legs, Corrie and Ceili picked through the rocks beneath the surface in search of mussels. Most of the edible shellfish had been discovered and devoured. But each day, every day, the sisters found something clinging to the underside of a rock or growing on the pilings or the jetty.

October 1846 brought storm after storm to the West. Each big blow deposited the edible varieties of seaweed known as *dulse* and *carragheen* upon the sand. When tempests churned the sea to a roiling froth, making the quest for nourishment from the sea impossible, the two sisters picked nettles, sorrel, and charlock, common weeds growing in the cemetery beside the Church of St. Nicholas. There was nourishment in such things, Corrie had learned from her mother. But though they remained alive, their flesh melted away.

As the sisters scavenged, daily burials took place within yards of them. There were no coffins, and, like the dead of the workhouse, common folk shared a common grave and a dusting of quicklime to speed them on their way. There were no wakes anymore. No one keened as they had in bygone days. There were too many dying lately to mourn.

At night Corrie and Ceili slept among a hundred strangers, crowded beneath the Spanish Arch across from Claddagh Quay. Beneath the noses of these starving folk, the produce of Ireland was loaded onto ships and carried away to feed the English.

There were times in the dead of night when Corrie rose from their communal bed to sit alone and stare at the ships. Guards patrolled the quay. Smoking their long clay pipes, they joked and talked together, leaving the dock and the gangplanks and the decks of the ships unwatched.

It was the carelessness of the guards that gave Corrie hope when other children her age simply gave up and died.

"Maybe me and Ceili can sneak past them fellows," she prayed. "Maybe, God, your Honor, you can make them look t'other way while we two sneak on board and then . . . to America with us!"

❀

Hand in hand, Joseph and Kate stood beside the cross of St. Brigit. Below them lay spread the remains of Ballynockanor, the dip of the river valley, and the sweep of the land away west toward Burke Park. The sun was just dipping below the Maumturk mountains.

"It's very beautiful this day," Kate said softly.

"That it is," agreed Joseph. His words carried conviction, but not force, like a single, perfectly clear note of music dying away in the air.

"And romantic," Kate added, linking her arm with his.

He nodded without speaking.

"But you did not bring me out here to speak of beauty or romance, did you, Joseph?"

"I did not," he admitted. "I brought you here to say the hardest words I have ever spoken."

"Say them quickly then, for until you do you carry the burden alone."

"We must leave this place," he said. "The apple trees we planted must feed the grandchildren of others. The failure of the second crop has done for us. For a time I thought we might muddle through, but I see it cannot be. The cost of supplies for another year is more than four thousand pounds. There is not so much money in Galway, let alone in the pockets of the Burkes."

Letting her eyes drop to the collapsed shell of the Church of St. John, she studied the graveyard awhile, especially the graves of her dear ones: Mother, Da, sister, and infant son, and the rest. But when she spoke it was of the living. "You cannot mean we will let our people fend for themselves?"

"No," he said quickly. "Never that! You and I could live on in Ireland if we did that, but I would never view my reflection again without shame. No, I mean to sell it to Mahon, and even though he will only pay two thousand pounds, it is enough to take all of us . . ." He swept his hand over the whole country between the river and the mountains. ". . . To take us to America. Unless . . ." His voice faltered.

"Unless what?"

"Unless you will hate me for giving up. But I tell you, Kate, I do not see what else there is to do."

Kate squeezed Joseph's arm and made him look into her eyes. "I think you are the noblest man in the world," she said. "I think wherever I go, however we live, as long as I have you, I am content. It will be hard to say good-bye, but this place is not Ballynockanor any longer. It is on our hearts." She pointed at the graves. "And even those we leave here for a time go with us in you and me and Tomeen and Rosie. We are the life of the land," she said. "Not the soil. It never was."

It was late, and the only two voices in the Great Hall of the Burkes belonged to Joseph and Charlie Nesbitt. "Sorry to keep you up late," Joseph apologized.

"It's no bother, Squire," Nesbitt returned. "Since givin' up the sea, I still cannot sleep more than four hours without wonderin' why my watch has not been called on deck."

Joseph nodded at this bit of information. "It is your experience in the navy that decided me to call on you," he said. "That, and the fact I can trust you completely."

Nesbitt stood at attention, his feet braced wide apart, leaning forward slightly, as if on a quarterdeck in a tossing ocean. "You can count on me, Squire," he affirmed.

"Here it is, then. We have lost the struggle to hang on to Burke land and to keep our people fed. I have decided to sell the lease, and there is no other buyer in sight than Major Denis Mahon."

Nesbitt scowled at the name but said nothing.

"I have also decided to take everyone . . . all five hundred of us . . . to America," Joseph continued. "We'll need to charter a ship. It must be seaworthy and the captain reliable. We have only two thousand pounds with which to bargain. Now you see this must be kept dark until it is accomplished."

Tumbling instantly to the reasons for secrecy, Nesbitt said, "Indeed I do! The people would panic, likely riot. A man facin' an amputation must be told at that moment that only if he has the operation, will he live. And too, we must never let the enemy know how weak we are . . ."

"Or Mahon might go back on the agreed price in favor of lettin' us starve," Joseph concluded. "Galway City tomorrow, then. And with the blessin' we will get everything concluded soon. But till then, no word to anyone else."

"Aye, aye, mum, it is."

It took Charlie Nesbitt no time to locate ships willing to carry a load of paying passengers to America. Captains who commanded loads of cotton or tobacco bound for England could scarcely afford to take their vessels back to the New World in ballast, so turned to human cargo if nothing else presented itself. The question was, how to find the right man and the right ship?

Already there were the horror stories: Irish emigrants crammed eight across into space enough for two. Foul drinking water, moldy provisions, damp, unclean conditions: these added up to disease and death on ships like the *Elizabeth and Sara*, which had sailed from Killala in July. Her manifest showed two hundred twelve souls, but she actually carried sixty more than that. Instead of twelve thousand gallons of drinking water, she had half that amount, and it brackish and leaking from unsound casks. None of the promised provisions were ever distributed . . . none. Forty-two people died on the voyage, fifty more of the fever after the ship docked in Canada. It was said that most of the passengers were farmers evicted from Mahon lands.

Some were already calling these floating dungeons "coffin ships."

Nesbitt caught sight of a former shipmate, bosun of a navy frigate on which Nesbitt had served and now, minus a leg in a shipboard accident, keeper of the channel entry lights at Galway City harbor. "Ahoy, Buckland," Nesbitt called.

"Why, it's Lieutenant Nesbitt!" the man exclaimed with enthusiasm at the reacquaintance. "How are you, sir?"

"Tolerable, Buckland, tolerable."

After an exchange of pleasantries and a discussion of how many cargos of cattle and hogs continued leaving Irish shores for English tables, Nesbitt asked about passenger-carrying vessels.

"Some terrible doin's," Buckland said, understanding the concern. "Unseaworthy tubs skippered by them as would have been flogged out of any proper service. For my money, sir," the former bosun offered, "there's not but one choice if you want to see your people come safe to harbor. What you want is a coffin ship."

Nesbitt looked at the bell buoy clanging in the channel and wondered what word Buckland had actually spoken. "Come again, bosun? It sounded like you said *a coffin ship*."

"That's right, sir. And won't cost you near as much as them others, neither."

"Buckland," Nesbitt persisted, "are you feelin' well? Do you ever have fever from the leg wound?"

"What? I'm fine, sir. Coffin ships is what you want. Himself is in port aboard the *Nantucket* right now."

"Who is?"

"Haven't I been tryin' to tell you, sir? Nathaniel Coffin. He's skipper and owner of the sweetest sailin' ships out of New England."

Captain Coffin was easily located and certainly remembered Joseph Connor Burke. Within a half hour the deal was struck, and Nesbitt was on his way back to report success.

The meeting Joseph held to announce the sale of Burke lands to Mahon was too large to be held anywhere except in the Castletown market square. The city center was packed and buzzing with rumor and anticipation.

Joseph stood on a wagonbed for his speaking platform and wished again that he had Daniel O'Connell's eloquence when it came to swaying crowds. Better yet, it would be nice if Daniel himself could be present and do the talking for Joseph.

As Charlie Nesbitt called the third time for attention Joseph looked over the faces in the crowd, many of them people he had known his whole life: Father O'Bannon, Joe Watty, Old Flynn, the blind piper, O'Brien . . . they were Ireland and Connaught and Galway . . . good men. Molly Fahey and Widow Clooney and Mrs. O'Shaunessy, all looked up expectantly to hear what he had to say.

And then it was time.

"You know how things stand with Ireland," he began. "Especially here in the West."

"Because the English, God rot 'em, want us to starve," someone shouted.

There was a rumble of agreement in the crowd, and Joseph feared a riot might develop before his eyes. "Daniel O'Connell said . . ." The throng stilled again at the invocation of the Liberator's name. "O'Connell said from the beginnin' that we must look to our own . . . that we must do for ourselves. And so we have done these many months past. You have borne the hardships patiently without complainin'."

"Much!" Molly yelled, to the delight and laughter of the crowd.

"Aye, Molly," Joseph acknowledged. "Not much. And you have done what has been asked of you to keep this valley safe through perilous times." There was much head-wagging at this as memories of the barricades and the awful winter came forcefully to the minds of all. "But," Joseph said with a sigh, "it is not enough."

"Let's take what we need from Mahon and the rest!" a strident voice shouted hoarsely.

"You know that is just what they want," Joseph said. "An excuse to shoot us down or carry us off to Australia." The crowd murmured its concurrence; everyone there knew Joseph himself had been victim of such a plot. "But in a manner of speakin', we *will* take what we need from Mahon," he continued, then hurried on over the renewed buzz. "There is a ship . . . *Nantucket* is her name. She will carry to America all who want to leave. There will be enough money over to give each family a bit of a start in the New World."

"You're sellin' out to Mahon?" O'Flaherty yelped in disbelief.

This was the crucial moment. "Yes," Joseph said. "But not sellin' you out. Kate and I and our family will be goin', makin' a new life, same as you, givin' up our home, same as you. But here's the way of it: in America you can own land, farms, businesses. A man can make somethin' of himself. We can worship in our own way, and there is no state church to tell us we cannot, no state church demandin' tithes, no government teachin' our children that their grandfathers are savages and their fathers drunkards. I won't lie to you. The way ahead is hard, and we've all had letters from kin over there sayin' the old hatreds die hard. But to stay here means it is we who will die, yes, and our babes too."

Even those who had shouted against Mahon and clamored for rebellion were silent, thoughtful, so that when Joseph spoke again, it was in a much quieter voice. "We will leave our homes here," he said, "but we will take our families and our songs and our history. And who wish to remain and trust to the justice of Mahon or the mercy of the English may do so, but . . ."

He was not allowed to finish the sentence. The crowd, as one, began to clamor, "To America! America! America!" and the pact was sealed.

∽ 27 ∽

Sneaking past the barricades was no challenge for Kevin, who had grown up running the hills of Ballynockanor and taunting the authorities to enforce curfews.

Besides, no one thought of St. Brigit's hill as anything other than a place of pilgrimage; it was not a main road to anywhere.

The previous times Kevin had approached the mossy boulder behind the stone cross, it had been to leave money for the aid of the Burke folk. It was true this time, but the quantity was minuscule. Things were so bad in the whole country that robbery had grown unprofitable. Anyone with any resources had left the country for more pleasant surroundings. Those who stayed had nothing worth stealing.

After keeping back enough for himself to live, Kevin had exactly six shillings to share with his brother, and he had the notion that there would be no more after that.

He reined Savina to a willing halt and dismounted on top of the message boulder.

The scrap of paper that protruded below a hand of grey-green moss caught his eye at once. Unfolding it Kevin read: *Kev—We are escaping to America* . . . Then the note assigned a time and location to meet in, of all places, Galway City.

Kevin weighed the shillings in his hand even as his thoughts balanced and sorted through the unexpected news. At last he replaced the shillings in his pocket and refolded the note, absently tucking it into a saddlebag. Once more on Savina, he retreated back down St. Brigit's hill.

The dividing of the loot from the latest holdup caused Daniel Grogan's face to shed its pallor and his spirits to lift for the first time in months. "It's enough!" he exulted. "I've got enough to go to America . . . me and me beauties. Finally we will give the back of our hands to Ireland and its landlords, rot 'em. It's America for us."

O'Hara and Kevin continued counting silver and copper coins into stacks of fives and tens.

"Come on, then," Grogan implored. "Lend me your horse. I've not seen me babies these many months. I'm afraid for 'em. Since I've got the passage money, I cannot rest another minute before settin' 'em free."

Kevin did his best to act stern and unyielding, but the truth was he could not imagine abandoning his younger brother and sister to such a place as the Galway City workhouse. The stories of disease and abuse that came out of that pit of degradation were too awful to contemplate.

"All right," Kevin agreed at last. "Only see you have her back to me by tomorrow night. My brother's left me word that he needs to see me."

"I promise," Grogan said earnestly. "And after that ye'll never see Daniel Grogan nor his beauties anymore this side of the New World."

Grogan was left waiting in the outer hall of the Galway workhouse for nearly an hour, pacing beneath the steady gaze of a portrait of the young Queen Victoria. Her pale eyes looked disapproving somehow. Bejeweled and well-fed, her image mocked the stark poverty that passed daily beneath her.

Grogan patted the leather pouch tied off to his belt and tucked inside his trousers. Eyeing the visage of the English queen he muttered, "A fig to yerself, ma'am. Beggin' yer pardon. No queens or kings in America, see. Takin' me girls there, I am."

The tap of well-soled boots sounded in the corridor. It was the Reverend Banbreak at the door.

"Good day to ye, yer honor." Daniel Grogan tipped his hat.

Banbreak replied with a clearing of his throat.

Grogan continued, "As yer honor was sayin . . . no false hopes. I've come for me girls. I've enough in me purse for passage to America. I'm takin' Corrie and Ceili and Megan upon the next tide away from this cursed land." He rocked back upon his heels and slid his fingers excitedly along the brim of the hat. "So I've come back for 'em, y'know, and I'll be thankin' yer honor to tell me beauties that their da is come. That he's waitin' here to take 'em to the New World."

Banbreak eyed him with disdain and let him finish before he replied, "Your children are not here."

"Not here . . . but yer honor said . . ." Grogan's grin vanished.

"We cannot keep anyone against their will. The two oldest . . ."

"Aye, Corrie and Ceili."

Banbreak flicked his fingers at the irritation of their memory. "They left."

"Left? But . . . when . . . why?"

"Some time ago. Ungrateful wretches. Left. Most likely starved by now."

"But . . . but . . . why . . ."

"How should I know?"

"And what of wee Megan? That's the youngest. Did they leave her behind?"

"In a manner of speaking. Yes. She's dead, you see." This information was offered coolly, as if the conversation was about the weather.

Grogan steadied himself against the wall. Queen Victoria glared imperiously at him, like he was a beetle to be stepped upon. At last he sighed the word. "Dead."

"Quite. Fever carried off a number of inmates."

"When?"

"There were so many, really, Grogan. How should I remember one out of the many?"

Seized by a wild fury, Daniel Grogan clenched his fist and glared at the cleric as though he would kill him. "You . . ."

"See here." Banbreak's demeanor was unruffled. "It was unavoidable."

Staring, Grogan thought it through: how wee Megan had died without her da or mother beside her. Then it came to him: a strong certainty that Megan was in heaven with Annie. He inhaled raggedly.

"Where . . . is she buried?"

This question amused Banbreak. "There were too many . . . we could not possibly identify every body in every grave. She had a decent burial. According to the rites of the church."

Grogan's eyes narrowed. He stared hard at the clerical collar. "The church, is it?"

"The two other girls . . . they simply would not obey the rules after that. They left, and good riddance to them."

The faces of Corrie and Ceili swam before Dan, accusing him of something less than love, of accepting the idea that this was unavoidable. "Corrie. Ceili," he muttered, staggering toward the exit. "Got to find 'em."

Kate, holding Rosie like a bird upon her arm, walked the long miles to the ruins of St. John's and to the churchyard, where much of her heart lay buried. All the long day, since Joseph had left for

Galway City, she had thought of nothing but saying good-bye to her home. It was like a death.

The unrepaired caved-in roof of the church where generations of Donovans had worshiped was the final sign to her that they must leave.

She swung back the groaning gate as she had done countless times before. Glancing upward at the autumn sun, she knew that by now the signing of the documents would be nearly completed.

Even this hallowed place belonged to Mahon.

Perhaps one day a bard would sing this story in the long history of Galway. Perhaps he would find the truth of it in the lives of the common folk who lay buried here and those who were forced to walk away.

Until that day the winners would write the history of this terrible time. Those who ruled would give their own particular twist to what happened here. History would seem to have been acted out only in the marble halls of capitols and castles.

Only a few would carry away the truth that the conquerors and their judges were mostly the guilty ones in this great drama. Those who called themselves the law were lawless. In the graveyards and in the stone walls of the courthouses of Ireland, truth would lie mute. The history they wrote would be written without the assistance of witnesses who lived and died here.

Kate stood over the graves of her dear ones. Whole lifetimes were concealed beneath the sodden leaves. Their memories were dust. Tales told in the shade of a tree or by the hearth would be gone with the old light.

What was left to the future generations would be documents defining dates and boundaries, "On this day, 1846, Joseph Burke sold his land to Major Denis Mahon. Beginning at the bank of the Cornamona and continuing . . ."

The voices of the folk of Ballynockanor would be as silent as the dust. Life, carried to the sea by the river, would take root somewhere else. All that had been here would be forgotten. Like beams and thatch, Ireland had fallen in upon itself. The loss of the Burke lands was only one tale among ten thousand. Centuries of con⁺inuity had collapsed today, and yet the world would hardly notice.

Kate sighed, praying that one distant day, sweet Rosie would grow old and have a dozen great-grandchildren. That sitting by her hearth in an unnamed city in America, Rosie, wizened and quaking, would recite the miracles God wrought for His beloved Ireland and the brave deeds of those who had fought for freedom.

Perhaps, Kate thought, she would lean down from her place in heaven and listen to the old, old tales beside the fire.

The Galway City town hall was the administrative center of English rule for the area. On hand in the courtyard were such reminders of English law as the permanent scaffold for hanging Irish rebels and the iron cage in which the bodies of the executed were displayed as a warning to would-be rebels. Both noose and gibbet currently were empty, but their presence alone gave notice that English justice in Ireland was seldom tempered with mercy.

At the moment, facing the loss of everything he knew and loved, Joseph felt there was no mercy to be had from either politics or nature. Both had conspired together to drive the Gaels out of Ireland at last. It was the mercy of God alone that any Irish survived the ministration of Trevelyan and others of his sort.

He stood at the base of the stone steps, hesitating. Joseph's fists were clenched as was his jaw, his whole being steeling itself for what lay ahead.

Martin, flanking him as did Charlie Nesbitt, said, "Is there truly no other way? Would it not be better to be buried on our own land than live in a foreign country?"

His refusal to accept the loss of home easily was somehow helpful to Joseph. When the last Burke who would be lord of Connaught spoke, it was as much to convince himself, as for Martin and Nesbitt's benefit. "Life is about people," he said, "and not about things or places or land. A river that rises in the mountains only to die in a bog is a sad, useless thing, Martin. We must be like the stream that bursts through all dams and finds its way to the sea. To a new life in a new way."

Inside the recorder's office Mahon, Richman, and Gann were already waiting, smirking. "So, Burke," Mahon exulted. "You see I've won at last."

"Have you?" Joseph asked quietly. "I wonder." He took the pen and with a hand that betrayed no quaver of doubt, signed the document that transferred the Burke crown lease to Mahon. He then paid a fee of ten pounds to the Crown for the official stamp.

"See that you and your tenants are out by Christmas," Richman warned, handing over the payment.

Smiling at last, Joseph said, "Why would anyone want to stay with yourself and Mister Gann? Have no doubts on that score. We are glad to go."

As Joseph and his companions left the office, they heard Mahon describe yet another village to be tossed. He reminded Richman to round up the band of destructives and armed constables and follow promptly, while he and Gann set out for home.

Joseph, Martin, and Nesbitt looked ashen, realizing that a like order would soon apply to them.

Martin tugged at Joseph's arm. "I also have some business to take care of before headin' back. May I have until three o'clock?"

Glancing up at the clock tower, Joseph reflected that the next time he saw it he would be boarding a ship to leave Ireland forever. "We must see to the provisionin'. Three o'clock," he agreed. "But no later."

With Gann driving the open-topped, two-wheeled carriage, Denis Mahon was in a triumphant mood. At a single stroke he had doubled the holdings of Mahon land and was getting the property in the form dreamed of by invaders for a thousand years: Ireland without the Irish.

On the drive past the workhouse he prattled happily about the changes that were to come. "By next spring we will have evicted the other tenants from our holdings," he said. "I can't remember ever being so perfectly content with the future. We will put this region on a paying basis . . . no tithes to collect, no carrying back rents, no Poor Law contributions to make. Sound business practices only, eh, Mister Gann?"

"Sound and sharp," agreed Gann. "I'm only sorry to see 'em get off easy. Best to crush 'em underfoot like the loathsome creatures they are."

As he said these words the carriage was approaching a crossing of the Cornamona over a stone bridge that dated to the time of Lord Richard Burke, he who had disappeared in the war with Cromwell's Ironsides. From out of the shadows under the willows spurred a man on a dappled horse. "You!" he screamed. "You killed me Annie and me beauties, and now you will pay for it!"

With that Daniel Grogan raised a dragoon pistol and fired at Denis Mahon from no more than ten feet away. The lead ball shattered Mahon's forehead and flung his body sideways into Gann and across the reins.

The unexpected thunder of the gun and the dead bulk jerking downward on the horse's mouth made the animal rear and pull sharply to the right. Trying to control the beast was out of the question, since Gann was already jumping to save himself. The buggy flipped up on one wheel, then continued over onto its side, pinning Gann beneath. His head and shoulders scraped along the edge of the bridge as his legs were wound up in the wheels and axle, much as one would scrape something off the sole of a shoe.

He was conscious and struggling to free himself when Steward Richman and the chief of the special constables arrived. Coming on horseback and having heard the shot, they galloped forward. Grogan, in a daze as he contemplated what he had done, heard their approach and waved the now-empty pistol.

Richman's companion raised a carbine and shot him out of the saddle. He fell to the ground, dead.

But the rescue did Jailor Gann no service.

The second shot was too much for the Mahon carriage horse, and he lunged forward again, winding Gann up in the wreckage before being dragged, flailing, backwards off the bridge. Cart and horse both landed atop Gann, crushing him completely. The body of Denis Mahon was draped over a rock nearby.

When Richman saw both men were dead, he turned his attention to the likewise motionless form of Daniel Grogan. "I know this man," he said. "Grogan. Evicted and run off some time ago. Mentally deranged? Perhaps, but more likely part of a conspiracy of Ribbonmen."

Catching Savina's reins where she stood at the river's edge, Richman noted, "And I know this animal too! It was Burke property . . . I tried to buy it once." Reaching into a saddlebag he found nothing of interest except a crumpled scrap of paper.

"'We are escaping to America,'" he read aloud. "'Will meet you at Monk's after the business is done.' And here it names today's date. Come on, then, Captain. We cannot do any good here, but we'll give the rest of the band of murderers a real surprise!"

Martin was pleased to find Kevin waiting for him at Monk's. He was less certain about the presence of Blue O'Hara. "I need to talk to you, Kev," he said with urgency.

"It's all right, Martin," his brother said. "You can speak freely in front of Mister O'Hara. What's this about America?"

"Joseph has sold the land," Martin began.

"That's old news," Kevin interrupted, "or do you mean he's sellin' more? Ballynockanor?"

"All of it!" Martin announced. "Joseph has sold everythin' to Mahon."

"Leavin' his people to fend for themselves, eh?" O'Hara grunted.

"Not a'tall," Martin said indignantly. "He's chartered a ship to take us to America. Took every last penny he could raise, but we're goin'. You too, Kev! We'll leave Ballynockanor, all of us, but we'll be together in America. What do you say?"

Stunned at the completion of what he had already concluded for himself, Kevin asked, "You and Kate and Mary Elizabeth? When do we sail?"

"Right away. But you must come home at once and show yourself to Joseph and Kate." None of the three noticed that conversation outside the snug had fallen silent.

"Today!" Kevin rejoiced, then looked thoughtful. "Or as soon as I get the dappled mare back. She is . . ."

"Stand still!" ordered a commanding tone that broke in on their conversation. Martin looked up to see the muzzle of a rifle in the hands of a constable. Two other weapons were leveled at O'Hara and Kevin. "I arrest you in the queen's name for conspiring in the murder of Lord Denis Mahon."

"What's this, then?" O'Hara blustered. "We've been nowhere but in this very spot."

The officer shook his head. "It won't wash," he said. "We heard the admission to ownership of the animal used by the murderer, and in the saddlebag we found the note that directed us to this meeting; and here you are."

Comprehension flooding his face, Kevin protested, "But that note was from my brother." He shut up abruptly as he realized the implication of what he had said. "Not Martin," he said. "Not him. He's got nothin' . . ."

"Come along quietly," the captain ordered. "We've orders to shoot if there is any resistance."

28

Something wondrous was happening.

Corrie and Ceili gulped down their meager meal of seaweed and
boiled mussels as a victorious shout echoed over the rooftops from
Courthouse Square to Quay Street. Torches appeared, bobbing
through the narrow lanes of Galway City to the Spanish Arch and
the cargo ships. A thousand people marched in the parade. English
soldiers followed warily, at a distance.

Was this the beginning of the riots every official had feared?

"What is it?" Ceili cried, her gaunt face alight with the excitement. "Is there food? Have they sent us somethin' to eat, then?"

Corrie grabbed her arm, and the two sisters joined the march.
Men and women were laughing, singing,

> *Major Mahon pleases me,*
> *His was a life of jollity:*
> *His tenants, many as he willed,*

He tossed them all from Connaught's hill.
Ah, but he's a wretched man
And now his soul's eternal damned.
He's dead, quite dead, in spite of wealth!
Let's drink a toast upon his health!

The tumult increased, and the song was sung again until everyone knew the words and joined in.

"But what's it mean?" Corrie asked a wild-eyed ragged man.

The man's index finger pointed skyward. Then he shook his head and pointed down at the ground instead. "Have ye not heard of Major Mahon, then?"

"Aye," Ceili shouted back as the roaring of the celebration nearly drowned out her voice.

Corrie explained, "Aye! We know him. 'Twas he who tossed us from our farm and made us what we are today."

"Then cry your pleasure to the heavens, young miss!" shouted the man passionately. "Sure! Major Mahon's dead. He who bought up all the West and starved us out . . . today justice of heaven has visited the divil!"

"Dead!" Corrie was happy for it, though she had never seen the fellow who had done her family such harm.

"Does it mean we can go home, Corrie?" Ceili's eyes shone in the torchlight.

Corrie did not know what it meant. She shook her head rapidly and looked at the ships standing alongside the docks. She did not think of Galway, but of America!

"How'd he die?"

The ragged man, grinning ear to ear, replied, "The brother of his lover, some say. Or an angry tenant. Rapparees, it is told. Or Ribbonmen. Others say it was his steward who arranged it. There is a curse on the House of Mahon, everyone knows. 'Twas the old Colonel Mahon who cut down the hangin' tree. No doubt there's a curse upon the whole lot of 'em now!"

There was no real answer. Only the rejoicing that one so evil and cruel was dead.

Corrie thanked the fellow and slowed her pace.

Ceili stumbled on the cobbles. The crowd was moving too fast, the emotion too high. Ceili was too weak to continue. The sisters fell away from the mob as they turned up Flood Street on their way back to the courthouse.

"Let's go back to the arch," Corrie instructed, taking Ceili's arm.

"Will there be food tonight?" Ceili implored. Always with any celebration there was supposed to be food, was there not?

"I don't think so. Nay." The booming of the song erupted again in the distance. "But all the West will be lit with bonfires in honor of the man who killed the devil this day."

Signal fires burned upon the hills beyond Castletown and Ballynockanor.

Kate, awakened by the eerie glow, stood at the window.

"What is it, sister?" Mary Elizabeth asked Kate from the doorway.

"Mahon's men, I suppose," Kate replied bitterly. "Gloatin'. Celebratin' the buyin' of the Burke lands."

Mary Elizabeth joined her at the window. "They say there's ten million times more land in America, Kate." Mary Elizabeth leaned against her.

"Then everyone from the townlands'll have their own." Kate was grateful for Mary Elizabeth's hopeful remark. Her own brain had been pounding the message that she and Joseph had failed, let down their people and their nation.

"I'm not scared." Mary Elizabeth raised her chin stoically. "Mad Molly says we're leavin' bondage."

"If Molly says it, how can we doubt?"

Mary Elizabeth exhaled slowly. "Where's Joseph and Martin then? Are they comin' back with Nesbitt tonight?"

"I expected them hours ago. Maybe they were too weary for the journey. And they'll be lookin' about provisionin' the ship."

Squinting into the light of a distant bonfire, Mary Elizabeth pointed. "It's Molly comin' there."

Kate hummed disapprovingly. Molly's daughter needed to take better care that the old woman did not wander about on nights when signal fires surrounded the valley. "Sure, and the fires have riled her up," Kate observed.

Molly came to the house at a jog. Spotting Kate and Mary Elizabeth, she called up to them. "The fires! Aye! Did ye see 'em then?"

Kate opened the window. "Come in to the kitchen, Molly. You'll catch your death."

"Catch death! Moths to the flame it be! Aye. He's singed his wings all right."

Kate and Mary Elizabeth hurried to let her in.

"Molly, what're you out for?"

Molly peered heavenward and stretched her hands to the fire for warmth. "Don't rightly know. But did ye see the funeral pyre?"

"Signal fires. Is it Mahon's men?"

"'Tis the vagabonds and tinkers. The tossed and the homeless. 'Tis the hungry and the nearly dead."

"What is it, Molly?"

"They're celebratin', don't ye see?"

"Celebratin'?" Mary Elizabeth quizzed.

Rubbing her palms together vigorously, Molly grinned. "Mahon's dead."

"Aye, Molly. Colonel Mahon's been gone for quite some time."

"Nay, Kate! Not that Mahon. T'other one I'm meanin'. The young one. Young Major Mahon. There's a curse on the lot of 'em since they cut down the tree. Dead as a doornail, God be praised! Whole countryside's lit up on account of it! Everyone from Roscommon t'Galway City is rejoicin'! Aye! Dead, dead, dead!"

"How do you know?"

"Claddagh brothers told me. They heard it from the Tinker."

Kate, doubtful, stepped outside into the cold night. Dead? Denis Mahon? Did that mean the land was not sold? The deed not recorded? Would they not be going to America then?

"Come in, Kate," Molly instructed. "It ain't over a'tall. Travail, ye see. Comin' to Ireland. Travail. Travail himself. We'll meet him face to face, we will. Ah, poor Martin. Ah, Kevin. 'Tis the gallows, sure. And there's no way to be free except the gallows. And then there's the girls. Poor things. But it'll be put right by and by. He has t'keep his promise, y'see. He gives his word like a fool, and then the whole world is waitin' t'see if he keeps it. He must. And the wee girl . . . she's no fool, that one."

Kate was about to turn her back on the spectacle when the Claddagh brothers emerged from the barn to hail her.

"Here's news," Molly shot. "They'll tell ye."

Speaking slowly, Simeon told her what he had heard at the barricade. Mahon was indeed dead. Killed along with Gann, just outside of Galway City. No one could say who had done the deed or why, but there were five thousand evicted tenants who would rejoice at the news.

And had Mahon died before he paid Joseph for the estate? Had the deed been officially recorded?

As to that, Kate would have to wait until Joseph and Martin returned home to know.

Charlie Nesbitt crossed the barricades into the Burke townlands at dawn. His cloak was splattered with mud from the night ride.

Kate, in the kitchen with Molly, Margaret, Tomeen, and Mary Elizabeth, looked up from the kneading of the bread as the sound of only one set of horse hooves came into the yard.

Moments later Nesbitt entered the house with Old Flynn and Simeon at his heels. It was plain from the expression on his face that things had gone wrong.

"Ma'am." He bowed to Kate. "The squire Denis Mahon is murdered, ma'am."

Kate, dusted with flour, nodded curtly. Fear knotted her stomach. "Where's Squire Joseph, then?"

Nesbitt swallowed hard. "In Galway City."

"Why has he and Martin not come home with yourself?"

"It's Martin. He's suspected, y'see."

At first, the meaning of his words were not clear in her mind. The thought of what he was saying was too impossible. "Suspected of what?"

"Complicity. Beggin' your pardon, ma'am. You should sit down."

Kate groped for a chair.

Molly worked her gums as if she would speak, but was silent.

"Martin! Somehow connected with this? Sure, and there never was a more . . ."

Nesbitt fingered the brim of his hat nervously. "Ma'am. It does not look promisin'."

"How can that be?"

"It's the horse, y'see. The dappled horse."

"Savina? The one he sold for forty pounds?"

"The very same, ma'am. She was found grazin' at the scene of the murder. And a letter from Martin was in the saddlebag. A letter . . . hear me now, ma'am . . . it was written to your brother, Kevin."

"Kevin. In America." The sense of it eluded her. Rosie cried from her crib, wanting to get up, needing to be fed. "Come to the point, Charlie Nesbitt."

"Kevin's not . . . well, he's not been in America for some time, ma'am."

Molly nodded. "Nay. Kevin's trampin' 'round Ireland. Come home, he did. Come to see Martin, he did."

Kate turned an astonished gaze upon the fey woman. "Molly. What do you know of this?"

"Swore Molly to tell no one . . . except to fetch Martin. Since it's out in the daylight . . . suppose old Molly can tell Kate. Travail, it is."

It made sense: Martin's surly behavior, his threat to go away with Kevin. "But Martin's been here with us. Here at the barricades. He's not gone away. Not even for a single night."

"Till now." Nesbitt shook his head. "They found the dappled horse, y'see, where the murder happened. 'Twas the same horse . . . they have it that Martin gave the horse to Kevin."

"Sold . . . forty pounds."

Old Flynn spoke up. "Richman offered twelve pounds. Savina weren't worth twenty in the best of times, I'm thinkin'. Though she's a fine animal . . . Forty pounds never made much sense to meself when the hunter fetched but twenty-five."

A bitter smile crossed Nesbitt's lips. "Forty pounds, ma'am. It never made sense a'tall. The cash came from Kevin, see. And from there . . . where'd Kevin get forty pounds?"

The crackling of the fire filled the solemn quiet.

Kate asked. "Where's Kevin?"

"With Martin, ma'am. In the Galway gaol."

"Ah. Sure. It would be the case . . ." Rosie wailed angrily to be let out. Kate drew a ragged breath. "And my husband?"

"He says to tell yourself he'll stay behind awhile. They'll need legal counsel, your brothers will. The squire'll arrange it. There'll have to be a trial, ma'am."

"And what can be the outcome, Nesbitt?"

The big man gave an almost imperceptible shrug. Lowering his brooding eyes, he replied, "It ain't good upon the face of it, ma'am. The horse, y'see . . . she's been seen at other robberies."

Charles Edward Trevelyan was at Dublin Castle attending meetings of the Irish aid committees and overseeing their work. He took such a personal interest in the details that he insisted any suggestions he referred to him for review, a process whereby critical judgments could be and were delayed for weeks or even months.

He had recently come out of one such meeting at which he had castigated the commander of the Cork coast guard station for diverting one hundred pounds of six-year-old ship's biscuit from government stores to feed a thousand starving islanders . . . without proper authorization. The chagrined officer promised it would never happen again.

"Mister Secretary," called Mr. Howard, a reporter for the *London Times*, "have you heard the news? Major Denis Mahon has been shot to death in Galway."

"Tragic," Trevelyan murmured, his voice laden with sympathy.

"I knew the late major—an upstanding man and a credit to his class and the nation. Is it known who the assassin was?"

"Better than that," the journalist said, "for they have already been apprehended. It is said to be a conspiracy of Ribbonmen, but the three perpetrators are already in custody."

"Good work, that," Trevelyan declared. "Is there more?"

"Judge Lewis will preside at the trial."

The words "the hangman of Kilkenny?" slipped out of Trevelyan's mouth before he caught himself. "Justice Lewis is a learned magistrate, none better. I must write him a message of support, reminding him of the importance, in these unsettled times, of keeping terrorists at bay. Thank you for the information."

Conviction!

The word of the verdict handed down by the hanging judge of Kilkenny circulated among the thousands of people who milled restlessly in Courthouse Square of Galway City.

Corrie and Ceili Grogan had a prime view of the spectacle over the rooftops. Along with two dozen other waifs they had climbed the stairs of a deserted warehouse to await the news.

"Look there," Ceili cried, pointing toward Mary Street on the southwest and Waterside to the northeast of the crowds.

Troops of English soldiers carrying rifles with bayonets at the ready marched quick-step toward the Courthouse.

"How many ye think there be?" asked a boy about Corrie's age.

Corrie eyed the two converging troops. "Five hundred," she guessed.

"Sure," Ceili said, satisfied. "There ain't as many of them as us."

Corrie warned, "But they have guns and bullets. 'Twould be shootin' ducks in a barrel if they fire into our folk packed there into the square."

The children, perched upon the ledges like pigeons, acknowledged that the arrival of soldiers did not bode well for the fate of the prisoners. If condemned to death, there was a sure promise that there would be a riot in the West. Weeks of threats had been backed by the murders of six land agents around the country. This, it was said, was retaliation for the arrest and trial of three innocent Irishmen. English reinforcements could only mean a severe punishment was in store for the prisoners.

Though Kevin Donovan, Martin Donovan, and Blue O'Hara had not killed Mahon, they were, nonetheless, celebrated as heroes in the West simply because they were on trial for his murder. As to the true killer of the despised landlord and his minion, the fellow had remained nameless, buried in an unmarked grave. He was quite unimportant to the drama being played out there.

It was widely suspected that the three in the prisoner's dock were no more than pawns. Justice Lewis intended to make an example of them before the people of western Ireland.

The redcoated soldiers were simply there to make sure the plan of Lewis was not circumvented by the violence of a mob.

The troops ringed the vast assembly in the square.

Mothers with children were shifted to the center of the crowd, while young, defiant men moved to the outer perimeter to face off with the enemy.

"Somethin's comin'," Ceili remarked.

At that, the mass on the courthouse steps were pushed back by a dozen constables. A hush fell over Galway City as the defendants were led from the building. A mighty cheer of support rose from the throats of the people. It echoed across the waters of the bay and frightened flocks of birds from their perches.

Rifles were raised to the shoulders of the guards as they took aim upon the gathering.

The bewigged court bailiff came blinking out into the daylight to make the announcement of the fate of the prisoners.

"Hear ye! Hear ye!" All fell silent. Corrie could clearly hear the distant announcement. "In the name of Her Majesty, Queen Victoria of England, Ireland . . ." At this point the crowd booed passionately. The bailiff, mindful of danger to his own life, continued unheard. Then the crowd grew quiet again as these terrible words were read:

"Insofar as they have been tried and found guilty, it is the judgment of this court that on December twenty-four of the year of our Lord, 1846, they shall be taken from their cells to an appointed place where they shall be hanged by the neck until . . ."

Once again the jeering of the mob erupted. Soldiers moved forward as the crowd threatened to set torches to the courthouse. The staccato popping of gunfire rang above their heads. Women screamed; men hit the ground in fear.

So much for the riot. Perhaps, Corrie thought, there would be burning and destruction on the day the men hanged. Many on the street predicted it would come to no good, that a violent end for many would ensue if these three died.

"Are they to die then?" Ceili asked.

"Aye," Corrie replied bitterly. She had never doubted the outcome of the trial. Justice Lewis was not known for rendering true justice.

The prisoners, manacled and ragged, were jostled down the steps and loaded onto an open cart pulled by an ox and guarded by more soldiers.

This was the first Corrie had seen these martyrs of Galway. She hoped the cart would pass beneath them along the Corrib before traveling on to Gaol Road and the prison.

The vehicle moved with difficulty through the packed streets.

As it neared, Corrie's interest stirred from an unattached curiosity to a passionate fury.

"Ceili," she hissed. "Do you see who it is in that cart?"

Ceili frowned and squinted but could find nothing in the faces of the three condemned men that piqued her interest. "Nay."

"That is the boy!" Corrie cried. "He who gave us his own coat at the Burke barricade." Corrie was still wearing it. Her other clothing had fallen away bit by bit. Not a day passed in which she did not give thanks to God for the boy at the barricade.

Now Ceili remembered. "Aye! Sure, and it's himself."

It was also the dear heart who had saved the baby from the lambing barn, Corrie knew. How then could such a one as this be condemned to hang?

It was unthinkable and yet, like all things impossible that had come upon Ireland, this was a reality.

For the first time since misfortune had first struck her family, Corrie Grogan began to weep. "Poor boy," she cried. "Ah, poor, poor boy! Kind and gentle fellow! Sure, and the world is ruled by the devil if such a thing can be! Angels in heaven! Lord of all! Have you forgotten us, then? Not the boy! Not he who saved my baby sister and then me and Ceili! If he is to die? Ah! We are lost! Lost!"

The sorrow continued unabated for hours after the procession passed by. Back in the shelter of Spanish Arch, Corrie sobbed and would not be comforted.

"Why's your sister keenin' then?" an old woman asked Ceili.

Ceili replied quietly, "All the host of heaven has wept for Ireland, and God has not moved to fight for us. Maybe Corrie's tears will cause Him to look and pity. She's never wept before. No. Not that I recall. Her tears must be worth somethin' more than all the others, then."

Reporter Howard of *The Times* accosted Trevelyan at the Dame Street entrance to Dublin Castle. "What are you going to do to prevent the West going up in flames?" he demanded without preamble.

"Eh? What?" Trevelyan returned, feigning a deafness he did not have in order to collect his thoughts. "What's this?"

"The three convicted for the murder of Mahon," Howard said, barely controlling his impatience. "Judge Lewis has set the date for their execution."

"Yes? What of it? Make an example . . ."

"On Christmas Eve?"

"Well," Trevelyan temporized, backpedaling, "Lord Justice Lewis is a strict . . ."

"And everyone admits that the one who assassinated Mahon was himself killed at the scene. The three condemned can prove they were nowhere near."

"Judge Lewis may have overstepped . . ."

"There is no more than circumstantial evidence to link the three to the crime . . . one of them is only sixteen or so years of age . . . and the proof of conspiracy offered was a horse and an ambiguous note."

"Lewis needs to be reminded . . ."

"And finally," reporter Howard concluded forcefully, "the talk in the streets is how the English state can pay for trials, special constables, and increased troops, and yet make no provision to feed millions of starving Irish men, women, and children. What will you do when the whole country goes up in flames, and everyone blames you?"

Secretary Trevelyan had heard enough. "The hangman of Kilkenny has clearly overstepped the mark," he said. "I think it is time for me to go to Galway personally and look into this matter. Christmas Eve indeed. What was he thinking of? If you'd care to accompany me, Mister Howard, you may collect information for your paper at first hand."

29

Kate reckoned they had been saying farewell to Galway for years, only they had not known it, had not admitted it.

On December twentieth, 1846, five hundred from the townlands marched up the long slope to St. Brigit's cross where Father O'Bannon said the mass, and the bread and wine of Christ's passion were shared among them for the last time in Ballynockanor.

The shroud of holy silence enfolded them, as all remembered the faces that went with the names carved upon the stones like fossils on the ledges of the cliffs. There were those who slept in ancient graves whom no one could remember. The living folk, descended from the Irish kings, were taking away even the soft language that had sung the old songs and told the old tales. Who would remember them now?

Molly promised Mary Elizabeth an angel would remain behind to tend the graves. Wild roses bloomed at the ruins of the convent, after all. Blackberries grew beside the shattered church.

Kate thought of her yearly pilgrimage to this sacred place and of those who had lived their lives from beginning to end within the sound of the river.

In four days Kevin and Martin would die together. The last of Ballynockanor. Joseph had paid to have their bodies brought home for burial. By then the ship would be far out to sea.

Each year when spring came who would be left here to remember the resurrection and make this pilgrimage? Who would remind the sleeping saints of Ballynockanor that they must be patient for a little while more? Who would be there waiting when Christ came, and they awakened?

High upon the hill Kate heard a bird call from the thistle, *Even so. Even so. I will, I will, I will . . .*

With the enormous swelling of the crowds coming in to witness the hanging of O'Hara and the Donovan brothers, there was no food to be found in Galway City. The best of the seaweed tossed up by the winter storms was gone. Cockles and mussels had vanished from every rock and piling along the waterfront.

Ceili Grogan was growing weaker by the day. She had taken on the look of the dying, Corrie knew.

The day before the hanging Corrie urged Ceili to her feet. "We're leavin' here."

Ceili sighed. "But why?"

"Because we're starvin'."

"What difference if we starve here or somewhere else?"

Corrie was adamant. "We're goin' north."

"But I can't. I'm a'weary, Corrie."

"You will come!" Corrie gripped her spindly arm and began to walk through Shop Street and then on to William Street toward the road out of town.

"Where y'takin' us, then?" Ceili found the energy to ask.

"Home."

"Home, is it?" Ceili staggered forward. "Goin' home to die, are we?"

"No! To find food." Corrie led on. "The Burke estate is sold, see. Mahon is dead. Everyone on the Burke townlands is set to leave. Sailin' on the *Nantucket* after the hangin', so I hear."

"What's that to do with us?"

"They're fine healthy folk, them as was behind the barrier. I seen them millin' about the ship. Now look, their houses'll be empty. Their barns. Maybe they've left somethin' behind. A sack of meal. Maybe seed potatoes. They'd not be takin' seed potatoes on the ship with 'em. We'll go there and . . . we'll find somethin' sure. Hole up in one of them deserted houses, we will. We'll stay until spring and plant our own little patch and . . ."

Ceili stopped in the center of the road. Her hands hung at her sides, her eyes glassed over. "But I can't, Corrie. I want . . . I gotta lay down, y'know? I'm . . ."

There was no holding Ceili up, no making her walk. She had given up, like so many others. Too many days without nettles or mussels or seaweed or fishheads. Too many days with nothing but air had finally taken a toll.

Ceili lay down in the ditch beside the road. Corrie, wrapped in Martin Donovan's coat, cradled Ceili's head and waited.

Darkness came. Ceili twitched; what was left of her muscles quivering as the last energy was used up in breathing.

At midnight Ceili said, "Go on the ship, Corrie. Go ahead. America. Like you always said you would."

"I'm goin nowhere a'tall without you, Ceili." She held her sister close. She was lighter than holding a feather mattress.

"But I want to see . . . Mother."

"Not yet!" Corrie cried, angry at Ceili for talking about dying. "I have a plan, Ceili! We can . . . no doubt they've left . . . seed potatoes . . . we'll plant . . . please! Ceili! Please! We can make a garden. Cabbages and stuff. Cabbage soup I'll make ye!"

"It's . . . almost Christmas . . ."

"Aye." Corrie rocked her. "Almost Christmas it is."

"And Mama . . . Megan . . . Da?"

"Aye. We're at home, we are. Sittin' by the fire. That's it. Spuds boilin', see. And the candle shinin'. And Mama tellin' stories from the Good Book. How Mary and Joseph . . . when they came . . . they didn't have a place for the Holy Child . . ."

There was a faint smile on Ceili's lips. "Poor sweet baby . . . Just . . . like . . . us . . ."

"That's right. That's right, Ceili. Just like us . . ." Corrie drew her sister close, kissed her forehead, rubbed her hands, trying to bring back the warmth. "But sure, see, I've got a plan, I have. We'll build a fire on the hearth . . . no doubt they left somethin' behind . . . some wee thing . . ."

It took a while before Corrie knew for certain that Ceili had flown way. Even then she would not let go for the longest time. There was no one else left. No one. Corrie sat holding Ceili until the sun came up. "Poor sweet baby," Corrie whispered at last. "No room in this world for someone sweet as you."

Like Moses leading his people to the promised land, Joseph, carrying Tomeen, walked at the head of the procession onto the dock in Galway City.

Kate, with Rosie on her hip, was at his side. Her head was high as the folk of Ballynockanor and Castletown passed the hungry and the dispossessed who had flocked by the thousand to witness the hanging of her brothers.

"Our folk are healthy," she remarked as the tall masts of the *Nantucket* came into view. "You did well to care for your own, Joseph." Unspoken in that observation was the truth that being fed and healthy, there was a greater likelihood that the folk of the Burke townlands would survive the ocean voyage. Nearly every other ship bearing half-starved emigrants had reported the deaths of one quarter to half of the passengers. Kate's gaze swept over children with round, happy faces, parents with strong arms and alert eyes. She could think of nothing but Martin, who had longed to go to America. How she hated Ireland at this moment! How she hated the English who cared more about cattle than people! She would not regret leaving. "God willing," she whispered, "we will not lose even one within our ark."

Captain Coffin greeted Joseph as an old friend. With a warm handshake the officer brought him onto the ship and left his mate to show the people their quarters.

"The tide'll be with us on Christmas mornin'," Coffin said. "Your folk will have a few days to get their sea legs and settle in."

Within the warmth of the coach, Trevelyan and Mr. Howard sped over the rutted roads toward Galway City. At every junction they had been approached by beggars until even Mr. Howard remarked that there was no way anyone could take care of so many. The urge to pity them had dissipated.

"It's what I've been saying since this began," Trevelyan instructed. "We must let nature take its course. God in his Providence has seen fit to remove the Irish from Ireland so a better race may rule. A sensible people, we English. Common sense tells us that this will pass."

"And how many lives will pass with it?"

Trevelyan raised his finger imperiously. "As many as it takes. A lazy bunch, these Gaels. Raise their potatoes, cut their turf . . . ah well, you know it already. Governed by their passions, Mister Howard. That is why we must take this journey, and you must report the outcome of it in its entirety in your paper."

"Indeed I shall." This last sounded like a threat.

"Then quote me in this. To give charity is to steal the dignity of the one who receives it."

"But if the one who needs it is starving?"

"Let him work for his bread." Trevelyan gestured toward the passing countryside. "This famine is the best thing that has ever happened in Ireland. It is the will of God, to my way of thinking. And you shall never see me offer so much as ha'penny to a beggar. I may extend help but not without making the recipient work for it." He was smiling smugly, certain he had won over this *London Times* correspondent through sound reasoning over the last few hours.

There were within two miles of Galway City when suddenly a girl of about fourteen appeared beside the coach. She was barefoot, wearing only an overcoat, closely buttoned to conceal she had no other clothing.

She began to run alongside the coach, matching the pace, stride for stride. It made no difference if the road climbed upward and the horses slowed, or if the downgrade carried it faster.

"We'll give her nothing," Trevelyan barked in irritation.

"She's asked for nothing," Howard observed.

Indeed, she did not beg but clenched her fists and set her jaw as she matched her speed to the horse. Always she ran with her face even with the window where the two Englishmen frowned out at her.

She was a beautiful thing, Howard noticed. Long blonde hair flowed like a mane behind her as she kept up with the jogging horse.

"Leave off!" Trevelyan shouted out the window at her. "We'll give you nothing!"

But she asked for nothing. Up the slippery grade, her fists clenched, her eyes set upon the road ahead in concentration.

"You'll have nothing from us," Trevelyan called to her again, then hammered his walking stick upon the coach to signal for the driver to speed up.

As the horse stepped up, so did the girl. She neither faltered nor lagged behind in spite of the increased speed.

Trevelyan shook his head in the negative, telling her the effort was useless. It was Howard's resolve that began to crumble. Did she see pity in his eyes? Did that look on his face offer her hope? A shilling would be enough to keep her alive for weeks.

Her complexion reddened with the torture. Fine aristocratic cheekbones she had—and such beauty, even if she was dressed in a tattered coat. She was running her heart out for . . . for what? But Trevelyan would not relent.

After the first mile Mr. Howard remarked, "Surely she's earned a copper."

"Earned!" Trevelyan exploded. "She's done nothing but play the footman. My father has stories of footmen in London running ahead of the coaches for . . ."

Howard snapped, "Have you no mercy, sir?"

"None at all when it comes to these cases."

"The horse that pulls this car is better loved than she."

"That may be. It is my horse. And were the girl mine, she would be properly dressed, fed, and educated. But she is not . . ."

"She is a child." Howard bit his lip as the coach ascended a steep grade. Yet another milestone was passed. "Two miles, sir. And she has never once begged for anything."

"But you know what she wants."

"To live."

"To live by the charity of others."

Like the spokes of the wheels the naked legs of the girl churned in harmony with the coach. On and on she went, always by their window, using her eyes only to find her way, never looking at the men, never imploring them for mercy. Her bare feet were bleeding.

"Just to live," Howard insisted. "Then offer her some job! If you cannot give her mercy, then be merciful! Surely you have a small task that will win her a Christmas wish. She cannot want much! I implore you! Mister Trevelyan! Sir! Stop the coach and let her in. Offer a little employment, sir! Or I shall leap from this conveyance and write of the hardness of your heart later!"

The girl was soaked with sweat, her eyes red. Gasping for breath, as last she faltered. Buckling from the pain, she coughed and doubled over. Still she continued to run dead even with coach and horse. Her fists remained clenched. There was dignity in her refusal to beg that made Howard frantic to help her.

Near panic, he said, "Sir, she will die if you do not stop this coach."

Trevelyan smiled. "I fully intend to stop. But first I must have some . . . some duty lined out for her to accomplish. How can I simply grant wishes? God and Providence may have sent her along beside us. I've come up with a brilliant idea. Certainly. It was God himself who brought her to us. She'll earn whatever it is I give her. You shall see in action, Mister Howard, what I have been preaching about this lazy, worthless race."

The runner was in agony. Mr. Howard could see that much. "Her determination will destroy her, sir. I see no laziness in that."

The conveyance slowed and halted just after the three-mile marker. The two English gentlemen offered no charity, but rather a civic duty for the child to perform. It was a while before the girl could speak.

"Have you a name?" Mr. Howard asked kindly.

"Aye, your honor. It's Corrie. Corrie Grogan."

There was only one thing Kevin and Martin Donovan had requested in their letter to Kate.

> *It is our last wish that we meet our end as patriots. Proud and unafraid we want to be gathered into the arms of our kin . . . Do not be afeared for us. Do not let the English see you weep. It would be best if Mary Elizabeth not come into the prison for our farewell. Bring Father O'Bannon and, if you can, bring us each a bit of soap and clean clothes to wear, for the English call us dirty Irish and mock us, though they do not let us wash. We want to meet the Lord in our Sunday suits, if you please . . .*

The last plea from O'Connell for pardon had gone unanswered. Kate and Father O'Bannon entered the Galway prison at six o'clock on the evening of December twenty-third. This, their last night on earth, was the first time Kate had been allowed to visit her brothers since the arrest. She shuddered at the memory of her visit to Joseph three years before. The jailors on duty were English soldiers, but their demeanor was not unkind.

Kate carried two bundles of black suits and shoes for her brothers. In a basket she brought a shepherd's pie and penny cakes, which she knew Kevin enjoyed. Great delicacies these were with many starving beyond the prison gates.

The jailor announced their visit before he opened the cell.

"'Tis your sister, the Lady Kate Burke. And your priest come to hear your confession."

The hinges groaned back, revealing the two haggard, ragged brothers sitting with an upturned bucket between them as a table. A single beeswax candle was half-burned. When that light burned away, they would spend their last night in darkness. A Bible, the gift of a Methodist preacher, was open in front of them.

They rose stiffly from the stone floor and each embraced Kate, holding her for a long time. It was, she thought, the way Tomeen held her when he was hurt or afraid. She was grateful the jailors allowed her brothers to share the cell, grateful Blue O'Hara was not here to see the tears flow freely from their eyes.

"Kevin," she whispered, wiping his cheeks with her thumb, "if only you'd told me you were home."

Sheepishly he wiped his nose on his sleeve. "Didn't want to get anyone in trouble, y'see." His half-smile dissolved into anguish. He embraced her tightly. "Kate! Ah, Katie! Look what I've done! Look! Martin is . . ."

"Hush," she soothed.

Martin retorted, "There's no one I'd rather die beside than yourself, Kev! I'm not afraid!"

Kate thought he was perhaps too young to fear. No, perhaps he was too young to feel regret, regret for a life not yet lived. Never to love or be loved. Never to have children, to watch them grow and celebrate every small achievement like a great victory. Never to see the New World . . . to know anything better beyond the suffering of Ireland.

"I'm sorry for one thing only, Kate," Martin said. "I've let down the baby Martin, ain't I? Promised him I'd live a long life for him. Nothin' I can do to change it though." At last he wept.

Kevin, sobbing like a child, laughed through the tears because he knew regret. "Ah, Kate. What a fine man our Martin has turned out to be! He's stood firm all through it. When I tried to take the blame, he'd have none of it." Hanging his head, he said in disbelief, "It was nothin'. I lent the horse is all. To be hanged for this . . ."

Father O'Bannon remarked, "You're bein' hanged for somethin' other than this, Kev. 'Tis a lesson the English are teachin' all of the Irish here. They've taught the Irish to hate. You're the lesson that they can and will do as they like. A million and more marched for our nation with O'Connell. Maybe a million or more of us will die of hunger before the year's past. There's only one difference between their deaths and your own. Both kinds of death are carried out by English political will. Yours is quick; theirs is slow. But don't hate them, Kev. Don't die with that sin upon your soul. Look here." He flipped open the Bible and began to read from Second Corinthians, chapters four and five:

> *We do not lose heart. For our light and momentary troubles are achieving for us an eternal glory that far outweighs them all. So we fix our eyes not on what is seen but on what is unseen. Now we know that if the earthly tent we live in is destroyed, we have a building from God, an eternal house in heaven, but built by human hands.*

As the priest read by the diminishing light of the candle, Kate felt the tension flow out of Kevin. And as for Martin, he sat down with her upon the stones and leaned against her as he had done in the days when Da told stories by the hearth.

"Y'see, Kate," Martin said when the old man finished, "I'm not afraid. And no regrets do I have. To die beside my brother, so he will not have to die alone. You mustn't worry about me, Kate."

Outside, the guard knocked the door. "Quarter-hour remainin'."

Father O'Bannon said to Kate, "I've confessions to hear. Ye'll not want your brothers goin' off with anythin' upon their souls."

Kevin said with an attempted smile, "Take Martin first. It'll take me a lot longer than a quarter-hour to be shriven."

O'Bannon patted him gently on the head. "Christ died for those sins already, Kev. They're forgiven since that day. Confession is . . . 'Tis a formality, this. So you can spit in the devil's eye when he tries to tell you you'll have to go along his way. Heaven is yours. The moment Christ heard you, Kevin, was when he cried, 'It is finished.'"

And it was accomplished. Confession, repentance, the joy of

forgiveness, a final breaking of the bread of Christ's body. In remembrance of innocence crucified.

Dear God, could this be happening? Was there no miracle left? No small glimmer of hope to cling to? Had every prayer gone unheard?

Kate offered the shepherd's pie and penny cakes to the brothers.

Kevin declined. "No use wastin' dainties on a dead man. Give it to one of them beggars outside the jail."

Martin concurred. "Sure, I couldn't eat a bite, Kate. You know how I get. All fluttery-like before somethin' . . . an exam like . . . at school. I'll tell them all . . . Da, Mother, the baby, Brigit, Sean . . . I'll say you love them still . . ."

She could not force a reply. She left the clothes and shoes. The door was flung back; the guard beckoned. One last embrace . . . until heaven.

Christmas Eve.

High noon on the day before the birth of the Christ child.

The bell in the Church of St. Nicholas remained silent.

There was no proclamation of peace on earth to men of good will.

The prisoners were marched out first, through the double line of nervous redcoats that ringed the gaol. The lane leading to the gallows was outlined on both sides by other soldiers eyeing the fist-shaking thousands over leveled bayonets.

The three figures, two of them in spotless clothing and with freshly scoured countenances, shuffled in leg irons and manacles. The trio were loudly cheered, but their features remained pale, pinched, and drawn. Kevin, coming first, looked straight ahead. O'Hara, in the middle, never raised his eyes from the ground. But Martin, the last in the procession of the condemned, never ceased to search the faces of the crowd.

Behind these came Trevelyan. A bellow of rage erupted from the throng at his appearance, and the mob jostled the guards.

Then on the step beside Trevelyan appeared a girl, a colleen of the

Irish, one of their own. Gripping her shoulder, Trevelyan urged her forward.

The crowd fell silent. What was this about? Where was he taking her, and what did it mean?

Those nearest the gallows found themselves squeezed into unexpected contact with the guards, who pushed back, then contracted into an even smaller circle when more people pressed in behind.

The prisoners mounted the steps precisely, to line up with the three dangling nooses.

A clergyman and the public hangman were also on the platform, but no attention was spared for them. Instead every eye was on Trevelyan and the child, who likewise climbed the thirteen steps.

"Terrorism and rebellion will not be tolerated," Trevelyan began. The outburst of rage drove him back a pace, as if the fury of the multitude would boil over at last, and he continued hastily. "But in this case . . . in this case," he repeated in order to be heard above the shouting, "it seems justice should be tempered with mercy."

What could this be? Armed soldiers and a hungry scaffold are not the stuff of mercy. What was he speaking of?

"The Crown is moved to make a show of clemency."

Cheers and sudden catches of breath burst forth, to be stifled quickly in the strain to hear what followed.

"Let gracious Providence play a role in who lives and who dies," Trevelyan intoned solemnly. "This child has agreed to perform a service for the prisoners. Watch and see. Let the prisoners turn around and clasp their hands behind their backs. Now," he said to Corrie, though his voice boomed over the throng, "take this coin." He flourished aloft a gold crown, its value evident by the way it sparkled in the December sun. "Select one of the men standing before you, and place it into his hands."

Corrie took the coin from Trevelyan. It was clear from the way the glow on her face matched the gleaming gold that she saw the opportunity to do great good, to repay a debt. She took the coin without hesitation and went straight to Martin's overlapping palms, then stepped back again, smiling.

"Hear the meaning of this action," Trevelyan shouted, pleased his drama was playing so well. "The mercy of the Crown dictates that two will have their sentences commuted from death to transportation. Only the one who received the coin must die."

"Die?" Corrie screamed. "I thought it meant he was to live. I wanted him to live."

"You have been the hand of Providence and must not question . . ."

"But you promised to grant me a wish if I did this for you, and my wish is for that boy to live and go to America."

"It's impossible," Trevelyan sputtered. "One must die."

"He promised!" Corrie implored the crowd. "He promised whatever I wanted, he would do."

The mob surged forward like a tidal wave about to overwhelm the shore. The captain of the guard stepped up and whispered urgently to Trevelyan, "If your intent was to prevent a riot," he said, "grant the girl's request. We are only five hundred against ten thousand, and none of us will live to see another sunrise if you do not act rightly."

Looking wild-eyed, Trevelyan called out, "I have given my word that Providence will direct the outcome. I must agree to the child's demand. The boy will go free . . ."

"And the others transported!" the captain hissed.

"And the others are to be transported, but they shall have their lives spared!"

The ebbing tide and a wispy topsail breeze wafted the *Nantucket* out of Galway Bay. The motion was so gentle so imperceptible, that to Kate, holding Rosie at the rail beside Father O'Bannon and Joseph with Tomeen upon his shoulders, it appeared the land was drifting away from them rather than the other way around.

Nantucket cleared the lee of the point, and her bow rose to meet the long Atlantic rollers. Captain Coffin shouted, "Hands to the braces, there! Main tops'l! Lively now, lively! Lay her on the starboard tack!"

"Lively!" Molly Fahey echoed with enthusiasms. "O'Rourke, give us a tune!" The fiddler, standing in the bows, and O'Brien, seated on the top of the capstan, burst into song:

One night when I was courtin'
I went upon a spree . . .

Nesbitt and the Claddagh boys, who had pitched into hauling of the braces, responded to the bellow "Belay!" by securing the lines. Then they were free to turn about and watch Paddy O'Flaherty dance an impromptu jig with Mary Elizabeth, while Widow Clooney made yet another futile effort to corral her children around the mainmast.

Martin, clothed in his Sunday suit in honor of this Christmas morning celebration, bowed slightly to Corrie Grogan. Since yesterday, in all her waking hours Corrie had not left his side except to bathe in the elegant tin bathtub that the captain sent down to the women's quarters of the ship. This morning she was transformed: dressed in a fine woolen coat, red calico dress, and bonnet, gifts from Kate and Joseph to welcome the sister of little Rosie to her new family, Corrie's porcelain skin shone, her face radiant with renewed hope and joy.

"Are you afraid of what lies ahead?" Martin asked.

"The Good Lord goes ahead of us," Corrie replied, watching the shoreline vanish in the mists. "I have found my baby sister, a blessed family . . . God has a path safe even through the sea. I will not look back."

"Nor will I," Martin agreed solemnly, "except to remind myself that miracles do happen."

She took his hand. Between the two was the unspoken understanding that each, somehow, was bound to the soul of the other.

The fiddle continued. Mad Molly spotted Martin and Corrie and capered to their station at the rail.

She sang in a croaking voice,

One night when I was courtin'
I went unto a spree.

With polished boots and fancy cocks,
I was dressed up to a tee . . .

Her wizened face split in a broad grin. "Sure, an' ye're a fine pair, fine, fine, fine!" Jerking her thumb up toward the rigging, she laughed. "See them there? The Holy Host. I thought perhaps they'd stay behind. But nay! They're all here, they are! Praisin' God this Christmas morn! And Corrie girl, ye've brought a new one along! Bright and lovely is he! Perched there upon the mainmast. Smilin' down upon ye, he is. Aye! There beside Martin's fair angel he sits."

Corrie and Martin followed her gaze to the vacant space of sky atop the mast. Corrie smiled as Martin took her hand.

"I do not doubt your word, Molly," Martin declared.

"That's a grand intelligent boy ye are," Molly replied.

Corrie concurred. "I saw him from the corner of my eye a hundred times or more. It is good to know I've not left my guardian angel behind." She touched the brim of her bonnet in salute and waved.

The gesture pleased Molly. "There's a proper girl, ye are." The old woman patted her on the shoulder. "Behind me, before me, to my right, and to my left. Above me, beneath me! Never fear. The angel of the Lord camps 'round those who fear Him. America! It is. We turn our eyes away from Galway."

The lively tune ended.

Molly raised her hands in exultation.

"People of Ballynockanor! 'Tis Christmas morn! Christ is born! Do ye hear the angels singin'?"

Silence fell as everyone on board the vessel looked skyward and listened. None but Molly had ever heard the angels, but now no one doubted her word.

Wind hummed through the lines. A Gaelic word, perhaps? Was that a whisper? There was no holy thunder, but the swells of the sea boomed a rhythm against the bow.

And then! A wonder it was! Eyes widened with awe as sweet Celtic voices drifted upon the breeze, singing in the ancient language the old, old song that was sung at every Irish hearth on Christmas day:

*This day you shall know that the Lord will come and
save us:
And in the morning you shall see His glory.
Tomorrow shall the wickedness of the earth be
abolished:
The Savior of the world shall reign over us. Alleluia!*

And so, these few folk left their home in Ireland that holy morn
with the blessings of God ringing in their ears. And with that blessing came the admonition:

*Even so! Even so!
Remember the River from whence you came!
I will! I will!
Remember the Sea which all are bound to cross one
day!
Fear not! Fear not!
Remember Christ the Savior, the child for whom
there was no room!
Even so! Even so!
He is with you and your descendants
Unto all generations . . . always!*

Thus ended a long, long tale of life and death, joy and sorrow in
Ireland. Thus ended the Chronicles of Galway, as a new song was
begun. Amen and Amen!

Historical
Epilogue

Though the good people of Ballynockanor sailed off for America in 1846, the Great Hunger continued for another six years.

At the conclusion of that period, surely one of the most horrific disasters of human history and still among the greatest mass migrations ever recorded, nearly one million had perished of starvation and disease and another one and a half million emigrated. These numbers are perhaps even more significant when remembered as fully *one-third* of the Irish race at the time.

Even today, a century and a half after the events, Ireland's population is only half of prefamine, preemigration levels.

Repeal of the Union with England failed, Daniel O'Connell died in 1847, and Irish independence remained an unattainable dream for another seventy years. Even today Northern Ireland remains the focus of bitter debate over how closely it should remain tied to Great Britain.

Charles Edward Trevelyan, who stands alongside Oliver Cromwell as one of the most hated figures in Irish history, retired in 1847 to write his memoirs, since by his own declaration, the crisis was over. Honored by the English government for his exemplary service, he insisted to the end of his life that the best response to the disaster was "to do nothing."

Calling the famine "the work of an all-seeing Providence" was Trevelyan's excuse to allow children to starve to death. We must be careful that we never see God's will in our own failure to do all we can to "feed the hungry and clothe the naked."